LAST TRAIN HOME

JANAY BRIDGES

For my younger self,
you can have it all. You might just have to lose yourself a little bit first.

CHAPTER ONE

I WAS MOVING AT FAST as I could, folding the shirts meticulously as the team screamed in my ear. The walkie was the bane of my existence, and my coworkers used it far too often. I realized that even though I felt like I was exerting myself heavily, I was still folding the same shirt.

I looked down, my hands covered in age spots and my veins protruding. They were large and deep blue, crossing over my bones. My skin was transparent, looking like most elderly people I knew. I looked around in confusion. I was frightened. I searched for an exit, noticing the store was growing dark and dusty. Suddenly, the store turned into an outdated shop that I didn't recognize.

I woke up practically heaving and pooled in sweat. I had been tortured by the same nightmare for weeks now. It always starts with me hunched over and folding clothes in a large department store.

It's hard to tell, but it seems that I'm living out of the department store, because there is always a kitchen where the Gucci bag display should be. Or perhaps that is the eccentricity of my subconscious. It feels like I'm folding the clothes in a panic, but I'm actually moving at the slowest pace possible.

No matter what I do, how much energy I exert, I can't pick up my pace. I wake up in a pool of sweat every time. My heart racing. Today was no different as I roll over to silence the alarm on my phone. I exhaled loudly, relieved that it was just a dream. I laid in my bed, trying to analyze this recurring dream (and my life in general). Maybe this was my subconscious filtering the normal fears from my mind, or maybe it's from late night binge eating while watching Pride & Prejudice for the millionth time.

Either way, I am awake, staring at the ceiling to find I am not elderly and folding clothes in an upscale department store. But rather I am 28 years old, single, and living alone in my overpriced studio here in Beverley Hills. I do, however, spend my days folding designer clothes and styling the rich and famous.

Most girls my age would give anything for the reality I'm living: A thriving nightlife, running into celebrities on brunch outings, and a closet full of Jimmy Choo's. But after almost eight years of living here, the truth is that I never aspired to any of this.

After graduating high school, I applied to the furthest colleges from my hometown in Connecticut. My dream had always been to live within tube distance from work, maybe stopping to grab a coffee and scone on my way to a beautiful office, at the perfect public relations job in London. That dream still lives on but was postponed when I got rejected from King's College and instead was accepted to UCLA. It was aspirational of me to assume I would get accepted to any study abroad program. I had always maintained a fairly high GPA but I was far from a valedictorian.

· · ·

Unfortunately, I had to work a full-time job throughout high school to afford anything outside of an essential. My mom was a single parent, raising me on a teacher's salary. My father was never in the picture and as my mom said, "Was the least bit interested in funding my upbringing."

I often wished I had that paternal figure to make up for the lack of connection with my mom. She couldn't keep a man around for more than a few weeks. She was naturally hot-headed and possessive which never failed to run them off. When I was close to graduation, the reality of me leaving her sank in. She wouldn't hesitate to give her two cents about my choice to move away. My whole life she had taught me to be wildly independent and to never "lean on a man for anything". Which only applied until I was ready to leave. That's when the narrative changed.

Suddenly, there was a laundry list of things that could go wrong and I would be all alone to figure them out. This couldn't have pushed me away more. I also refused to move to New York City, like most of my peers had. I couldn't blame them for being enticed by living so close to a major city like New York. It had never been that exciting to me though, not like London had and it was still too close to home.

So, I went with the first school I was accepted to, UCLA. I knew it would be unlike anything I was prepared for but I didn't expect to hate it this much. My suburban upbringing did nothing to prepare me for LA. My first year in LA had been quite a culture shock and with the industry I'm in, I had no choice but to assimilate.

Now, after eight years here, LA had only proven to be the smelliest, season-less, and most superficial place I've ever lived. I'd always felt that I was made for something bigger that I couldn't accomplish by staying in my hometown, but I am not a health nut, influencer, or aspiring actress. I was just a girl with an unutilized degree and a dream. Los Angeles had seemed like a fun, short-lived prospect when I made the deci-

3

sion to uproot my life here. But in reality, I'm working a dead end retail job, loveless, unmotivated, and feeling hopeless.

I wanted to use my major and build a future for myself. You would think that in a city like Hollywood, they would need as many PR workers in the field as most cities need nurses but alas, I'm sat sending my fifth job application this week. No bites.

I'd been working at Saks Fifth Avenue and doing personal styling on the side to make ends meet (or to finance my shoe collection, however you want to look at it) ever since graduation. I looked at my phone to check the time. *Shit!* If I was late today, that would be the third time this week and my second write up this month. I had one hour to get ready and get to work. *Those write-ups don't mean anything. They wouldn't fire me. They need me. The commission they would lose from letting me go would be detrimental.*

I continued to stare at the ceiling, thinking about how desperately I needed a vacation. My mind wandered to the last trip I'd taken, to my favorite city, London.

I'd only been able to afford a London trip twice while living in LA. Both times were equally euphoric, lighting a fire in me that doesn't seem to be extinguishing any time soon. During my trip, I took my time marveling at the architecture and eating at local pubs as much as possible. I made conversation with shop owners and patrons of their businesses trying to live like a local. I made a few friends doing too and still kept up with most of them on social media. I lived every overcast day abroad to the fullest, especially the second trip where I spent 10 blissful days in London. I closed my eyes, trying to imagine it all again.

I couldn't help but see that handsome blonde figure in my head. I'd invited my then boyfriend, James. A tall, blonde heartthrob from Upstate New York, with a heart of gold. At the time, we had only been dating for a few months. We met at UCLA in the Arts Library; I was taking an elective class and James was an Arts major. I still vividly remember the first time we met. He commented on my *Dictionary of objects and Symbols in Art* textbook.

"The depiction of a cultural rebirth" he said. I had the book open to "The Birth of Venus". I was sitting down at a large table studying. I jolted as I heard his voice, even though it was just above a whisper. I immediately melted when I looked up at him. He was as beautiful as a painting himself.

His hair was like a wheat field, blonde and thick. I remember his bright blue eyes glistened behind his long lashes. I sat there for a moment in silence before saying, "umm, yeah, I was just getting to that part." It was all I could manage to say. He'd caught me off guard.

But he had a softness to him that made me feel safe. He was warm in nature and had manners unlike any guy I'd ever met. It took me by surprise.

I still remember what he was wearing. A grey pair of chinos with a white t-shirt tucked in, along with a pair of penny loafers. His style was unique and I admired him for it. It was timeless. Old money, Ralph Lauren vibes.

"Sorry, I didn't mean to startle you. I'm James." he said and extended a hand. I shook it gently and asked him to join me. We sat in that library and talked for hours. We connected instantly over our love for surrealism and being from the East Coast. We got absolutely no studying done that day. Although, I felt that I had with how passionately he spoke about his studies. James told me about his dreams of becoming a curator and moving to Paris one day. "I've heard the fourth is the perfect place to live, if you manage to find a place."

"The fourth? The fourth what?" I asked. James laughed until he realized I had no idea what he was referring to. "The fourth arrondissement, its a district. There are 20 within the city." He explained. He said that he had interned at a small gallery there the summer before Fall semester and fell in love with the culture and the 'pain au chocolate'. James was wildly intelligent and completely well-rounded.

"You should definitely see Paris one day." He smiled.

I remembered it so clearly. Of course I wanted to experience Paris. Mainly to see if it lived up to all the romantic movies I'd seen. I'd always wondered if it truly was the city of love.

James and I ended up dating for two years before I broke it off. I often have flash-backs of the night I ended things. I'd spiraled after he told me he was moving home for the summer. He wanted to apply for jobs and see his family. I didn't believe in long-distance relationships then and I still am not sure if I do. I certainly couldn't imagine moving back East either.

I still picture those sad blue eyes begging me not to do it. Begging me to come with him. He gave me all the reasons to stay, but I couldn't. I couldn't stand the thought of moving back to the coast. I thought it would be easier to just break it off then and there, before we became too serious, not realizing until now that maybe we already were. He was my first love and just like the movies portray, there's nothing like it. But I was career focused then, I still am. I'm sure he thought I was heartless and second-guessed our whole relationship after the fact.

I had no idea if he ever actually moved to France, or if he was still on the East Coast, but I was scared of missing out on my own potential, or stunting his.

So I broke his heart the night we graduated UCLA. I was depressed for months after, but I knew it was the right thing at the time. We were young and there was so much life to live. I was never able to truly say that he was "the one". But I knew that it was real love.

Somehow, despite all of that, I still ended up here. Miserable. Single. And ironically hating the dating scene, all while wishing I **had** found 'the one' already.

It was exhausting dating in Hollywood and my career was

unfulfilling. To think that a budding romance could've distracted me was ridiculous in hindsight.

Here I am, three years later, working a job in luxury sales at Saks Fifth Avenue, with a useless degree in communications.

There was one silver lining to all of this, Hanna Robinson, my one and only friend. Hanna is a gorgeous southern belle with the hair like a Victoria's Secret Model. She's got the height to match too. Most would look at this sweet model-esque creature, and never guess that she sells provocative feet pictures to pay her way through college. Most would never guess she'd never been in a serious monogamous relationship, or that she sustains five-plus 'sugar daddy' arrangements to afford her lifestyle. I am not judging. I admired how shame-lessly she hustled.

Meanwhile, I live paycheck-to-paycheck and work two jobs to sustain my own lifestyle. Not to mention, my credit card that was practically maxed out at the moment. Hanna and I met at Saks Fifth Avenue four years ago, junior year of school at the height of her modeling phase. Back then, she was still doing freelance gigs here and there for sketchy photographers in the city. However, she gave it up after one too many uncom-fortable encounters with photographers. I suppose manipu-lating old men out of their generational wealth seemed was a better gig.

Hanna and I were drawn to each other instantly. We both had a mutual dry humor and a love for fashion. I still remember what she wore the first day of work; a cashmere sweater from The Row and a pair of leather pants. I'd been eyeing that sweater for months prior, but couldn't pull the trigger because of the price. Her style was simpler back then. I remember her fragrance too, she wore Dolce & Gabbana Light Blue. I remember what I had worn that day too. I wore a J. Crew turtleneck with a pleated Dior skirt and a pair of Monolo's (the only pair I own) that I got on Ebay. I paid for everything on credit. I couldn't imagine showing up in anything less than designer.

Back then, I thought living in LA meant that anybody and everybody knew and cared about fashion. It's hilarious how naive I was, or that I even cared about something so superficial. I'd always had expensive taste growing up. A taste that my lower class family couldn't support. I'd always been thrifty enough and found a way to replicate designer looks on a Target budget.

I snoozed my alarm for the 5th time and shook off the memories of James and all the other flashbacks I was having. I decided to get myself together for the sixth consecutive shift at the store this week. I hastily cut the tags off my new dress and steamed it while my coffee brewed. I looked at the clock again. 10:20am. I shoved a protein bar in my mouth and started on my hair. I quick blow-dry would have to do. I doused my scalp in dry shampoo and massaged it vigorously. I swallowed the rest of my protein bar and started on my makeup. I heard my coffee pot steaming and poured myself a hefty cup. I looked at the clock once more. 10:40am. *Shit!*

I knew it wasn't enough time to get there with traffic and my makeup was only half done. "Owe," I yelped, burning my tongue on my coffee. I raced back to the bathroom and finished my makeup as fast as I could. I ran to my closet, desperately searching for a pair of matching shoes. I grabbed the nearest pair of pumps and slipped them on. I took one more generous gulp of coffee as I searched for my keys. *Purse, phone, sunglasses. Keys! Where are my keys!* I sifted through the junk mail on the counter, not there. I dumped out my large tote bag, not there.

The time was slipping and I knew I was going to be late no matter what. *Ah! There they are!* My shiny Louis Vuitton keychain was reflecting in the morning light. I swiped my keys from my bedside table and ran out the door. I rushed past my neighbor Miss Breyer and her standard poodle. "Jessica, slow down! You almost knocked me over." She yelled. "Sorry, Miss Breyer!"

I clicked the down arrow five times.

"Come on, come on." I whispered to myself. Finally, the doors opened. I tapped my foot all the way down to the lobby and ran out as soon as the doors split open. I ran as fast I could to the parking garage. I fumbled with my keys before peeling out of my parking spot. It was 11am. I was officially late.

My boss was going to have my head on a platter. A designer platter nonetheless. I raced through traffic, cutting off people left and right. I circled the parking garage of the department store for what felt like forever. Of course I couldn't find a single spot. I settled for the first one I could see on the top story. I raced out of my car and into the elevator of the garage. I glanced at my watch. *Shit!* It was a 11:30. A whole 30 minutes late. My toes were being pinched by my shoes as I raced inside. I zig-zagged through the store, inconspicuously hiding behind clothing racks. I felt something pinch my ass. "Ouch!" I hissed.

I spun around to see Hanna standing behind me. "Oh, you're in deep shit, Chadwick." She said with a half smile. "Hanna! Please tell me Herb isn't here, please." I begged. Her half smile dropped. She ran a hand through her perfect hair and sighed. "I have bad news for you, my friend. He's waiting for you in the office." She said, looking at the ground. I groaned in defeat and sauntered to the back room. I found my locker and placed my things inside of it and took five reluctant steps towards the office. *Knock. Knock. Knock.* "Come in." Herb's sassy voice called from behind the door that was ajar.

I cleared my throat. "Good morning, Herb! How are you?" I said in a forced chipper voice. "Have a seat." He said flatly, without looking at me. "I am so sorry for being late. I promise it won't happen again. I couldn't find my keys and then I spilled my coffee-"

"Jessica, you're fired." Herb said, cutting me off.
My stomach dropped. "What?"

I knew my tardiness was higher than normal lately, but this was retail. I'd covered so many shifts, worked countless holidays, and never made a fuss. This couldn't be happening.

"I'm sorry but your tardiness and lack of care this last month is unacceptable. You've missed multiple styling appointments and it's not a good look for the store. I want to be top in the district. If I'm going to do that, I need a strong reliable team. One that's dedicated and professional. I'm sorry." Herb said, looking up at me slowly.

He adjusted his blazer and began typing on his computer. I sat motionless with my mouth open. I thought I was going to be sick. "Please clean out your locker by the end of the day." He added before leaving the room. I sat in complete silence for about five minutes before I got up from the chair. Hanna was lurking around the corner. "*Im fired..*" I said in shock. Her eyebrows raised as high as her botox would allow. "Fired? How?" She asked, sounding surprised. I knew she was trying to make me feel better. It was no surprise at all. I had been unreasonably late more times than I could count. Apparently Herb was keeping score though.

I walked to my locker in silence, Hanna's heels clacking behind me. "Too many tardies, he said. I've really been trying my best, but all these extra shifts have been burning me out. I guess I couldn't keep up." I said, the blood leaving my face. I had been working overtime to save up for a trip to London. I'd saved up just enough for a plane ticket. I saw the ticket disintegrate in mid air, knowing it was all for nothing now. I slowly filled my tote with the items in my locker and stared at the magnetic name tag on the door. "Jess, don't you worry! Look, I have just the guy for you. All you have to do is go to dinner-"

"Hanna, stop. I'm not like you. I"m not interested in that.

No offense." I said, curtly. I was tense. "Fine. Just trying to help." Hanna said, rolling her eyes. I couldn't believe this.

All my credits cards were nearly maxed out and rent was due in two weeks. "What, am I going to do?" I asked, mainly to myself. I couldn't bare the thought of using my savings on bills instead of a flight. "Look, we'll figure this out. I can come over at the end of my shift and help you sort this out, ok?" Hanna said, reassuringly. She was being a good friend and I was being a bitch.

"I'm screwed. I'm so screwed, Hanna. This is bad. Like, really bad." I whispered in a panic. The shock was wearing off and reality was setting in. I turned around to face Hanna, work belongings in hand.

"Thank you. I'm sorry for snapping. I've just never been fired before and you know I've been saving for this trip and now….now it's all for nothing." I said, a lump growing in my throat.

"Look, you've still got a check coming. That should buy you some time to find *something*. This is LA! There's got to be someone out there willing to hire someone like you. Maybe reach out to some clients and do some more personal styling."

Hanna was being optimistic. I wasn't in the mood to be optimistic yet. So I nodded instead and said I'd see her tonight. I slowly walked out the building with my head down. Once I reached women's dresses, I looked up and around. I watched as the line at the cash wrap grew. The store was playing the same song it played everyday at this time. A wave of relief washed over me suddenly. This was the last time I would have to hear this stupid song or muster the energy to make it though a nine hour shift. After all, this job was only ever a place holder for my dream job. I sighed as I exited the building with my bag full of junk. There had to be something better than this.

CHAPTER TWO

I woke up to the sound of an email alert and the feeling of the sun beating down on me. I must have left the curtains open last night, after one too many glasses of wine with Hanna. We had stayed up far past midnight laughing, crying, and searching for endless jobs on Indeed.

I needed to sober up and get vertical. I had applied to at least 60 jobs. Half of which, I wasn't even qualified for. Half of which, probably wouldn't accept my drunkenly filled out applications. I rubbed my eyes and forced myself to keep them open. I reached to my bedside and grabbed my phone to see it only had 10% battery life, but opened my email, regardless.

A wave of excitement ran through me as I read the subject line to an email from ***danielmcdowd@barnesburton.com.*** The email read

---

Jessica, we would love to move forward with the interview process for the role of remote assistant/assistant at Burton Barnes Productions. This role requires immediate fulfillment, so we ask for full transparency about interest on your behalf. If this role is still of interest to you, we will be holding interviews tomorrow at The Beverly Hills Executive center and your interview time slot is June 13th, at 12:30pm. Please respond accordingly and thank you in advance for your time and consideration.

Best,

Daniel McDowd, Lead assistant, executive of onboarding Burton Barnes

---

I sat up quickly and nudged Hanna awake. *This couldn't be. An application response already?* It had been less than 24 hours since I applied. Hanna groaned as she cupped her forehead "Hanna, someone emailed me back about a job! I need to respond quickly. Wake up. What do I say? Wait, no, I know exactly what to say. Short and sweet is best and of course I'm free tomorrow" I said to myself. I was filled with anxious excitement.

Hanna rubbed her eyes and pulled up her bra strap as I typed away. "Wait, Jess, let me see what you're talking about." She groaned. She grabbed my phone and scanned it over as she rubbed her eyes once more.

"Okay, this is good. I know exactly where these offices are, too. They're by the surgeon's office, where Richard's ex-wife got completely botched. I'm just confused why it's at a co-working space." She said. Richard was one of Hanna's clients, you could say. He seemed to be the one getting the most attention as of late. She was fond of him, although she would never admit it to me.

"Maybe because it's a remote position?" I shrugged. I didn't care. I was just excited to already have a job prospect. I paused. *Could this be a total scam?* I grabbed my laptop from the floor and sat in silence while I google searched the address for the offices. "Oh, wow, you're not going to believe this, H."

I scrolled through the Google images. A quick search lead me to find that it is, in fact, legitimate and is a successful indie British film production company, with head offices in London.

LONDON of all places. My stomach dropped. It was the place my heart longed to go back to and stay for good. "Good or bad? It's too early for me to interpret your tone," Hanna said, as she began rummaging around my kitchen.

"Very good.. it's a British film production company. Their headquarters are in *London*, which is why they don't have a permanent office here." I replied, eyes glued to the screen. I sat there for a moment with my mouth wide open. I couldn't shake feeling that I was meant to apply for this job. My termination was quickly becoming a blessing in disguise. It didn't matter how under qualified I was. It was a start. Hanna slammed down a mug onto the counter and walked towards me. "Jess, I told you it could be good!" She squealed, motioning towards me. I smiled and shrugged in response. Not allowing myself to get my hopes up too soon. Hanna handed me a hot mug of coffee. "Shit!" I spat as the mug burned my skin. I sat it on the table next to me. I was consumed with my research. She leaned over my shoulder and pointed to one of the images I was scrolling through. I was swiping through the movies the company had produced.

"Oh, I recognize that one. I saw that movie on one of me and Richard's first dates." She said. I caught her gaze.

"That is the second time this morning you've mentioned Richard. It's 9am" I replied. I wasn't intending to be rude, but I found it odd that she was bringing him up at all. He was a client, not her boyfriend. God forbid. She broke eye contact and cocked her head up in a sophisticated air. "I think I'm just excited for Milan. Anyway, you have to email them back and confirm this interview and then we're going to find you the perfect outfit. None of this all black, contemporary-art-museum curator aesthetic." She said, clapping her hands together.

The moment the words left her mouth, I couldn't help but instantly think of James. I think she realized her use of words too. *Art. Museum. Curator.* We hadn't talked about James in ages. I didn't like to, and she knew that. It was one of the few sensitive topics of mine, as much as I hated to admit it. "Hey! There's nothing wrong with my looks okay? After all, it got me the job at Saks," I said proudly, as I shook the thought of James off, pretending not to be bothered. We both have very different personal style. My style has always been modest and a bit mature for my age. I wasn't sure why that was..body image issues? *Only being interested in older men who actually read and don't hang around bars until 2am? Dressing for myself rather than the male gaze? Who was to say?* Either way, I'd never be caught dead in half the trendy garbage most girls my age wore.

"No, I'm not saying there's anything wrong, obviously we both work in fashion. You're stunning. You have great taste. But I'm just saying, we need something fresh... a little va va room." She said, as she made a squeezing gesture in the air with her hands. What she was squeezing, I wasn't completely sure, but I had a good guess.

She was vigorously shuffling through hangers in my closet like a madwoman. Her eyes got wide as she handed me a dress I'd had in my closet for a quite a while, but never worn. It was a Jason Wu knitted midi dress. Not too sexy. Not too modest, but it accentuated all the right things. I had been saving this dress for something special, like a first date, but seeing as romance was nowhere near the horizon, it was a better contender for the interview.

"Hmm maybe, is it too special for a first interview?"

I slid it on and examined myself in the mirror. I liked how I looked, which was surprising. I liked how confident I felt in the dress and suddenly felt silly for saving it for a special occasion. I felt like someone who was on her path, someone who knew what she wanted and had a plan to get there. "No! It's perfect! Here, take your Never-Full to dress it down a bit."

An hour or so had passed, and we compared accessories over a few more cups of coffee and delivery bagels. We decided I'd wear stilettos and not pumps. We discussed potential interview dialogue and creeped Daniel's Instagram before Hanna left, and I sat down to respond properly to the email.

Daniel, thank you for considering me for this role as I am highly interested. Please take this as my confirmation to attend my interview slot for tomorrow at 12:30pm.

Best,
    Jessica Chadwick

Sent. I instantly felt a sense of excitement I hadn't felt in so long. The potential for something new and opportunistic was making me feel superior. All doubt had subsided and was replaced with the anxiety of being in the interim. This was my typical fashion. I always allowed myself to get caught up in the future, creating scenarios in my head about how things might go. This only ever lead to anxiety and a deep spiral even though these scenarios never ended up coming to life.

I found myself obsessing over the potential of this new career opportunity. I researched the company for hours to distract from my anxious thoughts. I also stalked the executive assistant, Daniel McDowd, on Instagram once more. He was medium height, slender, and dark-haired. His style screamed new money and according to the photos of him at his "family home" in the Cotswolds, I'd be correct. I only knew of the Cotswolds because of Vogue. I had never been there.

I winced a little bit at photos displaying Daniel's pastel shirts and preppy style. Most of his photos were at what seemed to be a putting green. His conventionally handsome features seemed to makeup for the poor style. I was typically attracted to more understated men, but I couldn't help but be a little smitten by him. I knew how extremely unprofessional this was, but I couldn't help myself. If it's one thing I do well, it's romanticizing and fantasizing every detail, stranger, season, and interaction of my life, on a good day. Hanna loved to remind me of it too.

I glanced over at the clock to see it was already 6pm. I became nervous as I found myself imaging all the ways I could potentially fuck this up. I'd never been an assistant before or worked in any similar circumstance. I have helped dress celebrities but never outright worked for them. I let out a sigh and started talking myself down. I began to think about how that is a good thing and how the nerves and racing thoughts only mean that this could be something really great. I had friends who interned and assisted for major publications and worked their way into significant role. I knew that this job could potentially lead me into one as well. If I played my cards right, I could be the company's next Publicist. I reminded myself that I had nothing to lose and everything to gain.

CHAPTER THREE

I TURNED off my alarm and began getting ready for a last-minute pilates class I'd booked the night before. It was the first workout I'd done in weeks. It was also the first self-improvement I had done in months. I'd always wanted to do pilates, god; I envied the mob of Lululemon wearing moms & influencers strutting down the boulevard in the early hours of the day.

Their hair was somehow always perfectly in place, makeup minimal but obvious, and their skin glistening. I would be lying if I said I wasn't slightly nervous to take a class with a bunch of people I didn't know. Most classes I had gone to in the past, felt competitive and unwelcoming. I began combing my hair back and taking a round of deep breaths. I thought about how the class might go and my interview later today. I couldn't help it. I had been feeling all the normal anxiety that comes with the prospect of a new a job. This was completely new territory I was charting. I had known nothing but fashion for so long despite having all the book knowledge for public relations. Not to mention, I excelled at running social media for local businesses during college. The boutique I had worked at when I first moved to LA, had asked me to run their social media (without a raise, I might add) and I did such a great job that they begged me to do it after I had graduated too.

I walked to my favorite coffee shop down the street to put my nerves at ease. The street slowly started to bustle around me from the morning commuters. The cool morning breeze kissed my skin as I strolled into the coffee shop. I ordered my usual iced matcha and sat at a small table near a window. I took my time sipping my drink. I couldn't remember the last time I had been up this early.

I casually checked my watch, realizing I had ten minutes until my class started. I chucked my cup in the trash and rushed out. I walked to my class thinking about all the new possibilities this new job could offer me. I quickly began daydreaming of myself hopping on the tube before work. Walking to a pub after work for a pint. Walking through the markets of Portobello Road on the weekend. I could see myself strolling Oxford street, being swept up by the bustle. Nothing would make me happier.

I let my thoughts consume me all the way to the studio. The walls were mirrored from top to bottom. The space was pristine and spacious with 10 reformers in two single file lines. I chose the one closet to the door that would offer the best view, in case I found myself lagging behind. I hadn't worked out in forever and I knew I was going to hurt tomorrow. I struggled through the entire class and was glad once it was over. I checked my phone as I wiped the sweat from my forehead. When I unlocked my screen, I noticed I had an unread text from Hanna saying, "Don't kill me but I told Drew you'd be available tonight for that blind date." I rolled my eyes. Of course she would tell him that. I knew she thought I was lonely or just needed to get laid but I was truly fine being alone. I had always been that way. Right now the last thing I wanted to entertain was a man. I was too nervous for my interview to even have the capacity to be mad at Hanna now.

So, I decided not to respond and table the conversation for

later. As soon as I was in my apartment I stripped off my workout clothes and ran to the shower. I took my time making sure that every last detail of my appearance was polished as I got ready. After about five spritz of perfume I grabbed my purse and looked myself over in the mirror. My hair was slicked back into a neat bun and my gold jewelry tastefully shining against my knit dress. I smoothed the front of dress out and looked myself in the eye while saying *"you've got this."*

I heard my phone buzz loudly. I opened it quickly, knowing it was Hanna waiting for me downstairs. I took a deep breath and made my way out. A sudden feeling of relief washed over me. All of a sudden, I felt like this was truly the beginning of something pivotal.

I checked my reflection one last time before hopping out of Hanna's Porsche. I couldn't help feeling like a kid again as she shouted from the car window, "Call me when you're done and I'll pick you up!"

I was grateful to have a friend who cared about me this much. She was the only friend I'd made here in the last few years. Hanna was the only one that felt like home too. There were a few acquaintances I had made along the way, but all of them felt shallow. Not to mention, in LA it's hard to trust that anyone has your best interest, so I preferred to keep my circle small.

I gave Hanna a nod and a wave as I strutted inside and exhaled deeply. *Breathe. Just remember to breathe.* I was always good at acting more confident than most, maybe because at the end of the day, I saw everyone as equals, but today I was nervous. Insecure.

The initial sight of the office was impressive. The smell of Dyptique candles permeated the common area that was lavishly decorated with fresh bouquets of peonies. The furniture was modern and chic, with large leather armchairs in the waiting area. A large fridge was filled with glass bottles of Aqua Panna and San Peligrino.

I stepped out of the elevator to see a disinterested face sat behind a giant iMac, applying lipgloss. The girl couldn't have been any older than 21 and had enough lip filler for the both of us. I straightened my bag onto my shoulder. "Excuse me, I am here for an interview with Burton Barnes."

"Name." She said, without looking away from the computer. Not a question but a statement, rather. I gave her my name as I picked a piece if invisible lint from my arm. She pointed to a velvet green couch and said, "Have a seat and listen for your name. Mr. McDowd will grab you when they are ready for you." Her voice was grew pleasant but her lack of eye contact and body language told me she was probably just as jaded as me.

I said thank you and made my way over to the couch. I took a moment to double check that I had my resume in my bag as well as my phone. I checked my Cartier watch, that read 12:10, and looked over my shoulder to see three people sitting at a long table. Glass walls encased their office space so that you could see everything happening inside. The room was bare, only having a table and 6 leather office chairs. As soon as I looked up, I noticed a familiar face. It was Daniel from the emails. The face I had only known from creeping on his insta-gram. My cheeks flushed as I realized he was far more hand-some in person. He carried himself well. He had definitely matured since his last post, that was undoubtedly a few years old. His jaw was cut to perfection and his style was impeccable.

I settled into my seat and looked away as I realized there was nothing to be embarrassed about. There was no way he could know about my internet prowling and besides, how do I know he didn't do the same thing to me? I saw from my peripheral view that the group had shaken hands and were saying their goodbyes. A wave of nerves ran through me as I knew I was next. I took a deep breath and relaxed my jaw. The candidate they were currently meeting with was a woman, seemingly older than me, and who could use a styling session or two. And although her taste in clothing was lacking, she could definitely be more qualified than me. Either way, at least I knew I'd make a good first impression. She walked out of the office space as the other two remained seated. She passed me and gave me a meek smile and kept her gaze down. Something about her stature told me all I needed to know about how her interview went. I got excited as I realized that this interview would probably sway in my favor. I sat up straighter in the chair and lifted my chin. I uncrossed my legs and removed a hair from my dress as a silky British voice asked, "Are you Jessica Chadwick?"

I looked up quickly and stood. "Yes, I am, I'm here for my 12:30 interview,"

I reached out a hand to introduce myself. Daniel firmly grasped my clammy hand. "Right, it's a pleasure, Miss Chadwick. Shall we get started?"

He smiled as he motioned towards the glass room. His presence was oddly captivating and his voice was calm as he pulled out my chair. He introduced me to the woman sitting across from me. Her hair was short and red. Her thin lips were painted with a ruby colored lipstick. She examined me thoroughly as she reached out a hand. Daniel said, "Celeste Smith, COO and backbone of this operation, no doubt" in a firm tone. Daniel laughed awkwardly, still speaking, as she sat there quietly. I could tell he was trying to ease whatever tension was happening in the room. He looked at me and then back at Celeste. Finally, she spoke and gave a taught smile. "Jessica it's great to meet you. Can we get you a water or coffee?" She asked. American. Her accent was American and her voice monotone. "No, I'm fine thank you." I breathed and looked towards Daniel, waiting for him to take the lead.

Truthfully, I could've used a water but I didn't want to delay this interview any longer. I was anxious as hell. Daniel gave a nod.

"Right, then let's get started with the interview. I'm going to ask you a few questions." He said as he placed his arms on the table. "Okay," I said in a confused tone and looked to Celeste and then back to him. Celeste was seemingly unfazed.

"What exactly are you looking for? I have to admit that the online description was pretty vague."

Daniel met my gaze. "We are looking for a personal assistant who can help our CEO in day-to-day tasks but also travel frequently and at a moments notice to help with various coordinations. The ultimate candidate will have the utmost discretion while on the job. It is long hours but is undoubtedly a great opportunity to network and travel. Not to mention, the competitive salary, which is negotiable." He looked away and towards Celeste. All of this was still so vague to me, but before I could open my mouth to speak, Celeste said, "This role is for a prominent actor and writer. At times you may be expected to travel for weeks alongside him, predominantly in London. Working this intimately with him, or any actor in general, can present challenges and sometimes be quite exhausting. We need someone who is radically gracious, discreet, and professional. Above all else, we need someone who isn't judgmental."

She kept her gaze on me. *Predominantly London? That was all I needed to hear.* There was an awkward pause before I said "There's nothing I haven's seen in LA, I can assure you of that."

I laughed, trying to ease the serious energy that filled the room.

Daniel chuckled and shrugged, joining in my efforts before Celeste responded. "I can imagine. This job also requires open availability. You can think of it almost as an 'on-call' position. I imagine this is why we have had trouble keeping it filled" She said.

Daniel scratched his head, looking away from us. I sensed there was something I was missing.

"You might work up to ten days in a row depending on the season. How do you feel about that?" Celeste asked. I honestly had no reservations about it. All of this sounded appealing and fresh compared to my current situation. And if it could get to me to London, I had no reservations. However, I wanted to know WHO I would be working for exactly. That would be the true deal-breaker.

"It sounds exactly like what I am looking for but I have to ask, who exactly would I be working for?" I asked. "We would be happy to tell you after you agree to a background check and an NDA." Daniel said, taking back the conversation. He straightened himself. I'd lived here long enough to know exactly what an NDA was. "We would also love to bring you back in for a second interview, where we would ask you to agree to these terms and offer up more information." He said. Celeste nodded and added, "We wanted to give you a disclaimer before starting today's interview. Now tell us about yourself and your job history. I see on your resume that you currently work for a department store?" She looked up at me, seemingly unimpressed. I nodded and replied, "Yes, I am a personal stylist and carryout various managerial duties as well, but as you can also see, I have a major in Public relations." I said, not daring to mention the fact that I'd recently been fired. I went on to tell them more about my job experience, my move to the LA, and college as Celeste multi-tasked on her iPhone and Daniel gave me his undivided attention. There was a blatant seductiveness in his gaze that made me a little uneasy, but I found it flattering, nonetheless. It had been sometime since I had that much undivided male attention, sadly. It helped that he was devilishly handsome and had that

British accent. I rambled on for a few more minutes until Celeste interjected to excuse herself. She thanked me for meeting them and quickly excused herself before answering a phone call. Her exit immediately left me feeling worried.

Daniel looked to the doors and then back to me. "She doesn't mean to be dismissive. She is usually running three operations at once most days. But she trusts me nonetheless." He said. I shrugged. "So that's why she left early?"

He smiled, "I suppose so... or maybe she knows already that you're a good fit." He said, reassuringly. Doubtful. I knew he was only saying that to make me feel better. I looked down, feeling uncomfortable. "Thank you." I said in a sheepish tone. My mouth was so dry from all the talking.

"Do you mind if I take you up on that water now?"

"Absolutely," Daniel said. He shot up to grab one from the fridge, briefly leaving me alone in the room. I allowed myself to slouch and take a deep breath. I wiped my clammy palms onto my thighs. "So, are you free tomorrow?" He asked as he swiftly re-entered the room. I blushed. "errr—I" I stuttered, feeling confused. "For the second interview? How does 10am work?" He asked. My cheeks flushed as I realized he was talking about the interview and not a date. Clearly it had been FAR too long since I had anyone as me out. I shook my head and picked up my bag to sling over my shoulder. "Oh, yes, of course. Thank you for your consideration. Ten is great." I stood up, straightening my dress and trying not to seem embarrassed as I smoothed out my hair. I caught his gaze, stopping at my boobs just as I looked up. I paused for a second.

He smiled devilishly, "Great, see you tomorrow, Miss Chadwick" I shot him a smile and made my way to the elevator. I checked my watch before clicking the button for the ground floor. I had been here for almost an hour and thought that was a good sign. Before the door could close, a strong veiny hand smacked in between them to keep them from shutting. I jolted back as a voice said, "I know this is very forward but would you like to get dinner tonight?" Daniel whispered in between the doors.

My eyes were undoubtedly wide. "Yes." I said, without hesitation. "Great, I'll call you," he said cooly, pointing at me as the doors closed. I was in disbelief and let out a quiet laugh. Once the doors shut, I covered my mouth and looked up. I knew I had been picking up on some kind of energy from Daniel. I couldn't believe he was being so forward. I couldn't believe *I said yes*. I grabbed my phone to call Hanna knowing good and well that she would be elated by this information. I dialed her and quickly hung up, realizing the date she had already set me up on was for *tonight*.

CHAPTER FOUR

WE TOOK our seats at Nobu as I prepared myself for the round of questions about to come from Hanna. I took an Uber to meet her for lunch after the interview. She decided to get her nails done while waiting on me and it took longer than expected, in typical Hanna fashion.

We placed our drink order, and I told her about the incident with Daniel in the elevator, feeling partly excited and partly embarrassed.

Hanna snapped her chopsticks apart showcasing her glossy new set and smiled. "So is this the start of your very own romcom?"

Just as she asked, the server came back with our drinks and placed them down without interruption. I took a large swig of my martini and ran my hands through my hair as I avoided eye contact. "Well, I don't know about that." I sighed, knowing full well I didn't want this to go anywhere but feeling a little guilty for enjoying the attention. "I cannot believe what came over me in the moment, but I just agreed. No hesitation at all! What if this compromises my chance at this job?"

I threw my hands up, and Hanna grabbed my elbow to assure me I was overreacting. "Jess, this is how men are when they're attracted to someone. This will probably *get* you the job. Honestly, I would be glad that he had the audacity. It's hard to come by, trust me." She said as she rolled her eyes. I had a feeling there was more to that comment than I cared to know. She had been spending a lot of time with Richard lately. I shook the thought of them together and thought about how she was right.

I've never experienced a man being so confidently forward. It was nice not to be chasing someone, but I felt slightly offended by her comment. I didn't *need* a man to land a job. But I knew she meant no harm. That's just how she was and I knew expressing any type of feeling about it would only cause an argument.

I took a deep breath and focused on her point. Normally, in my experience with men, they're passive or play silly games and I am extremely turned off by that. As any woman *should* be. It was exhausting dating anyone my age here in LA, but on the contrary, the older men didn't aspire to anything serious either. Maybe this is why I had completely sworn off any men my age recently, turning down any blind date Hanna had to offer.

I had no idea how old Daniel actually was, but my guess was 3 or 4 years older than me. I based this guess off the date stamp on his University graduation picture that I saw on Facebook. My god, he was so incredibly handsome, but I knew I was crazy for entertaining any romantic thought of him (or for creeping his social media). Still, my mind wandered about his short black hair that was perfectly cut and groomed and his clothes that were nice and pressed too. He had sparkling green eyes and thick brows to accent them. He was pretty fit from what I could tell, under all the suits he wore. I told Hanna about the odd tension between us. I described the energy flowing through the room. I also told her about the very obvious gaze at my chest. Which, I still felt a bit awkward even re-telling.

Again, she saw no issue with this behavior. She let out the largest laugh I had ever heard from her which turned a few heads from the table next to us. "Oh, he is *sooooo* into you. You guys are gonna bang. I have money on it."

I rolled my eyes and chuckled.

"Can you please not use the word *bang?*" I whispered, taking a sip of my drink. I know she just wants me to loosen up and date for fun but it was hard for me. I have always dated for love, or the idea of it, and didn't really know another way to be. I was a pure romantic at heart. I enjoyed my comfortable little life for what it was, but I knew I was stuck in a rut too. My weekends comprised of reality show marathons accompanied by Trader Joe's wine and frozen pizza. A wild night for me would be dinner and drinks and bed by 11pm. My party days were long gone.

The waiter came by with two complimentary shots of saki from the bar. "From those two gentlemen over there." He said, placing the small glasses on the table and pointing across the room. Hanna whipped her head in that direction and squealed, waving sensually at the men. I turned my head slowly to see two middle-aged men in cheap suits smiling back at us. I sighed deeply and lifted my glass to cheers Hanna "To new opportunities," I smiled, trying to riff off her excited energy. She clanked my glass and gave me a wink before tossing back a saki shot. "to new opportunities! AND GETTING LAID!" She screamed as half the restaurant turned to look at us. The two men at the bar yelled in reply "Alright!!"

"*SHHHHHH!!!*" I hissed. "I cannot sleep with Daniel!" I whispered as the server laid our sushi rolls down on the table in front of us. "I'm joking. You know, you really should have a couple shots. You're pretty tense." She said, smiling like the Cheshire Cat. I took a bite of my ahi tuna and replied, "and you should really eat. I think that saki is already getting to you."

She laughed before dunking a her roll into the soy sauce. "Hanna, you do realize this means I can't go out with Todd tonight? And I will NOT be the one to break it to him!" I pointed a chopstick at her.

"Oh, that's right! Even I forgot I had set you two up already. Well, don't hate me for giving him your number." She said. I sucked a piece of edamame and shrugged. "I don't hate you. I've ignored many men and he won't be the last." I replied.

"He's so boring anyway. You won't be missing much." Hanna added. My eyes widened and I felt my voice go up a pitch.

"Then why on earth did you insist on setting us up?" I asked. I wasn't one to waste my time with anyone, let alone a blind date. "Because Jess, you've got cobwebs in your panties. I can see it when you walk!" Hanna was definitely borderline tipsy now, but I couldn't help but laugh. She snorted loudly and I swear I saw a piece of rice fly from her mouth.

"That is NOT TRUE!" I said, as I threw the empty edamame pod at her. I let out a laugh and reached for another one. "Jess, come on, it's been years since James." She said, leaning back in her chair.

I felt my stomach slightly drop as the words floated towards me. It grew silent between us. I felt like everyone was staring at me. I looked down at my lap. I avoided looking up at Hanna, but I could feel her gaze piercing through me.

"So, what? You think I'm still hung up on a relationship from college? It was puppy love. I work 40 plus hours a week, *I'm busy! I'm stressed!* I don't have time to play The Dating Game. Dating just isn't a priority for me right now, and besides that was years ago." I yelled. Hanna sat in silence, staring at me. As I caught her gaze, I could tell she felt horrible. "You're right. I'm so sorry for bringing it up. I wasn't thinking... maybe I am a bit tipsy. But you know you can still have love for someone and not be IN LOVE with them right? You're lucky to have loved anyone at all. You're lucky to know what that's like. What you both had was special." We looked at each other for a moment longer. Hanna normally never had much of a serious tone, especially when it came to relationships or love for that matter. She wasn't the emotional type and she definitely didn't wear her heart on her sleeve like I did. I'd never given much thought to the fact that she'd never had a serious relationship, or that she'd never been in love. Part of me felt guilty for that. I didn't realize until this moment that we had never actually talked about it.

I was suddenly having some sort of epiphany about her sleeping around and always being so casual with men. I'd never personally agreed with her lifestyle but I'd never judge her for it either.

"I think I need to be cut off now."

Hanna pushed the porcelain vase of saki away from her and looked down at her lap. I dropped my chopsticks onto my plate and let my head fall back as I exhaled. "No, no, it's ok. You're right. I need to put myself out there more, but it's not because I'm not over him, H." A half-truth. "It's because I truly haven't found anyone I can stand to be around for more than one date. Find me a guy who is a classic romantic—who wants to swoon me and listens to oldies, like Frank Sinatra and Dean Martin. Find me someone with passions and aspirations other than to 'be famous'. Someone who would lend you their jacket when its cold, hold the door, and ask to kiss you on the first date rather than assume you're going to hook up with them. Look, I have entertained multiple blind dates by you but I think I'm done for awhile."

I picked up my chopsticks and took one piece of sushi and shoved it into my mouth. Hanna sat there, still and silent. "Have you ever been in love?" I asked, cutting the silence with a sharp knife. She looked down at her food and flipped her hair over her shoulder before whispering "I think you'd know."

She said it without looking at me. I couldn't help but feel sorry for her.

She was clearly embarrassed and I felt embarrassed too. *How could I not know if my closest friend had ever been in love?* I'd never seen her act this way, meek and ashamed. She cleared her throat and straightened up in her chair, coming back to life, almost in a robotic way.

"Anyway, what are you going to wear tonight?" She asked. I took it as a clear sign not to press.

"I'm going to go there tonight, wearing this, and keep it very professional. Mark my words." I said, taking another bite of my tuna roll. I obliged her emotionally avoidant ways. *Just sweep everything under the rug. No need to speak on the emotions that filled the restaurant.*

"You can't be serious! You're not even going to change? I think I'd change my day clothes even just to have dinner with my mom." She scoffed. I gave her a glaring look.

"No! I don't want to seem like I care, remotely. Changing would definitely imply that I wanted to impress him. I want it to merely seem as though he's just a quick pit stop on my way home." I said, leaning my torso closer into the table. Even though this is the impression I *wanted* to give, part of me couldn't help but feel excited about the idea of a hot British guy asking me to dinner, but I wouldn't let Hanna know it. "I will say, and mark my words, Daniel cannot be more than a work crush. I still feel silly for saying yes," I was talking with my mouth full as she hung onto my words.

"Maybe I will try and set him straight tonight about all of this." I added. Hanna almost spit out her water "you are the least domineering person I know but good luck with that." She said. I couldn't help but laugh because she was right. "Well, its never too late to start...dominating" I said, looking up from her, cackling.

. . .

I could feel the alcohol settling into my blood stream. Just as we both let out a laugh I felt my phone vibrate loudly on the table. I opened the message from the unsaved number.

> Hi, Jessica. This is Daniel McDowd from Burton Barnes. Can you meet me tonight at 7:30 at Datare's? xx

I gulped down my last bite and turned the phone towards Hanna so she could read. The blue light from the screen lit up her big blue eyes with wonder.

"Ah! Speak of the devil! What's with the 'xx'?" She asked. I rolled my eyes.

"It's a British thing, a closing salutation, I guess. Don't read into it." I said, clicking the lock button on my phone. Despite me advising her, I couldn't shake the nervousness that had sunk into my stomach. I was intrigued by Daniel and also by the reasoning behind this dinner. It was all so abrupt and sudden and obviously very forward.

The waiter placed our bill on the table and Hanna insisted on picking it up. I didn't fight her on it. After all, she was driving a brand new Porsche and I was still in my 2015 Lexus from college.

We finished lunch and decided to take a stroll down to our favorite gelato shop. I got my usual: one scoop pistachio and one scoop Fior Di Latte. Once Hanna stepped up to order she got her usual scoop of Limone and stopped there. "What, just one scoop?" I asked quietly. "Yes, just one. I'm leaving for Italy soon!" She said, as she stood up straight and smoothed out her stomach. I rolled my eyes because all the gelato in the world couldn't make her fat, and she knew it.

"Well, I'm sure you will make up for it there." I said as we walked out of the little shop on the corner. "Do you want to walk for a bit?" She asked. I nodded and scooped a spoonful of delicious coffee flavored gelato into my mouth. "So, you know you didn't recount anything about your actual interview?"

My eyes nearly popped out of my head when I realized she was right. "Oh," I tapped the side of my head with my palm and swallowed my bite. "I was clearly caught of guard by how it ended more than anything, but the interview was good. A bit awkward at first and a little vague." I said.

"How so?" Hanna looked as confused as I felt. "Well, there was a woman who sat in, Celeste, she's the head of something. I don't even remember now. Anyway, she seemed very uninterested and busy and didn't even stay for the entire thing. They asked me a few questions, just the typical kind and then basically stated their terms."

"Which were?"

"I would have to agree to working essentially an 'on-call' schedule and would have to sign an NDA before even getting a second interview. I'm essentially assistant to the executive assistant, Daniel, who works directly with this celebrity apparently."

I ate another scoop of gelato before continuing. "They said most of my time would be spent in LA, but that I would be required to fly to London at some point." I said. I heard Hanna coughing and extended an arm to pat her back. "Are you okay?"

"*LONDON?* You didn't lead with that?!"

"Well, no, because I thought you'd be more interested in the whole horny co-worker thing?" I said, scooping more gelato onto my spoon.

"Besides, I haven't gotten the job yet so I'm trying to keep expectations low." It took me a second to realize she had stopped walking. I turned around to see her stopped in the middle of the sidewalk. "This is big. This is huge. Jess, I'm happy for you." She said. I didn't realize how badly I needed to hear those last few words until this moment. I smiled and put my arm around her shoulders "For once, I'm happy for me too." I smiled.

———————

It was 7:40 when I had strolled into the Italian restaurant Daniel chose. I had intentionally waited in my car as to not seem eager; I was still in the exact outfit I'd worn to my interview and lunch with Hanna. I tousled my hair a bit in the car, just for theatrics, and noticed how the effects of the saki were still lingering. I walked up to the host stand and told them I was meeting someone and gave them Daniel's name in the most mundane tone. As I did this, I saw him standing in his tailored suit, leaning over the bar, laughing loudly at whatever the bartender had just said.

I slid into the barstool next to him, waiting to see if he would notice me. As the bartender's eyes shifted to me Daniel's head turned in immediately.

"Jessica, darling! I thought you were going to stand me up for a moment there."

I felt satisfied that he noticed my tardiness.

"Oh, I'm sorry, I lost track of time. It's been a busy day."

I said, avoiding eye contact and nonchalantly placing my purse on the back of the chair. The bartender took my order and Daniel sat down next to me, unbuttoning his suit jacket in the process. I looked around the restaurant, admiring the soft glow of the lighting and the view of the busy street.

"This is a nice place" I said, sipping my dry martini. He nodded, taking drink of what I presumed was whiskey on the rocks.

"I normally don't oblige coworkers when they ask me out. I have a strict rule about not shitting where I eat." I said, cooly. I knew I was being a bit brash but I wanted to set boundaries straight away and prove *I could* be domineering. He almost spat up his drink "Well, we're not coworkers yet you know." He winked. "So, why did you decide to ask me to dinner after just meeting me if you weren't going to tell me I had the job?" I partially joked.

"Because you're absolutely stunning. I couldn't help myself." He smirked. I should have been flattered but something about his tone made me feel uneasy. I took another sip of my drink and avoided eye contact. I could tell he felt awkward by how he shifted in his seat. The silence had grown long, and I wasn't going to be the one to break it.

"Right, the real reason is that you seem far more capable than our other candidates. We tend to hire the same sort of character for this role and sadly, none of them have stayed longer than six months. Celeste is apprehensive to hire you, due to your lack of experience. I, however, think that's exactly why we should hire you."

Part of me got nervous hearing that. *Was this mystery celebrity the ultimate boss from hell? Was Celeste the absolute bitch that she seemed to be? Was Daniel a nightmare to work with?* I didn't understand.

"You see, quite honestly, a monkey could fill this position, that is, if they could understand the nuances of it. Like I said, most people don't last long."

"Well, that speaks to the company I'd assume." I said. Daniel knew exactly what I was implying. "Well, not entirely which is why I wanted to talk to you outside of the office, on a personal level. Jessica, this role can be stressful exhausting at times but it can also open many doors. Its fun and exciting and it pays fairly well. I want to hire someone who isn't too sensitive to a high maintenance team or who crumbles under the pressure of a 50 hour work week." I took a sip of my drink and raised an eyebrow "Well, if we can discuss salary I'd be more inclined to accept an offer." I said.

"Absolutely. I know exactly what they'd offer you as I'm the one who typically sends over the offer letter from HR." He took a large swig of his drink, nearly finishing it and leaned in to say "Don't you also want to know who you're working for?" His breath confirmed that he was drinking whiskey. The smell was intoxicating.

"Well, of course." I said sensually, removing an olive from the small metal cocktail skewer. He raised his eyebrows

"See, I knew you were smart from the moment I saw you." He had a twinkle in his eye. "No you didn't. You just thought I had great tits." I said, with a little liquid courage. I couldn't believe how blunt I was being but I felt a high, knowing I was going to have a job by the end of this. I could feel it. His eyes grew wide and he laughed.

"You've got a mouth on you, eh?" Clearly he was neither confirming nor denying his stare from earlier in the interview. He smacked the bar with the same veiny hand that stopped the elevator door earlier today. Daniel called the bartender over. "We will have another round, cheers!"

I bit into the last olive and finished the last of my martini wondering if we were ever actually going to get to dinner.

"I did my research on the company, but truthfully, I'm not too familiar with who I will be working for." I said, steering the conversation back to the reason we were here. Or at least the reason I was lead to believe we were here. Daniel looked at me with wide eyes "Really? As surprised as I am, that actually works in your favor. Obviously we never want to hire major fans as it's a conflict of interest."

"Naturally." I said, just as the bartender set our second round down. I refrained from taking another sip as I felt my ears getting hot, a sign I was getting tipsy. I am the ultimate lightweight.

"So the person you'll be working for is Roger Barnes. He's a comedian, actor, and writer. I'm sure you've seen something he has starred in or wrote." I caught Daniel staring at me and felt myself staring back before shaking it off. I was familiar with most indie cinema but terrible with names. Regardless, the name didn't ring a bell. "The name doesn't sound familiar, but I'm sure if I saw him I would recognize him. What has your experience been like working for Roger?"

"Its been fantastic. I've worked for him-er, the company, for about eight years now. He pays well, takes great care of the team, and he's very *hands-on*. He treats everyone as equals as well, but he can be very demanding. If he's hard on you, that means he sees something in you."

I had a feeling any boss would have to be 'hard' on Daniel. I couldn't explain why, just an intuition. "You'll meet him tomorrow during your second interview. He likes to get a sense of who we're brining on and often has the final say."

Daniel took a swig of his drink and ran his hand through his dark hair. I found myself staring at his jawline for a moment too long because when he turned my way a smile painted across his face. "Your eyes are stunning," he said and raised his hand before brushing my hair behind my left ear. I felt a wave of heat pulse through me. I quickly replaced his hand with mine

"Oh, thanks," I said, and looked down at my drink. I was here for business and I intended to keep it that way.

"So, uh, the interview, is there anything I should know?" I asked still looking at my drink. "Right, it should be fairly brief and they may even ask you to start immediately. We need this position filled before September. As far as questions, just the simple ones to indicate your job performance, etcetera."

I didn't know if it was just me, or the drink, but watching his lips move was making me hot. I took a large swig of my drink and flipped my hair over my shoulder. "Okay, seems reasonable," I swallowed, hard. He extended his arm and placed his hand on my shoulder. It was warm and hard and I couldn't help but lean into it. "Don't be nervous. Everything will go smoothly." he said in a low voice.

I felt myself pulsating. I had no choice but to excuse myself. I was losing my power, whether he knew it or not.

"Um, ok, wh-where is the bathroom?" I asked, with a dry

mouth. "Just around there." Daniel said, breaking eye contact to point to the left of the bar. His face was painted with confusion as he watched me squirm in my seat. I shot up and grabbed my bag.

"Great. I'll be right back."

I walked as fast as I could in my heels, until I saw the gold 'W' on the swinging door. I clambered into the pastel pink bathroom and hunched over the porcelain sink. "You've got this. Pull yourself together." I said, to myself in the mirror.

I felt dizzy all of a sudden. I took a paper towel and dabbed the sweat pooling under my pits. I grabbed another one and dabbed my forehead before splashing cold water onto my face. I didn't know what was coming over me. I was normally repulsed by men like Daniel but it had been so long that I'd been with any man that I think nature was taking over. Mother Nature was doing everything in her power to make me procreate tonight in this modern Italian restaurant. She definitely didn't care that it was with my future co-worker either.

I took a deep breath before cupping a small amount of water from the sink and drinking it.

I suddenly remembered reading a Cosmo article about how men hate red lipstick. Something about it being messy and off-putting so I immediately started rummaging my bag. I always carried a red lipstick with me as it was my go-to color. I hadn't worn it tonight because I had been going for an effortless look but I decided to slap some on as a deterrent. I found the Chanel rouge at the bottom of my bag and carefully applied it. I took another paper towel and blotted my lips before going back to the bar. As I approached Daniel, I saw a plate of food on the bar that he was picking at. I sat down beside him and cooly said, "Where were we?" His eyes grew wide as he clearly noticed something different about my face. He shoved a piece of bread into his mouth. Bruschetta, he ordered bruschetta.

He offered me some of the appetizer and I took a small bite to keep my rouge in tact. Thankfully, he said nothing about the lipstick. We spent the rest of the evening talking about the position and what it entailed. I learned that Daniel handled a majority of the large-scale assisting duties; like meeting with actors and potential writers, hiring, and so much more.

He explained that I would be handling the everyday tasks for Roger and also the team at the office. According to Daniel, award season caused tensions to be high and to-do lists long. He gave me a ball park range of what they'd offer me for a salary and it was 60% more than what I was earning annually, side gigs included. This was enough to have me leaping at the role but I didn't want to seem too eager. We finished our second drinks and chatted for awhile longer about the company and eventually about ourselves. We had talked for so long that neither of us ever ended up ordering food. Instead we had two or three more rounds of drinks. I don't know why I obliged but as soon as I felt it sinking in, it was too late. The red lipstick must have done the trick too, or so I thought until Daniel and I walked out to the street.

Once we stepped out in front of the restaurant, my head began spinning. I swore he had leaned in for a kiss, just before I got a wave of nausea and doubled over. Before I could even think twice, I hurled my body forward and puked bruschetta all over Daniel's leather shoes.

Clearly alcohol, nerves, and dairy don't mix well. Daniel called me an Uber after I cleaned myself up in the restaurant bathroom. I was beyond embarrassed and still too tipsy to walk straight. I left the bathroom where Daniel was waiting to assist me. After apologizing profusely, he shoved me into the car and slid next to me.

"Daniel, I'm fine, really. I can get home on my own." I slurred. He laughed and straightened his suit jacket.

"I'm not so sure you can."

I rolled my eyes and leaned my head against the window. The cold glass felt good on my face. I must've fallen asleep on the ride home because Daniel was soon shaking me. "Right, come on then." He said, as he helped me out of the car.

"We're here. You think you can make it up alone?"

I certainly didn't want him following up into my apartment, but thought that a gentleman would insist. Maybe he wasn't a gentleman. My apartment was filthy and I wasn't quite sure I even trusted him enough to breach that level of comfort.

"Yes, I'm fine. I think I'm sobering up now." I tried my hardest to say it with confidence. He didn't fight me on it, thankfully. Instead, he walked me to the entrance. We said goodbye and I made the trek up to my floor. By the grace of god I made it to my front door. I stumbled in almost face planting on the tile in my kitchen. I felt incredibly sick. *Was I truly a lightweight or was it food poisoning?* I stumbled to my closet and tried to take my heels off before falling to the carpet. I managed to get the first one off before getting completely dizzy. I stopped for a moment and took deep breath. I eventually got the other one off and tossed it behind me. I stood up while trying to remove my dress over my head. I stumbled around before losing my balance and falling back into a rack of hangers.

"Owww!! *FUCK!*" I yelped as the wooden hangers dug into my ribs. I released my grip and allowed myself to fall into my clothes. The hangers clanked together and a few of my bags fell and toppled onto my head. Suddenly something inexplicable came over me, and I was crying. I fell back onto my floor, letting the tears flow. All the emotions that had been festering over the last few months were finding their way out now. All the sadness and frustration was bubbling up and spilling over.

I stared at the ceiling for awhile before finding the strength to get up. I drunkenly wiped my arm across my face, removing the tears and snot. I finally got my dress off and threw it to the floor. I was thumbing through my clothes to find an old tee shirt to sleep in, my balance faltering. My eyes grew wide and I blinked hard, trying to focus my drunken vision. I pawed through every item, making my way to the far end of the rack.

In front of me hung a large grey men's blazer. One that had been hanging there for a couple years now. I buried my face into the heavy cotton as I realized who's it was. I sobbed into the fabric, letting it soak up my tears. It still smelled like him. It still smelled just like him. Clean and woody. It was the blazer James had left in my car the night of graduation. He always ran hot. James took it off before the ceremony. I remember finding it the next day and bringing it inside. There was no chance he was coming back for it and no chance I'd be able to reach out to him. I couldn't bare talking in circles over again and I knew any contact would lead to that. I also didn't know if I would be strong enough to keep fighting him. I needed a clean break from him.

I winced at the flashback of that night. I had blocked it all out until now. All the memories were suddenly racing back. I tugged the blazer loose from the hanger and wrapped it around my half naked body. I sunk back to the ground and hugged my knees into my chest, practically heaving as I did so. I rocked myself back and forth for comfort, curling my toes into the carpet. I felt more alone in this moment than ever.

I should feel happy that I was starting new and exciting career but instead, I was deep in the sadness of having no one to share it with.

CHAPTER FIVE

I SAT IN MY CAR, checking my reflection one last time. I realized my hands were clammy when I pressed my fingertips to my under-eyes. They were puffy from the drinking and my Chanel eye masks didn't seem to make a difference. I smoothed my hair down to my scalp one last time and checked to see if I had any red lipstick on my teeth. I opted for the color once more just in case vomiting on Daniel's shoes wasn't enough of a turn off.

I made my way into the building and up to the elevator, just as I had yesterday. I was wearing a thick black cardigan tucked into a mid length pleated skirt. I wore the only pair Louboutin's I owned, despite how hard it was to walk in them. My flat feet always ended up killing me by the end of the day. The elevator doors opened to the same smug receptionist from yesterday. I approached the desk. She instantly stood up before I could say a word, seeming more attentive. I could only assume it was because Roger was in the building. I couldn't blame her for switching up her performance because it was the singular reason I was wearing black. I couldn't afford sweat marks seeping into the lining of my bra. I was extremely nervous after dinner with Daniel.

I had no idea how this interview was actually going to land. "Hi, Jessica?" She asked nervously before I could introduce myself. "Yes. Hi, I'm Jessica Chadwick. I was here yesterday for an interview--

"Yes, Mr. Barnes is waiting for you. Right this way." She said. Her tone was far more pleasant than before. I followed her into a different conference room than the one I was in yesterday. This one was much smaller furnished with a desk and two leather armchairs. The room was plain and bare, making it obvious that it was rarely used. I sat down and placed my purse on the floor. "Mr. Barnes will be with you shortly." She said, closing the door swiftly behind her.

I fidgeted in my chair wondering where Daniel could be. There was no sign of him here at the offices and no text from him on my phone. Maybe that was a good thing. I jumped slightly at the sound of the door opening, breaking my train of thought. I turned my head as the person I could only assume was Roger, entered the room. I was instantly taken aback by his presence. He had that subtle star quality about him that made you want to stare. I stood quickly and shut my mouth that seemed to be hanging open. "Hi, Jessica, I'm Mr. Barnes, Roger Barnes." He said, in a deep performative voice. I let out a nervous laugh and grabbed the hand he had extended. He shook my hand with a slightly firm yet tender pressure. His hand was soft and warm, unlike my clammy one. As soon as I realized how clammy it was I quickly removed it. His eyes were small and brown, piercing. I found it hard to look him in the eye at first glance. I was surprised at how nervous I was becoming as I found myself fidgeting a little too much. I slowed my breathing and tried to focus on just that. Soon enough, I was able to sit there in my normal disposition and just observe him.

Roger's skin was bronzed and smooth with the normal amount of wrinkles a man of his age would have. I assumed the tan was from whatever recent holiday he must have gone on. His hair was salt-n-pepper and sat just below his earlobe. The room was so small that we stood merely a couple feet apart. I could smell his cologne, fresh linen scent with a hint of musk. It was intoxicating yet subtle. He was wearing a beige blazer with a a white shirt underneath adding to the glow of his skin.

"Terrible joke, I apologize." He said, running a hand through his hair. I felt my mouth open once more involuntarily.

"I— um pleasure to meet you, Mr. Barnes." I stuttered.

He looked me over once before motioning for me to take a seat. I suddenly realized that I recognized him from a movie that I'd seen years ago. It was an indie film shot in the style of a documentary. In the film, he and his co-star road tripped throughout the English countryside, trying renowned and obscure five-star restaurants.

"Will Daniel be joining us as well?" I asked, looking at the chair next to me. "Erm, no, unfortunately Daniel is sick. He came down with a stomach bug I'm afraid. He texted this morning."

Shit.

"Not to worry though, he speaks highly of you and assured me that you're a great fit." Roger smiled a reassuring smile, waving a hand in front of him. He interlaced his fingers, cradling his chin on top of them and looking at me in silence momentarily.

"I'm sorry," I breathed, letting out a slight laugh and looking down at my lap. "I just realized what movie I recognize you from. It's actually one of my favorites, but I haven't seen it in years. The one where you travel throughout England trying those five star restaurants. I'm sure this is a butchered description. I apologize." I finished speaking as he leaned back in the chair behind the desk. He smiled.

"It's the one that was mostly improvised, no set script."

He crossed his arms, silently. "The Journey." He said softly.

'juuurhney'. I loved his accent. "Yes!" I said, as I snapped my finger. "Not many people are familiar with that one.

They typically know me for my more obnoxious charac-ters." He said, his eyes dancing on me. I averted my eyes to the floor and smiled as I brushed my hair behind my ear. I could tell I had flattered him somehow.

"Well, I guess you could say I have obscure taste. The film was so aesthetically pleasing as well. I think that's what I loved most."

I looked back up to see his eyes still on me. "Not to say your performance wasn't equally great." I added softly, forcing myself to look him in the eye. I kept his gaze, feeling nervous as I did. He laughed and waved a hand to reassure me that he wasn't offended. "So, when can you start?" He asked.

His words shocked me. Either this company was extremely desperate or I had made more of an impression than the other candidates.

"I—um, you don't even want to see my resume?" I asked, bending forward to grab my folder from from my bag. I it in the air for a moment before he nodded his head.

"No, I trust my team and I have a good feeling about you. You have good taste in film." He said, with a smug smile. I sat there in disbelief. I placed my letter of recommendation and resume on the desk, anyway. "Well, here is a letter if recom-mendation...for your records. And..ummm...I can start tomorrow?" I said, sounding confused.

He glanced down at the papers and then back at me. There was another long pause. "Well, thank you for these. Right, that's perfect." He stammered. His accent was enticing and different from Daniel's. I assumed it was because they were from different parts of England. His voice was more mature and adenoidal. He stood up from the desk.

I grabbed my purse, following his lead. He reached out his hand once more for me to shake. "Pleasure to meet you and... erm, welcome aboard." He said softly, allowing his hand to linger. There was an inexplicable tension between us that I began to feel. I looked into his eyes and let out a sigh.

"Thank you so much. It was great meeting you."

Roger opened the door slowly and motioned for me to exit first. I took a left down the hall and sauntered towards the elevator, feeling his eyes on me. I looked back slowly to see that my feeling was on par. Feeling satisfied, I shot the receptionist a smile and stepped into the elevator.

CHAPTER SIX

I HAD OFFERED to purchase Daniel a new pair of shoes about 100 times, but he consistently declined. I was embarrassed for thinking he was trying to win me over, or get laid. It was still a possibility. We had only just met and he was direct about how attractive he found me. It didn't matter if it was just the alcohol talking.

On second thought, it was a good thing that my drunken behavior had deterred him, at least for now. After accepting the role, Daniel explained that the first few weeks of work would consist of me shadowing him. The thought of us working so closely together made me nervous. I stood on the corner, anxiously waiting for Daniel to pick me up.

I straightened the tote on my shoulder as I saw a silver Audi pull up in front of my building. It was him. Daniel insisted on carpooling as it wouldn't make sense to drive separately, since I had no idea where I was going. He gave me a wave and I swiftly reached for the door handle. I slid into the leather interior. A heavy scent of musk and tobacco hit my nasal passages. I never understood men who doused themselves in cologne. "Good morning," I breathed, as I buckled my seatbelt.

"Good morning, miss Chadwick." Daniel said, in a chipper tone from behind his ray-ban's.

"Have you had your coffee this morning?" He asked.

He smiled while peeling out from the side walk. I gripped my door handle. "Uh, nope."

His driving was terrifying me. "Well, we can't have that. I know a good spot that's on the way."

"What exactly is on the agenda today," I asked, still gripping the door handle for dear life.

"We've got to pick up and deliver a few screenplays from the townhouse, pickup some personal items, and then we will head to the office to get your laptop and work cell. There is a possibility for me to attend a logistics meeting over zoom with Celeste. She's just landed in London." Daniel said, quickly. He was speeding like crazy as he spoke. Just as he finished his sentence as he ran a red light.

I ran my fingers though my hair as we pulled up to the coffee shop. I was thanking god that I'd made it in piece. We stepped out of the car and made our way inside the bright and minimal shop. Daniel kept his sunglasses on as he ordered a flat white, and gestured for me to place my order. His tone was flat and clipped towards the barista.

"I'll have the same, thanks." I said, and reached for my purse only to be interrupted by Daniel's strong hand halting me.

"Company perks," Daniel said, as he waved his black card to the barista. I nodded and smiled nervously, as I waited for him to finish the transaction. Once our drinks were ready, he scooped them both up and handed mine over. Daniel yelled "Cheers!" To the staff as we left. I took a sip of my latte and asked where our first stop would be. "It's in a neighborhood called Brentwood. Are you familiar?" *Am I familiar? It is one of the most beautiful neighborhoods outside of LA. But also the most pretentious.*

"Yes, I think I've been to a dinner there once or twice." I

said, cooly. Daniel didn't pick up on my sarcasm. It was a 30 minute drive to Brentwood, without traffic. The typical congested roads made that drive an hour long. During that hour, Daniel took as many as eight work calls. He discussed everything from meetings to movie set locations. The blaring ring of the cellphone through the car bluetooth startled me every time it rang.

As soon as we were north of Sunset, I knew we had to be close. We approached a gated neighborhood as the car was softly humming the talk radio station. Daniel rolled down his window to let the guard know who we were. The guard smiled and looked at me.

"I see you have a new friend with you."

"A new colleague. She will be making the trek out here soon for Mr. Barnes." He said, quickly correcting the guard. The guard smiled and made a bit more small talk before opening the gate. We whipped past about 50 houses. I thought about how easily I could get lost finding this place in the future. *Thank god for Google Maps.* We pulled in to the drive of a modern three-story townhouse. The house was a grey metal with black finishes.

The ceilings were high and the walls were made of windows. The house was stunning but still modest for LA.

"Here we are," Daniel said, as he put the car in park and swiftly got out.

"This house is great. Is it the resident bachelor pad?" I asked.

Daniel smiled as he turned the key and looked at me

"Are you referring to me or Roger?" He laughed. "Both?" I said, with upward infliction and shrugged. We stepped inside and I gazed up at the modern light fixture. It painted a glow on the foyer. The decor was minimal and very chic.

"I've only known Roger to be with one woman in the last 5 years I've worked for him. And as for me.. that's confidential," Daniel winked.

I looked around noticing every piece of furniture had brushed gold hardware. The walls were wallpapered in bright colors too. This place definitely had…flare.

"Where is the restroom?" I asked. That long drive after a flat white was proving to be a bad choice. "Just that way," Daniel said, pointing.

"Thank you," I breathed as I rushed around the corner with my stilettos clacking loudly behind. I entered the bathroom that was wall-papered with a colorful print of gummy bears. A bit off-putting, but fun, I suppose. I had no idea what type of person Mr. Barnes was, but if his house was any representation of him, he seemed eccentric. What I did know, was that he was devilishly handsome.

I finished using the toilet and fixed my hair in the mirror. I washed my hands with the lavender scented soap and tried to find my way back to Daniel. He was leaning over the grey granite countertop, talking on the phone and muttering something about estimated arrivals and departures. Once he saw me, he told whomever was on the receiving end that he had to go. He lifted a manilla envelope and yelled, "I've got what we need," And made his way towards me.

"And what exactly is that?" I asked, nervously. "The screenplays! We are dropping these off at the office for some producers to come and review. You'll be doing a bit of this on your own soon. Protect them with your life." He said, pointing a serious finger in my direction. "Of course." I breathed. I should've known that's what he meant. It was in the itinerary for today. He handed them off to me and I followed him to the door. I felt some pressure sinking in. *Was I really cut out for this? Were they going to realize how under qualified I am and give me the boot?* I chewed the inside of my cheek as my thoughts consumed me.

We made our way back to the office so Daniel could attend his meeting. We planned to drop off the screenplay in the process. I quietly rode up the elevator with Daniel. As soon as the doors opened, he turned to me.

"This is somewhat of confidential meeting. If Celeste wasn't attending virtually I would have you sit in, but since she is, I was thinking you could finish our tasks for the day. We still have some items on the agenda so you could get them done for me or take a long lunch. Up to you."

I looked at my watch and decided it may be best to start on the errands. The mention of Celeste made me uneasy. I was under enough pressure today trying to remember everything.

"I don't mind getting the tasks done." I said. Daniel reached his hand in his pocket and handed me the fob for his car.

"Right, here, you'll take my car and pay with your company card for whatever items you purchase. I need you to pick up a few things at Hudson Grace for the townhouse, a couple things at Whole Foods, and an item at Tiffanys. Can you handle that?" He said, with a wink as we stepped out of the elevator. I was making a mental list of everything he was saying. I only hoped I could remember.

"That sounds easy enough but,"

Daniel interrupted me. "I've already texted you a list. Be back within two hours and try not to scratch the car, okay?"

He gave me a devilish grin and strode into the glass encased office. The one I'd just had an interview in days ago. He began shaking hands with some unfamiliar faces as I turned and made my way to the elevator. I slid into the driver's seat and let out a satisfied sigh. I rode in many Audis before, but never driven one. It felt nice compared to my old car. I pulled out my iPhone and saw the instructional text from Daniel.

> Two beeswax candles, one hand soap, one
> bottle of 2005 Barone Reserve cab sauv from
> Hudson Grace. Two prepared meals from
> Whole Foods (freezer bags in the boot), and a
> bracelet from Tiffany's under my name.

> Don't miss me too much, x

I had another text, from Hanna.

> Good luck today! I am sure you look hot. I
> want to hear all about it.

I smiled and rolled my eyes before responding. I carefully shifted into drive and headed to my first stop. I'd never been to Hudson Grace, but it was immaculate inside. It was as simple store with a masculine feel to it. I took in a long breath of what smelled like vanilla and gardenia, as the shop owner made her way to greet me. She was petite and round and had short curly hair that perfectly framed her face. I quickly found the items on the list with her help. I patiently waited at the cash wrap, while the shop owner carefully wrapped the wine. She placed it in a red box and tied it with twine. S

"I put a box of matches in there, on the house."

She gave me a gentle wink, accentuating her crows feet, and I thanked her. I wasn't used to this sort of treatment here in LA, but I suppose when people think you have money, they treat you differently. *Daniel's car. The black company Amex.*

I rushed to my next stop, only having an hour left to complete the list Daniel gave me. I couldn't shake the need to move with urgency to prove myself competent. I wanted to prove I was more than capable of going above and beyond for this job, because I had a feeling it was already unlocking doors for me.

After quickly making my way out of Whole Foods, I sped

through traffic to make it to Tiffany's. As I drove down Rodeo drive, I realized I had thirty minutes to grab the item and be back at the office. *Shit.*

I rejoiced as a Bentley pulled out of a parking space close to the entrance. I quickly parked and thumbed through my phone for the instructions. *I had to get this right.* I was meant to pick up a tennis bracelet under Daniel's name and drop it to the townhouse later this evening.

I approached the tall concrete building and grasped the large silver door handles. My freshly manicured nails glistened in the reflection. I'd seen the classic Audrey Hepburn film, 'Breakfast at Tiffany's' and had always dreamt of owning the classic heart-shaped charm bracelet from Tiffany's. I'd always secretly dreamed of recreating that opening scene from the movie too. I think most girls did. But I'd never actually stepped foot inside the store. I made my way to the counter where a slender, long-haired blonde was showing an older couple a few beautiful pieces.

In a hurry, I blurted out "Excuse me, I'm here to pick up a bracelet."

The woman and couple turned towards me and stared. "Is there someone who can help me with that?" I asked, more politely. I caught a breath and waited for her to answer. The woman and the couple turned back to the sales associate. "We're really not in a hurry, go ahead and help the girl." Her tone was warm and reassuring. The sales associate, who's name tag read, 'Gretchen' gave me a fake smile and asked for the name of the order

"Daniel McDowd."

Her eyes immediately met mine. "I know exactly where that is. Excuse me one moment." She said. She opened the gate that was keeping her enclosed in the case, and sauntered towards the back of the store. I had a feeling that Daniel either made frequent purchases here, or frequent stops for Mr. Barnes. I sighed as I checked my watch and adjusted my dress.

Gretchen soon approached with that classic little blue box. She opened it and asked me to examine it. I really wasn't sure what I was looking for. I was just told to pick up the jewelry, but I didn't want to seem unsure of myself, so I opened the box and silently looked the item over. It was a gorgeous tennis bracelet, platinum with diamonds throughout. "3.04 carats. Platinum silver. Did you want to try it on?" She asked. I almost hesitated as a reflex, but then thought it would be harmless. I'd never worn Tiffany's before, but who wouldn't want to? Gretchen doesn't know who, or what this is for, so I nodded.

"Yes, absolutely."

She wrapped it around my wrist gently and clasped it. I turned it around to see it better in the light. It was beautiful. It felt good, natural almost, to be wearing it. The feeling it gave me was inexplicable. "Diamonds look good on you," Gretchen said, as she turned to greet a customer. She knew that I didn't own any real diamonds. I could tell.

Although that was unfortunate, I knew she meant well. I unclasped the bracelet and carefully put it back in the box. "Everything looks good," I said, confidently and went to reach for my company card "Oh, it's already taken care of. Just sign for it here and you're good to go." She gestured an iPad towards me.

"Oh, of course. How could I forget?" I said, nonchalantly. She quickly and delicately wrapped up the box and placed it inside a small bag before handing it over. I brushed my hair behind my ears and thanked her, as I made my way out of the store.

I jumped into the car and checked the clock. I had 20 minutes to get back to the office. I was going well over the speed limit when my phone rang. I fumbled with the bluetooth system until I heard Daniel's voice. "Hello, love, are you there?" Daniel's voiced chimed. "Yes, yes, I'm here. Hello?!" I yelled, as I ran through a red light. *Shit.* I was never that great at multi-tasking. "Great. Listen, we have finished a bit early and the plans for today have changed. How far out are you?" He asked.

"I'm about ten minutes away. I'll be there very soon!"

"Wonderful. I will fill you in when you get here. Cheers." He hung up the phone before I could say goodbye. Thankfully, it saved me from having to figure out how to end the call. I wasn't used cars as modern as his. The dashboard looked like a spaceship.

I pulled into a Parking space in front of the building and grabbed the Tiffany's bag. I was walking so fast that I could feel my breath catching. I stepped into the empty elevator and grabbed my Joe Malone fragrance from my bag and gave myself a spritz. After today, I knew I was probably running the risk smelling less than fresh. I took a second to catch my breath.

The door chimed and I stepped out and straightened my hair. I met Daniel's eyes through the glass of the empty conference room. He snapped his laptop shut and quickly made his way to me

"What are you doing with that in here?" He asked, sharply. My cheeks flushed. *Shit. Was I not supposed to bring it up?*

"I-I didn't want to run the risk of leaving in the car. I'm sorry." I whispered. He grabbed the bag and leaned in closer.

"We just like to keep things as confidential as possible in the office." He turned his head to look at the receptionist. "You never know who could be watching." He said. He straightened his shoulders and gestured towards the elevator. "After you," he said as his hand grazed my mid back, guiding me in though the doors.

"Oh, okay." I said, softly. I felt my hands grow clammy. I shifted away from his touch. I had no idea what could've been so confidential, but I was new and didn't think it would be appropriate to pry. "I will make sure to use better judgement next time. Again, I'm so sorry." I said, as I looked up at the ceiling. I caught Daniel's reflection and looked away.

"It smells amazing in here. Is that you?" He asked.

"Oh, um,"

I awkwardly sniffed my wrists and pretended that I didn't completely douse myself seconds ago. I was grateful for the subject change though. "It smells like earl grey tea!" He said, raising his eyebrow. "Oh, you're good."

I laughed and extended my wrist for him to smell.

"It's earl grey and cucumber, Jo Malone." I said. Daniel looked me in the eyes and took a whiff. He lingered a little longer than I liked and then stepped to the side. I shrugged it off, pretending not to notice. "Fantastic! Right, so plans have changed just a bit. The writers have made a few changes to the screenplay, and it needs to be reviewed before we can pick it up. So we might be working a little later than expected. That doesn't interfere with your evening does it?"

He tapped his laptop to his thigh a few times without making eye contact.

"No, not at all." I smiled. I said it without thinking. I was only slightly annoyed that I wouldn't be binge watching The Great British Bake Off and polishing off the wine in my fridge.

The doors opened with a *ding* and he lead the the way as we stepped out.

"Wonderful," Daniel smiled, as he held the lobby door open. "I've opened up times for the film team to go over Roger's schedule. I'd like you to sit in and take as many notes as possible. It will help you feel more familiar with this whole world." He said.

A wave of nerves rushed over me. This job was starting to feel like real, and I couldn't tell if I was becoming overwhelmed or excited. "Well, I'm glad I packed a legal pad then." I said, nervously. I smirked at him as we got into his car. He laughed and whipped his car into the street in his usual chaotic manner. We sped down Gower street, the palm trees whipping by and Daniel's music blaring. It was giving me a headache. I never thought I would be taken aback by the glitz of a filming studio, but as we approached the large white stone building, I started to feel that sense of magic that everyone talks about. There's some kind of 'larger than life' feeling that overtakes you. I wasn't much of a film buff, but I did enjoy a good drama or documentary.

He put the car in park and waited for me to meet him on the driver's side. We entered under stage number eleven and took the second floor to a large room. The room had a white table with a thick stack of papers in the middle. In the corner, were cases of Fuji water bottles stacked high on top of a mini fridge. The room was lit with awful florescent lighting.

Daniel sat his laptop on the table and unbuttoned his suit jacket. "Right, the writers and Roger will be here in about fifteen minutes. So, do you mind putting out some water bottles? I'm going to catch up on some emails before we get started." He said, as he sat down.

"Eh, absolutely..um did you say Roger will be here as well?" I asked. I tried my hardest to sound nonchalant, but the nerves were getting to me. I had only met Roger once and now I would be in an intimate, confidential setting with him. *My boss* who happened to be a prominent British celebrity.

"Yes, he has to approve any changes made since it's his production company." Daniel said, without looking up from his laptop. Normally, I'd expect a bit of banter from Daniel, but he seemed to be preoccupied. I was relieved that he wasn't picking up on my nerves, I thought. I took off my blazer and draped it over a chair. The room was stuffy and warm. My anxiety wasn't helping either. I brushed my hair over to one side of my shoulder and bent down to the mini fridge, hugging the water bottles close to my body. The cold felt good against the heat of my skin. "How many people are we expecting?" I asked, as I turned to look at Daniel. His eyes were glued to me, or my body, I couldn't quite distinguish the difference. I ignored his glances as to pretend not to notice. He looked away.

"Ten." He said, in a soft voice, swallowing hard. There was something so mischievous and overtly sensual about Daniel. I would be lying if I denied his good looks and demeanor, but I wanted to remain professional, despite whatever he wanted.

I placed the bottles in uniform on the middle of the table and stood there awkwardly. I was so nervous at the thought that Roger would be in the meeting today. I am not easily impressed or intimidated, but found myself nervous in Roger's presence. When we met, I was impressed by his humble attire and attitude. I found it hard to make eye contact with him. He was so handsome. And the accent, *god, his accent!*

I walked over to my bag, shaking myself from my daydream, to grab my notepad just as two men walked in. Daniel chatted with them and invited them to sit down. He motioned for me to do the same, without making an introduction. He pulled a chair out for me, right next to him. The rest of the men filtered in and were quietly chatting until Mr. Barnes walked in. They all greeted him warmly as he waved and shook hands with the men at the table. They weren't just colleagues, they were friends.

Roger was wearing a white linen button-down, a cabby hat, slacks, and New Balance sneakers. He looked polished but casual. He sucked his teeth, creating a faint smacking noise before saying, "Right, so, there's been a few changes to the screen play so let's have a run through it once more. Daniel, could you hand them out please?"

He scratched the back of his neck, his glance moving from the men to me, briefly. Roger seemed tired and ready to be over with this meeting. Daniel jumped up quickly and started disbursing the stack of papers on the table. I sat there awkwardly twiddling my pen. I shifted my eyes towards Roger, just as he quickly made a glance at me, once more. I fought a nervous smile as he looked away, clearing his throat. He straightened his collar and sat down.

Something about Roger was wildly intriguing to me. He was handsome and stern, but he had a sweetness to him. As a comedian, he was curiously quiet and reserved, which made me feel even more out-of-place in this testosterone-filled room. Determined to appear busy, I scribbled 'screenplay run through notes' on my legal pad, and tried my best to look busy.

The meeting started and the men tossed ideas back and forth, bouncing off each other's wit and humor. I watched closely, taking note of everything, even when one of them jumped up to act out a particularly hilarious scene he had in mind. I hadn't been told what exactly I was supposed to be notating but I figured to just be as observant as possible. Daniel interjected ever so often, while typing away on his laptop. Suddenly, the room fell silent as Roger cleared his throat and said, "Okay, let's do a read-through shall we?" His eyes landed on me and I felt a sudden jolt of panic.

"Jessica, was it? Why don't you help us by reading for the photographer on page 89?"

At first, I laughed, thinking it was some kind of joke. But as the men stared at me in silence, I realized he was serious. Daniel leaned back, folding his arms with a smug grin on his face. "

Take it away, Jess." He said, as if Daring me to fail. I felt the blood rush to my ears and cheeks, but I had no option but to go ahead. Thumbing through the text, I took a deep breath to steady my nerves. The lines were simple and minimal in comparison to the rest of the screenplay. But even though I'd never taken a theatre class in my life, I was determined to make a good impression.

As I read, I felt the weight of the room's scrutiny, knowing that as a newbie, all eyes were on me. As I reached my last line, I finally relaxed in my seat, taking another deep breath. I felt relieved that it was over. I also felt a pang of annoyance that Roger hadn't remembered my name, or at least, pretended not to.

I tried to shake off the feeling and turned to smile at Daniel, the only familiar face in the room. Daniel attempted to smile back, but was interrupted by Roger saying, "Excellent job, everyone. I'm happy with where it's at."

Roger dismissed everyone, his eyes lingering on me. The men slowly filtered out and chatted amongst themselves. I got up to grab my tote when Roger said, "Jessica, you're a natural. We should replace you with Natasha."

His attention to me made my cheeks flush. I knew he was trying to break the ice and couldn't be serious.

"Yes, I really feel like this could be my breakthrough." I said, sarcastically. I was shocked that that he was making conversation with me. It wasn't because I didn't feel worthy. I had styled hundreds of celebrities at Saks and knew that being famous didn't mean that someone was automatically better than me. However, something about him made me nervous. He smiled wide at me in response and nodded. He quickly returned to his conversation with one of the men and I took it as a cue to walk away. I noticed Daniel watching our interaction from the corner of my eye. I threw my tote over my shoulder and walked over to him.

"You didn't tell me there would be acting involved on my part." I said, begrudgingly. He snapped his laptop shut and buttoned his suit jacket. "Like he said, you were a natural. I honestly had no idea he was going to have you read. This was definitely a first." He assured me, in a hushed voice, just as Roger called him over. Roger handed over a thick, stapled pile of paper to Daniel. Daniel nodded and looked at me. "Jess, are you ready?" He asked. Roger and Daniel both stared in my direction as I shyly nodded. I adjusted my skirt before walking towards them, both of them awkwardly staring as I did this. I checked the time on my watch, 5:30pm. I guess it really was going to be a late night. We still had to deliver the screenplay to the townhouse. I didn't understand why we couldn't just give it to Roger now, but I refrained from asking any questions. We slid into the car and Daniel turned to me to say, "Do you mind coming with me to deliver the screenplay? I would enjoy the company. If not, then no worries. I can always drop you home." His eyes were glistening towards me. I hated that he was so handsome. *Gosh.* I would've loved nothing more than to head bak to my apartment. It had been a long day and I had a bottle of wine that was beckoning me. But, I decided I better prove how eager I was to learn. Also, some crazy part of me wanted a chance to snoop around the townhouse. I wanted to see how Roger really lived, no matter how creepy that seemed.

"No, I don't mind at all, on one condition," I said.

"And what is that?" His eyes widening at my ultimatum.

I frowned, "You buy me dinner. I'm starving." I said, as I clicked my seatbelt. My stomach had been growling for hours. He laughed and started the engine "Buy you breakfast and dinner? Just call this a long date, why don't you?" He said, jokingly. I cocked my head sideways. "Not when it's on the company dime".

"touché." He breathed. "touché."

We decided to takeout sushi and I let Daniel order for us. I pretended like the restaurant he chose wasn't a place where they knew me by name. I practically lived on delivery from this place.

He ran inside to grab the food and I quickly searched my bag for my phone. I sent Hanna a text telling her I was working late and having dinner with Daniel. Since I knew I'd be working late, and unable to respond, I expected to get a rise out of her. I smiled to myself and put my phone away.

This was the most excitement I had felt in months. Meeting my celebrity boss, shopping with someone's Amex, trying on fine jewelry, and dinner with a handsome man in a townhouse. *Is this really my job? Is this really what I'm going to be paid to do from here on out?* Just weeks ago, I was convincing a reality star to buy the new Marc Jacobs bag so I could use the commission to buy groceries.

Suddenly, Daniel opened the door, interrupting my train of thought. He placed the large paper to-go bag in the back seat.

"What kind of music do you listen to?" Daniel asked.

I always considered that to be a personal question. I think music preference directly speaks to your personality. It tells a story of your life in a way. Maybe that's why I was hesitant to answer.

"I like a lot of different music." Was all I said. I don't know why I felt uncomfortable telling Daniel that I mostly listen to vocal jazz, but I did. He nodded and reached for his phone in the cup holder. His knuckles grazed my thigh. My eyes grew large, for a brief moment, and I quickly looked away. Kanye West began blaring through the speakers and we were whipping through traffic again. It wouldn't be my first choice for a night drive, but I didn't mind it. Daniel didn't strike me as a fan of Paul McCartney or jazz so what did I expect?

We whipped past palm trees as the sun was slowly faded. With every long and sharp turn, I found my eyes getting heavy. Finally, we passed security and pulled in the driveway of the townhouse. A gigantic light fixture, on the second floor, lit up the front, illuminating the driveway. Daniel grabbed the food and told me to follow him inside. "Is Roger not home?" I asked, as he punched numbers into the keypad lock.

"No, he shouldn't be home until quite late." He assured

me as he pushed the door open. I followed him into the kitchen where he placed the food onto the bar. I looked up and around, taking in the decor once again.

"The light fixtures are fantastic, aren't they?" Daniel asked, proudly. Honestly, I found them to be mismatched and gaudy but would never dare to express that. "Mhmm" I managed. "I had them designed especially for this place." I heard a cork pop, as I made my way to the bar stools. "Fancy a bit of wine?" Daniel smiled, as he began pouring it into a glass. "One glass won't hurt, but I have to warn you that I am a terrible lightweight."

"Brilliant," He chimed, as he poured me a glass.

"I'll get the things from the boot, go ahead and eat." He said. I tried to refuse, but he insisted on taking care of it. I shrugged and reached for the edamame. *I was starving.*

After a few bites, I decided to plate our sushi rolls. I caught a glance of the wine bottle and realized the bottle was a 30-year-old vintage. I almost spat. I'd enjoyed nice wine before, but nothing this luxurious. Why would Daniel uncork something like this on a causal night? Daniel quickly returned. I helped him unload the items, realizing that the Tiffany's bag was not among the rest. I stopped myself from asking where it was. Instead, I excused myself to the bathroom. I wanted to see if the bag had made it back here somehow.

I made it to the hallway where I took my heels off quietly. I passed the guest bathroom and kept straight down the hall. On the left, was what appeared to be a guest room. There was a full-sized bed with a large tufted headboard. The walls were dark with crown molding and a large sliding glass door outlooking the side of the pool. There was a bag of golf clubs in the corner and a large grey chair with an ottoman. I covered my nose at a familiar overpowering stench. *Daniel's cologne.* This must be his room. I kept straight past the room to find a moderately sized gym. There was a rack of free weights and a treadmill, accompanied by a large caddy of towels and a mini fridge. After seeing how nice the setup here was, I didn't blame Daniel for wanting to stay here with Roger. I'd been absent long enough for Daniel to assume I was doing more than use the toilet.

I put my heels back on and headed towards the kitchen. Halfway there, I ran into what felt like a brick wall.

"Woah, slow down there, love! I thought you may have gotten lost down here," Daniel's hands locked onto my shoulders.

Embarrassed, I said what came to mind immediately.

"Oh, no, sorry. I had to fix my contact lens."

A lie. I didn't even wear contacts. I tried not to make eye contact, but he found my eyes and stared into them. "They look fine to me, darling." He said. His breath was hot and smelled of wine.

"All good. Let's eat. I'm starved," I said, releasing myself from his grasp. I casually scratched my head. I walked into the kitchen and noticed the sun was completely set now. The glow of the pool was lighting up the beautiful backyard. We sat in unison at the bar and I took a hefty swig of wine. It was smooth and oaky and exactly what I need to calm my nerves. I took a few bites of my yellowtail.

"You know, I think this is the most eventful first day Ive ever had."

I was trying to deter from the fact that I was snooping around he and Roger's bachelor pad.

Daniel polished off his first glass of wine, nearly pounding the glass on the bar. "I'm hoping that's a positive statement," He said, letting out a breath. I laughed

"Absolutely. I mean it. I know it can probably be chaotic at times, but it definitely beats retail." I said, shrugging. He looked at me, catching my gaze as I sucked a pod from an edamame shell. The energy in the room suddenly shifted. I was feeling the wine set in. My cheeks were warm and my body more relaxed, but my stomach was uneasy. *Was it the yellowtail?*

"Well, I am certainly glad you feel that way. I'm glad to have you on the team," He said gently, as he dropped his left hand to my knee. I froze.

I quickly crossed my legs. He caught the hint and removed his hand. "This is really good sushi." I said, to fill the silence. I enjoy a bit of flirting, but this was crossing a line. *First the stare, then the forwardness at the restaurant, and now making he was trying to make a move?*

Sure, Daniel was conventionally handsome but *that was it.* He ignored me and poured himself another glass of wine. I sat there quietly in shock, not knowing how to come back from that gesture. I also couldn't help but remember he would be driving me home soon. I pretended to check my watch out of habit and realized it was 8:30. It was officially the longest work day on record for me.

"You know, I should really head back into the city if we're finished for the day,"

I stood up, refusing to make eye contact, and ran my hand through my hair. I reached for my tote and began looking for my phone. Suddenly, I felt his warm hand on my low back. I spun around, only to have Daniel's hands quickly move to meet my cheeks.

He pulled me into his body and planted his wet lips into mine. I couldn't help but linger for a moment, in utter shock, before pushing him away from me. It felt good to be kissed in this way, but this was *WRONG.* Before I could raise my voice in protest, I heard the beep of the front key pad and the closing of the door. We both stood in shock before we heard the deep and nasal voice of Roger.

"Daniel, do you mind moving your car to curb so I can," his voice echoed as he came into the light of the living room. As he spoke, his eyes landed on us, cutting off his sentence. Embarrassment and shock ran through me and I was frozen. His gaze flicked from me to the wine glassed and then to Daniel, before shaking his head and then looking down at the floor, rubbing the back of his neck. I couldn't help but think of how bad this looked, especially on my first day on the job. It seemed like everything good in my life was doomed to fall apart. I braced myself for the worst. There's no way I wouldn't be sacked after this. *Shit. Shit. Shit.*

"Ah, Jessica, hello. Sorry, am I interrupting?" He said, in a tone that was vaguely sarcastic.

Daniel cleared his throat, "No, we were just dropping off the screenplay and having a quick bite to eat."

He walked to the opposite side of the bar and grabbed a thick folder and handed it to Roger. He smiled nervously as the silence that followed was heavy with tension. "Along with a bottle of my most expensive wine, I see? Right, well, thank you for dropping that off." Roger said. Roger parted his lips and raised his brows, as he looked us over. I fidgeted with my blouse and looked down at my shoes, trying to avoid eye contact. Daniel broke the silence with an awkward laugh. "Absolutely. I'll clean up and then we will be out of here."

He quickly started cleaning, tidying the space as fast as he could. Roger turned and began walking to the stairs but stopped halfway, resting his arm on the railing. "Oh, and Daniel, a package came for you today. I put it in your room next to the golf clubs." I looked at Daniel, who was painted with embarrassment. He did, in fact, live here with Roger. By the look on his face, he didn't want me to know.

Roger's stare seemed like a warning sign of some sort. His voice echoed through the silence of the kitchen as he ascended the stairs. My embarrassment was quickly mixing into rage. Not only had we been caught kissing, but now I looked unprofessional too. I stood there silently as Daniel trashed the food and put the wine glasses into the sink. There was no way I was going to offer to help after this disaster. I pulled out my phone from my tote bag, trying to look busy as I replied to a few messages from Hanna.

When I heard the jangle of Daniel's keys, I made a beeline for the door, my heels echoing loudly on the marble floor. Daniel followed closely behind me.

CHAPTER SEVEN

"SLOW DOWN THERE," Daniel whispered under his breath, moments after I stormed out of the townhouse.

"You're disgusting you know that," I spat, as I grabbed the car keys from his hand. "What do you think you're doing with those?" He scoffed.

"The smartest thing I've done all day. You really think you're fit to drive after three glasses of wine?" I got into the driver's seat.

"Calm down. I'm not a lightweight and I am English, after all."

Daniel smiled with his arms wing-spanning beside him, attempting to make some joke out of this. I slammed the car door. He slowly made his way to the passenger's side and got in. "Look, I didn't mean to upset you," He said, as I whipped the car into reverse. I peeled out, looking past him and straight out the rear window. I didn't care if Roger heard, even if he did, he would assume it was Daniel and that satisfied me.

"*Oi, slow down!* This is a rental!" Daniel yelled. *Of course it was, pretentious ass.* "That move you pulled back there was disgusting and well planned out, I'm sure. That kind of shit is what could potentially lead to me losing my job!" I yelled. He started laughing. "You think you'll be fired for having a few drinks and dinner with me? You really need to get out a little more." He scoffed, adjusting his jacket.

I pressed my heel deeper into the gas pedal as we exited the neighborhood. "I have no idea, but it sure as hell doesn't look good for me. This whole thing was premeditated, Daniel! And you know it! I mean, you live with Roger! You failed to mention that."

"Look, I had no idea he would be home tonight. I write his schedule for Christ's sake! Besides, do you think a boss who allows his employee to live with him would be the type to easily sack someone? I hardly see how me living with him has anything to do with this." He said, in annoyed. I felt his eyes on me as he turned his head but I refused to look at him. I was whipped crazily past every car on the highway. He had somewhat of a point, but I was still fuming from this whole event. "Jess, slow *down.*" He said.

"Fine. I'll let it go, but I don't appreciate you coming onto me like that. Seriously, can't you take a hint?" I scoffed. I felt the rage bubbling within me. "I'm sorry. Maybe I did enjoy a bit too much wine." He said, as he ran a quick hand through his hair.

Oh, so now he's admitting that he drank too much? Blaming his actions on the wine was such a cop out.

"Did you really need me to come here with you tonight?" I asked. I knew the answer already, but I wanted to hear him say it. I took a deep breath in an attempt to calm down. I realized if I didn't cool off that *I* would be the reason for losing this job. I reminded myself that Daniel has been the executive assistant for five years. He probably held more weight than I knew within the company.

He sighed before saying, "Truthfully, no, I didn't. However, I enjoy your company and I did give you an option, remember? I didn't force you to come here or lead you here under false pretenses. I thought we were just having bit of fun, getting to know each other."

I clenched my jaw as hard as I could, avoiding saying the offensive thoughts in my head. I sat in silence, waiting for him to explain himself further, but he didn't. I didn't believe him one bit. No man would be as thoughtful and charming as Daniel upon meeting a new female coworker. It wasn't platonic and he knew that.

I quickly approached my street and parked the car to the curb. My blood was boiling and I just wanted to be alone to process all of this. I couldn't even look at him.

"Look, I'm willing to put this behind us and act as if nothing happened, if you are," I sighed and closed my eyes. I was exhausted and the wine didn't help. I just wanted to get into bed and worry about this tomorrow.

Daniel raised his eyebrows and nodded.

"Absolutely. Right."

I couldn't believe that he was acting so nonchalant. This probably wasn't the first time something like this had happened to him. I had a feeling I was the first one to deny him, though. I reached for the door handle and Daniel said, "Wait, how do you expect me to get home?"

I grabbed my tote, stepped out of the car, and threw it over my shoulder. I looked him in the eye before slamming the door shut.

"Call a cab!" I yelled, over my shoulder.

I raced to my apartment without looking back. My feet were absolutely killing me. I continued up the hill as fast as I could. I'd been in these shoes for 12 hours. A record high for me. I reluctantly slipped off my shoes and walked into the elevator of my building barefoot. I didn't even have the capacity to be disgusted at my feet. The cold marble felt good on the pads of my feet, but the feeling of the carpet on the 8th floor made me nauseous. I could only imagine how much grime was caked onto it from the other tenants. Finally, the vision of my front door felt like a finish line. My heart skipped a beat at the sight of a vase with bright pink peonies. On my welcome mat sat a crystal vase full of them, along with a card. I quickly opened the small card.

"I hope your first day was amazing. I'm proud of you! Talk soon. Love, H."

For the first time in forever, I didn't want to tell Hanna every detail about my day. It was still surreal that I wasn't working beside her anymore. Typically, I would be on the phone with her immediately after a day like today, but I had to decide if this was even something worth sharing. I didn't have the capacity to talk now. If I didn't fully know how I felt about it, then I sure as hell wasn't going to share it with Hanna. I knew I was angry and disgusted, but I also knew these feelings were reactionary.

I peeled off my dress and stepped into the shower. The sound of the water hitting the tile was almost deafening in my silent apartment. I scrubbed every inch of me as vigorously as possible. Every scrubbing motion was fueled by rage. I replayed what had happened tonight backwards and front. Over and over. Trying to view it from all angles. I'd thought about until the water turned cold.

The clock on the oven read 11:30PM. I groaned with exhaustion.

As I gulped down my water, I realized that if this career was important to me, as I expressed to Daniel, I had to compartmentalize this situation. I couldn't let it get in the way of my future, but I wasn't going to forget about it either. *How could I?* On one hand, I couldn't help but slightly blame myself for engaging in the flirting. I enjoyed being adored by Daniel on some level, sure, but things had gotten out of hand. *A kiss, really? From someone I'd only known a few days?* It was crazy. I'd never even kissed on the first date before, let alone with a coworker! I was old-fashioned that way. It was something not many people knew about me, not even Hanna.

I paced in my studio and began to think about the lack of romance in my life. Maybe that was a factor that played into what happened. I knew the implications of me accepting a late work night dinner with Daniel. Truthfully, I enjoyed Daniel's company too, when he wasn't being a tipsy fool. Any warm feeling towards Daniel was completely wiped from my thoughts, when I remembered the look on Roger's face. When he saw me sitting at *HIS* bar, in *HIS* home, with an expensive bottle of *HIS* wine. I wanted to die. I don't think I've ever felt that level of embarrassment in my life. I was wincing as it replayed in my mind.

I looked around my small apartment and thought deeply about what I wanted. I saw my full-sized bed that just barely met the black kitchen tile. Gosh, it was such a small space. I didn't even have room for a kitchen table. Half of my studio was all glass windows that wrapped around to touch my closet door. I had a small table with a 32 inch flat screen on it and very few possessions, apart from my wardrobe. My closet was large for a small place like this, but I still had to keep half my shoes under the bed. I turned, facing west, and wondered how I'd ever get out of here. The view was the only redeeming factor about this place. I knew I'd miss it once I was gone.

Five years ago, I thought I'd hit the lottery with this apartment. I thought moving thousands of miles away from home would bring me all the happiness I needed. I also thought ending my relationship was a good career move. It was the only loving and respectable relationship I'd ever had. Little did I know, that I'd be here.

I thought a lot of things would be different than they are now. As I looked around, I couldn't help but wonder when it would all change. I unwrapped my hair from towel and made my way back to the bathroom. I combed out my hair and thought about all the time I had spent here. I thought about the very few people I'd even had in this small space. Despite that small amount, I had many memories to show for it. My stomach dropped as I realized most of those memories were with James. I quickly shook myself from the flashbacks of us in my small bed, eating takeout or having our morning coffee. I knew the only way to fully move on from my past and this tiny apartment was to keep a cool head, and not do anything to compromise my new job. I decided right then, in the silence of my studio and in the glow of the car lights, reflecting off my walls, that I did want this job. I wanted to prove myself, if I'd get the chance. I wanted to travel, find love again, and get out of this shoebox apartment.

With that decision, I knew I had to be strategic. I needed to be aware of the perception of me and Daniel's work relationship. I needed to seem unbothered to Daniel and I needed to somehow prove my worth to Roger. I pulled out my phone to check my email and found the subject line:

'This weeks itinerary' and scrolled to tomorrow's agenda.

- *9:30 AM meet at Office*
  - *9:45 attend meeting and take notes (Jessica)*
  - *11:00am book transportation for team (Daniel & Jess)*
  - *12:45 Lunch*
  - *2:00 drop final scripts to studio (Jess)*
  - *3:30-5:00pm admin*

I sighed with relief. Tomorrow wouldn't be another long day. I looked at the clock. If I went to bed now, I could still get seven hours of sleep. A heavenly thought after the day I'd had. I laid my head on my pillow, my icy cold, damp hair making me shiver. I watched as the car lights reflected off the buildings and onto my ceiling, knowing I wasn't going to get a wink of sleep.

CHAPTER EIGHT

TWO YEARS earlier

I placed my finger tips closer to the air vents to defrost them. Although I had missed the chill of a New England Autumn, it had been a long time since I had been back to enjoy it. James had invited me to spend Fall Break with him and his parent's in Saratoga Springs, his home town. I'd never visited upstate New York and jumped at the opportunity. I couldn't bare the thought of spending Thanksgiving with my family. I hadn't told my mom the truth, of course.

How could I? I didn't need to hear another guilt trip from her.

I was finally old enough to not feel guilty about making my own plans for the Holidays. I'd spent plenty of years watching relatives have drunken outbursts and I'd had my fill of mediocre sweet potato casserole too. Instead, my mom thought I would be working, an excuse she was used to hearing since I had moved to LA. Working in fashion left no room for enjoyable holidays and lengthy time off. I turned on the seat warmers of the Volvo rental, and watched as James made his way out of Starbucks, juggling our drinks. We had taken a red eye from LA to NY and were beyond exhausted.

I felt like royalty as he carefully slid into the nice car, both drinks balancing in one hand. I quickly grabbed one to help, not knowing which was mine.

"They were out of oat milk so I got you soy is that ok?"

I nodded happily as he swapped our drinks, so that they were correct. "Mmm.. its so nice to enjoy a warm drink with frost on the window." I admitted. James let out a soft laugh.

"Yes, it is, isn't it?"

He took a sip of his usual. A venti vanilla latte with an extra shot. For someone who came from such an affluent background, he was a simple guy. I liked that about him. His father was one of the top heart surgeons in New York and his mom was an interior designer who had been featured in *Better Homes & Gardens* a handful of other well-known magazines.

"What has gotten into you?" He asked. I must've been smiling at him a bit too long.

His big blue eyes were glistening as I looked at him, a bit of latte foam lingered on his top lip. I lifted my hand to his face and gently swiped my thumb over it.

"Nothing. I'm just really grateful that you invited me here."

I took a large sip of my pumpkin spice latte, burning my tongue. He smiled to himself sheepishly before he extended an arm across the headrest and pulled me close.

"Me too. Even though I know you're just in it for the Volvo joy ride," he joked, putting the car into reverse. I tossed my head back and let out a laugh. "Now, what would give you that impression?" I said, sarcastically as I pressed the music icon on the touchscreen. I adjusted my seat dramatically and got comfortable as the soft music began to fill the car. The sad thing was, that I'd never been in a car this nice and he probably had no idea. I was sensitive to the fact that something so mundane to him excited me. I'd also never flown above coach before this trip, so this was one of many firsts for me. I tried to fight him when he gave me the business class ticket weeks ago.

It was no use. He not only intended to spoil me but I'm sure he refused to fly coach. It was odd to think I worked and lived in a world that was much more elevated than a life I'd ever known. And now I was dating a man who knew no different. This was his baseline.

"My parents have texted me only about a hundred times to make sure you were still coming," He said, casually placing a hand on my thigh.

I felt a slight butterfly sensation in my stomach. I knew they adored me and it felt so nice to know that sense of belonging. I'd only met his parents a couple times. Mostly, over dinner when they'd come to visit him on campus. It was a rare occasion as they were both so busy but each time we'd spend hours talking about design and LA food culture. James' dad was a foodie with a bottomless pit for a stomach. While his mom was a wealth of design knowledge. They were both so incredibly down to earth that I felt silly after first meeting them. I remember being so nervous that I wore a black turtleneck, on one of the hottest days of the year, to avoid my sweat marks showing. His dad was tall and fit, with wiry salt & pepper hair that had never seen a day of styling product. His mom was petite and blonde with emerald green eyes. Her smile was as warm as sunshine, something she no-doubt gave to James. Then there was Ethan, James' little brother who didn't resemble either of them. He was four years younger than James, and a total sweetheart, when he wanted to be.

"Awe, of course. I couldn't turn down an opportunity to see your childhood home and ask your mom to show me your naked baby pictures," I laughed, poking his side.

"Okay, for the last time, Jess, that won't be happening," He said, as he rounded a corner.

"Yeah, we'll see about that." I said. He took his eyes off the road as we came to a red light to look over at me. I placed my hand on top of his and squeezed it. We road the rest of the way without a word, just Ella Fitzgerald and Louis Armstrong playing singing to us on the radio.

I relaxed into the headrest, taking in the landscape around us. There was nothing more breath-taking than a New England autumn. The leaves were vibrant orange and picturesque. The beautiful brownstones and historic victorian houses, were unlike any I'd ever seen. This place had the small town charm straight out of an episode of *Gilmore Girls*. We were driving down historic main street, something James pointed out, breaking the comfortable silence. It was the most charming street I'd ever seen. There were quaint restaurants, small bakeries, and antique shops that were beckoning me. "Wow" I whispered.

"Pretty neat, huh?"

"My mom used to take us to that little cafe right there every Christmas break. She would pick us up from school and get us our first hot chocolate of the season. It was our tradition. It's still the best in town. You've gotta try it." He said, emphatically. I could tell he was excited to have me here. I felt honored that he was so proud to show me where he came from. I couldn't say the same for myself. Before I knew it, we had turned down a secluded road leading to a large iron gate. It was at least twelve feet high with a large 'L' monogrammed on the entrance. We approached the gate closer and James rolled down the window to type a code into a silver callbox. I was utterly amazed at the grandeur of the estate. I looked ahead to see a beautiful three-story victorian house. It was no doubt built in the mid 1800's. It was like something out of the Great Gatsby. It was whimsical and charming, but also spooky. The grass was still lush, despite the season.

It was nearing 5pm and the sun was setting, showcasing the glow of the lights inside the house. The main driveway was large and circular with a patch of grass in the middle. There were two large light poles, the kind you'd find in Central Park. They sat on either side of the front drive, making this place seem like a movie set. There was a black range rover parked out front next to a bright red Porsche. I assumed the Porsche belonged to his mom, Alice.

We drove past them and parked to the left side of the house just as my nerves set in. "Well, here we are," James said, as he killed the engine. He opened his door and walked around to open mine. I sat with my mouth open, gawking at my surroundings. I stepped out and reacquainted my top jaw to the bottom one as I fixed my hair.

"You look beautiful, Jess." James said, in a reassuring way before kissing my forehead.

"Thanks, I just feel a little messy after all the travel."

Not true. I was anxious for some reason. I felt like there was some sort of pressure for me to perform this week. I stood there with my arms crossed, marveling at the hundred-year-old brick as James grabbed our luggage from the trunk. I tied my trench coat, a thrifted Burberry find from online, one of my most prized possessions that I pulled out specifically for today. I followed James as he motioned me towards the porch. "Jess, are you nervous?" He asked, as he sat out bags in front of the door. He seemed concerned.

"Sort of, I—I don't know why. I mean, gosh this house is beautiful."

I was deflecting. He kissed me before I could finish my thought, just as the porch light came on. I heard the turning of a door handle followed by a creaking sound. "Oh, come on you guys couldn't want until you got settled in?" It was Ethan. I jumped back from James, my hand instinctively covering my mouth. Ethan had matured quite a bit in the last six months since we'd seen him. A once scrawny version of James' younger sibling now seemed to be a beefed up version of Mr. Locke. "Ethan, don't be a creep. I hadn't even rang the door bell yet. How did you know we were out here?" James said, jokingly as he grabbed our bags and walked over the thresh-old. Ethan slapped him on the back in that weird masculine way that guys do to welcome each other. I followed behind. "I saw your headlights, Genius," He scoffed, before yelling to the house "The lovebirds are here!"

I felt my cheeks get hot and began laughing nervously. We stepped into the entry way and James sat our bags down on the marble tile. Leave it to Alice to replace what was probably a wood floor with Italian marble. The Foyer also had a large crystal chandelier with small pearls decorating the hardware. Everything in the foyer was an antique and probably worth more than my whole wardrobe, maybe even my whole apartment.

There were four hallways extending from where we stood and I could already tell I'd be getting lost during my stay. James turned around to grab my hand, making me feel like an timid child. I tucked myself into his side as we made it down one of the hallways. I heard the click-clack of heels heading our way and that warm voice called out,

"Is that the sweet Jessica I see?!"

Alice's petite frame came into vision beneath an archway, lit by a gorgeous sconce. "Wow, good to see you too, mom" James said, lightheartedly as she embraced us both. She stepped back to get a look at us. I straightened my hair once more out of nervousness.

"I caught them making out before they even stepped foot inside." Ethan said with a smug grin, leaning against the wall.

"Oh, we were not!" I said, reassuringly.

"Ethan! Stop that. One day you'll be in love too and you better hope that's the least I ever catch you doing." Alice said. "Oh, ew! god, mom." Ethan and James said in unison. I couldn't help but let out a laugh.

"I knew that would shut you up. Ok, enough, I have canapés waiting. Follow me!" Alice said.

I looked at James and he gave me a reassuring nod, placing a warm hand on my low back as we were lead into the living room. "Will Robert be joining us?" I asked eagerly. I absolutely adored Alice, but Robert and I always shared the same humor and made good conversation.

"Oh, yes, he's just finishing up some paperwork in his office. He will join us for dinner." She said, reassuringly. Her petite hands rested on her elbows, displaying a beautiful gold Cartier bracelet.I smiled in response.

We entered a cozy space with a large fireplace that was lit with a roaring fire. There were two large mismatched armchairs on either side of an oak coffee table. It was all so lovely. It was unlike any house I'd ever stepped foot in. Alice had a gift for using eccentric antiques to make a space cozy yet elevated.

"I know you are probably hungry after all that traveling, so please help yourself," She motioned to a silver tray with miniature quiche and cocktail napkins. I immediately went to grab one as to not seem rude. I was still full from the latte and my appetite was shot from the nerves. James and Ethan quickly followed my lead.

"Mmm these are delicious." I said with a mouthful.

"I'm glad you think so! Norma got them from Trader Joe's. There's more where that came from too, so help yourself!"

I was stunned that Alice would ever step foot inside of a *Trader Joe's*, much less serve it to us, but maybe I was being judgmental.

"Norma is our housekeeper," James said, smiling at me and shoveling another quiche. Ah, so maybe she hadn't ever stepped foot inside of a *Trader Joe's*.

"She's a lot more than a housekeeper to us! But she's on vacation this week" Alice chimed in.

I nodded in silence. I found myself looking around at the exquisite architecture of the house. The ceiling seemed to go on for miles. The second floor spiraled around the living room, encased by solid oak railing. "Impressive isn't it?" James asked, in my ear before giving me a gentle kiss on the cheek.

I was almost shocked by the amount of affection he was displaying in front of his family. He'd never been one for PDA.

"This house is beautiful... I'm speechless, Alice." I said, as I caught her gaze and stepped away from James.

"Thank you, dear. So much history, so much work has gone into it. It's nice when you can appreciate your own home after years of curating homes for others."

Alice took a sip of wine.

"Oh, dear! You both are still in your coats. Sorry, without Norma I'm a useless hostess." She sat her glass down and sauntered over. I placed my napkin on the coffee table and James helped me out of my trench.

"Here, mom, I've got it."

He took both of our coats and disappeared.

"Lovely Burberry, is it vintage?" Alice asked. I nodded silently. Alice admired my dress and ran a hand down the arm, remarking that it was cashmere. She didn't just know interiors it seemed. She was well versed in fashion too.

She continued to compliment me on my outfit and taste as we had a few more appetizers. She poured me a glass of red wine and I finished it within minutes. It was the most delicious wine I'd ever tasted. A Bordeaux, if I wasn't mistaken. I didn't know too much about wine, but I knew that was the exact type I liked.

"You like the wine?" She joked, noticing I'd finished my glass. I giggled. "Oh, yeah, it's delicious. I promise I'm normally not this…thirsty. Is this a Bordeaux?" I asked. Alice sat her glass down on the table before answering.

"Yes! I pulled out a special bottle just for this occasion."

Suddenly, I felt a warm hand on my shoulder. James' sweet voice said, "Are we the special occasion, mom?"

He gave me a squeeze. I looked up at him from behind and smiled nervously. I wasn't used to being the center of attention. I didn't like it.

"Well, of course! It's the first time you've brought a girl

home. And not just any girl, *Jessica.*" She said, smiling our way.

I wasn't sure why his parents loved me so much. I hadn't spent a significant amount time with them, but I guess the time I had spent was enough to make a great impression. We did connect quickly, talking nonstop, and sharing laughs. It felt like an unspoken bond that most people are lucky to make few times in life. I was certainly lucky to be making that bond so early on. These were good people from what I knew so far, so I decided to relax and enjoy it.

"Thank you for saying that, Alice. It means a lot. I am so grateful to be here with you guys for the break. It's a nice change of pace." I said with my hand on my heart. I knew James was frozen with pride right now. I didn't even have to look at him to know it. I could feel it. As the time passed I thought about how James was extremely lucky to have been raised by them, and to be loved by them. His family was the most important thing to him and to have their approval was like an early Christmas gift.

It was hard not to be envious of this in some small way though. I didn't have many family members I was close with, much less a strong parental unit to impress. The only approval I sought out was that of my friends. "She's pretty great." James said, softly and squeezed both my shoulders. "Yeah, yeah, Jess is great. What's for dinner?" Ethan asked, sarcastically. I let out a laugh.

"Those protein shakes aren't keeping you so full these days?" I joked, while pretending to flex my muscles. Everyone bellowed with laughter and Ethan rolled his eyes before saying, "Clearly not! Besides, I still have lots to gain, baby!" He joked, flexing dramatically, twisting his torso.

Ethan was captain of his Lacrosse team and definitely the star athlete of the family. James had a naturally fit and slim build, but I wouldn't bet on him making a sports team. What he lacked in athleticism he made up for in intellectualism and romanticism, that was for sure.

"I'm making my specialty tonight, lasagna." Alice said, breaking my stream of thoughts.

"By speciality she means one of the few things she can cook." James said, jokingly. "Hey, it's better than nothing! We still have about twenty minutes before its ready. Let me show you both to your rooms." Alice said.

I gathered that meant we wouldn't be rooming together. Maybe I shouldn't have assumed we would be sleeping together with how traditional his family seemed. We followed Alice up the closest stair case that was carpeted with a cream and black speckled pattern. The brass rods that secured the carpet to the steps was beautifully patinaed. I would have to guess that they were as old as the house.

Every detail of this house was so meticulously chosen. I wondered if James' grew up noticing he was surrounded by this beauty, or if he took it for granted.

We followed Alice, for what seemed like forever, until we reached a dimply lit hallway. A bright red runner ran over the polished wood floors.

"You both will be staying in the East wing, where James spent his younger years."

"Yeah, you don't wanna know what he looked like before puberty hit," Ethan teased.

"Oh, I think I do." I laughed, as I elbowed James in the side. James rolled his eyes. "Mom, I can take it from here. We will be down when dinner's ready."

I was shocked at how direct James sounded, but I'd be lying to say I wasn't relieved. All this travel had me wiped out and unable to keep up appearances for much longer. The wine wasn't helping.

"Okay, okay. I can take a hint." Alice said, with her hands waving in front of her. "Come on, Ethan, I need your help in the kitchen." She whispered. They made their way back down the hall into descending the stairs and out of sight. I took a deep breath and looked at James, who had his hands in his pockets. His broad shoulders soon found my arms around them, hugging him tightly.

"Ugh, I'm exhausted." I mumbled, into his firm chest. He rubbed my back softly. "The coffee didn't perk you up like usual?" He asked. I peeled back to see his devilish smile.

"Clearly not," I nodded.

"So, where's *my* room?" I asked. I knew that he could tell I wasn't absolutely thrilled with that distinction. "This way,"

James lead me to a set of French doors with large crystal knobs. "After you." James said.

I opened both doors to see a lush king-sized bed with a large fabric headboard tall enough to climb. The room was wallpapered with turquoise satin that took my breath away. The room was encased in thick crown moulding that matched the large chandelier handing above us. There were two lights on either side of the bed that were made to look like candle sticks. I felt like I was living out of an episode of *Downton Abbey*.

"Pretty impressive. Huh?" James whispered. He could tell I was in awe with the luxury of the room.

"I can't believe you live here." Was all I could manage. I turned to meet his eye, his hands in his pockets again.

"Oh, my room isn't nearly this impressive. Mom just wanted you to have the best guest room." He said, running a hand through his thick hair. He looked more handsome than ever.

"I don't believe that one bit," I said, playfully as I put my hands around his torso. "Well, I guess I'll just have to show you." He whispered, as he grabbed my and pulled me in for a kiss.

He lead me back into the hall and straight across the way to his room. "Oh, how convenient." I said, as he opened the door. "Don't get any ideas about sneaking over here..lets say, when everyone in the house is asleep, or drunkenly passed out by 12am, okay?"

I let out a laugh. "Okay, whatever you say." I replied.

His room was slightly smaller than mine, but not by much. It was simple. Still, it was much more elegant than any room I'd had growing up. The walls were a deep red and printed with the same satin pattern as mine. His bed was decorated with a fluffy white down duvet. The pillows were large and billowy to match, beckoning me to lay down. There was a small fireplace on the west side of the room with picture frames and awards on the mantle. His whole adolescence was displayed perfectly there. To the left of the fireplace was a giant bookcase. In the middle, was a small, modern looking record player. I raised my eyebrows. I was surprised to see the ratio of records to books on display. His extensive collection was amazing. I walked over to it and ran my fingers across the row of multi-colored spines.

"Those are the classics. So, if you're looking for Frank, that's where he lives."

I smiled at how well James knew me. I also loved that he enjoyed the same type of music as me.

"This is impressive." I said, as I turned around and looked up at the ceiling. Instead of a chandelier, he had a large white circular lantern. "That's interesting," I said, pointing up at it.

"Yeah, I begged my mom to let me replace the chandelier after my trip to Japan." He said.

"When did you go to Japan?" I asked. "My sophomore year of high school." He laughed.

"To be honest, it wasn't my favorite trip. I just fell in love with the minimalistic way they decorated. Everything was so streamlined and calm. My mom was just surprised that I finally showed an interest in her line of work, so she got me this." He said, gesturing at fixture.

"I love that." I smiled and let out a sigh. I took a seat at the foot of his bed.

I laid back, throwing my arms over my head.

"Wow. I could stay here forever. How did you ever manage to leave?" I asked, as I suddenly felt James' hand on my left boot. I craned my head up to see James on his knees, slowly taking off my shoes.

"Hey, what are you doing?" I asked, trying to wriggle free.

"I'm just helping you to get more comfortable," he whispered. "Are you now?" I smirked down at him. He took my boots off and placed them uniformly to the side of the bed, and began running his hands up my thighs. I was surprised by what he was doing. I let out a soft moan before stopping him.

"James, your parents are down there. And they'll probably be calling us soon." I said, trying to steady my breath. This wasn't like him to be so spontaneous or careless. I sat up as he said, "We have time."

He pushed me back down onto the bed. I giggled nervously. "James, what's gotten into you?" I asked, putting my hands on his shoulders.

"You just look so good on my bed. I can't help it."

His tone was almost desperate. I was exhausted, but I was also incredibly turned on seeing him like this. This had to be fulfilling some wild fantasy of his. I lifted my hips to pull my tights down, obliging him. My butt was ice cold and fully exposed in my thong. His eyes grew wide, like a kid on Christmas, as he watched me struggle to remove my tights.

I began to want him just as badly as he wanted me. I felt a warm wetness pooling in my groin. I looked down to see his pants growing larger by the second too. He couldn't unbuckle his belt fast enough for either of us. He tried to pull my sweater dress over my head and I stopped him at my black lace bra. "We don't have time." I said. He knew what I meant. I reached into his underwear going straight for what I wanted. He groaned as I did this. He pulled me closer, my legs straddling him briefly before he pushed me back down onto the bed aggressively. My body sank slowly into the marshmallow-like comforter. He grabbed the backs of my knees and hoisted my hips up to meet his. Finally, he was deep inside me.

"God," he breathed to himself. My tights were hanging around my ankles still, stretching to their limit. I let out a whisper of a moan before he cupped my mouth to silence me. He reached down and nearly ripped my tights off. Leaving my bare legs free to wrap completely around his waist. He pushed me further up the bed as I grabbed onto his hair for dear life. I tried my hardest to be quiet. He felt amazing against me. I felt like I was evaporating with each thrust. He grew larger by the second and before I knew, it we were both pulsating against each other trying not to make a sound. I whimpered against his hand as he breathed heavily into my neck. Just as we finished, a low beeping noise came from somewhere in the room. I heard Alice's voice over the intercom telling us it was time for dinner. James quickly shot up and buckled his belt. He ran to the intercom and pressed down on a button. My head was spinning.

"We"ll be right down." He breathed into the speaker box mounted onto the wall. His hair had fallen into his face and was slightly messy. I don't think he'd ever been more attractive than in this very moment. I sat up on my elbows still trying to catch my breath

"Do you have a bathroom in here?" I asked.

"Of course. Right through here." He sighed, still trying to catch his breath. He opened up another set of French doors, displaying a gorgeous marbled floor and a white clawfoot tub. I tiptoed around, until I realized the floors were heated. Of course they were. I turned to shut the door but James stopped me briefly to give me a kiss.

"I'll be quick." I whispered into his lips. I sat on the toilet, looking all around me. His bathroom was small but equally as breath-taking as any other room in this house. I stared at my reflection in the mirror, noticing how beautifully flushed I looked. I cleaned myself up and washed my hands feeling increasingly aware that my legs were bare. There was no way I was putting those tights back on. I hoped my dress was long enough that no-one would notice they were missing. I couldn't help myself from smiling at what we'd just done. James had always been a great lover but I'd never seen him so passionate.

I opened the doors to find him sitting cross-legged in a large leather chair. I walked over to him, stepping in between his legs and lacing my fingers with his. He looked up at me with a large smile.

"That was incredible but now I've worked up an appetite."

James pulled me into his lap. I gave him a kiss and whispered, "You mean more of an appetite?"

He laughed against my lips, sending a wave of chills down my legs. He rubbed them away and patted my butt before standing us up. "Lets get down there before they think something is up."

I hopped up quickly with him. James lead the way out of his room and down the stairs, my stomach growled all the way to the kitchen. We weaved through what felt like ten hallways before reaching the dining area where his brother and parents were. They had already served themselves and were patiently waiting. I Immediately caught Robert's vision as he stood to greet me with open arms. "There she is!" He cheered, as he opened his arms from across the table. We took our seats across from Robert and Ethan with Alice at the head of the table. James pulled out my chair and reached for the bottle of wine at the table, immediately pouring himself a glass. He remained standing and soon lifted his glass.

"I want to make a toast. To my beautiful parents, for hosting us this weekend, to a lovely holiday together, and to the love of my life Jessica." He said. My cheeks flushed immediately. I'd never him say I was 'the love of his life'.

"Aweee." his parents cried in unison as Ethan began shoveling his food, inattentive. "Cheers, everyone. Were so happy you're here. All of you." They said.

I was overwhelmed with gratitude, but couldn't help but get this uncomfortable sinking feeling in my stomach. James' words kept replaying in my head as I ate my food. *Why was I so uneasy? I loved James. I really did.*

"You two look so refreshed. Did you take a Power Nap or something?" Robert pointed out, shaking me from my thoughts. I immediately turned red before James quickly interjected

"Yep. Wine and a quick nap will do that to you." He said, cooly. I sank into my chair with relief and my heart pounding.

"The lasagna is insane, Alice." I said, nervously to change the subject. *Insane?* I'd never used that as an adjective in my life. I shoveled another bite into my mouth and she thanked me. We spent the rest of dinner catching up and exchanging stories, deflecting from the previous question.

Soon, Robert and Alice were telling me all about James' quirks as a kid and his many accomplishments. My face hurt from all the laughter and genuine heartfelt energy filling the room. They were incredibly proud of him. I could only imagine how good that felt.

My ears were getting hot as I tossed back one more glass of wine. Alice served us doppio espressos as I asked them about how they met. Robert told me their whole love story as the minutes turned to hours. They met in college, just like us they pointed out. Robert was knee deep in his residency and Alice was finishing up her degree at the New York School of design. They had met at a bar amongst mutual friends and were inseparable ever since."I didn't know you two met at a bar." James said, sounding shocked. James kept his warm hand on my thigh all night long. Occasionally squeezing and gently caressing it. I tried not to squirm away but I felt like I was suffocating.

James was being exceptionally clingy throughout dinner, in a way I'd never seen from him. I began spiraling about this whole week meant. We'd been together for a year and a half now, but I had a feeling it was extremely significant to him and his parents. Even though it was a milestone, I felt overwhelmed by the weight of it.

We finished off our coffee and finally said our goodnights. As James and I walked to the stairs I let out a large yawn.

"Its, been a long day, huh?" He asked, pulling me to his side.

"Yes and these stairs are my worst enemy, currently." I said, stepping away from him. Suddenly, I was horizontal and James was holding me tight to his chest. I let out a screech and began to laugh.

"You're giving Ethan's new muscles a run for their money." I said.

"I think it's the other way around, love." He huffed. We reached the top of the stairs and he sat me down gently. He ran a hand through his hair, putting it back into place.

"Is there anything you need before we go our separate ways?" He asked, in a light tone. "Are we really sleeping in separate beds? I thought that was just for show." I joked, feeling partially relieved. I needed some time alone to think.

"Well, that was the plan. I thought you might want your own room and my mom spent the whole week making sure it was up to standard. But if you'd rather stay with me, I think we could pull it off." He said, smiling. I was being inconsiderate. Alice had really put a lot of thought into me being here this weekend and it showed.

I stood there in silence for a good moment before apologizing.

"No, no, it might do me well to have a night to myself. It is a beautiful room too." I said, honestly. We stood there a moment longer before James grabbed my hand. "Do you want to listen to a record first?" He asked. "Of course." I said, with a smile. This was a ritual of ours. One that he'd started but that we'd neglected this semester. Life had gotten so busy for us with graduation approaching. He lead me into his room by hand and made his way over to his collection.

He slid a vinyl from the shelf and blew some invisible dust from it. I heard that brief static before music echoed from the speakers. Frank Sinatra was suddenly cooing and I couldn't help but let a large smile grow on my face. He turned to me and extended his arms to invite me to dance. I wrapped my arms around his neck and we began swaying.

"You know, I'd be lying if I said sex in your childhood bedroom wasn't the best I've ever had." I said. James grinned, forming a small dimple on his right cheek.

"Seeing you here, in that dress, with my family being so excited—just ignited something inside me. I don't know what it was, but I needed you right then." He admitted. I said nothing. I was flattered and at a loss for words. "I'm sorry if my family came on a bit too strong tonight. I think they're happy that I'm happy for once." He said. I knew what he meant. He had shared how miserable college was for him. How it was hard for him to make friends and he got homesick frequently. Both of us hated LA but I never got homesick.

"No, it's ok. I mean, it was a little off-putting at first. I-I'm just not use to that kind of thing, and at dinner.. I swear you were going to propose or something." I laughed. I felt his body tense up. He was silent for a second too long.

"James, please tell me I'm crazy." I said.

"Of course I wasn't going to propose, but maybe don't act so taken aback by the idea."

He was clearly offended.

"James, I'm sorry. I'm 24. Sure, I want to get married one day, but it's nowhere on my radar right now. I mean, I still work two jobs and..." As the words came out I knew this was adding fuel to the fire. But it was the truth. "We haven't even graduated yet and I don't even know where I'm going to be working next year," I continued.

"Okay! I get it! Let's talk about something else." He said

looking anywhere but my eyes. "Hey— hey, listen, I love you. We don't have to think so far ahead though. Okay?" I said, softening my tone. Almost pleading with him. I tilted my head inviting him to look at me. He nodded slowly.

"I'm getting tired." he said. He dropped his hands from my waist and turned around to stop the music. I stood there with a pit in my stomach. I pushed my hair from my face. "Are you upset with me?" I pleaded. "No, no. I'm just exhausted." He sighed, rubbing his forehead. A lie.

I was glad we were in going to be in separate beds tonight. "Okay, me too. Goodnight."

I turned to the door and his hand was on my shoulder in an instant. He turned me around and kissed me gently without a word. I kissed him back and slowly made my way to my room. Seeing it a second time felt just as good as the first. I sat on the bed and removed my shoes. My hands were clammy from the conversation we'd just had.

I searched the room for my suitcase, and found it on a satin covered stool next to a gold vanity. The vanity was decorated with empty antique perfume bottles and a silver hairbrush. I opened my suitcase and began rummaging through it to find my makeup bag. I was dying for a cigarette. A nasty habit that James had no idea about. I rarely ever smoked anymore, but brought a pack of them, not knowing how this week would go. I was all nerves and it proved to be a smart choice. I looked for the bathroom, praying my room had one. Sure enough, there was a tall set of doors with gold tassels hanging from the knobs. I pushed them open and almost fell to my knees at the sight of a large white clawfoot tub, that sat underneath a window and an angled ceiling. There were large white towels rolled up like you'd find in a Scandinavian spa, and full bottles of designer toiletries. I stole a soap tray from the sink and placed my pack of cigarettes on it.

I began running the bathwater, admiring the vintage inspired knobs. I stepped into the scalding water and leaned over the tub, my breasts grazing the cold marble, and cranked the window open. I shivered at the cold air as I looked up and around, making sure there were no fire detectors in sight. I lit the cigarette with my vintage lighter and took a drag, as I soaked my torso deeper into the water. I contemplated the tiff me and James had gotten into and wondered what my future could look like.

I kept circling back to the main fact that I truly didn't know. I felt that my options were endless, I had a million directions to go. Some would only feel so lucky, but I was overwhelmed. I knew I loved James dearly but he was the only guy I'd ever loved or taken this seriously. It left me feeling uncertain on whether or not I was comfortable with that. I finished my cigarette and and dunked my head underwater. I didn't want any evidence of the cigarette left on me in the morning. I scrubbed my nails aggressively with soap and then drained the tub. I began my skincare and brushed my teeth vigorously before slipping into a short silk nighty. I'd only brought lingerie, in hopes that I'd be with James. I was so tired that my vision was becoming blurry. I crawled into the large bed made for a princess, and dozed off before I could give it another thought.

The rest of our week was filled with a grand tour of Saratoga. James didn't bring up what we spoke about on our first night. Instead, he showed me around town, took me for hot chocolate at his favorite little cafe, and kept me company as I attempted to knit for the first time ever. I was going stir crazy and needed some kind of project. I had attempted to make a bright red scarf with a wool yarn I'd picked up at a local shop.

James insisted on buying me an artisan knitting needle set at *The Nosy Needle*. I mentioned that I wanted to learn, but that I felt I didn't have the time. Little did I know, I'd have plenty of time to learn on this trip. I was admiring the bright red yarn and turned my back to find him purchasing a needle set for me.

"I'll take that red yarn too." He said, to the cashier, motioning towards me. It was a sweet gesture, so I didn't fight him on it. The scarf came along decently. Thankfully, I was a fast learner, but I had no expectations for it to be something wearable.

The following days we sat in the reading room of the house, drinking endless cups of coffee and silently enjoying the each others company. James read ahead for his classes, out of pure enjoyment, spitting out random factoids to me period-ically. I admired how much passion he had for art and school in general. I couldn't say the same for myself. I majored in what I was good at, but it didn't excite me in the way it did him.

"How's it coming along?" He asked, looking over his Horn-rimmed glasses. He always looked so good in his glasses. He looked like a 1950's journalist taping away on their type-writer. I held up the nearly finished scarf.

"Well, let's just say, if I develop carpal tunnel by the end of it, it might be worth it."

He laughed, relaxing into the pillow behind him. "It's extraordinary for a beginner, not that I'd expect any less."

He winked, running his fingers over the crimson wool. I gave him a gentle smile and moved my gaze towards the window. I was becoming bored. Nearly three hours had passed in this room. I was restless and not used relaxing. We laid on the cushioned bench beneath the window with our legs parallel to each other. Like sardines in a tin. He sunk his head back into his large text book and began reading again. I lowered my needles and yarn in my lap, and slowly slid my foot into his lap. He was unfazed until I began moving my toes around. He lowered his book and smirked at me. James laid the thick book on the ground and I immediately crawled on top of him, letting the scarf fall from my lap. I bowed down to kiss him, my legs straddling him.

He pushed me off slowly "My parents are home." He whispered against my lips.

"That didn't stop us before," I smiled and leaned in for another kiss. For a second, I thought he was going to oblige me but he gently lifted me off of him. He got up and walked over to shut the door. "Yes, but we weren't on the same floor as them." He added gently. He grabbed the scarf and the knitting needles from the floor and handed them back to me.

"But you look so handsome in those glasses. I can't help myself," I pouted.

He sat down slowly and soon we were both sitting cross-legged, staring at each other. We hadn't had sex since our first night here. It wasn't normal for us. He seemed a bit distant and I was hesitant to ask why. I felt like I knew where it would lead us and I wasn't willing to go there. I was happy he hadn't brought up that same conversation from our first night here. I was enjoying myself for now, and wanted to keep it that way. So, I quickly picked up my knitting and looked away from him.

"I'm close to finishing this anyway." I said, acting disinterested. James stared at me a moment longer before patting me on the knee and returning to his reading. I was relieved that he didn't continue the conversation further.

I finished the scarf later that day while Ethan and James played a round of badminton with their dad. His mom and I had cozied up to the fire pit with a glass of wine. She was flipping through a book of samples for a client that desperately needed new curtains before Thanksgiving, apparently. I occasionally caught James and his dad motioning to me and Alice. They smiled, seeming happy that we were bonding silently. I'm sure Alice was happy too as she's always been outnumbered with these boys. We spent our last two days staying up late with Ethan, watching old family movies (much to my amusement) and binge eating pastries from the local bakery. James was in better spirits as the week progressed and was back to his normal self by the end of it.

Thankfully, our sex life had followed suit. But once we began boarding our plane, I couldn't shake my racing thoughts.

Was I even good enough to marry him? Was I just imaging that he would want to propose to me? What would he think of my mother? What would HIS parents think of my mother? I spent the plane ride home feeling like this was all moving too fast. *Even if we weren't moving too fast, would I ever be ready to show him where I came from?*

James had no reason to think I was ashamed of where I came from. I hardly talked about it. I dressed and carried myself well and my apartment in LA was nicer than his, too. Sure, my car was older but as far as he knew, I was content. And I wanted to keep it that way, for now.

CHAPTER NINE

After about a week, Daniel and I were back to our normal banter, acting as if nothing had happened. Luckily, Roger was back to business as usual too. But it was hard to push out the thought of Daniel's awkward face heading towards my lips. I would be lying if I said I wasn't glad that Daniel would be away for a week.

He was on vacation and I was left with double the duties in the office. The seemingly overwhelming workload proved to be easier to handle than I thought. I couldn't decide if it was the fact that I had learned quickly, or if Daniel had been pawing his duties onto me this whole time. I felt like I was the only one who knew how to efficiently tend to Roger and the whole Burton Barnes office. I'd only been working here for about two months, but it felt longer, somehow. I'd done more research on the company, worked many late nights, and sat in countless meetings. Observing. Listening. Reading social cues. Picking up on all the lingo the team used.

I felt confident at anticipating Roger and Celeste's needs. Although, Celeste's were far more outrageous. Roger liked to have simple coffee or tea throughout the day, plenty of water for everyone at meetings, dry-cleaning done (but not hung), and his four cars routinely maintenance and detailed. That was the extent of his needs. Celeste needed seven ice cubes in her drip coffee. If there was anymore, or any less, she knew. Her lunch order was meticulous and longer than a CVS receipt.

My days consisted of helping Daniel arrange travel for Roger and the production crew, along with getting lunches for the office. Roger had been at the townhouse quite a lot these last few weeks. He often asked my opinion on his outfits and began requesting my styling advice before any big meeting or interview. I was glad we'd finally made it farther than pleasantries. We'd also made it a bit further than work-related conversations too. "Coffee is excellent this morning, Jessica." Roger had made an effort to tell me as I sorted his mail. I enjoyed styling him more than anything else on my to-do list. This week he would be leaving for London to attend a charity gala and I was asked to prepare his outfits for the trip. I started to feel the pressure of doing all the preparations alone. *What if I forgot something? Who would be here to notice?*

The workload for this week had finally proven to me why two assistants were needed. I took a sip of water and went back to separating copies of a screenplay that needed to be delivered this evening. I looked at my watch to see that it was already 3pm. I hadn't eaten all day. My stomach growled as I thought of all the tasks I had left to do. I decided it was going to be another late night anyway, so I threw my bag over my shoulder and made my way to the elevator. I had been to the café downstairs almost daily these last few months. It was out of convenience, but they also made an amazing club sandwich.

I strutted to the elevator catching my reflection on the way. *Yikes.* I fixed my posture and ran my hands through my hair. I was on day three of a blowout and my dry shampoo was working overtime. I desperately needed a shampoo and prayed I could squeeze one in this week.

My new salary had afforded me an impeccable new wardrobe and a few more Jimmy Choos, but my self-care was lacking. After stepping out of the elevator, I immediately pulled out my phone to book a hair appointment. I decided it would *have* to work with my schedule (aka ROgers schedule).

The doors opened to the lobby of the building and I noticed a familiar car parked out front. It was Roger's. My stomach dropped for a quick second. It was 3:00pm. He was normally in meetings at this time. I took a deep breath and brushed it off, thinking that the odds of someone having the same car as him in LA was probable. I approached the café, only to see the back of a familiar head, wearing a grey cabby hat. My hands became clammy. Seeing him outside of our normal setting was disarming. I wanted a moment to relax and enjoy my lunch without performing or being in work mode.

Which was laughable because I typically read and responded to emails during my lunch anyway. I made my place in line as my stilettos clicked behind, giving me away. I prayed Roger wouldn't notice me. Naturally, he turned around at the sound of them. I blushed. I nonchalantly tapped through my phone as I waited in line, avoiding eye contact, pretending not to notice him noticing me.

To my surprise, he didn't approach me, but rather walked towards the opposite counter. I sighed in relief and stepped up to order. "Hi, Jessica, your usual today?" The worker asked. Clearly I had been coming here too much. The staff knew my name and my order.

I saw Roger's head turn in my direction. *Shit.* I kept my head down and began rummaging through my bag. I nodded in response "Mhmm. Thanks."

What is your problem? He's your BOSS. Go talk to him. I decided to acknowledge him and stop acting ridiculous. I stood up straight, shifting my bag on my shoulder. Roger was standing there, hands in his pockets, a tweed blazer. He looked good. He always looked good. So distinguished. Nonchalant.

I was halfway to him before I found myself on all fours. "*Owe!*" I yelped, as my palms smacked the dirty floor tiles. I must've tripped on something, my hands catching my fall. Suddenly, Roger's hands were on my elbows, lifting me up from the floor.

"Christ, are you alright?" He asked, quietly in my ear.

The warmth of his touch made me dizzy. I slowly came up from my knees and dusted them off.

"Yeah, I'm fine. I think. There must've been a napkin on the floor or something." I said, smoothing my hair down.

I looked up at him.

"Thank you. This is completely embarrassing."

He smiled at me warmly. "Oh, no. It just looked like you had lost your contact sense or something. No one even noticed." He joked. I laughed, feeling relieved at his humor.

"So, what's on the menu today?" He asked, changing the subject.

"A club sandwich. The usual as I'm sure you heard." I said, motioning to the worker behind the counter.

"That happens to be my usual too. Look, I know you've got a full day, but did you want to join me for lunch?" Roger asked. My checks got hot and I felt a wave of nerves run through me. Unable to find an excuse not to, I blurted "Absolutely."

Play it cool. He's just your boss. It is normal to eat lunch with your boss. Your boss who happens to be an attractive middle-aged British comedian.

"Angela, can you make those orders dine-in? Thanks." He said, kindly to the girl who took my order. He motioned to a table in the corner. An inconspicuous seat. "This is your usual spot too, I'm guessing?" I asked.

"Yes, surprisingly enough, I'm not often noticed here. It's a quaint little spot." He said. I took a sip of iced tea.

"You think it's really due to the location?"

I got a twinge of fear, thinking the joke wouldn't land. He crossed his arms and did that lip- smacking thing he does, before letting out a chuckle. *Phew.*

He shrugged. "Fair, point." He said.

The cafe worker, Angela, brought our food over. They made small talk as I checked the time. Roger looked my way. "Are you needing to be back at the office soon?" He asked. *Had he forgotten the itinerary for the week?* I looked up and shook my head

"Oh, no, I'm sorry. I'm trying to stay on top of everything while Daniel is gone. But I guess I can't be off track if I'm having lunch with person who employs me." I said, with an animated shrug.

Moreover, I hoped this lunch wouldn't interfere with my hair appointment. I took a bite of my sandwich.

"Precisely. If you want, I could ask you to send a few emails, or make a few calls for me while we eat. Only if it would make you feel better." He joked, gesturing towards me.

"No, I appreciate the thought though." I laughed.

There was a long pause as we both chewed our food. I wiped a bit of mayonnaise off my mouth before asking, "I saw your convertible out front. What brought you out this way?"

"I was meeting up with a friend and then decided to take a drive. I know you're trying to enjoy your lunch, but I can't help but ask about the flights for this weekend." He said. *Oh, no. Had I forgotten something? Did I book the wrong times?*

I swallowed my bite hard. It hurt going down.

"Oh, I have the confirmations pulled up on my laptop back at the office. Let's see.." I said, trailing off as I opened my notes app, hoping everything was correct. "I have a one-way for you, Mark, Johnathon, Wesley.." I named off the rest of the team, one-by-one. He interrupted me before I could finish.

"No, that's great Jessica. Look, I'm going to need you to add one more." He said, looking at me straight on. I felt a sudden urgency from him. I held my breath. I pulled up the browser on my phone and didn't look away from it. "Ok, no problem let me see here...what's the name?" I asked. There was a long pause. I looked up at him, my eyes wide. I blinked waiting for his response. "Jessica." I blinked.

"Yes?"

"No, it's for you, Jessica. Choose something in first class that's suitable."

My heart stopped.

"I need you to go to London with us. With Daniel gone, I fear I may still need an extra hand. This gala will have lots of press for the company as this new production rolls out, and there's always something unexpected that comes up when I'm in London." He said. My heart was in my stomach and I was frozen. I knew that this would eventually, but I didn't expect it to be so soon. I had been so hyper-focused on doing a good job, that I hadn't even thought about the fact that he may need an assistant on this trip.

He seemed impatient by my lack of response.

"Look, I know we didn't give much warning, but I hope you understand why we would need you there this weekend. I hope this doesn't effect any of your plans."

I shook my head in disbelief.

"No, absolutely not. Sorry, it's just been a long day and I am still processing. I would love to come to London. I will book the flight as soon as I am back to the office." I said, in shock.

I wiped my hands on my legs nervously. Work trip or not, I'd been dying to get back to London and it was happening sooner than I could've imagined. "Brilliant. Look, I will send over a list of hotels we use and you can make accommodations for yourself. I'll need to have my tux in order the day before for any tailoring as well. Thank you for understanding.

I've got to run, but it was great running into you and we'll chat soon." He said, patting my shoulder as he got up. Roger waved goodbye, leaving his half-eaten sandwich behind.

I sat there staring at my food and began laughing. I think I was hysterical. I hadn't been this happy in so long. *I was really going to London.* The weight of nerves and happiness was overwhelming. I didn't care how large my workload was going to be, *I WAS GOING TO LONDON!* I shot up from my chair and rushed back to the office as fast as I could.

I dialed Hanna as soon as I made it to the conference room. I was close to tears. She was obviously overjoyed for me, and offered to drop me off at the airport.

"I would take you up on that, but they're giving me a company car." I said.

"Ooo, you're making it up the ranks, Jessica Chadwick."

Of course, I would be arranging all of this for myself BUT STILL.

I hurriedly packed the copies of screenplays into their separate envelopes and made a pile on the glass table. I looked at my digital planner checking off the tasks I'd done. Looking at the items left, I added everything I could remember from lunch with Roger.

- *Buy my plane ticket*
- *Make hotel accommodations for team*
- *Make hotel accommodations for me*
- *Check in with Liz in PR *CC Celeste* and make sure communications are sent over to myself and Roger for review*
- *Get location lists from Roger*

I decided to finish the rest of the days work at home. I scooped up the screenplays that needed to be delivered and

and made my way to the studio. So many thoughts raced through my brain on the way. *I needed to pack for London. What would I wear? What hotel would I be staying at? I'm flying first class for the first time ever.*

There was hardly any time to plan my own outfits after organizing Roger's. I knew this trip was happening as the perfect opportunity to prove my skillset to Roger and the team.

I realized, almost instantly, that this could be *what I really wanted*. This could be the job to move the needle of my happiness. I put my car in park and reached for the stack of envelopes. I entered the studio and made my way to office #4. At the desk, was the familiar face of Mary. A plump woman with a gentle smile and cat-eye glasses. We'd become familiar with each other over the last couple months. I'd made many deliveries to the studio as this current production gained momentum. Her face was a constant among my ever-changing tasks throughout my day.

"Jess, how is your Monday?" She asked, without looking up from her computer. I hesitated telling her the news, but I couldn't help myself. "Very busy..." I said, with a tone of suspicion as I leaned over the desk. She raised her eye brows, creating three hard horizontal lines on her forehead.

"Looks like I am going to be joining the team in London this weekend. Daniel is gone." I said, in a nonchalant tone.

I plopped the thick stack of envelopes onto her desk. Mary cleared her throat, looking me up and down before saying, "You're kidding?"

Not the response I was hoping for.

"Most assistants don't get that opportunity for at least a year. No matter how many NDA's they sign. Consider yourself lucky." She said, pointing a finger at me.

She went back to her typing before I could respond. I knew she was probably right. I guess my efforts to prove myself since that first week had not been for nothing.

"*Really?* Well, I definitely do, that's for sure. Anyway, can you get this to mark today? Thanks."

I smiled and turned on my heel, pushing my thick rimmed glasses up to my eyes. Before I could cross the threshold Mary said, "Make sure you soak up every minute, kid."

I smiled to myself and turned back her way. I gave her a silent and sincere nod before leaving the building.

After rushing my way through traffic, I was in the comfort of my own apartment. I poured myself a glass of sparkling water and cracked my laptop open. I had ten unread emails. I clicked the blue icon to find the top one was from Roger. My eyes widened. I still wasn't used to getting emails directly from him. The subject line read '*Travel Details for Jessica*'

Something about him using my full name made me smile.

"*Jessica, below is the itinerary for our trip. I will need you to fly out Wednesday to ensure enough time for all events. You will be attending the gala Saturday evening with myself and Arthur, so please make sure to pack accordingly. The dress code is black tie. If there is anything you need to prepare (before or during the trip) please use your company card. I look forward to working with you this weekend. Thank you for understanding. Please give me a call if you need anything.*"

I read it again. '*I look forward to working with you this weekend*'. Roger was looking forward to working with *me*. I was excited, despite all the responsibility weighing on my shoulders. I quickly booked my flights along with hotel accommodations. I looked at the location of the gala and then mapped out the closest hotel. I wasn't expecting there to be too many options, at such short notice, but I didn't know they'd be *this* slim.

Trying not to panic, I saw there was a suite available for the dates I needed. I booked it fast. This was all working out. I looked at the time. 7:20pm. After I replied to a few more emails, my work day would be done AND THEN I'D BE HEADING TO LONDON. I looked at the weather for the week in London, highs in the late 60's and lows in the 50's. *Heaven.* I sighed with happiness knowing I would soon be in a chunky cable knit sipping breakfast tea.

I was relieved that Daniel wouldn't be tagging along the first half of this trip. He was probably hooking up with multiple women by now, and vomiting off a yacht somewhere in Ibiza. I shook my head at the thought.

I started pulling pieces from my closet and building outfits. After about twenty minutes, my bed was a mound of wool, polyester, and silk. I had upgraded my wardrobe over the last couple months, but nothing was suitable for London, much less a black tie gala. I knew I had to make time to buy something new. I recoiled at at the thought of going back to Saks to shop after being fired, but it was my only saving grace.

As much as I dreaded shopping there, I knew it was my only option on such short notice. I knew that store like the back of my hand. There was a silk slip dress I'd had my eyes on for a minute. This could be the perfect opportunity to purchase it. After pulling a few casual pieces from the pile on my bed, I realized I definitely needed more. I decided I would skip lunch tomorrow and buy everything I needed. I might even stop at Louis Vuitton for some new luggage to celebrate.

I grabbed my phone off the plush duvet and texted Hanna asking if she could help me. She responded quickly, she was already pulling dresses for me. I knew she'd be excited to help. I sunk into my plush

down comforter and took a deep breath. The words '*I look forward to working with you this weekend*' on repeat in my head.

CHAPTER TEN

MY NERVES WERE STARTING to get the best of me as I took a conference call via bluetooth. I drove down Wilshire boulevard, ticking off my daily errands for the office. *Coffee run, prep conference room for Skype calls, and pick up dry-cleaning for Roger.*

These last few months had flown by at the agency. I never realized that working with so much freedom would be fulfilling. When I was fired from Saks, I was devastated. I never dreamed it would be possible to be picking up coffee and dry-cleaning for a celebrity.

Then again, I had no idea I'd ever even want to be working in this type of role, or that it could lead to something bigger. I was able to drive Daniel's Audi most of time too, which was a huge perk. He was mainly stationary at the office now, attending meetings and sending emails. Meanwhile, I went up a tax bracket just by making sure Celeste's latte was extra hot with *'no foam whatsoever'*. She was hard to please, so the pay increase definitely made up for her constant scoffing and back-handed remarks.

I pulled into a nearby Starbucks drive through and muted myself. I ordered my usual: *a grande iced coffee with extra ice and cream.* Daily coffee was also a company perk.

I was going to be on a flight to London in less than 48 hours and had so much to do. Being over caffeinated was the only way to get through the day. I tapped my fingers impatiently against the company credit card as the team went on about semantics. I never gave much input on these time-consuming calls, but was required to take detailed notes and email them over to the team. I learned quickly that no one read those emails. I normally enjoyed hearing the team bounce ideas around, but today my mind was elsewhere.

All I seemed to think about was the outfits I'd be packing for the trip, or which mascara would stand up against the humidity of London: *the waterproof Chanel or YSL?*

I pulled into a parking space and chugged my coffee until the meeting neared it's end. I bobbed my head at the sound of a producers voice.

"Jessica, we are thrilled that you'll be joining us this weekend! Safe travels across the pond!"

The rest of the team echoed his sentiments. I assumed it was Mark by his accent. He was the blonde one from Manchester. I cleared my throat.

"Thank you all very much! I hope to see you there."

I'd made my way from silent eye contact to small talk with the team, but didn't think I was on first name basis with any of them, much less a passing thought. I'd be lying if I said it didn't give me a little ego boost. I no longer felt like the new girl. I suddenly felt like I was reaching a new level within the company.

I wrote out my final notes on my phone and headed down the street towards Saks. Hanna insisted I come in to find a few new dresses for my trip. Most of my clothes had become slightly baggy since I started doing pilates.

I walked inside the old familiar building and kept my sunglasses on. I felt a sense of pride coming here as a shopper rather than an employee though. I'd made it a long way since my termination here.

My Chanel flats made a distinct clatter as I walked through the different departments. There she was. *Hanna.* I saw her thick golden hair before she saw me. She was wearing a pair of wide leg trousers and a tight, off-the shoulder top.

"Jess, look at you! Did you start getting blowouts again? You look great!" She said as her hands went up for a hug. She looked me up and down once more.

"Yes, but honestly, it's because I don't have the energy to do my own hair these days."

I embraced her. She smelled like fresh linen and gardenia. We hadn't seen much of each other these last few months. I worked long days and she was consumed by her escapades involving Richard. She rolled her eyes

"Oh, poor, *baby.* You're forced to get your hair done."

I let out a breath of annoyance before I clapped my hands together and looked her in the eyes.

"Ok, H. We have one hour to find the perfect dress and maybe a few other things. I have been so busy at the office I can hardly keep up with what day it is."

My voice trailed off as I thumbed through the nearest rack of blouses. "I know. You've been working so much I've hardly seen you much less, heard from you. I knew this job would be exciting but I can't believe you're already going to London!!" She squealed.

Hanna bobbed her head above the rack to get my attention. I knew I seemed distracted but I couldn't help it. I was so hyper-focused on getting the perfect dress and getting on a plane. I didn't want to look like an assistant. I wanted to be completely unrecognizable. I felt a rush of excitement switching back into the gear of a stylist. I'd always had an innate sense of what looked great and what didn't. What proportions worked best with certain body types and how to apply color theory. Growing up, I'd always loved and adored nice things, I just didn't grow up in a family that could afford to give them to me. I always wanted the most expensive outfit, the nicest school supplies, and to decorate my room with everything from high-end furniture catalogs. That hadn't subsided in the slightest since moving to LA, but working retail didn't afford me all of the luxuries I wanted. It usually just afforded me the clothes that were often charged to my credit card.

This job at the production agency made me feel like I was finally living the life *little me* dreamed of. One that I deserved.

Working around celebrities and other people of high status in the industry made me want to be fully seen too. Their confidence rubbed off on me somehow.

Snap! Snap! Hanna flicked her fingers in front of my face.

"Are you evening listening to me?"

"Im sorry, Hanna, I am paying attention. My mind is just elsewhere. I've just got emails to send by 2:30 and i've got a million other things on my mind, so show me what you've got."

I motioned to the fitting rooms. Hanna lead the way without a response. She opened the black velvet curtain, one that I typically wasn't on the other side of. I saw about ten dresses elegantly hung across the rods. My eyes immediately went to the long red silk material in the middle. "Oh! *THIS!* This is exactly what I had in mind. I was looking at this one online. Alice + Olivia gown right?"

I pulled the fabric close to me examining it. Hanna stood with her arms crossed and a smug look on her face.

"Yeah, I knew you'd love that one. It's stunning. I also pulled some more modest pieces, like Getti, since I know that's usually what you land on." She said.

I turned to her. "Not this time. I think I'm stepping it up a notch. It's celebratory." I smirked.

"Oh, is that so? Are you sure it's not so Daniel can admire your new Pilates bod?" She asked with a wink.

"Oh, god no!" I practically spat. I shivered at the thought of him. Daniel and I were on better terms and had decided to put that whole experience behind us but, it would always live there in the back of my mind.

"He's in Ibiza, anyway. I thought I told you this? And thank you for noticing." I said, smoothly as I positioned my hand from my hip to my waist. I knew I'd become more toned lately, but didn't think anyone else would notice.

"No you didn't mention that." She said, grabbing another dress from the rod. She looked me up and down before she whipped the curtain back, enclosing us together.

"Oh, sorry", I breathed.

"I really have been going non-stop these past few months."

I took off my top in an instant and began unzipping my pants.

"Holy shit," Hanna whispered. Startled, I jolted back.

"God, what?!" I asked, looking around us.

"Your body! It's almost enough to convince me to start working out," she said.

I rolled my eyes and caught my breath. "Also, to answer your question, no you didn't tell me that minor detail. I can hardly catch you for more than 30 seconds these days."

She was right. I had been completely consumed by work. "I know. It's been crazy. We will catch up over proper sushi boats and saki soon." I said, patting her on the shoulder.

I slipped one foot into the skirt of the dress and then the other. Hanna stepped closer, helping me get my arms in and straightening out the cowl neck. She synched in the waist with the paper thin strings on the back. The dress felt like water running over my skin.

I looked at myself as my figure became more apparent to me in the mirror. I don't remember ever looking this good. My arms were thinner, more toned. My legs had always been nice and long but they were more slender now. The dress looked better than I had imagined in my head. It had been awhile since I wore something this sexy—I really had no reason to. My eyes gazed from my legs up to my collar bones and I ran my hands down the front of the dress. It fit perfectly and felt like second skin. It was elegant but understated and sexy. "You don't think this is too sexy for an assistant attending a charity event?" I asked, my eyes still on my reflection.

"No, it's perfect. Not too much. Not too little. Besides, maybe it will attract the gaze of a hot British bachelor who will ask you back to his flat." She said as she smacked my ass.

"Oh, I wouldn't mind that." I laughed.

"I would like to try on a few more though, just to be safe. There's a few more events on the team calendar this year and with the way things are going, I might be able to attend those too."

I smiled at the thought. She pulled another gown from the chrome bar on the wall. This one was long, heavy black fabric with only one shoulder. "Is this the Rosetta Getti?" I asked.

"Yes, also a good choice. My favorite. A little more modest though." She said, from behind me. I slipped into it carefully and she zipped me up. I loved how this one looked on me too. *Understated, chic, and sexy.* The fabric was heavy but taught on my body. I tried on the rest in her lineup to to appease her, knowing exactly which ones I'd end up with.

"Ok, I'll take them both. The Getti and the red dress. I have about 30 minutes to spare and I need to run to Louis Vuitton for luggage."

"I see the new salary is treating you well. I'll start ringing you up, boo." She said, with a wink.

"Thank you so much." I said, as I slipped my foot into my shoe. I grabbed my phone from my bag and smoothed out my hair as I read a text from Daniel.

missing you ;) xx

I rolled my eyes. It was the last text I was expecting. I couldn't pretend his persistent advancements weren't a little funny, or flattering, but I didn't want to give him the satisfaction. I also didn't want to take any chances of him trying to plant one on me in front of Roger again. I had hoped we would be on normal terms soon but wishful thinking when it came to Daniel. I'd been keeping things cordial since the incident. I was warm enough to be on his good side and cool enough to seem explicitly professional.

I decided not to respond and made my way to the counter. Hanna had elegantly prepared my gowns. She was patiently waiting for me just as she would for a guest. She didn't announce my total, but it was displayed on the card reader: *$2,095.* Not bad given my past purchases here, and I wasn't second guessing it for once, or splitting between credit cards. I typically had to choose between new shoes or eating out. I usually landed on new shoes.

I felt good spending this money on the other side of the register. "Jess, I'm so happy for you." Hanna said. She smiled a genuine smile as I waited for a "but" That never came.

Hanna walked around the corner and we shared a long hug. I was shocked to be hugging her for a second time today. "You're just saying that because I helped you make your daily commission,"

We both laughed.

"Now go to England and do whatever British people do and have FUN." She said, shoving me away.

I sent my last email before shutting my laptop. It was the night before my flight and despite my fatigue, I knew I wouldn't sleep at all. I triple checked that my bags were properly packed and ran through my list once more. I took out my luggage scale for the second time, making sure the weight was accurate. I'd always been such a pack rat and I couldn't bare the embarrassment of paying extra fees. Instead, I packed three large suitcases to lug around.

The clock read 9:02 as I sat on my bed, over looking the lit-up city. I curled my legs in to my chest and sat there for a moment on my bed. I watched the car lights pass and reflect off my walls, as I often did. I felt grateful for everything happening, no matter how fast it seemed. Out of pure boredom, I reached for my phone and opened Daniel's message from earlier. I decided to reply.

> "I'm not surprised ;)"

Partially for fun, and partly to keep up the charade between us. I hated his guts and he was none the wiser, which is exactly how I wanted to keep it.

CHAPTER ELEVEN

I MADE my way through LAX wheeling my new luggage behind me. I was wearing leather loafers, one's that I never envisioned myself affording anytime soon. I felt more luxurious than ever.

And let's not forget about my beautiful cream coat, belted to perfection like a high-end robe. I knew I looked good, and I was relishing every moment of it. I was flying first class, thanks to Roger's generosity. *Was it because of our undeniable chemistry, or was it just a friendly gesture?* I know he probably would've done the same for Daniel, I thought, reminding myself that he was *my boss*.

I couldn't believe what I was thinking. I shook my head at the thought that Roger had done it as some grand gesture for me, cringing. Although, *he had been in the press for taking coach seats on the trains in England.* So, why would he insist on me taking first class? Was he trying to impress me? I knew he was quite humble at his core. *No, Jess, STOP.* It's not like *that.* I couldn't help my mind wandering. Roger had an endearing energy about him, not arrogant like Daniel. He was dangerously magnetic. His allure was unassuming. Roger was soft in the way he spoke, but equally stern. He was unconventionally handsome. He was obviously funny, as any comedian would be. I'd seen a couple of his films since beginning my work here, for research, of course.

I shook myself once more, trying to focus my mind elsewhere. As I settled into my seat on the plane, I tried to distract myself by scrolling through my phone, mapping out our day 1 itinerary. As soon as I landed, I would check into my hotel and pick up Roger's tux from the cleaners. I needed to rush it to the tailor before the team met up for dinner. My night would be free but I was advised to be "On-call."

I knew I would be exhausted, but the idea of exploring London had my mind reeling. I'd spent the week bookmarking places to visit and wanted to see as much as possible.

I decided to find a movie to occupy me on the flight. I flipped through the touch screen stopping on one of my favorite films, James Bond; *Goldfinger*. Sean Connery was exceptionally attractive in this film, I'd almost forgotten. I mouthed Bond's line when he meets Pussy Galore, "I must be dreaming." He says. I'd always loved that line. The thought of being a Bond girl, with all the attention and admiration, made me smile to myself.

I must have fallen asleep. I was gently nudged awake by a flight attendant as she offered me a hot towel. I wiped my hands and then held it to my face to wake myself up. I glanced at the time on the screen. I had slept a solid seven or eight hours. I looked out my window to see a mossy green landscape unlike the one in LA. A view I had missed for far too long.

This moment felt a bit surreal seeing as how weeks ago I was staring at the ceiling of my studio, having an existential crisis. I slipped back into my shoes, my legs feeling stiff. I gathered all my belongings, checking twice that I hadn't forgotten anything in my enclosed seat.

I looked out the window once more and felt my stomach bubble with excitement. *I was here.* I was *in London. Finally.* I made my way off the plane briskly and rushed to find baggage claim. Surprisingly, I remembered exactly which direction to go.

After a good thirty minutes, I had my luggage. It was comical watching me lug three large suitcases through Heathrow airport, I'm sure. By the time I reached the arrivals my hairline was drenched with sweat. I patted my forehead with the back of my sleeve and looked for my driver. I finally saw a short elderly man holding a sign with my last name.

"Hi—Hi! Im Jessica!"

I must've shouted due to the sudden change in his glum expression. Maybe I filled the stereotype of being a loud American. I didn't care.

"Alright, Jessica, I will take these." He grunted, opening the trunk and avoiding eye contact. Perhaps he had already had a long day or maybe the Brits weren't as friendly as I remember. As he piled my bags into the car and I took a seat inside. It was the classic, small black limousine you see in all the movies. I felt luxurious sinking into the black leather around me. I laid my head back and let out a sigh. I watched as people met their loved ones or looked around with confusion at the arrivals gate.

My daydreaming was interrupted with the sound of the driver opening the car door. Soon, we were bobbing and weaving through the busy streets of London. I was mesmerized by the distantly familiar architecture around me. The feelings this city had evoked inside me hadn't seemed to fade one bit. The air was just as damp as I remembered. The streets were as busy as too. The magic was still here in every detail of the city. The sun was going down, casting a beautiful glow against the pavement. We reached the hotel I had booked for myself— it was even cuter in person. It was located in Westminster and had that classic stone architecture that was distinct to London.

The driver stepped out quickly after turning on his hazards. He opened the trunk and placed my bags on the curb. Just as I turned towards the hotel, someone I assumed was a hotel employee approached me with a luggage cart.

"Hello ma'am, can I help you with these?" He asked in a sweet voice. I smiled at him and nodded as he guided me inside. He followed me to the front desk where I stood with my booking email displayed on my phone. There was one person in front of me who seemed to be getting directions to a place close by. Finally, the concierge waved me forward and welcomed me.

"Hi, yes my name is Jessica Chadwick and I have a reservation for one in the King Suit." I said cheerfully, flashing him my phone.

He nodded politely and began tapping his keyboard.

"I'm sorry, can you spell your last name for me?" He asked in a confused tone.

"Yes, C-H-A-D-W-I-C-K. I'm sorry is there a problem?"

"I don't seem to be finding your reservation in the system." He responded, keeping his eyes on the screen.

I felt my stomach drop. This wasn't how I had wanted to start this trip. I had booked this last minute, sure but the booking was confirmed.

"I don't understand, sir, the booking is confirmed." I pressed.

"Right, but there must have been some technical error, I'm afraid. Did you happen to use a third party site?" He asked, seeming unsympathetic now.

I felt my hands grow clammy and my blood pressure raising.

"I-erm perhaps, but either way it was confirmed. There

must be something you can do. I have three suitcases and I'm here on business." I pleaded.

I looked at my phone once more to make sense of this. It appeared that *I had* used a third party site, as most other hotels were completely booked for this week. It was last minute and I had no other choice. I looked at the calendar, racking my brain at how this could possibly be happening. *It was London fashion week. Shit.* How could I have not realized?

"Of course, let me see what we have available. With the timing of this weeks events we may be booked up." He said.

He kept his eyes on the screen. I understood that they only had so many available rooms but weren't people in these rolls supposed to be as accommodating as possible? This guy couldn't have cared less. He continued clicking away at his keyboard and squinting every few seconds.

"I'm sorry Miss Chadwick, we seemed to be completely booked until tomorrow." He said, without feeling.

I scoffed loudly.

"This cannot be possible! I just flew ten hours on a red eye. What am I supposed to do until tomorrow?"

I pleaded as I motioned towards my luggage. I didn't want to use this card, but it was my last hope. I rested my elbow on the desk and leaned in.

"You know, I hear on business for *Roger Barnes* and I don't think he would be too pleased with how his employee is being treated."

The man looked away from his computer slowly and looked me up and down.

"Ma'am, I'm not sure who that is, but I can assure you that you're being as fairly treated as any other guest at our fine establishment. Now, what I *can do* is suggest a few other hotels that may have accommodations for you." He said calmly.

I let out a huge sigh, feeling embarrassed.

"Alright." I huffed in defeat.

"But it has to be in central London. It's absolutely vital to my itinerary, please." I said, smacking my hand against the counter.

The man made a disgusted face and gazed back at the computer. "Well, unfortunately I know full well that there will be *no vacancy* in central London, but you can try your hardest just across the street at Wilmington Hotel." He said and pointed out the window.

I stood in shock that this was happening. I had two hours to pick up Rogers dry cleaning and make it back to dinner, all while trying to find new accommodations.

To avoid making a scene, I silently stepped away from the desk and over to my luggage. The bell hop gave me a sad look and unloaded my luggage from the cart.

"Thank you for your help." I whispered.

"Not a problem, ma'am." He said, giving me a fake smile and rolled the cart through the double doors.

I began to freak out. *How was I going to handle this?* It was my job to arrange proper accommodation for myself and the team and I'd failed. I wanted to call Daniel. *I needed to call Daniel.* I felt like he would know exactly what to do, no matter how much embarrassment it'd cause me. Part of me didn't want him to see that I'd messed up without him. I had worked so hard to prove I was capable. I didn't want to give him the satisfaction of knowing I needed him. The alternative was to call Roger, which I absolutely couldn't bring myself to do. He was my BOSS and I couldn't bare the thought of looking incompetent. I let out a dramatic groan and dialed Daniel.

It rang five times before going to his voicemail. I hung up and immediately dialed again. *Nothing.*

I rang him once more and my eyes grew wide as he picked up. "Hello? Who is this?" He yelled into the phone.

"*DANIEL!*" I hissed, in a low tone as to not make a scene. "*DANIEL I NEED YOUR HELP!!*"

"Who is this??" He screamed, again. I held the phone away from my face to avoid damage to my eardrum.

"DANIEL, IT'S JESS!! MY HOTEL RESERVATION FELL THROUGH AND I DON'T KNOW WHAT TO DO!" I

The concierge looked directly at me.

"Oh, Jessica, darling, *is that you?* Do you miss me already?" He cooed in a drunken slur.

I rolled my eyes.

"Yes, yes, listen I don't have anywhere to stay!!" I repeated.

"Look, love I can't hear you! Call Roger!" He shouted with music blaring behind his voice. It was so loud that I had to keep the phone away from my ear. Finally, he hung up and I was left with one last hope before calling Roger.

I grabbed all three of my bags in the clumsiest way possible and stumbled out of the lobby. I walked through the entrance of the Wilmington Hotel feeling hopeless. It seemed to be more of a five star hotel, unlike the three star one I booked, or thought I had. There was a massive crystal chandelier hanging from the ceiling. It lit the foyer perfectly, accenting the black and white marble floor. I took a deep breath and walked up to the front desk. I put on my most confident air as I approached the female concierge. I fixed my hair and rubbed my lips together.

As I quickly approached the woman, she looked up at me warmly. *Ok, this is a good start.* She looked kind. Her eyes were a gorgeous green. I felt hopeful when I saw her smiling back at me.

"Good evening, miss." she said in a thick Irish accent.

"Hi, there. I just came from the hotel across the way. I had a room with them, but they seemed to have overbooked. So, they sent me this way in hopes that you would have something. You see, I'm an employee of Roger Barnes," I said, before she interrupted me.

"Oh! You're slagging me! He's the fella that does that silly anchorman bit, eh?"

I smiled back at her.

"Yes! He's the one! So, you see, I'm here on business for him and I basically have nowhere to stay. I could call him and have this all sorted, but he likes to keep a low profile. I'm sure you understand as someone who probably sees hundreds of celebrities a week." I said, attempting to boost her ego.

"Ah, don't you worry, las, let me see what I can do."

She looked at her computer, typing ferociously. I was stunned at the contrast in manners from the previous hotel to this one.

"Okay, so we are quite booked at the moment but I could get you in tomorrow right at check in for our deluxe sweet." She chirped.

I was excited at that first until she finished her sentence.

"Oh, I see. Well, I've just landed and I need to get in *tonight*." I said, feeling defeated.

I knew what I was going to have to do.

"I apologize, miss. We'd love to have you stay, and potentially get an autograph from Roger Barnes, but unfortunately that's all I can do. You could always try a hostel." She said, her face grimacing.

She knew it wasn't what I wanted to hear. Her genuine kindness was the only thing keeping me from bursting into tears. I always cried when I was furious. I hated that about myself.

"I appreciate you trying. Truly." I said, a lump forming in my throat.

I grabbed my three large suitcases and walked over towards the entrance. *Should I stay in a hostel? Or Should I swallow my pride and call my boss?* I felt defeated and jet-lagged.

With a hefty sigh, I took out my phone and dialed Roger, my hands trembling. It rang the longest three rings I had ever heard in my life. His sultry adenoidal voice projected from the other side.

"Hi, Jessica. Is everything alright?" He asked.

"Umm, hi, Roger." I said, in a shaky voice.

The moment the concierge heard me on the phone, she looked my way. I could tell she was eager to hear our conversation.

"Not exactly..I guess there was some technical error and the hotel is refusing to give me a room. I've tried every surrounding hotel and no one has a room available until tomorrow. I'm so sorry for-"

"Not to worry, where are you right now? Send me your location and I'll pick you up." He said casually, before I could finish. I was in shock that he wasn't biting my head off. That wasn't his style though, not as far as I knew. He didn't call me incompetent or insult me like he could have.

Roger hung up before I could respond. Maybe I was being too hard on myself. Either way, I was curious to see what his solution would be. I hoped he had some glamorous apartment in the city. That was probably wishful thinking, but I refused to stay in a hostel for even one night. I had heard too many horror stories about things like bed bugs and stolen luggage.

I quickly sent Roger my location, starting our first text thread. There was something exciting about it. He immediately responded saying he would pick up his tux and be there to get me in fifteen minutes. He sent me his location back. *Shit.*

All of this hotel nonsense kept me from picking up his tux. I was glad he at least remembered. Eventually, five minutes of waiting on the curb turned into fifteen, and just like that, a sleek black Porsche appeared. The driver had on classic black ray-bans and a ball cap. It was Roger. He gave me a casual wave and smiled. My mouth went dry. I smiled back before looking at the ground, feeling embarrassed. He stepped out of the car and made his way towards me.

"Hello. You're still here in one piece, I see." He said, clapping his hands together.

"All in one piece but I feel like a wreck after all of this." I said, as I motioned to the hotel. Roger reached for the two suitcases that sat next to me and made his way to the back of the car with them. I followed behind him.

"Well, not to worry. We will get everything sorted." He said, grabbing the third suitcase from me and lifting it into the trunk.

I was in awe of his kind and calm demeanor. I looked him over as he stuffed the bags into the car. His dark wool sweater had a white shirt peeking out of the collar. His Adidas were the same shade of his sweater, a forest green. His pants were slightly wrinkled, giving him an effortlessly put together look. He was crisp and clean. He was a silent type of wealthy. It was the sort of thing only a trained eye could see.

The sound of the trunk closing jolted me from whatever daze I was in. "Rright, shall we head to dinner?"

I nodded quickly and headed to the passenger's side, reminding myself that it was now on the left. I slipped into the soft leather and buckled myself in. I felt like a damsel in distress being saved by him and part of me was satisfied that we would be arriving to dinner together. We drove for a few minutes in silence. Traffic became increasingly worse as we made our way through London. I was amazed at how sound-proof his luxury car seemed to be. Every swipe of Roger's hands on the wheel caught my attention. I looked over to see him making a glance in my direction. I smiled to myself. I could tell he was trying to be inconspicuous. We had never been in such close quarters for so long. There was tension and it was undeniable now. I decided to break the silence. I didn't want things to be awkward and I also didn't want to be an imposition.

"So, do you have any suggestions for accommodations tonight? I spoke to someone at the hotel across the way and they said they could at least get me in a room tomorrow. However, that might require you to give an autograph or two."

Roger raised an eyebrow in my direction. He looked back at the traffic.

"Well, as long as it's just and autograph." He joked.

"Right, I've also called every hotel on our roster and can confirm they're fully booked. I can see you've been resourceful too. Don't worry, these things happen. So we have two options," Roger said. I was glad he added that last bit, as I didn't feel I was living up to my job expectations.

"Yes, I have. It's impossible with fashion week," I responded, looking at my palms. "So what are those options?" I asked.

"Well, I know it's not the most ideal situation, but you could stay with me—er—in my guest room."

I felt my stomach drop and suddenly my cheeks were hot. *He couldn't be serious?*

"Now, I know it's unconventional, but it might be our only logical option. It's quite a roomy house and the guest room has a private bathroom as well. We wouldn't even need to see one another unless absolutely necessary."

He rubbed his index finger over his mouth slowly, while looking ahead. I couldn't believe what I was hearing, but I would be crazy to say no. After all, being forced to stay with him was a lot better than staying in a hostel, which was my only other option at this point.

"Or, perhaps you wouldn't mind staying in a hostel. Not that I advise it." He added.

"Quite honestly, it might make work a bit more convenient for you this week, I might add, staying with me. Again, I know it's not ideal Jessica— I do apologize."

I shook my head dramatically. How could I even question staying with him?

"No, no, that's very kind of you, Roger. Thank you. Your guest room sounds like paradise compared to a hostel."

Roger let out a chuckle. I was glad he found that amusing.

"Well, I can only hope so. I promise it's not as much of a

bachelor pad as the townhouse, that's for sure. That's more for Daniel's sake, as I'm hardly there." He added.

"I never thought it really reflected your essence, now that you mention it." I admitted. "Daniel is obviously more colorful, that's for certain. My taste in interiors is more understated. The sweets wallpaper was definitely a point of contingence when styling the town house."

I let out an uncontrollable laugh.

"Oh, I almost gasped the first time I saw it. It feels good to admit that."

"I don't blame you. It's a huge female deterrent. Why do you think Daniel is single?" He continued.

We both were laughing now. I knew there was no way he could've picked out that heinous print.

"I can assure you that staying in my guest room will be much less headache inducing." He said.

"It sounds lovely." I replied.

We were moving quickly now. The sun had completely set. I sat in silence, taking in the scenery and imagining what his house would be like. Black taxis, stone buildings, and lovers strolled down the sidewalks that we were passing.

"How was your flight?" Roger asked, breaking the silence.

"It was great. Thank you. I actually slept though most of the flight for once." I beamed, adjusting my seatbelt and looking his way. He had a half smile painted on his face.

"Very good." He muttered. It was entertaining to observe him. *Was he nervous?* He was so reserved that it was hard to tell. Yet, there was an inexplicable tension in the air that seemed to appear out of nowhere. I realized we were pulling to the curb in front of a beautifully lit building. Without a word, Roger exited the car and quickly made his way to my side, opening the door for me. I could only assume that our age difference was what afforded him such great manners. It felt nice to be treated with care.

"Thank you." I breathed, combing my hair behind my ear. His jaw flexed and he motioned me away from the traffic.

"Right, here we are." He said, opening the navy blue double doors of the restaurant. We walked in and I followed his lead, remembering he'd made the reservations for the team- the team that would be joining us soon. *Right because you're working, Jess. Get it together.* It was hard not to think about the fact that I was arriving with Roger, and would be going home with him too. It was all I could think about.

As I looked around the beautiful restaurant, I remembered Daniel saying it was Roger's favorite. Apparently, it was a tradition to eat here the moment he landed back in London. I could see why. It smelled heavenly and it was equal parts cozy and elegant. The tables were all candlelit and draped with white tablecloths. The chairs were tufted and lined with brown velvet fabric. In the corner, was a live pianist tinkering away.

We followed the host down a narrow hallway where Roger motioned for me to walk ahead of him. His elbow brushed the fabric of my sweater. I felt my breath catch slightly. I could feel electricity in his touch. I swallowed hard and kept my eyes on the back of the hosts head.

We entered a private room with larger tables and were instantly greeted by the team.

"Aye! You made it!" They cheered to Roger.

The men smiled gingerly at me and told me to have a seat. Thankfully, Celeste was nowhere in sight. Roger's closest friend and fellow comedian, Arthur Burton, motioned for me to sit next to him. He had a warm and inviting smile. Roger sat on the opposite end of the table, immediately engaging in conversation with the other men. I felt like a fish out of water. I was the only woman, new to my position, and I was feeling jet-lagged.

"You look lovely for someone who just got off a red eye. Maybe I should fly more." Arthur said, leaning in. He was animated and welcoming.

"Well, that's refreshing to hear. I feel like a mess." I laughed, sheepishly.

I checked the mirror across from the table, to make sure my hair was in place. Arthur slid a glass of red wine towards me.

"Here, this should remedy that." He said.

I took a large swig knowing it couldn't hurt. Delicious. I took off my coat and turned to drape it over the back of my chair. When I turned back around, I caught Roger looking my way. I immediately averted my eyes, and adjusted myself in my chair.

I asked Arthur to hand me the breadbasket, not only because I was starving, but because I wanted to keep my hands busy. He took a slice as well and asked me what I thought of London. I told him how I'd been here before and that it was just as wonderful as I remembered. I liked talking to Arthur. He had a gentle spirit and a childlike nature about him. He was just as funny as Roger, naturally, but a bit more self-deprecating. Their dynamic was an interesting one, but I understood how it worked for them.

Arthur was less conventionally attractive and not as critically acclaimed. He was happily married with kids, something I had learned at dinner. Roger on the other hand, was clearly more attractive and a bachelor, as far as I could tell. After googling him, I learned that he was once married at a young age and divorced just three years later. He had a teenage daughter too, not that he'd ever mentioned her. Roger was incredibly private.

We spent the rest of the evening enjoying our delicious food and drank three bottles of wine. Roger kept stealing glances towards me, and after my third glass, I let myself steal a few too. There was a definite chemistry between us. It wasn't just in my head anymore. I knew it. It also frightened me.

"So where did you book yourself in Jessica?" A large man, from the opposite side of the table, asked.

Was it John? Or William? I couldn't remember. I realized Roger was staring daggers at me now, and I felt myself pause for far too long. I was frozen. Not a single thing came to my mind. It was blank.

"Isn't it the Hoxton, Jessica?" Roger offered, before taking a leisurely sip of wine.

I smacked my forehead.

"Ah, yes, sorry, guys! The jet lag is setting in." I said.

I laughed, playing along. Obviously I knew I couldn't tell them the truth, but I felt weird being dishonest. I also felt like an idiot for not coming up with any sort of hotel name. I finished my last bite of risotto and the men went on talking about whatever writers and producers talk about.

Arthur and Roger were at each others throat with some impersonation of Mike Meyer's and the table was enamored by it. I tapped away silently on my phone.

Finally, the check came and Roger paid the bill. The men left one-by-one until it was just myself, Roger, and Arthur left. They were talking about the event we were attending tomorrow night. I reached for my purse and took out a compact and my lipstick. As I touched it up, I felt Roger's eyes on me. I looked his way and quickly put it away. I tried not to smile but it was amusing. He seemed distracted by me, and I could tell he was trying his best not to be.

"Sorry, Arthur, repeat that." He said, as I hid my smile.

I slipped my arms back into my coat just as Arthur said, "I really think we should discuss it tonight and go over the edits they sent over. Just once more in case we get ambushed by them tomorrow." He urged.

"Who's ambushing you two?" I asked.

They both looked my way and Roger took a deep breath. He leaned back into his chair and folded his arms. His looked wildly handsome. "This director and producer, who have been on our case to finish scripting a film for them. It's a bit of a long story, but if you do insist we talk tonight you can head back to the house with me." He said, looking towards Arthur once more. I felt my stomach drop and I knew my eyes were wide now.

Head back to the house? Where was I going to hide? In the trunk? I sat in silence as Roger did that thing where he rubs his forefinger back and forth over his top lip. He was thinking deeply.

"I do, I really do." Arthur urged.

"Right, well, I guess that's what we should do. You can meet me at the house. I have to drop Jessica to her hotel." He said.

I sat in silence, stunned. *How in the hell was this going to work?* Arthur looked at me and back to Roger.

"Erm, right, well, let's get on then." He said, seeming suspicious.

I could tell he thought it was odd but didn't want to draw any attention to it. Very British of him. I felt a bit of relief as we all got up without saying another word about it. Roger and I loaded into his car once more in silence.

"Sorry about that. There was no way around it." He whispered.

I smiled at him in agreement.

"So, how exactly is this going to work?" I stuttered.

"It's fine. Arthur will get to the house first and you'll go in through the garage. It takes you straight to the guest room."

Thank GOD.

He pulled the car into drive and turned the radio on. I sat with a million thoughts swirling my head. I was definitely awake now. I was terrified. *Why couldn't we just be honest with Arthur?* I didn't like feeling as though I was doing something wrong. It made me uncomfortable. I quickly remembered how much more uncomfortable I was at the thought of staying in a hostel.

"Dinner was excellent." I whispered, trying to change the subject.

He loudly sucked in some air before responding. He did that a lot, one of his few ticks I'd picked up on.

"Oh, wonderful. It's a hidden gem. I'm glad you enjoyed it and the wine too it seems." He joked.

"Hey, you were the one ordering bottle after bottle."

"I could tell the wine was getting to you when you laughed at all of Arthur's jokes. You shouldn't stroke his ego, you know?" He said.

"I actually find him very funny and charming!" I argued in Arthur's defense.

Roger seemed to be the one with an ego. I knew he was joking, but there was always a bit of truth sprinkled in. He wished the attention had been on him.

"Well, lovely. That makes two people then. You and his wife."

Our banter had momentarily distracted me from the thought of having to sneak through Roger's garage soon. My palms began sweating and my mouth went dry. Roger was so sure that this would go smoothly, but I wasn't as optimistic. I'd always been clumsy and heavy-footed.

Finally, our surroundings became much more secluded from the hustle of the city and the roads began winding. We approached a three story house made of stone. Roger drove the car into the circle drive and parked behind Arthur, who had luckily beat us there. I swallowed hard and attempted to break the silence.

"Wow, it's beautiful." I whispered.

Roger killed the engine and turned towards me.

"It's no castle but it's home to me." He smiled and opened his door. "Wait," I whispered, and grabbed his elbow.

"How exactly is this going to work?" I asked.

"Not to worry. Just as soon as you see me enter the front, I'll go in and open the garage for you, then it should be clear for you to come. The guest room is just straight down the hall, third door on your right." He said. I tried repeating it in my head. Somehow, I couldn't get past how he pronounced garage. *Gar-idge.*

The jet-lag had sat in and I was fighting to keep my eyes open. I prayed I wouldn't fuck this up. Roger gave me a reassuring smile before he walked to the front door.

I was anxious to see how the this would play out. Just a few hours ago, I was asleep first class and now I was about to be sleeping in Roger's home. I shut the car door quietly. *Okay, you've got this, Jess. It's a large house, the odds of Arthur seeing you are slim.*

I decided to take off my shoes to avoid making any noise. I tiptoed down the driveway and to the garage door. Roger was out of sight, but the garage was still closed. *C'mon, C'mon.* I pleaded.

Suddenly, I heard a familiar voice.

"It'll just take a sec, Roger. They're in my car." The voice shouted. *Fuck. It was Arthur.* I looked around, panicked. There was nowhere to hide and I had no time to run back to the car. Quickly, thinking on my feet, I ran to the opposite side of the garage door, hiding behind a wall that faced a small garden. Just as my foot touched the dirt, I heard a small ticking noise. *Oh, god.*

Water was soon soaking me from head to toe. *Sprinklers.* I covered my hand to my mouth, trying not to scream. The freezing water was soaking my clothes and turning the dirt to mud under my bare feet. I took a deep breath before a stream of water blasted me in the face. Finally, I heard the closing of a car door. Arthur must have been out of site as it was followed by the electric buzzing of the garage opening. I wiped the wet muck out of my eyes and walked into the garage. I let out the breath I'd been holding in. The sound of water dripping followed every soggy step I took. I wanted to be angry, but I was too cold, tired, and wet to be angry. Finally I heard the low groan of the garage door opening. Just as I looked up from my soggy feet, I saw Roger's eyes through a crack in the door. He slipped through, shutting the door behind him.

"Christ! Jessica…I'm so sorry." He whispered.

"This is just perfect. First I'm left destitute by my hotel, and now I'm standing in my bosses garage, soaked to death, and in hiding." I said, in a monotone voice. Roger began laughing. I looked at him like in disbelief. "You're really laughing right now? I mean, *look at me!* There's MUD IN MY TOENAILS!" I shouted.

He put a hand to my mouth, still trying not to laugh. It was warm and soft against my wet face.

"Shhh." He said, stepping away from me and releasing his hand.

"That was inappropriate of me. Let's get you inside."

I was suddenly aware that my nipples were hard and piercing through my shirt. I folded my arms and followed him into the house. The smell of musk and wood enveloped me. It smelled how most old houses did, in the best way possible. It smelled like him. It was warm too. I made it to the end of the lengthy foyer to see the beautiful living room to the right of us.

There was a large velvet couch and a couple arm chairs perfectly positioned next to one another.

"Right, Jessica, the guest room is just this way." Roger whispered, as he motioned to the right of us. I followed him down a long hallway, stopping at the third door to the right. He came to a quick stop and cleared his throat. Roger opened the old wooden door to the guest room. I quietly brushed past him, my shoulder grazing his.

"Look, I'm sorry about Arthur. I had no idea he would need to go to his car. I tried to stop him, but I couldn't. This is all a mess. I'm sorry." He said, softly. Seeing the comfort of the guest room, I melted and accepted his apology.

"This is great. Thank you." I whispered, brushing my wet hair behind my ears.

I saw his eyes quickly dart from my chest back to my eyes. I crossed my arms.

"You're welcome. Do you have what you need? Let me grab you some towels." He said, in a nervous voice. He was scrambling to make sure I was comfortable. Our roles were suddenly reversed.

"I think so. Towels would be great and maybe a raise." I said, sarcastically.

He nodded and quickly turned to leave. The room was charming, with a full-sized bed that was undoubtedly an antique. As nice as it was, I prayed it had a private bathroom. I turned around just as Roger made it back with an armful of towels. I rushed over to grab them from his arms.

"Thanks," I breathed, as my fingers grazed his forearm, sending a buzzing sensation down my back. They were icy cold against his hot skin.

He stared at me silently before pushing up his glasses and looking away. He cleared his throat again.

"Oh, and the bath is quite old, so you have to slowly turn the knobs to get the right water pressure." He explained, motioning with his hands in the air. It was cute to see that my unexpected stay was making him nervous. Surely, this was extremely out of the ordinary for him.

"Right, well, I'll let you get settled. Arthur and I will just be in my office going over a few things. Please help yourself to whatever you need and I'll see you in the morning." He said, lingering in the doorway a bit.

"Okay, got it. Thanks. Oh, wait. My luggage. It's still in the car," I said, with panic. He snapped his fingers.

"Bloody hell, right, I'll grab it for you once Arthur is gone. I could lend you something of mine in the mean time." He said.

I felt bashful about sleeping in something of his, but I had no other option.

"Sure, that will work." I said, my fingertips resting on my

chin. Roger nodded and left the room swiftly. I let out a breath before closing the door.

I couldn't help but smile to myself. It was one thing to make a man nervous, and another to have it be Roger. I began rummaging through the drawers in the bathroom, hoping to find some sort of toiletries. The first drawer had a bottle of high-end shampoo and conditioner. *Yes!* I scooped them up in arms.

Curiosity soon got the best of me, and I was opening every drawer. There was a box of Sainsbury's tampons— *his daughter's I assumed,* and a toothbrush with a half a tube of toothpaste. There was also boar bristle brush with hair in it and a tube of lipstick, in the shade 'Bordeaux'. *Hmm.* I swatched it on myself, not my color, I thought. I put it back in the drawer.

I opened one last cabinet to find a bottle of generic micellar water and some Chanel moisturizer. It wasn't much, but it was enough to get me through the night. The tub Roger was talking about was a gorgeous clawfoot tub that stood a few feet from the toilet. I turned the knobs just as he said waiting as the water pressure soon became harder. I immediately ran my icy fingers under the hot water. I peeled my gross, wet, and mud-stained clothes off and threw them in the sink.

Finally, I was soaking into the boiling bath water when I heard a knock outside.

"Y-yes?" I asked, instinctively covering my breasts with my hands.

"I'm just going to put some linens and clothes on the bed for you. So sorry." Roger's voice called from the other room.

"Thanks!" I yelled, my voice cracking.

Once I heard the bedroom door click shut, I used the loot of toiletries I'd found and drained the bath. Feeling like a brand new person, I wrapped myself in a towel and opened the door to find a soft white shirt folded on the bed. Next to it, was a set of blue boxers and a few fluffy towels and a note that said, "You're definitely getting a raise."

I smiled wide and held the shirt up to smell it. It smelled nice. I slipped into the items he'd laid out for me, both swallowing me whole. I rolled the elastic of the boxers up three times to fit me better. I looked at myself in the mirror and couldn't help but laugh. If I went back to my first week of work, to tell myself about the night I'd experienced, I wouldn't believe a word of it.

CHAPTER TWELVE

IT WAS THE NEXT DAY. I stood looking at myself in the mirror. I'd spent the last few hours getting ready for the gala. I wanted to look perfect.

This was the largest event in my career so far and I was nervous. I hardly slept the night before, my adrenaline was still pumping from everything that had happened. My mind was flashing scenes of Roger's face from the restaurant as I tossed and turned. A picture of his smile stamped into my mind.

I smoothed my hair back once more, allowing it flow in one single wave down my back. I'd done my best with the old curling iron I found in this guest room. I gave myself another spritz of perfume before putting on my jewelry. The Swarovski crystals accented the color of my dress beautifully. I normally didn't wear red, but I couldn't pass up this dress after seeing it on myself. Hanna's reaction alone was enough to sell me. It was perfect. The hue complimented my dark brown hair perfectly too. It hugged my curves in the most flattering way, while dipping low enough to expose a little cleavage. I checked the clock, seeing that we had just enough time to get to the event. I grabbed my clutch and headed to the living room. I looked like a movie star in comparison to the mud-soaked toad I looked like last night.

"Roger, I am ready to go! We should probably be leaving by now," I yelled into the hall. My head was tilted down, watching my shoes as I sauntered to the living room.

"Right, how do I look?" He asked, as I rounded the corner.

His voice made me jump. We met in the middle of living room. Both of us speechless at the sight of one another.

The glow of the pool lights reflected onto the ceiling and danced over Roger's face. I looked at him, his arms extended out to his sides as to present himself. I smiled. His arms dropped as I caught him noticing *me too.*

"You look absolutely dapper, I must say." I said.

I was being modest. He looked devilishly handsome in a tux. I raised a hand to groom his shoulder. He froze and slowly blinked as I stepped in closer. "There." I said.

I smiled at him and met his eye line. He softened and straightened his bowtie. He smelled good. Woody, musky, and peppery. I felt my palms start to sweat and my throat was becoming dry. I stepped back, composing myself.

"Thank you," he breathed and looked away.

"You look quite lovely, Jessica." Roger said, in a low voice.

He motioned to the door.

"Shall we?"

His 1960 Jaguar E was parked at the front of the drive. It was the most stunning car I'd ever seen. The color was a pale, mauve green and the interior was a cream colored leather. I went to reach for the passenger handle when Roger quickly stepped in to open in for me. I slid in, without a word.

I felt regal with my silky dress rubbing against the smooth leather. The top was down and a gentle, frosty breeze caressed the hair around my face. Roger sat himself inside and started the car. The vibration of the engine sent a wave of excitement through me.

We whipped through the winding roads in silence. The tension between us was slightly uncomfortable. The only noise was the purr of each acceleration of the engine. I had spent the last 24 hours in Roger's house, learning more about him through the pictures on his wall and the food in his fridge. Not through conversation. He had stayed tucked away in his office all day and told me to make myself at home.

I looked out the window, watching the trees and the brick buildings whip by. The sun had just set and the sky was in-between a deep blue and dusty grey. My favorite time of day. I enjoyed the near-constant overcast in England. I found comfort in it. I exhaled as Roger's voice broke the silence.

"You know, I don't really care for these large events."

He kept his eyes on the road as my ears perked up.

"Why's that?" I asked, turning to look at him.

I was genuinely curious. I knew most celebrities disliked the way the media meddled in their personal life, but I found it hard to believe they didn't care for events like these. Just as much as I found it hard to believe Kylie Jenner doesn't want to be famous.

"I think I would much prefer something more intimate, with people I actually liked. For instance, a nice dinner of sorts. It seems these events are just popularity contests. It's always the same actors kissing the asses of big name director's to play yet another outdone breakthrough role."

I tried not to smile at the way he pronounced *"asses"*. I sat there feeling a bit embarrassed at how excited I was to attend, but I understood what he meant. I'm sure being in the industry this long, and knowing the intricacies of it, could leave you jaded. I turned my head slightly towards him.

"Does Arthur feel the same?" I asked.

It was the only response I could muster. I didn't have much to contribute to the conversation.

"I doubt it. He loves rubbing elbows and telling a poor one-liner as much as possible." He said, laughing.

Roger took his eyes off the road momentarily to look my way. It was obvious that Arthur was the more social of the two, but I didn't see anything wrong with that.

We approached a large stone building. A quick google search, the night before, told me the building had been here since 1828. I felt in awe of it. I'd never seen something so beautiful and grand in my life. Women in beautiful gowns climbed the stairs alongside men in tuxedos. Limos and other luxury cars line the entrance. The valet took Roger's car and we made our way up the stairs.

I clung to his elbow for dear life. My breath became short there were butterflies in my stomach. Photographers were clicking the shutter of their cameras, blinding me. I hadn't stopped to think about the fact that we would be photographed together.

After a moment, Roger unlocked his arm from mine and walked slightly ahead. Clearly, he wasn't comfortable with us being photographed together. I could feel him angling his body away from as we approached the entrance. I understood but felt a wave of disappointment. *What did I expect?*

We walked in and my jaw almost dropped to the floor, distracting me from what had just happened. The venue was even more stunning inside. There were two grand staircases lit up by large, vintage chandeliers. The walls were decorated in gold framed paintings and crown moulding. There was live music in the center of the foyer as everyone filtered into the beautiful space. I was truly in awe. I had made it. I worked hard, a lot harder than Daniel, and had taken a risk to get here. Roger's arm extended in front of me to guide me to the main event room.

"After you." He said.

I smiled and shook myself out of the trance I was in. I looked down at my heels as I entered the room. They were the tallest I'd ever worn and I was terrified of falling. I took a deep breath as my anxiety was getting the best of me. My palms were wet with sweat. I wasn't quite sure what my job was tonight, or if I had one at all. I decided to stand back and observe, regardless. As we made our way further in, a warm and friendly voice called out to Roger. I could tell from the tone and Welsh accent that it was Arthur. We turned around to see his infectious smile and a beautiful woman buy his side. A blonde with large eyes and a plump figure. He greeted me first, to my surprise.

"Jessica, you look absolutely gorgeous! Much too gorgeous to be standing next to Roger." He said.

I laughed in unison with his wife as Roger stood there with a look on his face and shook his head.

"Well, thank you. Is this your wife? I don't believe we've met before." I asked.

"Hi, I'm Deborah. Lovely to meet you," She smiled.

She was open and kind. Her warm nature was a perfect match for Arthur.

"Hi, I'm Jessica, Roger's assistant," I said.

I extended a hand and she shook it with a bewildered look. I noticed her eyes darted quickly from Roger to me, so I quickly excused myself to grab a glass of champagne. I needed something to calm my nerves anyway.

"Would anyone like a drink?" I asked, and walked away before anyone had time to answer.

I felt like a fish out of water. I noticed Arthur already standing with a drink in hand. *I'm an idiot.*

As I turned my back and made my way to the bar I heard Arthur say, "She's quite hospitable, isn't she? It makes sense she would be your assistant" He joked.

Roger chuckled before saying, "That she is."

I grimaced, I didn't like being the butt of a joke. I stood at the bar, impatiently waiting to get the waiter's attention.

"I just assumed she was Roger's girlfriend or...something of the sort. I'm glad she made that clear." I overheard Deborah say. "Come on Deborah, have you known Roger to bring any of his previous girlfriends to these events?" Arthur said.

"Fair point." She replied.

"Look, it's a great opportunity for exposure and to gain experience as a new assistant. She needs to get accustomed to this world. Daniel is also gone, so I needed the help." Roger said.

I saw him shrug as I headed back their way with two champagne flutes. I decided to come in with a change of subject. I couldn't bare what I was overhearing.

I noticed Deborahs's earrings twinkling in the light of the chandelier and complimented them.

"Thank you! They're from this lovely little shop in North Hampstead." She said.

I handed Roger a champagne flute and took a sip of my own, noticing my hand trembling.

"I've never been to Hampstead. It seems beautiful—from what I've heard" I said to Deborah.

"Oh it is!" She mused.

"Absolutely marvelous. Roger you must take her if you have time. You know, since you're in London."

Her tone was nervous, as if she'd overstepped.

"No, I don't think we'll have time for that. I have lots of work to do. I'm only here for three days anyway, but that sounds lovely."

I tried to emphasize that I was here solely for work. I shot Roger a reassuring look. Deborah stepped closer to me and looped her arm into mine.

"Well, if you decide to extend your trip, I would love to show you around. There's this charming little boutique where I got the most gorgeous dress," She rambled on.

Roger began talking to Arthur about who all had arrived. They threw a few jabs at each other, as they normally do, and then made their way across the room, leaving us behind.

"So, where are you staying dear?" Deborah asked.

The question caught me off guard. I felt like she was prying. I tried to remember the name of the hotel Roger had used last night.

"Oh, errm, the Hoxton!" I said, quickly.

"Ah,"

"Well, if I were you, I would've booked The Browns. Much nicer. Since your on company expense, it's only fair," she winked.

I sighed with relief at her cheery disposition. She wasn't prying, she was just opinionated. "I will definitely remember that next time."

I gave her a reassuring smile. She continued to tell me about her favorite places in the city. After the 100th suggestion, I became bored. I appreciated her efforts but it was getting tiring. The thoughts whirling through my head overtook her voice. I wanted to take in the evening and explore the venue. It wasn't out of character for me to wander off at most large parties, anyway. Most importantly, I wanted to see what Roger was getting up to.

Roger and Arthur were still occupied with their mingling, so I excused myself to the restroom so I could touch up my makeup. Deborah insisted on following me. We looped arms again and I took her lead. I looked over my shoulder before exiting the room to see Arthur and Roger smiling our way. It felt nice to think they might enjoy the fact that we were getting on.

We entered the ornate bathroom and I searched for my Chanel compact. I hardly ever wore this much makeup. I'd always preferred to keep it natural. Just as I lowered my compact, I saw a familiar face enter the bathroom. My stomach almost dropped at her presence.

I wasn't often intimidated by anyone, but Celeste had a way of doing just that. She had an air about her that made my stomach turn. I couldn't ever quite place why she had this effect on me, but I was always on guard around her.

Initially, I had tried to win her over by exceeding her daily needs at the office. I would surprise her with her favorite lunch or coffee. It was all useless. I never heard a single 'Thank you' or even a smile. She avoided eye contact with me as much as possible. Daniel had warned me to never expect these things from anyone on the team, but especially *from her*. We were there to service and support without the need for recognition. The company ethics were written this way for good reason, of course, but I hated not getting a shred of recognition. It was dehumanizing, but that was the business. Celeste knew I was the "help" and didn't want me to feel any different.

Without smiling, Celeste said 'hello.' She walked in front of me to get to the stalls. I squinted. Her shade of lipstick resembled the exact one I'd found in the drawer of Roger's guest room. I shook my head. It had to be a coincidence. I could also be mistaken. She was wearing a maroon floor length gown and her hair was in a low up-do. The gown she was wearing was definitely not flattering for her figure, or her skin tone.

"Hi, celeste. How are you?"

"Very well, thank you." She said, curtly. She placed her hand on stall door to push it open. *I froze.* Just as she opened the door, the sparkle of her bracelet caught my eye. My eyes grew wide, as I realized why it kept me fixated; the white diamonds, the silver, and the cut of the design. It was the exact tennis bracelet that I had picked up from Tiffany's during my first week at the company. Another coincidence that didn't feel so coincidental.

"Alright then, off we go" Deborah said, shaking me from my stare. I nodded at Deborah with my mouth open, and followed her out. We stepped back inside the main hall, my head still whirling as I grabbed another glass of champagne from a caterer.

Roger and Arthur were standing alone now talking amongst themselves. As we drew closer, the image of Celeste in the bathroom replayed in my head. I immediately felt myself disassociating.

"You alright, dear?" Deborah asked.

She met my eye line. I nodded yes and met her eyes briefly. There's no way its the exact same bracelet I thought to myself. There was no way. But the coincidence was uncanny. The men noticed us drawing closer.

"Now what kind of trouble have the two of you been into, eh?" Arthur asked.

"Oh, just the usual girl stuff," Deborah said, nudging me and smiling.

I stole a look from Roger and tried to keep my thoughts at bay. *Keep it together,* I thought. Deborah quickly dropped her smile, realizing something was off. Roger was observing me closer too.

"We saw Celeste in the ladies room, I thought she wasn't able to attend the event tonight?" I asked.

I couldn't help myself from blurting it out. I felt surprised at myself as the words fell out. Deborah looked at Arthur, then Arthur at me as I stood looking at Roger straight on. His eyes quickly darted to mine and then he looked away, seeming unfazed.

"Oh. I haven't seen her."

Roger seemed equally as surprised as me, but suspiciously calm. I could tell from the look he gave that it was the truth, but my gut was telling me something else. It didn't make sense. I know we all had lives of our own but we did, in fact work together. Maybe I was out of line for assuming there was anything going on between them, but that's immediately where my mind had gone. So what on Earth *was* she doing here?

"Right, well enough business for tonight. I want to have some fun. Deborah, darling, have a dance with me, will you?" Arthur asked, putting his glass on the nearest table. Deborah rolled her eyes and whined.

"Art, my feet are already killing me and you know I'm no good. I'm fine with my drink, right here."

Arthur looked disappointed and turned to me.

"Jessica, how do you fancy a turn about the room?" He asked.

I was still frozen as my mind tried to sort out this mystery. I snapped out of it, painting a smile on my face. I laughed before obliging him. "That is the wrong use of that reference, but how could I say no to you?"

He seemed surprised by my answer. I grasped his hand. I was no good at dancing, but I was dying to show off my dress and finally enjoy myself. I handed my champagne flute to Deborah after downing what was left of it. Roger stared at me in bewilderment. "Don't run away with him now, love, you'll regret it soon enough." Deborah joked.

I gave a half smile and made my way to the floor with Arthur. The band was playing *Sway with Me*, one of my favorites. I enjoyed Arthur and could see why he and Roger got along so well. Not only as business partners, but as colleagues.

He twirled me around as I drug my feet along and laughed at all of his witty quips. He pulled me in closer as the next song was much slower. His gestures were respectful and gracious. He was a total gentleman and I felt comfortable with him, as if I had known him for quite some time. The platonic closeness of it all. We did a 180 and I saw Roger staring daggers at us, and pretending not to as soon as he caught my gaze. I looked away as quickly as he did and was jolted by Arthur's.

"He's rather fond of you I think." He said, with no specific tone that I could decipher.

I didn't meet his eyes as I faked a smile. The words made me uncomfortable. Not because I didn't think it was true, but because I knew it was. Arthur's words had only confirmed what I'd been feeling.

"I've never seen him take so kindly to an assistant before..well, apart from Daniel for whatever reason. The difference is that Daniel doesn't deserve it." He said.

My eyes darted to his just then. Obviously Daniel didn't deserve it. It was bold of Arthur to admit it, especially to me.

"I thought I was the only one who held that opinion." I muttered.

"I enjoy working for Roger, er, the agency, I guess I should say. I get to wear nice dresses and dance with handsome comedians." I added in an attempt to lighten the mood.

That brought a large smile Arthur's his face. As charming as I thought Arthur was, I knew he probably wasn't used to compliments. Apart from the ones his wife gave. God knows Roger wasn't handing them out. There was often a popularity contest between Roger and Arthur too. It was a part of their bit, but sometimes I felt Roger took it too far. Arthur laughed and replied with a Hugh Grant impression, to no surprise of mine. Suddenly, Roger was standing near us with his hands in his pockets.

"Alright, Arthur, enough harassing my employees." He said, cooly.

"Oh, did you want to cut in, Roger? I don't think I've seen you dance before." Arthur said, sarcastically.

Roger puffed up his chest and adjusted his bowtie, without making eye contact. I smoothed my hands against my dress.

"I'm actually getting tired, you guys. Arthur is hard to keep up with out here." I said.

I patted him on the shoulder and looked and looked at Roger. Deborah made her way over just as Arthur gave me a parting kiss on the cheek.

"Arthur, Lilly James has just arrived and you promised me you'd introduce us." She said as she tugged on his arm. Arthur shrugged at us while being pulled away.

"Duty calls." He said.

"Who knew Deborah was such a Cinderella fan?" I joked.

I got a breathy laugh out of Roger. The first one to date. He ran his fingers through his short salt and pepper stubble, scratching the skin beneath, and met my eyes for a long moment. I held his gaze, refusing to look away like I had been.

"I think I need another glass of champagne, would you like one?" I asked.

"Yeah, after you," Roger gestured for me to lead him.

I grabbed two flutes from the caterer standing nearby and invited Roger to cheers. *Clink.*

I took a generous gulp as he took a small sip.

"Ah," he sighed, parting his lips widely and adjusting his glasses on his nose.

I watched him closely, noting how effortlessly handsome he looked. I felt the other glasses of champagne setting in. I think Roger had caught on to that as well.

"You alright?" He asked.

Roger's inquisition turned to concern.

"Oh, yeah, I feel fine," I responded, taking another sip from the crystal glass and remembering I'd eaten nothing since lunch.

"Right, well, we've got a long day tomorrow," Roger said, taking a small sip from his glass.

He quickly sat his glass down before taking mine and grabbing my hand. I stared at him in confusion, wanting to finish my glass.

"Shall we head back?" He asked, rhetorically.

I knew we should but I didn't want to. He was right. We had an early morning tomorrow. Roger had an interview for a local TV network in London, followed by an interview with a journalist from British GQ. It was the start of a small press tour about Roger and Arthur's new film. And that was just the first half of our day. So, I surrendered. I was caught off guard by his stern temperament and equally as attracted by it. I nodded in response and followed him out of the venue. I squeezed his hand firmly, enjoying the intimacy of it. I couldn't remember the last time I held someone's hand.

I suddenly felt like all was right in the world. That feeling quickly faded as a picture of Celeste creeped into my mind. I stood closely to Roger as the valet pulled the car around, trying to shake my disdain. I felt a deep shiver roll over me as a breeze caught us. I hadn't thought to bring a coat for tonight. Without a word Roger removed his suit jacket and suddenly placed it over my shoulders. It was warm and smelled like him.

"Thank you." I breathed.

He grabbed my hand once more and lead me into the car. I watched him carefully as he made his way to the drivers side.

I felt myself staring, clearly I was more tipsy than I realized. The way the chilly breeze caught his mid-length hair was enough for me to throw it all away, right now for a kiss. I knew it was the alcohol that was impairing my mind. *You're being crazy, jess. Stop. Besides, a woman never makes the first move.* It was a rule I lived by.

I slumped into my seat and we drove off in silence. I decided to turn on his radio. I pressed what looked like a small button with a 'play' symbol and Witchcraft by Frank Sinatra gently started flowing from the speakers. I clapped my hands together in excitement.

"You like Frank, hmm?" Roger asked.

"No, I *love* Frank." I said.

I hummed along, letting the lyrics to fall out of my mouth without embarrassment. I looked over at Roger. He was smiling at himself just as Frank sang, "*and although I know its simply taboo, when you arouse the need in me..*" I pointed at him, belting the lyrics loudly. I was making a fool of myself, but I didn't care. I was in London, in the most expensive dress I owned, whipping around in a vintage car with my devilishly handsome boss. *No. I wasn't supposed to think about that last part.*

The energy became lighter in the car. He joined in and

tapped his fingers gently on the steering wheel, as we flew down the winding roads. I'd never seen this side of him. At this point I wasn't sure it existed.

"I love this bit right here," Roger said, turning the volume up.

The song ended and faded into another. I didn't want the drive to end. This was bliss. It was a feeling I had been chasing for so long and almost gave up on. I felt like the luckiest person in the world to be here. I was finally hitting a peak after years of valleys.

We sat in silence for a second. I felt my stomach drop at the sound of the next song. It was my favorite. 'Strangers In The Night'. A sudden melancholy fell over me. I couldn't believe it. It still reminded me of James. I tried to focus my attention back to Roger. To this moment.

Roger rounded the car into the drive and killed the engine. I adjusted his jacket onto my shoulders, feeling uncomfortable.

"That was a lovely evening," he whispered, turning towards me.

"Oh, so you actually enjoyed yourself for once? Maybe you just needed someone like me on your arm." I said, forcing a smile and tapping his shoulder. His gaze shifted to my hand and back to me. He smiled at me as we sat in silence. The tension grew thick. My palms became sweaty. I looked at his mouth and back at his eyes. My mouth opened slightly but words failed to come out.

They didn't need to, because after a second had passed he gently raised his left hand to my cheek. It was warm. I caught my breath before he gently pressed his lips to mine. *This wasn't real. It couldn't be. I must've fallen asleep on the way home.* I opened my eyes slowly to see him pull away from me. *No this was real. Very very real.* I rubbed my hot lips together and tasted him. I couldn't believe this was happening. I couldn't believe that I wanted it to. My melancholy had melted into lust.

Roger exited the car in silence, and lead the way inside the dark house. My heart was beating out of my chest as we entered the foyer.

Roger wasn't talking. Why wasn't he talking? He flicked on the lights. It was the only sound made between us. The house was a different sight to be had tonight. The grand piano had a light reflecting on it from the pool in the back.

"I think I'll light a fire and have some tea before heading to bed. Would you like some?" He asked.

Finally he spoke. I was at a loss for words. I nodded, standing there in silence. I walked towards the piano and began to remove my shoes, before placing them gently next to the bench. I took a seat and tapped a finger on the F key, letting the note drag out. It was one of the few notes I remembered from my lessons as a kid. I caught Roger's his head turn towards me as he stood in the kitchen. I let my fingers dance on the keys a moment longer, still unsure of what to say. *Maybe he didn't mean to kiss me. Maybe he was in the kitchen kicking himself.* I waited until he turned back around before I looked over at him. He placed two mugs carefully onto the counter and plopped tea bags into them. His back was facing me as I sat there staring. He poured the steaming water into each cup carefully. I stood up and walked into the kitchen barefoot, my footsteps filling the silence. I looked around to distract myself from Roger.

The East wall was made of old red brick that could've easily been 200 years old. The island was large and white with a golden honey wooden top. Opposite of the island, was a beautiful Inglenook fireplace that sat under a rounded archway. Two plush white chairs sat uniform in front of it with a small cushion in the middle. It was a beautiful room that I could see myself wasting hours in. I further understood why he didn't socialize much. I wouldn't want to leave this setting too often either.

My thoughts were interrupted by the sound of Roger starting the fire. The vision of his silhouette tending to the fire was captivating. His bowtie was undone and hanging loosely over his shirt. He rubbed his hands together for warmth as I heard the fire crackle.

"Ah, lovely" he whispered to himself.

He turned my way and looked at me standing in complete silence. "Why don't you make yourself comfortable and I'll grab our tea," He said.

"Okay."

Roger kicked off his dress shoes by the island. He turned and handed me my mug. The thick, white ceramic was still very hot. I shifted it in my hand and followed him over to the chairs.

He took the one to the left and I sank into the right, curling my feet underneath me, his jacket still wrapped around me.

"Do you play often?" I asked, in reference to the piano.

His eyes moved from the fire to me, and then quickly back to the fire. "Not very often. It came with the house." He said.

He cleared his throat.

"And do you play?"

I laughed and admitted that I wasn't musically inclined.

"So dancing is the only thing you're trained in?" He asked, in all seriousness.

I almost spat out my tea. "Oh, god no! Why would you think that? The only thing I'm trained in is department store sales. I mean, and PR of course." I snorted.

I let my head rest back on the chair and relaxed my shoulders.

"Well, you seemed to know your way on the dance floor with Arthur. So, I could only assume." He said.

He shrugged at his obvious attempt to flatter me.

"Are you jealous of my time with Arthur tonight? I ended up being more of his date than yours."

It was a bold thing to say but the champagne was talking,

not me. It was also bold of him to kiss me in the car, no matter how badly I wanted it.

His eyes held mine.

"But look who you came home with."

I couldn't believe it. I'd accomplished far more than just catching Roger's eye tonight. His smile turned devilish as he took a large sip of tea and rested his head against his thumb and forefinger, pulling the skin of his left temple taught. I couldn't help but think I *could have* gone home with someone else, if I really wanted to. I could've sorted out other staying arrangements. But I didn't. *He could've sorted out different arrangements.* Surely, he knew that by now. It was a choice. The ice we had been skating on was so thick until this very night. I felt it getting thinner with every crackling of the fire.

Roger sat his mug on the floor beside him, and lifted his legs to the plush ottoman, relaxing deeper into the chair.

"Rob said you're quite fond of me. Is that true?" I asked.

I took another sip of tea. I could be bold too.

"One could say that."

He rubbed his middle finger and index finger back and forth on his lips, making me want another taste of them.

"But are you fond of me?" He asked.

His accent gutting me at that decibel.

"One could say that," I whispered before taking another sip. I lifted my legs to meet his on the ottoman. My right leg barely grazing his left pant leg. I felt the warm and buzzing electricity from his covered leg to my bare one. My dress slid off my legs and draped onto the floor. I didn't care if any part of me was exposed. I invited it, in fact.

I felt more comfortable then I should in this moment, sitting straight on from him. It was the boldest I'd ever been in my life. I brought my knees up slightly, allowing my dress to come further up my thighs and cascade onto the ground. He watched me and removed his bowtie from his shoulders. He took off his glasses and placed them onto the arm of his chair.

I cocked my head back against back of the chair and closed my eyes.

I relaxed into the cushion for a split second before feeling a warm soft hand caress my ankle. I let my eyes stay closed, as to not seem too caught off guard by his touch. I couldn't believe what was unfolding. His hand slowly slid up my leg onto my knee before as I let out a low breath. The moment was electric. I opened my eyes to see him coming forward onto his knees, as if he were kneeling in front of me. He pushed the ottoman towards me so that it was touching the chair.

I pulled my dress above my hips, exposing the black string of my thong, inviting him in. We weren't using words to communicate and I liked that. He looked down and then up at me, still kneeling, before running his hands upwards to meet my waist, pushing my dress further up to meet the bottom of my breasts. I gasped. I lifted myself up to my elbows looking up at him slightly towering over me. A warm heaviness pooled in between my thighs as I lowered myself so that the backs of my knees hungover the ottoman. Each one now on the outside of his hips. He moved to stand in between them and I reached up to tug him closer until our lips were touching. He pressed into my face and pulled away to exhale. His warm, sweet breath showered over my face. My lipgloss transferred to his lips, causing them to slowly pull apart. He began kissing down one side of my neck as I kept reaching up for him.

Suddenly, his fingers were grazing me and drawing lazy circles outside of my underwear. I began throbbing at his teasing. I forced his lips to meet mine so he couldn't see me reaching for him. I cupped the outside of his crotch and he breathed deeply into my neck. I struggled to unbutton his pants but didn't stop until his fullness was out. I sat up, my head in line with the fullness of his cock. Roger wrapped his arms around me and began kissing me with more intensity. I felt my the straps of my dress fall off my shoulders and his lips immediately landed in their place. I almost couldn't stand the heat building between us. There were no thoughts in my head. My body was moving automatically. I started unbuttoning his shirt and watched as his skin was slowly exposed to the light of the fireplace. I looked him in the eye and paused in bewilderment. Almost as if to ask if this was really ok. I didn't wait for an answer.

His chest was fully exposed now and inviting me to trace my lips across it, so I did. He pressed his lower half against mine, both still covered by the fabric of our underwear. I could feel the stiffness of him and it was almost enough to ruin me. I clawed at the elastic of his underwear and pulled it down to expose him. Roger quickly did the same to me. He touched the wetness leaking out and lingered before entering me. I thought my whole world collapsed around me. It had been years since I'd been with anyone, much less someone his age.

After the first few thrusts, I carefully lifted my dress above my head and he threw it on the chair behind me. It landed on his jacket. My breasts were fully bare in the light of fire. He slowly slid in and out of me, as my body was sprawled out over the plush fabric. I pulled him down closer to me and ripped his shirt off of his arms. We were moving much faster now and I felt him growing larger inside of me. I opened my mouth around the side of his neck and let out a small squeal, trying to be quiet. I was on top of him gripping the arms of the chair for leverage. I swayed back and forth until he was in the deepest part of me. I collapsed over the left side of the chair, as I tried to catch my breath as we finished. My head began to spin, so I rested it in my hand and propped my elbow up on the chair for support.

Roger looked up at me and brushed my hair out of my face, and behind my ear. I let my cheek lean into the heat of his hand and grazed my lips against his inner palm. I pushed myself off of him. I stood up and then sat in the chair across from him and let out a sigh. We both laid there in silence staring at each other naked, catching our breath.

We were now each in the opposite chair from when we started. Our clothes were draped over the furniture and our tea, no doubt cold. I stood back up and reached for his pressed white shirt that was on the ground. I put it on and stood there staring at him briefly in silence before excusing myself to the bathroom. I felt my way around the guest room until I found the light switch. I felt dizzy and exhausted.

After using the toilet, I brushed my hair back and looked at myself in the mirror. I didn't recognize myself and I couldn't tell if that was a good thing. I didn't recognize where I was. *Was this even real?* I wasn't sure how the rest of this night was supposed to go, but I knew there was no going back now. I felt my mouth water and suddenly I was nauseous. I ran to the toilet and heaved viscously. The champagne hadn't agreed with the emptiness of my stomach. I wiped my mouth on the sleeve of his shirt and stood up. I washed my mouth out with water and took a large gulp from the faucet. Looking at the clock, I realized we would need to to be up in just five hours. *Shit.*

I felt dizzy and disoriented. I decided to pick up my clothing from the other room and get to bed. To my surprise, Roger wasn't there. I quietly kneeled down to grab my heels and dress from the chair. "Jessica," his low voice vibrated from somewhere in the house.

I jumped at the sound of it.

"You can leave that for the morning." He said.

I clutched my chest and spun around. "Oh, god. You star-tled me." I replied.

"Oh, no sorry, sorry. Just leave it," he said, waving his hand.

Roger was standing with a towel wrapped around his waist. His hair was still wet. As he smoothed it away from his face. His chest was glistening in the light of the fire.

He must've gotten bored waiting for me while I was vomiting in the guest room.

"Unless, of course, you want to stay in the guest room." He added.

An indirect invitation. I shook my head 'no'. Honestly, I didn't know what I wanted but I knew wouldn't be able to sleep a wink. I silently moved in the direction of his room, following behind him. It was a simple room, clearly decorated by a man. The bed was tall and plush with a red love seat at the foot of it. There were no pictures hanging, the walls were just bare. The carpet was soft against my cold and tired feet. I waited to see which side he slept on and took the opposite. The left. He peeled back the down comforter and wiggled in. I slid in right next to him, taking in the crisp earthy smell of the bedding. We laid here in silence both completely exhausted and processing what had just occurred. I opened my mouth to speak just as he switched off the lamp on his bed side. I quickly shut it.

"Goodnight." Roger whispered.

Clearly there was no conversation to be had. Thirty minutes ago we were like magnets and now I felt like I was sleeping next to a stranger. I felt my gut sink. I wanted to ignore it. I knew I should ignore it or I'd never get to sleep. I just wanted to lay here for the next few hours, before I turned back into his assistant.

CHAPTER THIRTEEN

I woke up in a state of panic before noticing the time on the analog clock. *6:05am.*

I had enough time to shower and get ready before preparing for our press day. I rolled over and let out a sigh of relief. Roger's room looked better in the daylight. I turned my head to see that I was the only one in bed. I was still wearing his white button down, the smell of my vomit still on the sleeve.

The smell was enough to have me hurling again. I felt exposed in the light of day, so I decided to button up the shirt. I tip-toed out of his room and made my way back into the guest room. I practically ran on my tip toes until I reached the room, trying not to make a sound. I closed the curtain around the antique bathtub and turned on the faucet. The steaming water felt amazing against my scalp. I stood there scrubbing myself as quickly as possible.

After doing my hair and makeup, I grabbed the cashmere turtleneck and leather midi skirt I had draped over the chair. The skirt fit me like a glove. I pulled on my leather Chanel knee high boots and zipped them up. I looked good. I gave myself a few spritz of perfume before grabbing my laptop and heading to the kitchen. I let my heels announce my presence. *Click, click, click.*

I hoped Roger would hear me and pop out from wherever he was. We hadn't spoken a word since last night. I chewed on my nails for a moment.

When Roger didn't magically appear, I grabbed a mug from his cupboard and poured myself some coffee. The pot that was still hot and full from whenever he'd made it. He couldn't have been up much longer than I'd been.

I opened my laptop and quickly ran over the itinerary before checking my email. Sitting at the island in the kitchen, I knew I needed to be in work mode, but I felt that the silence left me feeling awkward.

I cupped my coffee mug close to my chest and searched for Roger. I rounded the corner of the living room to find his office door ajar. I stepped into the doorway slowly and knocked. His head was blocked by his desktop and he was muttering something.

"Right, right. I understand that," he said to someone on the phone.

I took a quick glance around the room and noticed his awards sitting behind him. They were on a shelf with a few framed pictures, one of which was him in full costume of his most famous role, 'The anchorman'.

"Alright, look. I've got to go. I'll call you later." He said.

"Good morning," I said, crossing one leg in front of the other and leaning against the doorframe. He looked up from his screen briefly, brows lifting above his glasses.

"Good morning," he smiled and cleared his throat.

"I've reviewed the schedule for today and sent reports out to the team." I said, in my sweetest voice.

I sensed his nervousness as I spoke, looking directly at him. *Why did it have to be this way?*

"Right, wonderful. Thank you very much. I'm just reviewing the questions the network sent over last week."

His look was pensive and serious as he read. I nodded and stepped further in, looking all around the room and admiring every figurine and picture. I wanted to make a joke about why he hadn't reviewed the questions last night, but I wasn't sure if we were acknowledging last night at all. Comedy was always a go-to crutch of mine. His too I would've assumed.

He stood up, taking off his glasses. I looked at him for a long moment.

"Is that what you're wearing?" I asked.

It came out ruder than intended. Roger was wearing light grey chino pants and a tucked in button down with a black tie. "Perhaps not?" He asked, in confusion.

"No, sorry, you look good I would just make a few adjustments." I said, knowing I wanted to change the entire outfit.

He was simple, and I liked that about him, but I didn't want him looking so simple *on TV.*

"Ok, well, you're the stylist, after all."

He gave me a smug smile and looked at me, his eyes lingering on my skirt. He cleared his throat again.

"I would add a suit jacket and lose the tie. We have about 20 minutes before the car will be picking us up, if you'd like to change," I said, looking at my watch.

He peered back up at me innocently.

"Right, to the closet then," He said, standing up.

He motioned for me to follow his lead.

We entered his room and my eyes instantly pandered to his unmade bed. I felt a twinge of nerves run through me. I smiled to myself and kept my head down.

"Have a go," he said, and switched the light on in his closet.

Without a word, I began thumbing through the thick fabric of his suit jackets. Plaid, tweed, linen, and heavy cotton blends as well as flannels, lined the wall. A mix of his scent and the scent of his historical house coated the small room.

"Ah, this one is perfect!" I said.

I lifted a medium brown tweed jacket with dark brown elbow pads and handed it to him.

"That one's actually my favorite," he smiled, as he put it on and looked in the mirror.

He loosened his tie and whipped it off, flinging it over the mirror. I stood behind him, only seeing the top of my head in the reflection. Roger turned around to face me.

"Perfect," he said, as I brushed some imaginary lint from his shoulder.

We stood there closely, staring at each other in silence. He lifted his hand, grabbing my wrist slowly, his lips parting to say something just as a shrill ring came from my phone.

We both jolted at the sound that broke our dead silence. I shook my head as I looked at the unknown number on the screen.

"Oh, that must be the driver. I'll meet you out font." I breathed, his warm hand still on my wrist.

He loosened his grip. I let out the breath I'd been holding before answering the phone. I told the driver we would be right out and exited. I made my way to the kitchen, grabbing my tote from the counter briskly. I made sure I had my phone, iPad, train tickets and everything needed for the day. I raced out the front, half relieved, and half disappointed. *What was he about to do?* Part of me was reluctant to find out.

———

The car ride was quiet and awkward to say the least. Roger hadn't said a word since we left the house. *What was he going to say in the closet?* My curiosity was killing me now. I pretended to look busy as I thumbed through my iPad, constantly refreshing my email.

Roger sat quietly, staring pensively out of the car window. His previously attractive mystique was now annoying me. We pulled up to the large electric gates encasing the studio and I felt my nerves begin to bubble up. This was the second biggest day on the job. I'd rehearsed it so many times in my head before now, but somehow still felt a bit of panic. The security guard handed the driver two lanyards with badges for us. He handed them back to us and pulled up to the entrance.

"So, your dressing room is 1306 on the west side of the studio," I said, breaking our silence and putting the lanyard around my neck. "Ah, yes, putting on makeup. That's my favorite bit about tv interviews." He said sarcastically, trying to get a laugh out of me.

He smiled my way and I gave him a forced smile.

We entered the large studio where there were two sofas on a stage, surrounded by at least six cameras. The floor was glassy back and the lights were extremely bright on the stage. The back wall was made-up of six plasmas TV's to make one large purple monitor, with the local stations logo in the middle.

I took the lead to find the studio director who I had been in correspondence with this week.

"Ah, Jessica!" A voice called.

A woman with thick black hair and Tom Ford glasses strutted towards us. She was wearing a pink bandage dress that accentuated her plump, pear-shaped frame. She extended a hand to me and then Roger. *Tilly. Her name was Tilly.* I reminded myself. I memorized every name in the correspon-dence emails leading up to this week. Not only to impress Roger, but to impress whoever we were working with.

"Tilly, so great to meet you!" I beamed.

"Wonderful to meet you," Roger echoed in a smooth, nonchalant voice.

"Let me show you to the dressing room. How was your drive in," She asked, as her heels clicked loudly across the set floor, my boots were hardly keeping up with her.

"Lovely, thank you." Roger said in a short tone.

He was annoyed already. "Brilliant. Well, this is it. We will go on in 30 minutes sharp. Someone from production will fetch you shortly," Tilly said, as her arm was extended into the open room.

It was the same setup I'd seen on late night shows, small loveseat, black directors chair, and bright shiny bulbs. After we entered, Roger swiftly shut the door. We stood there looking at each other, and before he could say anything, I blurted, "I'm going to grab a water. Would you like one?"

I left the room before he could answer. Whatever he was going to say, I didn't want it done here. Not a chance. Not with a full day of work ahead of us. I took a left down the hall, as if I knew exactly where I was going. I walked for quite some time before finding a water cooler and filling up two paper cups. I figured I had killed enough time for the makeup artist to find him. I made the unfamiliar trek back and opened the door to the room. With one elbow, I pushed down on the handle, balancing the cups with both hands. I opened the door to find Roger being powdered and plucked by a team of two people. "Found the water cooler," I said, putting his cup on the vanity next to him.

"Great, cheers." He replied.

Without eye contact, I told him I was going to head to the stage and wait. He nodded silently watching me exit the room.I hated the tension that lingered from this morning. I was still reeling about what he could've said. *Was it that he might need to let me go because this was a conflict of interest? Or was he madly in love with me?* I almost laughed to myself at the thought of that. I froze.

That could be a possibility. OH, who are you kidding, Jess? You hardly know this man. You hardly know what he eats for breakfast in the morning. The more I thought about it, the more I realized that there was no way he would let me go on one of the busiest weeks of the year. Besides, HE came onto ME.

The stage was brighter than before, almost blinding. The anchor sat on the couch, getting her makeup done as well.

"Ten minutes to air!" someone screamed on the set.

I looked around sipping my water and taking in my surroundings. It was so surreal to be behind the scenes of a news broadcast in the UK. I opened my phone and messaged Hanna. I told her about last night with very minor details. It was about midnight in LA and that she was probably asleep so I was surprised to hear the notification of her response. *"WHAT!!! I knew this would happen! What was it like? How are you feeling about everything? Was it good? Tell me it was good."*

Ten minutes must've passed quickly, because I saw Roger approaching the stage from the corner of my eye. I locked the screen on my phone and watched him as he entered the room with such grace. I know he had been in the the industry for quite some time, but it still impressed me with how well he carried himself.

Maybe true confidence came from not giving a shit about being famous. The news anchor asked him the typical run-of-the-mill press questions about the film and he gave his long-winded responses sprinkled with stuttering and lots of eyebrow raising. He was passionate about his work and it seemed to be one of the few things that made him long winded. It was charming.

All of a sudden, my eyes widened, as a picture of me at the gala flashed onto the monitor behind them.

"And who is this lovely lady we saw you with earlier this week?" The anchor asked.

"Some say it's a new love interest." She added.

My body froze as I stood and watched the words come out of her mouth. Roger cooly looked behind him, raised his eyebrows, and chuckled.

"No, no, that's one of my assistants. She's actually here now, *working.*" he said, emphasizing the word. He was fuming but keeping a cool demeanor. Roger waved a finger as to gesture to the set and I held my breath, hoping no cameras would point at me.

"She is quite lovely though but no, just an employee of the company, unfortunately"

He searched for me behind the cameras but I had no idea if he could actually see me.

"Unfortunately, huh?" The anchor pressed on.

"No, you've got it all wrong. You've mistaken my tone. She's a lovely assistant." He said, sternly.

I stood there in shock, my breath halted.

"So for the folks at home, should we tell them you're still on the market then?" The anchor asked.

He chuckled in an annoyed tone, and shrugged his shoulders.

"Tell the folks at home, perhaps, to focus on my film coming out soon. Not my personal life. I assure you it's quite boring." He retorted.

Heat filled my cheeks and ears as they wrapped up the interview. Part of me wanted to be flattered at the fact that I was on local British TV. *I did look good*, but under these circumstances, it was beyond awkward. The reality of his words stung me, though. We had just gotten comfortable with each other, shared a heated night of passion, and hadn't even had time to speak about it.

The lights flashed brightly and the crew yelled 'cut'.

Roger almost leaped out of his chair. He walked off stage, ripping his mic off, without saying anything to the anchor. A makeup artist quickly ran to the anchor, giving her a touchup, and making it seem like it was just another days work for them. I could see in Roger's eyes that he was furious.

Tilly appeared out of nowhere and Roger seemed to be making a beeline to her.

"What the fuck was *that?*" He nearly shouted at her, pointing towards the stage.

My eyes grew wide and my mouth fell open.

"Ok—I" Was all Tilly could get out before Roger interrupted.

"This was supposed to be about the film. This is why I hardly do this *bloody shit*. You local stations love to pry to get a laugh and a little rating, meanwhile dragging my employees into your gossip segment." He hissed.

"Roger, *please*. I apologize. I had no idea." Tilly pleaded, looking my way.

"You'll be hearing from my lawyers. *Goodbye*." He spat.

Fuming, he made his way to me and swiftly yanked me by the arm. "Come on. We're leaving." He said.

I nodded and quickly strode alongside him. Seeing him so defensive was doing something inside of me that it shouldn't. A car was waiting for us out front. I slid in before him. He leaned in, slamming the door behind him. *"Christs sake!"* He yelled.

I shot back at his voice. I sat bewildered. I'd never imagined him so angry. He put his fingers on his nose, pinching it, and sighed. I decided to say something.

"You handled that very well." Was all I could say.

He rally did. He was calm and collected up until that last minute.

"I had to be. I was on *LIVE TV!* I don't want some ridiculous speculation sputtered about." He huffed.

"Right, ridiculous speculation of a boss having an affair with his assistant." I said, sarcastically and looked out the window.

It was my attempt to make some light of the situation. It might have been wildly inappropriate, but I couldn't help it. I couldn't bear pretending like nothing had happened last night at all. The silence became deafening. Roger didn't respond. I looked at him, waiting for him to say something. I crossed my legs and watched as he rubbed his middle finger and thumb over his eyebrows. He let out a deep sigh.

"It's about the principle" as his hands motioned in front of him, as if the principle was in this very car.

"It isn't right. The media has gone too far with this shit.

These interviews are unbearable enough as it is, without the petty gossip." .

I admired how serious he was, I had to admit. How deeply he was effected by an industry he was equally passionate about. I guess you can only be deeply hurt by something you truly care about though. He sat there looking out the window letting silence fill the car again. I knew he wasn't going to mention anything about last night now and I was at a loss for words anyway. It didn't seem like the right time to press it. I said nothing, knowing it wasn't my place to initiate. I was the assistant. That was all.

I sat in silence for about an hour while Roger and Arthur discussed scripts, screenplays, and ideas while throwing in the occasional jab at one another. I barely touched my food and spent most of the meal staring out the window. We were seated in the back of the restaurant, for obvious reasons, but our table was next to a large window looking out to a busy street.

I felt Roger glancing at me from the corner of his eye every so often. I wasn't an expert on body language, but I could sense that he was wondering what I was thinking. He seemed distracted as he kept asking Arthur to repeat himself. I knew he could feel my thoughts swirling in my head. *Or so I hoped.*

I finally met his gaze. I gave him a half smile and a nod before taking a large sip of my water. I was so deep in my thoughts that their conversation sounded like tv static. I was thinking of every possible scenario that would result from what we'd done and what he *didn't* say this morning.

We finished our lunch, or rather they did, and made our way outside and I focused in on their conversation.

"I think it could be a great opportunity to push the film. So what do you say?" Arthur asked Roger.

"Yeah, absolutely. We will look at the calendar and see how we can make it work." He replied.

He looked my way, insinuating the '*We*' was he and I—er, the team. I had no clue what they were talking about so I just said, "Of course. Absolutely."

I smiled my best smile.

We said our goodbyes and I walked to the car. Roger followed. We slid in and he instantly said, "So how do you feel about extending your trip?" I shook my head feeling numb.

"Oh, yes. I'm fine with it." I said, not knowing what I was even agreeing to. Either way, I knew if I was going to be dealing with all of this that I'd rather do it in England. Besides, I had no life to go back to.

"You know I don't need you there, but I would appreciate the company. I also think you would enjoy Paris this time of year. Or have you been before?" He asked.

I turned my head slowly. *PARIS??? We were talking about extending the trip to Paris??* My heart started to beat quickly. I blinked hard. I was paying attention now. There was no question in my mind about what we were doing, I'd be there.

"No...no i've never been to Paris." I sighed, shaking my head.

He was looking at his hands before lifting his head to say, "To be honest Jessica, I want you there. I would enjoy it."

I fixated my eyes on him. Trying to read him. Roger only met my gaze for a second before looking to the left out of the car window. I was shocked at what he said, but I knew that was about all he could give me. That was good enough for me.

Maybe we didn't need to talk about last night. I didn't need to know what he was going to say this morning in the closet. I didn't need to know where we stood or have clarity. That was enough for me, for now. I smiled at him.

"I would enjoy that too." I said, brushing my hair behind my ear.

He seemed slightly surprised by my answer and smiled back at me.

"Right, well, I will leave the arrangements up to you. We will need two nights in a central hotel. Daniel will be with us by then so make sure that we have appropriate accommodations. And try to book directly this time, okay?" Roger asked.

Shit. I forgot about Daniel. I had wasted the morning thinking about the least important aspects of all this, rather than the obvious one. Daniel. One whiff of me and Roger and I'd never hear the end of it. I wasn't even sure what he would do with this kind of information. Suddenly, I was fine never speaking about me and Roger *at all.*

CHAPTER FOURTEEN

I'D NEVER BEEN on a train before, apart from the NYC subway, which didn't really count. I'd always dreamt of riding a train through London, or any city in the UK, for that matter. All the European influencers I followed left me envious of how easily they could travel by train. To be a couple hours from Paris, London, or other surrounding cities was something I hoped they didn't take for granted.

There was something incredibly soothing about the city buildings and green pastures whipping by in the silence in the train car. The car was completely empty, apart from an elderly woman who sat five seats ahead of us. Roger had insisted we take the train, for privacy I'd assumed, or maybe he enjoyed the tranquility as much as I did.

I was finishing a cup of porridge. Roger often skipped his breakfast and opted for a coffee. I watched his lips purse as he blew into the open paper cup. I was sitting directly across from him. He looked good with his white button-up messily rolled up to his elbows. His hair was air-dried and laying wispy around his face. His thin framed brown glasses—similar to countless other pairs he owned—rose above his eyebrows when whatever he was reading became interesting.

The faint smell of sandalwood lingered in the air. He must've been wearing a new cologne. I looked over at him as he checked his large silver Rolex, before running his hands through his hair. I couldn't tell if he was anxious or just bored. I'd stayed in his guest room the nights leading up to Paris, but things had been strictly business since the incident at the TV station— a day I wish I could forget for many reasons. I'd be lying if I said wasn't craving his touch. I imagined him barging into the guest room and quietly crawling over me late at night. I fantasized about sneaking into his room too. Instead, I tossed and turned until my alarm went off.

I put away my iPad and began reading a biography I had packed about Frida Kahlo. After writing numerous papers about her in college, she became my favorite artist. I already knew everything about her, but I needed to look at something other than a screen. I took a sip of my breakfast tea and and crossed my legs as I skimmed the pages. Roger put his paper down and looked at me as I did this, his gaze lingering.

I was wearing my black turtleneck that fit snugly to my torso along with green, high-waisted wool trousers.

"Incredible woman...and artist," Roger said, breaking the silence.

I looked up from the book and smiled. We stared at each other for a moment. I hoped he'd add more to the conversation, but when he didn't, I asked "Do you have a favorite artist?"

"Not particularly, but her work is rather remarkable." He said, as he rubbed his forefinger and thumb under his chin.

I smiled back politely, surprised that he didn't have much to add. He went back to reading his paper. I found it odd that he didn't have an answer. Everyone had a favorite artist, *didn't they?*

I thought about his house for a second and how he didn't own any artwork. I guess it shouldn't have been so surprising.

Perhaps his favorite medium was performing arts, I thought, and vowed to dissolving my judgement.

I placed my book aside and crossed my arms, getting more comfortable. I decided to change the subject. Surely, we could connect through something else.

"Roger, where did you grow up?" I asked.

He raised his eyebrows in surprise at the question. I realized in this moment that we truly knew nothing about each other. I was desperate to connect.

"Just north of Manchester, in Middleton" He said, doing his tooth-sucking, lip-smacking thing and nodded.

"And where exactly are you from? Wait, wait, no. Pennsylvania right?" He asked with confidence, pointing his index finger.

I shook my head.

"New England of all places, Connecticut, actually. A town called Westport." I laughed awkwardly.

Roger really knew nothing about me apart from what I looked like naked and that I was good at making coffee, or that I knew how to steam his suits shirts perfectly.

"And you went to school for fashion and found yourself in LA, only to end up working in film? I did read your résumé, I promise." He said.

"Well, that's the short of it."

I looked out the window.

"I always loved fashion and thought I would want to work in the industry, until actually moving to LA and experiencing it first hand." I responded.

I paused a few beats before I finished my thought.

"I feel miserable in LA. I only chose to move there because it was the far from home."

His eyes widened at this and his face softened.

"I have a feeling I could relate to that on some level. Are you not close with your family? Not to say that even if you are, you can't have the desire to be far from them at times—I think most people feel that way.." he did that cute rambling thing he often did to make people more comfortable.

"I don't have much of a family." I said.

"We're pretty broken up. Gosh, this sounds like a sob story," I covered my face with my hand.

"But I promise it's not." I added, waving my hand in front of me.

"My father was never interested in being around. And I guess you could say my mother was the same." I said.

I hated talking about my family. It was embarrassing to say the least. I didn't want people to pity me. I wanted people to relate to me. That was all I wished to share. In truth, my mom had provided for me in all the essential ways a parent should, but emotionally she was absent. She spent her days working late and then coming home to veg out on the couch with a bottle of wine. On the weekends she'd pawn me off on my friend's parents so she could go on blind dates. They only ever ended poorly, at least from what I heard from her late- night phone calls with my aunt Rachel.

"Ah. So, where did you acquire your fantastic music taste?" He smiled a tight smile, that was borderline mischievous. I was relieved that he was changing the subject. He was no doubt referencing the frank Sinatra song we sang together the night of the gala. My stomach sunk at the thought.

"I'm not sure. I've always enjoyed older music. I think music was much more romantic and straightforward back then. I also watched The Lorence Welk Show late at night as a kid." I laughed.

It was true that I'd always enjoyed this style of music, but what had created a deeper fondness for it was James. I tried to push him out of my mind but I couldn't. Sinatra was the soundtrack to most of the memories we shared. For some odd reason, this trip was making me more nostalgic than I cared to admit.

"The *what* show?" Roger asked. I quickly realized that was exclusively an American TV show.

"Oh, sorry. I think that's just an American thing. It was a popular music show with a big band." I explained.

"So, you're a romantic I assume?" He asked.

I slightly shook the thought of James out of my brain.

"Terrible, terrible, romantic." I responded and rested my head on my right hand. I bit my bottom lip.

"You must be too if you had Sinatra in your CD player." I joked. Roger shrugged in an a somewhat agreeing gesture. One thing about Roger was that he was ever ambiguous. He was smiling at me with that gleam in his eye that accentuated his crows feet.

"Why do you find LA so miserable?" He asked.

I thought for a second about how I wanted to formulate an answer. I brushed my hair back.

"Well, apart from practically having no seasons I guess the culture? It really does fit almost every stereotype you hear. I don't know— I just know I don't enjoy it."

I felt stupid trying to articulate this.

I felt my palms getting sweaty. I hated looking stupid in front of him. He was taking too long to reply.

"And after my years there, I think I'm entitled to that opinion." I added, sounding defensive.

"No, I absolutely agree. I know that the industry can be filled with untrustworthy sociopaths, believe me. It's much worse in Hollywood than it is in London." He said, folding his newspaper in his lap.

I was surprised by his response. It was far more eloquent than what I'd been trying to say. I think I was too afraid of sounding blunt. I don't know why I felt I couldn't fully express myself around him. "And how do you feel about London?" He asked.

"I love everything about it, unfortunately. The delicate

rain, the mild temperatures, the cozy pubs, and mass transit," I said, gesturing around us.

"Should I go on?" I laughed.

His eyebrows were raised again.

"Why is that unfortunate?—loving London?" He asked.

I hesitated answering honestly. I wanted him to know my plans for the future, on a professional and and personal level. I just didn't know how it would affect my current circumstance. Or our current circumstances.

"Its unfortunate because I want to live here. More than anything, but I don't know if that will ever happen." I admitted.

I lowered my gaze to my lap and fiddled with the ring on my middle finger. After a long silence he said, "Well, you're here now aren't you?"

I looked up slowly at him. I couldn't help but smile.

"So is that how you feel about London too?" I asked in response.

"I guess I assumed with your townhouse in LA, that you enjoyed being there more."

"No, I much prefer being here. I'm only in LA when I am needed by the team or if some director refuses to come to me. I mainly bought the house for Daniel. He's in LA quite a bit, helping the team there, and it's nice for me not to live out of a suitcase constantly. The townhouse is practically his. Or at least, he thinks it is. He on the other hand, loves living LA." He said.

Of course Daniel loved LA.

"When a man is tired of London, he is tired of life" Roger said.

I raised my eyebrows. "Samuel Johnson?" I asked, only knowing the quote from my endless hours of Pinterest scrolling. He nodded, silently.

"I love London for the exact reasons you do, but I hate not being able to have a fireplace. They've been outlawed due to the smog. That's something LA and London have in common, *smog*," He said, with a laugh.

"And we're taxed for practically breathing it seems too. Apart from that, it doesn't get better than London. But I do prefer the countryside, which is why I don't live in Central anymore. Fresh air and green grass is therapeutic for me and I'm just a drive away from the city." He added.

"Although, my neighborhood isn't quite as popular as The Cotswolds, it's home." Roger said.

I knew little about the Cotswolds, apart from the fact that most British celebrities had country homes there. David and Victoria Beckham to be exact. I knew this thanks to my Vogue subscription.

"I'm sure the Cotswolds are lovely but so is your home." I said, softly. There was another long pause and Roger shifted his gaze to the window for a minute or so. Finally, he turned his head and looked at me.

"Jessica, there's actually something I wanted to talk to you about." My cheeks got hot.

I felt my stomach drop. *What on earth could it be? Was it the conversation he was avoiding days ago?*

"Daniel is needed quite a bit at the LA offices." He said, easing my tension. I bit my cheek and waited for him to finish.

"I don't have anyone here, in London, who is *hands-on*. I find myself needing someone rather frequently. I tend to lean on interns a bit too much."

I'd hoped these interns he was referring to were men. I sat still in confusion. What was he getting at? *He couldn't be talking about me, could he?*

"We both know Daniel's performance hasn't been up to par since you've been on. I was wondering if you knew why that could be." Roger said.

I was blindsided. *How should I know why Daniel's job performance wasn't up to company expectations?* I was slightly annoyed now.

"I want to have someone who I can trust in London. I need a sharp mind and someone who can follow through every time." He continued.

He gave me an incredulous look. I felt that the undertone of the question was pointed.

Part of me felt offended. As if it were my fault. The other part of me felt that no matter what, I needed to be honest and professional. A laughable thought after what we'd done.

"No, honestly I could ask you the same about Daniel. I just assumed there was leniency allowed with him because of his tenure, you know, because he's been with the company so long."

I looked nervously down at my lap once more. I hoped I wasn't overstepping. I couldn't tell what Roger was insinuating, but I felt like it had something to do with that kiss all those months ago. The one between me and Daniel. The one that sent me into an absolute spiral about losing this very position. Surely after the other night he wouldn't still be worried about *that*. I didn't care for Daniel, but I didn't feel comfortable outing him in some way either.

"Right, well I need someone here in London. I'm spread thin with everything." He said, completely glazing over the subject of Daniel.

I wanted to laugh. *Dry cleaning and having five hour long expensive dinners was so taxing apparently.* I took a deep breath, feeling relieved that he wasn't pressing any further or that my position wasn't somehow compromised.

"Would you be willing to split most of your time here?" He asked.

My eyes nearly popped out of their sockets. I found it difficult to speak. *He wanted ME to work in London?*

"I wouldn't ask if you hadn't mentioned your disdain for LA and I'd rather not hire someone new." Roger said.

My head was spinning in a million directions so I just blurted "Yes, yes of course." I felt my heart pounding so hard that I could hear it. I couldn't believe how fast this was all happening. I wanted this more than anything though. My own feelings aside, I knew this moment would eventually come. Daniel had explained it all to me that night at the Italian restaurant. But he said it could take YEARS to get there. At least, thats how long it took him to move to LA.

"Please don't mention anything to Daniel just yet. I am still working out the details. Its complicated." He said.

I nodded in agreement.

"Of course."

I couldn't help but feel that this last week had played a part in his decision making.

"Is this what you were going to say this morning, in the closet?"

I hesitated on the word closet.

"Yes, well, that was the main bit," He said, clearing his throat. I could tell he didn't want to elaborate further.

"Why are you so lenient with Daniel?" I asked.

I figured now was a better time than ever to ask. I knew it might've been a misstep, but I needed to know.

"It's complicated." He said, firmly, adjusting his collar.

Just as he answered, the train came to a stop and our location was announced overhead.

"Right, here we are," He said, as he stood and put on his thick tweed jacket.

Roger threw his long maroon scarf over his shoulder. It was similar to the one I'd made James all those years ago. I looked away from him. I reached for my coat, feeling his hand brush mine, sending a warm rush through my stomach.

"Allow me," he said, and gestured to help me thread my arms through. I turned to face him, we stood inches apart, our noses practically touching.

"I'm glad you asked. More than glad." I whispered.

"Glad that I asked what, exactly?"

Roger's face was so close that I felt his warm breath on my face. It smelled like coffee. I swallowed hard before answering.

"Im glad you asked me to extend the trip to Paris."

It was silent for a moment longer before I added, "And glad that you asked me to work in London."

He responded with a warm smile and guided me into the aisle. I was embarrassed my his silence. I shouldn't have said anything. He grabbed our bags from over head.

"I'm just happy you obliged." He finally said, without looking at me.

We checked into our hotel and got settled in our separate rooms. Mine right next to Roger's on the 3rd floor. I laid my toiletries out in the bathroom and hung up my clothes. I sifted through my bag to find my perfume and gave myself a few sprays.

We had an hour before Roger's first meeting, so we decided to grab a cappuccino and walk the city. I was in awe of everything I saw. The narrow streets were cobblestone and brick laid. I could feel the breeze of every car or bicycle that whizzed by me. The streets were lined with quirky and colorful shops. I loved the juxtaposition of modern brands inside buildings that have stood in the city for hundreds of years. The area was congested and lively with shoppers and storekeepers alike. I'd look up occasionally to take in the surroundings. Mostly, finding black metal terraces lining every window with someone sitting outside with a glass of wine and a cigarette. Some of the apartments above were covered in ivy and lush greenery. I was taken aback by how magical every-thing looked, it wasn't how I'd imagined Paris. It was better.

I caught Roger's eyes on me just as a smile painted his face. I laughed and elbowed him.

"What is it?" I asked, brushing my hair behind my ear.

"You're going to trip if you don't keep your eyes on the ground." He said.

"It's lovely though, isn't it?" He asked.

"I've never experienced anything like it." I admitted.

I wanted nothing more but to lace fingers with him and stroll blissfully down the street, but I couldn't bring myself to do it. I swallowed hard and tried to focus on how happy I'd felt just moments ago.

"So, what coffee shop are you taking me to?" I asked, in a forced chipper tone.

"This one," he said extending his arm to his side. He gestured to a turquoise blue painted shop. A large 'M' was stenciled on the front window. A few people were enjoying their coffee or working on laptops. The quaint coffee shop was warmly lit and minimally designed. The pastry case was filled with mountains of fresh pastries. My mouth was salivating at the sight of the pain au chocolat, and Kouign-amann, that was delicately displayed.

We decided to split a pastry. Roger stepped up to the counter and ordered our drinks in French. I wasn't surprised that he spoke the language but it was still impressive. I interrupted him before he could finish his sentence.

"Et une pain au chocolat, s'il vous plait. Merci." I said.

And gave him a wink. He looked at me in surprise.

"Absolutement, madame."

I thought of correcting the man, but I refrained.

Roger smiled.

"I thought you'd never been to Paris?"

He put his wallet away.

"I haven't but I never said I didn't speak French." I smiled.

"Ah, impressive." He said, putting his hands in his pockets.

I shrugged not wanting to admit that I could hardly speak past a third grade level. We walked out into the busy street again with our coffees and pastry. After a few blocks, we approached a park bench. Roger suggested we have a seat to finish our coffee. It was the most delicious cappuccino I think I'd ever tasted. We tore our pastry in half, our fingers grazing, making me nervous.

"Thank you," I whispered, before I ate my half in two bites.

"How will I ever be able to enjoy an American pastry again?" I asked. I rolled my eyes in ecstasy while chewing. Roger let out a deep laugh, probably the most genuine one I'd heard from him.

"You won't. You'll spend your days cursing every one you come into contact with that isn't this one." He said, with a mouth full.

We sat laughing while the breeze picked up around us. My hair began whipping around my face and the parchment from the pastry bag went flying. Neither of us bothered to get up and chase it.

"Oh, no!" I yelled.

I turned to Roger. He was staring at me and raised a hand to my face, gently brushing my hair behind my right ear. I felt my breath become uneven as he leaned in to kiss me. I gently kissed him back. His lips were cold.

I was in disbelief that Roger was being so bold in public. He was clear that whatever this was, it shouldn't be public. As bad as that made me feel, I'd never say. It's just how it had to be. I knew the ramifications, for both of us, if this were to get out.

I suppose in Paris there wasn't much likelihood for this to be exposed. Just as Roger pulled away, the sun disappeared causing a grey overcast. A light drizzle began to fall but we sat still in silence. "We should head back to the hotel. The meeting's in an hour." He said, in a gentle tone.

I nodded, saying that I was exhausted and would probably take a nap.

That was partially true, but for the most part, I just wanted to be alone with my thoughts. A sudden sullen feeling had come over me. I knew how unfortunate that was, to feel this way in such a beautiful city. I couldn't help it and I couldn't place it either.

We strolled back to the hotel at a leisurely pace. Roger pointed out how 'marvelous' different building structures were and made pointless small talk. He never really rambled like this unless he was nervous. I wasn't sure what had gotten into him.

We were about a block away from the hotel when it began pouring rain. I knew Paris was notorious for random showers, but neither of us had thought to bring an umbrella. Roger suddenly grabbed my hand and took off running. I let out a playful shriek and tried to keep up with his stride. We finally reached the spinning doors of our hotel. I let out a sigh as we squeezed into the same window of the carousel. He bumped against my backside, almost tripping. I let out a laugh.

"Oh, god! Sorry." Roger breathed, into the back of my head.

His mouth was grazing my hair. We stepped into the lobby and I shook my arms in front of me, flicking the water off. I turned to look at Roger just he ran a hand through his hair. He sighed loudly catching his breath. I stared at him blankly, feeling entranced by how sexy he looked in his soaked clothes.

"*Bloody hell.* That was invigorating, eh? Should we head up?" He spat, as he read his watch.

His glasses were covered in water droplets and I could barely see his eyes. He took them off and dried them off on his shirt, exposing his navel area. I nodded still entranced by him and panting. I followed him to the elevator and we rode in silence all the way up. The doors opened and I stepped off first. The hall was so narrow that we had to walk single file. I approached my door just as I heard Roger yell, "Christ!"

I turned to see him patting his pockets and looking around.

"I've seem to lost my key card." He said.

He continued looking around in shock, before I told him I had a spare. Roger looked at me, a single bead of water dripping from his temple onto his shirt.

"Have you? Oh. That's great. It must've fallen out of my pocket during all of that." He said, wiping his face.

"Would I be a good assistant if I wasn't prepared for this kind of situation?" I asked, as I swiped my key and opened the door. "Besides, I'm paranoid that these sort of things will inevitably happen, so I ask for extra keys."

Not mentioning the fact that I was just as capable of misplacing a key card. We stepped into my dimly lit hotel room. I took off my jacket. My clothes were soaked along with my hair. I wanted to strip naked right then and get into a hot shower. The bed was beckoning me with the two red velvet throw pillows and plush white comforter.

It was positioned between two large wooden wardrobes that fused into an awning above the bed. There were two small incandescent sconces inside the awning, with a small patch of wallpaper.

I bent over slightly to open the drawer of the desk. I caught Roger staring at me intently, as I fished for his key card. He cleared his throat. I felt a drop of water roll down my cleavage and I pretended not to notice, knowing his eyes were following it. I slowly turned to him, handing him the keycard in what felt like slow motion. I looked up at him, holding my breath. Roger let his fingers graze mine for a long moment, before pulling me into him. I looked up at him in surprise.

"You have to go," I whispered.

I knew it's what he should do, but I wanted him to stay. No matter how much I'd hate myself for it later. Suddenly, his hands were around my face and his lips were on mine. I leaned into the kiss and then pulled away.

I took a step back and looked at him, catching my breath.

He looked at me with earnest eyes. He rubbed his hand over his mouth and then his chin.

"I'm sorry.." He whispered.

I stood there in silence and began wringing my hair out. A stream of water dripped from my ends to the floor. My thoughts were swirling now, between giving in, and *never* doing this again. I didn't like what it was becoming. I didn't like me.

Either way, my clothes were becoming uncomfortable and I was cold. I sat down on the bed and began unzipping my boots.

"You've gotta go," I said again, avoiding eye contact.

I meant it just as it sounded, but I knew he thought I meant he needed to go to his meeting. I peeled my socks off just as I saw his shoes in my field of vision. My heart began pounding, the energy was shifting and I knew what was about to happen. I knew I wouldn't be able to stop it. I looked up at him and caught my breath. Without a word, he took off his jacket and threw it over the desk. He stepped closer and cupped a hand to my left cheek. I leaned into it, breathing in his scent. I could tell he was picking up on whatever deep state of thought I was in.

I looked up at him and before I knew it, may hands were on his belt, undoing it as quickly as possible. His cold fingers were suddenly grazing my ribs, peeling my shirt off and over my head. I felt goosebumps form on my arms, as I sat in my underwear unbuttoning his shirt ferociously. Finally, he was shirtless and I was pulling him down to me. *This was wrong. I shouldn't be doing this.* I slid back welcoming him onto the bed. *You can stop now.* He was on top of me and we were both gasping for air. *You don't really want this.* His stubble scratched my sensitive skin. I liked the raw feeling it gave me. He undid my bra and I removed it. I threw it across the room as he struggled to unbutton my wool trousers. I pushed them down past my knees and he stood, removing them off me completely.

I laid back, partially bare, in my black underwear. Roger climbed on top of me quickly and touched his warm chest to my cold one. I let out a deep sigh. The warmth of his skin undid me. I wanted him badly now, no matter what. His lips soon found mine and we were breathing each other in, unable to get enough. I tasted as much of his tongue as I could. I let my mind go blank as he moved my underwear to the side and entered me. Roger let out a low moan, and I wrapped my arms around his neck. My wet hair was cold against my now warm body.

His breath was becoming shorter, as was mine, and I felt myself getting closer.

"*Christ*" he whispered under his breath, sending a chill down my spine.

I turned my head to see his hand gripping the bedding firmly beside me. I rocked my hips back and forth, slowly. Suddenly he was pulsing inside me.

I fought the urge to hoist myself up to kiss him. Instead, I completely relaxed into the bed, motionless.

I looked anywhere but at him. He kissed me on the lips slowly and then stood up. Roger quickly got dressed as I looked for my bra. I was cupping my boobs, until he picked it up from the floor and handed it to me.

"I'm so sorry. I have to run." He whispered.

I told him I needed to shower and take a quick nap before tonight. Roger put his jacket on and smoothed out his hair, which was practically dry now. I turned to walk to the bathroom, just as he said my name.

I turned on my heel, raising my eyebrows in response.

"I'll see you tonight." His voice was smooth and deep.

I had a feeling he wanted to say more. I hated that it melted me. I hated that I was left pining for any morsel of affection he expressed. I nodded, faking a smile and carried on into the bathroom. I waited until I heard the door shut to start the shower.

I stood there half-naked, looking at myself in the mirror. The mirror began to fog. As I stared into my own pupils, the high I was riding began to fade into melancholy. I felt hollow. I had no idea what Roger truly felt for me, and here I was, giving him every ounce of me.

I stepped in to the hot shower and let out a deep breath. I'd never been one for casual sex, I wasn't wired that way. I was all or nothing. Knowing this about myself only meant that what was happening was doomed from the start.

I'd be crazy to think anything else, right? How could this possibly work?

A celebrity falling madly for his assistant wasn't a common love story. At least, not one I'd ever seen, or read about. The assistant or secretary was always just an affair, usually the catalyst for someone's divorce. Or even if things did work out, it never lasted very long.

My delusions were quickly fading, as I not only realized what this meant for me romantically, but professionally. If I expressed how I felt, what would this mean for my career at the company? I felt my anxiety heighten as my reality set in. I was falling—or at least I thought so, for my boss.

I felt a deep attraction to Roger's status and maturity, but was there anything left *after that?* I didn't like being a secret, but I couldn't deny that the mystery fueled this fire. It added to the passion, I couldn't deny that.

When I dissected what this was, there was hardly any depth to it. I knew that, anyone would be able to see that. We've hardly known each other a year and I only just realized the little we had in common. Sure, he liked Sinatra and he was handsome but that's all I knew. He was respectful too, but what man of his age wasn't? I turned off the faucet and quickly wrapped myself in a towel. I searched the room for a mini bar and only found a bottle of champagne in a bucket of melted ice. I popped the cork and tossed it over my shoulder. I took a swig of the bottle and wiped my mouth.

We had dinner in three hours, and I knew I had to compose myself and not let my mind run wild. Celeste and Daniel would be joining us, as well as a few other members of the company. I wasn't excited in the least to see Daniel. I knew he would at least be a diversion from all of this. I wasn't any more excited to see Celeste either.

I was exhausted. I decided to rest for a good thirty minutes before getting ready. I laid my wet hair onto the plush pillow and felt my eyelids instantly fall heavy.

I awoke anxiously to the sound of my iPhone alarm. My hair was still wet and sticking to the side of my face. I rolled over and out of my towel and planted my feet onto the carpet. I decided on a cream colored cashmere dress and a pair of stilettos. I knew I was among the overdressed on the team, but I didn't care. I was in Paris and had no desire to dim myself for anyone. I smoothed my hair behind my ears and put in some tasteful gold earrings. I kept my makeup simple, as I often did, but decided to wear my Chanel Rouge.

Once I was ready, I checked the time. The car should be here any minute to pick up me, Roger, and Daniel, but I hadn't heard a word from either of them. I sent a text to our company group chat and gave them the update. Just as I did, I heard a knock at the door. "Jessica, *darling*? Are you in there?" a familiar, cheeky voice sang on the other side.

I rolled my eyes and opened the door to find Daniel standing there. His arm was resting above the doorway. He was wearing a crisp black blazer and a white shirt that was buttoned a little too low, exposing a gold chain. He was wearing jeans and a pair of designer sneakers. *So flashy. So Daniel.*

This was the first time I'd ever seen him so business casual.

His skin was glowing and his hair was roughly tousled. A bit longer.

"You just couldn't wait to see me could you?" I breathed, pretending to sound annoyed.

Truthfully, I was relieved to see him.

"Heavens! You look delicious." He said, forcing his way into my room, his eyes dancing over me. I smiled to myself.

"Thank you and come on in, I guess." I said.

"Do you want some Champagne? We can't leave until Roger gets here."

I poured us both a glass before he answered.

"You're quite hospitable these days, Jessica. Getting the party started early I see?"

His sarcasm was oddly comforting. He walked over to me and took a glass.

"Cheers." He said, and took a generous swig.

I smiled and did the same. I kept my eyes on him, noticing how tan he was. "Right, listen, I love you dearly but I only came over borrow some deodorant." He admitted.

I choked on my champagne, as he looked at me in all seriousness. "No, really. I hate to trouble you, but Roger isn't here and I cant risk a chance of ruining dinner. I've misplaced mine it seems." He said, biting his lip.

I laughed and sat my glass down.

"What kind of person forgets deodorant?" I said, as I fished through my purse.

"I don't know, the kind that was in Ibiza for weeks and did so much coke he was lucky to make it back at all?" He said, grinning proudly. I'd truly never met a more audacious man in my life. I hated to admit that he was growing on me. I don't know if it was because I saw through it, or if it was some form of exposure therapy.

"Here." I said, making a disgusted face.

"Keep it. Think of me every time you use it." I said, with a half smile. "Are you sure? Is the French culture getting to you now? You're going without showers and protesting deodorant." He said, laughing.

I joined in and told him I'd get another one at the pharmacy around the corner that I'd been dying to see.

Just as I did I heard a faint beeping sound and my door began to open. My heart stopped realizing it was Roger. He looked at both of us. Daniel was frozen with the deodorant stick under his shirt. I gathered instantly that he was embarrassed by the fact that Daniel was with me. I knew he was thinking that it was somehow giving away our act.

Or was Roger worried that Daniel was in here for other reason?

If Daniel was clever, he'd realize that Roger had a key to my room. I looked at him in surprise.

"Oh, hello,! Sorry, am I interrupting?" Roger asked, putting up a charade.

He couldn't be serious. Daniel cleared his throat.

"No, no. I was just borrowing some deodorant from *Jess*...Jessica." He stuttered.

I swear Roger was the only person who could make him nervous like that. Roger's eyes traveled from mine to the champagne glasses and back to me.

"Yes and we were having a glass of champagne as we waited for you, Roger. Just wasting time." I said, reassuringly and in a calm manner. I knew his mind was wandering. I could see it on his face. He always kept such a cool façade when he was upset. That in itself was the giveaway. But he was jealous, cementing it in this very moment.He was naturally chipper otherwise.

"Right, well the car is waiting for us." He said, still standing with the door ajar.

I smoothed out my dress and cleared my throat. Daniel put the deodorant in his pocket and made a bee line for the door.

"I just need to grab my purse. I'll meet you both down

there." I said. They looked at each other and Roger gave me a nod.

"Daniel, how was Ibiza?" He asked, breaking the awkward silence as they left.

The door shut heavily and I let out a deep sigh. I searched the room for my small clutch and transferred my necessities to it. My phone, lipstick, and a key card for every room, just incase.

I saw the black Mercedes waiting out front. I slowed my breathing as I walked the gorgeous marble floor of the lobby. I approached the car while Roger stood outside of it, holding the door for me. I slid across next to Daniel, who was texting god-knows-who, about god-knows-what. Roger climbed inside and shut the door, squishing himself next to me. I found it almost laughable to be sandwiched between the man I was deeply infatuated with, and the guy who almost cost my me my job for a kiss. A guy who I suddenly didn't despise as much as the night he forced himself onto me.

We rode to the restaurant in a silence. Daniel tapping away at his phone screen, Roger checking the time incessantly, and me lost in thought as I looked out the window.

We reached the restaurant and all exited the car single file. Roger was quick to my side, putting his hand gently on the small of my back as we entered. The touch of his hand shocked me. *Territorial.* I liked that. Even this small gesture was out of character for him. I looked at Daniel to see if he noticed, but he was still distracted by his phone.

We entered the restaurant and I gave the host the company name. I followed Roger to the large table, already filled with guests. Most were unfamiliar to me. One familiar face called out, "There, he is! I saved you a seat next to me, darling."

It was Celeste.

My stomach almost dropped at the sight of her. I'd never heard her take such a soft, feminine tone. Roger immediately removed his hand from me and cleared his throat, adjusting collar. He raised a hand, gesturing hello to everyone.

"Hi....hi. right, thank you," He muttered.

I turned my head to look at Daniel who looked uncomfortable. Roger left my side and joined Celeste. Daniel took a seat at the opposite end of the table and I followed him, sitting next to him at the only empty chair. I couldn't help but feel that Celeste was going out of her way to make me feel like an outsider. I felt like me and Daniel were at the children's table and they were the *"gown up"* one.

I sighed and helped myself to the bottle of wine in front of us. Daniel leaned in close to me.

"Easy there.. we haven't even had our *amuse bouche* yet."

Ignoring him, I took a large sip of the red wine. It was delicious. Full-bodied and oaky. I felt my stomach growl and took a piece of bread from the basket on the table.

"Does Celeste always act this arrogant, or is it just when I'm around?" I said, to Daniel, not caring who heard.

His eyes darted and he cleared his throat, before responding.

"I don't think I know what you mean." He said, looking around nervously.

I didn't believe him. He clearly knew what I meant. I finished my glass of wine, and kept an unbreakable stare at Roger. I shoved more bread into my mouth and offered Daniel a piece. Daniel poured me another glass of wine. Roger caught my glance and held it for a moment, as I took a large sip.

I broke eye contact and turned to Daniel, touching his arm flirtatiously.

"Have some wine," I said, seductively as I poured him a glass. He smiled and took a drink.

"*My, my, Jess,* are we going to have some fun tonight?" He asked, painting a mischievous smile on his face.

"God, I sure hope so," I groaned, taking another sip of

wine.

I felt Roger's eyes on me, but I refused to look down the table. The waiter came by to take our order and I looked to Daniel.

"*Il sait ce que J'aime*" I said, to the waiter, keeping a flirtatious gaze on Daniel.

Daniel looked at me and back to the waiter in confusion.

"She said, you know what she likes, monsieur." The waiter said, in a thick accent.

"Oh, alright. I'll have the steak and she will have the salmon." He replied pretending to know. I hated salmon.

All I'd eaten in the last five hours, was a croissant, a coffee, and a glass of champagne.

Daniel was eating up every moment of this, from what I could tell. He had angled himself to face me and wouldn't take his eyes off me. His eyes were glistening with excitement.

By the time our food arrived, I was four glasses in. I poured the last bit of the bottle into my glass and cackled loudly, at whatever story Daniel was telling me. Roger and Celeste shot me a stare and I waved at them in a chipper manner. I cut a piece of the steak that Daniel ordered and fed it to him. He let out a forced laugh and looked around the room, slightly embarrassed. I took my napkin and wiped a non-existent crumb from his mouth, letting my thumb linger on his lip.

He grabbed my hand and slowly placed it back into my lap. Daniel leaned in, his strong cologne hitting my senses and his hot breath on my ear.

"Jess, keep it together, *ok*? Everyone is staring" he hissed, nervously and then pulled back.

He painted a fake smile onto his face and I straightened in my chair. The room was spinning. I waived a hand in front of me as to say 'nonsense'.

"I have a question."

"Yes?" Daniel, asked.

"Did you use two bottles of cologne tonight or just one?" I asked him. I laughed loudly and snorted. I'd waited far too long to use that joke. I took a bite of food and suddenly felt light headed. I took a drink of water and wiped my mouth, before casually looking down the table. Roger was deadpan staring at me. He wouldn't take his eyes off me. He was seething. *I could feel it.* He did that tick of his, where he sucks his teeth loudly and parts his lips.

As loud as the restaurant was, I could hear it in my head as I watched his mouth. I felt my purse vibrate and opened it to find my phone lit up. I could hardly focus to read it but saw Hanna's name. I opened it and responded as best as I could.

I let out a laugh and leaned over to Daniel.

"Do you wanna get out of here?" I asked, nearly falling into his lap. He put his hands on my shoulders to stabilize me.

"I honestly think that would be best. I'll call the car."

He got out his phone and tapped the screen vigorously.

I grabbed his glass of wine and finished what was left before standing up. I wobbled, almost falling over.

"I'll meet you outside." I said, and excused myself from the table.

"Wait!" Daniel hissed.

I walked as gracefully as possible over to where Roger was sitting and put my arm around Celeste.

"Thank you for a lovely dinner, you guys. Daniel and I are going to head back now." I said.

Celeste's eyes grew wide as she looked at Roger for an explanation. "Jessica, we rode together." Roger argued.

"Yes, and...and it was a little bit crowded. *Un peu...*" I slurred, making a pinching gesture with my thumb and index finger.

I patted Roger on the back, and gave him a big kiss on the cheek while looking Celeste in the eyes. It left a bright red mark on Roger's cheek. My Chanel lipstick, branding him.

Daniel was now at my side. He grabbed me firmly around the waist.

"I apologize. Someone wasn't cut off soon enough. I'm taking her back to the hotel." He said reassuringly.

He pushed me away from them and pulled me into him.

As he dragged me out of the restaurant, I was smiling to myself. We stood on the pavement for a second before he yelled, "*Jess, what the fuck are you doing?*"

I turned to him, offended.

"What am *I* doing? What are *they* doing?" I slurred.

"WHO?" He declared looking into my eyes.

"*Themmmm,*" I groaned.

"Jess, you're absolutely sloshed. I can't believe it." He said.

"Yeah, but you love it don't you? I thought you'd like this. You wanna *fuck* me don't you?"

Daniel stood there motionless, staring at me.

"Don't...don't answer that." I said, waving a finger.

"Jess, if you puke on these shoes, I swear I'll never talk to you again."

"You can't act like this. There were investors and producers in there and Celeste looked enraged." Daniel breathed.

"FUCK CELESTE!" I screamed, before he cupped my mouth shut.

"Jessica, please. Im begging you. Let's get you back to the hotel now."

The driver pulled to the curb and Daniel tightened his grip on me. He opened the door and shoved in me inside. He slid in behind me and buckled my seatbelt. Just as he did I looked up at him, his face an inch away from mine.

"Daniel," I breathed.

"Yes?" He whispered, his face still close to mine.

"No one wants to love me. They all just wanna fuck me...even you."

I said, as tears welled up in my eyes. Daniel sighed loudly

and plopped into the seat next to me. I began sobbing so hard that I felt sick. He extended a hand to my knee and patted it gingerly. I'd always heard that the English were cold and uncomfortable with this kind of thing, but I felt comforted by him. The last time he had his hand on my knee he was, indeed, trying to *fuck* me. Now we had done a 180, and I felt closer to him than I did Roger.

I grabbed his hand, aching for comfort. Daniel laced his fingers in mine and squeezed gently. We approached the hotel and he helped me out of the car. We walked through the lobby, slowly, his arm around my waist. I was drunker than I realized as I stumbled with every step. Once we entered the tiny elevator I told him I was going to be sick.

"No, Jess, *not again.* These are brand new shoes!" He groaned.

"Ok. ok..." I said, cupping my mouth.

"No, I'm okay." I reassured him, not knowing if I'd actually be ok.

We reached my door and I turned to look at him.

"No, no. Let's go to your room." I said.

He laughed.

"You can't be serious....*are you serious?*" He asked, after a long pause.

I knew he assumed it was a sexually charged request. I nodded yes.

"I don't want Roger to knock on my door in the middle of the night. I want him to think I'm gone." I said, clearing up his confusion.

He looked at me, puzzled.

"Why would Roger come into your room?" He asked.

As soon as the question left his mouth, he realized what I was saying. He was putting it together in his mind. I saw his brain working in real time. Daniel nodded silently and took me back to his room.

Once we were inside, I ran to the bathroom and puked up

every ounce of that expensive French steak. I wiped my mouth and washed it out under the tap.

"Everything alright?" Daniel asked, from behind the door.

I washed my hands without responding and opened the door.

"Yeah, I'm fine now that it's out of me." I said, my head pounding.

He made a disgusted face as I plopped onto his bed. He took off his suit jacket and sat in a chair across from me.

"Water....I need water." I groaned, cupping my forehead.

"Sparkling or still?" He asked, sarcastically.

I gave him a disapproving look and ripped the miniature water bottle from his hand. I took a large sip and sat up on my elbows. Feeling the room spinning, I laid myself back down.

"Aren't you going to explain why you're in my hotel room?" He asked, calmly.

It took a moment to process his words. Once I did, I decided I would explain everything. He knew the steaks when it came to outing me. It would be a loss for the company and for him. They'd be on the hunt for their 10th assistant this year, and Daniel would actually have to pull his weight. With all the joking and flirting aside, I knew Daniel got the clear message that I wasn't into him either. So the jealousy factor was out of the window, at least I hoped. I let out a loud sigh.

"Me and Roger have a relationship that exceeds the needs of the company." I slurred.

I opened my eyes to see him staring at me with a worried look.

"How—when did this start?" He asked.

"Mmmm, maybe about two weeks ago? Give or take." I said, before coughing and almost vomiting again.

"Oh, Christ, Jess." He said, as he tried to lift me up right.

I felt the room spin and my head began to pound.

"I need you to sit up. Come on now."

Daniel pulled me up to the headboard. His hands were

warm and his grip was surprisingly strong. His face was inches away from mine when I looked up at him. Mistakenly, my lips landed on his briefly. "No, let's not do that, okay?" He whispered.

If I wasn't so drunk I would've been shocked at his disapproval. I guess the cold shoulder really had done a number on him.

"I-no,"

I was struggling to find words.

"I was trying to—anyway, yes. Me and Roger have...been involved." I breathed.

Daniel's eyes dawned around the room. He sat down on the side of the bed beside me, and rubbed his forehead.

"Jess, I wish you hadn't told me this."

I looked at him and shrugged.

"It all makes sense now. How you were acting at the restaurant, I mean, I'd never seen that side of you. I thought Celeste was going to have a heart attack!" He laughed.

"But why do you wish I hadn't told you?" I asked.

I took a deep breath and he shook his head. He looked at me gingerly for a long second.

"Because I don't think it's wise. For obvious reasons but also.."

"*No!* No, no, no! You're the one who tried to come onto me during my first week! You *do not* get to judge this scenario." I yelled.

"Keep your voice *down!* I have apologized profusely for that. And part of me does regret it, believe me, but this is a whole other beast, Jess," Daniel said, running his hands through his hair.

His tone became very serious.

"Look, let's get you into a bath and have some tea, yeah? We can talk about this tomorrow." He suggested.

How British of him. He was avoiding the whole subject.

He grabbed a pack of cigarettes from the desk and began to light one.

"No, I will not. Tell me right now why you think that." I said, as he began trying to pull me up from the bed.

"No! STOP! STOP IT!"

"JESSICA! Get ahold of yourself! You've got to keep it down."

"Then tell me," I begged.

I begged even though I already knew. The way Celeste and Roger looked at each other, the way she melted for him and only him. It was the only explanation.

"Roger and Celeste...they're complicated but they're very much involved as well." He said, putting emphasis on that last word.

Daniel was gripping the sides of my arms tightly, practically shaking me as the cigarette hung from the side of his mouth. Daniel loosened his grip. He could see the sadness in my eyes. Even though I knew the truth of it, hearing it aloud crushed me instantly. I felt my whole world, my whole dream for my future crumbling around me.

All the time and work I'd put into this job, one I never even knew I wanted, was ruined. The emptiness I felt earlier was enough to ruin me. Now I was fully hollow. It cut me deeper because, in a way, I was free from it all. I was free from the pathetic longing. I was free from whatever fantasy I was entertaining with Roger.

I began sobbing hard at the thought. Daniel pushed me into his chest and my tears soaked his crisp shirt. The smell of his awful cologne flooded my nostrils and I almost hurled again.

"I know..." I whispered.

I pulled back from him and wiped my nose on my arm.

"How on earth did you know?" He asked.

"Can I?" I asked, taking the cigarette out of his mouth.

He watched me take a long drag as tears rolled down my

face. I walked to the other side of the room and cranked the window open, blowing my smoke out of it.

"I had a feeling..a feeling that she disliked me for more reasons than the obvious and at the gala...I ran into her. Roger said he had no idea she was there, which was odd in itself, but I saw the bracelet." I said.

"The bracelet?" He asked.

"The one I picked up from Tiffany's the first week at the office, remember?" I asked.

He nodded silently.

"Well, she was wearing it that night. Something just told me it was the same one." Daniel looked at me in amazement.

"Christ, I'd almost forgotten about that." He said, looking around the room and rubbing his forehead.

"The funny thing is, I assumed you got it for someone. I thought you were using company money to win some girl over or something." I laughed to myself, my sinuses becoming swollen.

"Jess, I might be a little forward, but I'm not a monster!" He spat.

Daniel got up to grab a bottle of water for himself and sat back down. "So what are you going to do?" He asked, earnestly.

"I'm going to take a bath and go to bed." I said, putting the cigarette out in the ashtray.

He nodded, not pressing the question any further.

"I'll start you some water then." He said, softly.

As I heard the tub filling up, I sat there pondering what tomorrow was going to be like. I'd embarrassed the hell out of myself tonight and I didn't have the energy to put up a façade. Tomorrow was a "free day" for me since Daniel was back, so I decided I'd send an email in the morning pretending to be sick. I'd planned to see some museums and do some shopping. I knew Roger had a full schedule, but I didn't want to run the risk of being needed last minute.

"Alright, Jess, all yours." Daniel called from the bathroom.

I stepped through the door to see him crouched down at the side of the tub.

"And keep the door cracked. I need to make sure you don't fall asleep and go tumbling under."

"Got it. And do you have something I can change into perhaps?" I whispered.

He held up a finger and began unbuttoning his shirt, revealing a full set of abs. I tried to avert my drunken eyes, but it was no use. He released his arms from the shirt and handed it to me.

"*Really?* I can't get a clean one?" I scoffed.

"No, because I've only packed what I needed and *you're the one* crashing *my room*. So it's this or commando." He said, walking to the bed.

I rolled my eyes.

"Perv. And hey, no peeking while I'm in here, okay?" I said, as I began to get undressed.

I practically fell over twice before I got my clothes off. I relaxed into the clawfoot tub and stuck my feet up on either side of the vintage knobs.

I heard a knock at the door. I quietly curled my legs into my torso. I froze in shock as I heard the sound of Roger's voice.

"Hi, have you heard from Jess? Is she with you?" He said, with an angry underpinning.

"Er. No I haven't seen her since we got back. She must be asleep, she was completely sloshed. I could hardly get her through the lobby." He said, over-explaining himself and laughing.

"Right, I think everyone at dinner was well aware of *that*." Roger said smugly.

"Well, I think she just wanted to end the trip on a bang. Why did you need her again?"

Daniel's wit was paying off. I couldn't help but think he

was purposely defending me. Did Roger seriously not consider how he'd look asking for me at this hour?

"Oh, right, I just wanted to make sure she had gotten back safe...and I needed to give her keycard back to her."

He sounded nervous, but it was a great excuse nonetheless. Roger was an idiot. As if admitting he had my key card to Daniel made any sense. Daniel reiterated my whereabouts and they said their goodnights.

I let out the breath I'd been holding and quickly grabbed the towel next to me. I got up as carefully as possible and wrapped myself. I patted myself dry and twisted my hair up in the damp towel.

"Nice save." I mumbled.

Daniel was in a set of navy Pajamas now.

"Jess, maybe this isn't a good idea." He said, with his hands up. "Well, I'm certainly not risking getting caught now. Look, I'll sneak out just after you guys leave for the casting, okay," I said, plopping down on the bed.

I was more aware of the fact that I wasn't wearing any underwear now. I caught Daniel looking at my thighs and immediately stood up to pull the covers back.

"Besides, he wouldn't dare try and get into my room, tonight after talking to you. It will be fine." I breathed, feeling myself sobering up and hoping I was right.

"You're right." He said.

"And If I get caught, I'm saying you held me hostage."

"Fair."

Daniel turned off the lamp. The room was dark, apart from the street light shining in. I felt my eyes getting heavy, but couldn't keep my mind from reeling.

"Daniel?" I asked, in a hushed voice.

"Mmm?" He groaned.

"I really think you should use less cologne." I whispered.

He rolled over in response, his butt grazing mine. "And you should really go to bed." He huffed.

CHAPTER FIFTEEN

I AWOKE in Daniel's room to find he had already left for the day. I checked my phone to find a text from him.

> "I hope you slept well. Drink some water. Talk soon."

I sighed and rolled off the bed. My head was pounding from the night before. The light beating through the curtains sent a singeing pain through my forehead. I looked at myself in the bathroom mirror, last nights makeup still painted on my face. I grabbed the small hand soap that was sitting on the counter, and vigorously washed my face. I patted it dry and stared back at myself for a long moment.

What am I doing? What have I done?

I buttoned up the shirt Daniel lent me, gathered my things, and rushed out of his room. I stormed into my hotel room to find a change of clothes. I pulled on whatever was closely hanging in the small armoire and bolted, stupidly forgetting my jacket.

I ran for the elevator with nothing but my phone. I had no idea where I was going, much less how to navigate my way through this city, but all I wanted was to get as far away from this hotel as possible. I didn't want Roger chasing after me, or anyone else for that matter. Not that he would.

I needed to escape *now* and sort the rest out later. I needed to clear my head. I doubted that last nights antics were ground for termination, but I wasn't sure if I could work another day alongside Roger. My emotions were surfacing now that I was sober. I felt my heart sink to the bottom of my gut. My eyes began to well up with tears. I was humiliated by how I acted the night before. I was better than that. On the other hand, if I hadn't humiliated myself who knows how long Roger would be stringing me along. I felt like an idiot for accepting the role in London so soon. I felt even more like an idiot for sleeping with my boss.

I should've trusted my hunch about Celeste and I should've never let Roger put a finger on me. I gave into whatever spell he casted on me, like a fool. There was no way I could take the job in London *now*. I knew I would never be able to put my feelings aside. I knew I'd be disgusted whenever I saw Roger's face. *But what was my other option?* I'd only been at the agency less than a year, and I highly doubted I would be able to use anyone as a reference if I left.

This year had proven to be the worst year of my life. Less than 24 hours ago, I was so close to my dream life. I could feel it unraveling. It was too good to be true.

I stepped into the elevator of our hotel floor, letting the tears flood over my cheeks. I manically pressed the door closure button, in hopes that no one would be able to enter the elevator with me. My vision was becoming blurry and I couldn't even see the button anymore. I heard the door close just as my warm tears welled over my eyes. I breathed in heavily and held it as a self- soothing moan escaped my mouth. My chest was beginning to ache as I realized I was holding my breath.

I was having a panic attack. My face became soaked as I

allowed the tears to flow. I was crying hard now. I crossed my arms, almost as if to hug myself, and leaned against the wall of the elevator. I watched the numbers decrease from three to two and then to one. I took a deep breath and quickly wiped my face, not wanting anyone to see me in this state. *ding.*

I saw the doors open before me and I hesitated. I had no idea where I was going or what I thought I was going to find. I second guessed myself for a moment before briskly passing through the lobby. I ran through the double doors of the hotel. The cold air bit my face sending a shiver through me. I had left in such a panic that I didn't think to grab anything, not even my coat. My white blouse felt paper thin as the wind whipped by me once more. I realized I was standing still in the midst of sidewalk traffic and started moving my feet, aimlessly.

After a few blocks, I looked up to my right to see a large green metal sign with the word 'metro' painted in the middle. I followed the sign until I reached a concrete staircase that descended underground, just like the ones in New York. I was directionally challenged there and I was sure that France would be no different. I stood at the entrance of the stairs with beautiful metalwork and antique circle lights lining the pavement. I reluctantly took the stairs down, feeling scared now. I shivered. It couldn't have been any warmer than 48 degrees. People were looking at me as I hesitated on the stairs. I shook my head. I didn't care what any French bystander thought.

I grabbed my phone and gripped it tight to my chest, thanking god that I even had it in my possession. The clacking of my heels echoed against the cement floors and off the tiled ceilings as I walked. I looked around at the beautiful architecture that was reminiscent of the 1930's, assuming that's when these tunnels were built. I took in the beauty around me as my teeth chattered. The green metal sconces that arched over the walkway lit the station with their rounded bulbs. I felt like I was walking through an old Hollywood French film. It was gorgeous.

I found myself thinking about how James would probably know when and how all this came to be. He would be able to tell me exactly what material the tile was made from or if the paint was the original job. He knew every fact about Paris and the art this romantic city had birthed. Tears welled up in my eyes again. I wish I knew someone here. I wish I didn't feel so alone in this beautiful city. It was a waste. I'd give anything to see a familiar face right now. It was wildly apparent as to why this city was deemed the city of love. It was oozing out of every piece of architecture. Every fresh baguette being transported in a basket. Every shared cigarette. Every street singer. Every group picnic on the lawn. It was all romantic and it was meaningless without someone to share it with.

I felt foolish coming here with the hopes that Roger and I would have some earth shattering romance. The kind I had only ever seen in an Audrey Hepburn film. The kind that made me melt, before a wave of sadness would wash over me, because I knew that could only be in the songs and movies. It couldn't be real. Or maybe it just means its not meant to happen to *me*. I was so pathetic. Crying in the streets of Paris because of a man I hardly knew. Feelings I'd developed way too fast and naively. My feelings were wasted on him.

I tilted my head back to cry, wishing it would stop. I think I knew deep down that this wasn't just about Roger, after all, we had nothing in common. He was a figment of something I'd conjured in my head. I fell for the *idea of him*, or who *he could be*, what I could be to him. I didn't fall for what he actually was and maybe that's what hurt the most. I had created this all. I'd projected a wild fantasy onto him, ruining my chance at keeping my dream job. I'd done it to myself. It was all a mess. I slumped forward to put my head into hands. After a second, I was shoved hard and heard someone scream, "éloignez-vous!" as they walked away.

Feeling shocked I moved out of the way and looked at the time on my phone. It was 8:30 now and people were beginning their morning commute. I pulled myself together and googled, "How to buy a metro ticket without a wallet"

I'd gotten the team to Paris, but didn't think I'd need to take mass transit alone. My google search showed that I could buy a ticket at a window and use an app on my phone to pay. I breathed a sigh of relief knowing I wouldn't be forced to head back to the hotel. One thing I greatly appreciated about Europe, was their efficiency and use of technology, something the states were sorely behind on.

After about five more painful steps in my heels, I saw what looked like a a ticket station. I approached the window and attempted my best conversational skills.

"Bonjour, je besoin acheter un billet, s'il vous plaîs." I said.

The stoic man behind the window gave me a nod and spat the total at me. I motioned to my phone.

"As-tu Apple Pay?"

The man was silent and looked slightly confused.

"You can pay with your phone, yes." He said in English, insinuating that I completely butchered my last attempt to sound French.

"Ok, parfait." I said, and sniffled as I pulled up my phone.

I bought a day pass, not knowing where I would end up or how long I'd be gone. Today was our last full day in Paris, and the team was scheduled to fly out midday tomorrow. I hadn't bought my own return ticket in hopes that Roger would ask me to stay. I felt so embarrassed at that thought now. I felt a lump growing in my throat. I felt like all the dreams I'd built in my head were being ripped at the seams now. One-by-one, in a tortured slow pull, I became helpless. I was back to square one. I realized I'd been standing under the lit exit sign for quite some time now, and hadn't committed to boarding a single car. The next round of cars came whipping by blowing a crisp breeze over my face, and whipping my hair all around me. I could barely see. I felt like if I didn't hop on now, I'd never get on. *Just go.* A gentle voice told me.

My hair was tangled all around my face and wet with tears. It had gotten so long over these last few months and I hadn't even noticed. I gathered it and twisted it over my right shoulder. I boarded the car in front of me and walked a few paces to the left to find a seat, keeping my gaze on the floor. I felt as though anyone who saw me would think I was crazy or pathetic looking. I looked like I was doing the 'walk of shame'.

I managed to find a seat in an empty row. Keeping my head down, I looked at my hands that were nearly purple from the cold, unlike my face that was swollen from crying. I took a deep breath, trying to relax, and placed my hands over my eyes. My cold flesh against my hot face was sobering. I moved my fingertips down to my cheekbones and began pressing down on them as I kept my eyes closed. Feeling more relaxed, I sighed while resting my head back on my seat. I slumped my body to feel comfortable and began watching the walls of the metro quickly whip by. I didn't know where or what my stop was. I had no more thoughts left in my brain. I was numb in more than once sense of the word. I'd get off when it felt right or maybe I'd just ride the train for hours. I looked slowly to my right, glancing around the car. I felt the blood return to my body. It was much warmer in here than in the station. My eyes surveyed the row of seats in front of me. A man in a fedora was reading the paper next to a petite woman with a dog in her lap. My eyes glanced over the figure that sat next to them. They darted back quickly.

I couldn't believe it. My stomach dropped to my feet and my eyes welled up once more, at the site of a tall, familiar, blonde haired man staring back at me. His blue eyes pierced right through me. I cupped my mouth letting out something inaudible. He sat motionless at the site of me. I saw him mouth my name. "*Jess*".

To see my name uttered from his mouth, after all these years, gutted me. Before I knew it, my eyes were burry and filled with tears again. I fell forward pressing my elbows into my thighs and plopped my head in my hands, as I audibly began to sob, not caring who saw or heard anymore. Even if I did, it was completely involuntary.

Just as I heard the train come to a stop, I saw a pair of leather Oxfords appear in the spaces between my fingers. Feeling defeated and helpless, I slowly attempted to look up at him, a man I hardly recognized but whose eyes felt like home. I couldn't believe it. His face was as warm as I remember that day in the library years ago. I was just as surprised to see him in front of me as I was back then. He looked at me, his expression becoming worried as he extended a hand to me. I reached out, trembling, and grabbed his hand. Time froze around us. We were the only two people in this train. We were the only two people in the world. I stood there, looking into his eyes with disbelief while everyone around us pushed and shoved their way out of the car. He stared back at me, his eyes as blue as the ocean, calming me just the same.

"It's you," was all I could say before I pressed myself to his chest.

He stood there motionless for a second before embracing me. I didn't care how I looked, or if I seemed crazy. I just wanted to be held by a familiar face.

"James," I breathed into his body.

"James." I repeated.

There was a quiet pause.

"Lets—let's get you home," he whispered in my ear, before gently pulling back.

His expression went from disbelief to worry. He guided me out the double doors of the car, keeping a strong hand around my waist. Those three words were like a warm winter coat, one that I desperately needed. *"Let's get you home."*

The words were a remedy to something I hadn't known needed cured. I felt tears streaming down my face again as we walked through the crowded station. I wiped them away quickly and gripped his hand in mine. I stayed close to his side like a scared child. James seemed taken aback by the gesture and then quickly relaxed into it. We climbed the stairs and made our way to the busy street above. He moved us to the side, out of sidewalk traffic and released my hand. James removed his trench coat and placed it over my shoulders.

"Where on earth is your coat?" He asked.

I looked down at myself and back up at him. He leaned in closer and dragged his hand from my shoulder to my cheek, letting this thumb brush just below my eye. I could see he didn't care. I could see the worry behind his eyes, trying to piece together how on earth we were both standing here, after years of no communication.

I stood wondering the exact same. *Was he just visiting? Did he live here now?*

"Back at my hotel along with my wallet and everything else." I said, breaking the silence.

I laughed nervously. I felt my knees tremble slightly beneath me. We stood there for a moment longer, his eyes locked on me.

"Come, come have breakfast with me." He said.

His eyes were still glued to me as I looked away. It wasn't a question. I could read his tone as easily as before. I could hear worry in his sweet voice. I nodded in agreement.

"Ok," I whispered.

He turned on his heels to lead the way. I couldn't believe any of this was real. I was taken aback by his confidence, something he never really had much of years ago. *How did he stumble into my life at the exact moment I needed him?* Our tether seemed to transcend across time and countries. I followed him down the street in silence, still in shock. I had no idea where I was but figured that the beautiful river below had to be the Seine. People below sat with their coffee and cigarettes.

After a few blocks, we approached a small restaurant. James spoke to the host in broken French and we were quickly seated inside the dimly lit space. It was a quaint but upscale bistro with large windows and velvet chairs. We were seated at a table in the corner that was enclosed by a large padded booth. It was cozy and intimate. I let out a large sigh as we sat down and put my forehead into my hands. *How was I going to explain any of this?*

"Jessica, what—I— how did you get here?" He asked, breaking the silence and shaking his head in disbelief.

I looked up at him and wiped my wet nose onto my napkin.

"Well, you see," I replied, and looked at my hands.

"That's a long story." I said, forcing a laugh.

I met his eyes, finding him motionless. I had no idea what I should say or how much information to give up. I'd hardly had time to make sense of it all myself.

"I'm here for work."

"Oh, okay." He said, looking confused.

James took a drink of water and waited for me to say more. He placed his elbows on the table, interlacing his fingers under his chin. He furrowed his brow, waiting for me to continue.

"Well, I don't know if it's a job I still have, actually. I might have gotten fired this morning." I said.

A half truth. He sat there, still listening intently.

"Today is my last day here and I left my hotel, upset, after speaking to— er, my boss." I sniffled.

"It's just been a long week. I'm exhausted and overworked and I wasn't thinking. I just stormed off because I'd had enough and all I had was my phone."

All of that was the truth, I didn't need to say anymore.

"Right, okay...okay. You don't have to say anything else if you don't want to." He said, waiving his hands in front of himself.

I forgot how large they were until now. He still wore the same leather watch on his left wrist.

"Thank you." I said, softly.

"We can eat, if you'd like, and then I can help you get back, alright?" He said, reassuringly.

I didn't know how to tell him that I wasn't ready to get back. I planned to stay out for as long as I could. I decided to see how long breakfast went and go from there.

"How are you here? How is this real right now?" I asked, my voice broken.

His expression changed to something inexplicable.

"I mean, what's going on with you?" I asked, nervously.

"Jessica, I live here. I have for awhile now." He said, matter-fact like. James never used my full name. Or at least, he didn't in the past. It made me uncomfortable to hear it from his mouth. But I guess we were on more formal terms now.

Our waiter came over before I could respond. James ordered a bread basket and some sort of omelette. I told him I'd have the exact same, unable to focus on the menu in front of me. We stared at each other in silence for a long moment. I decided to speak.

"I'm sure you're living out your dream here...curating some lovely museum and madly in love, spending you days like a true Parisian."

My voice cracked and my eyes were beginning to well up.

"Not quite...but not far off either." He said, sipping his water.

"I've built a nice life here, sure." He said, shrugging.

"That's great." I said, sniffling and wiping my nose on the back of my hand.

"I got an internship here shortly after graduation," he hesitated on the last word and cleared his throat.

"At the Modern art Museum of all places. I was recognized by a few organizations after curating a small exhibition that summer. Now I curate for an independent gallery in the Marais, where I also live." He explained.

"That's great James." I said, smiling with tears in my eyes.

I was truly overjoyed for him. I always knew he'd be

successful. "Jessi—Jess, why does that make you sad?" He asked.

His formal façade melting, with the use of my nickname. I used my napkin to soak up the tears before they ran.

"No, no, I'm not sad. I'm just very happy for you. It's what you always wanted and that makes me happy…. to know you got that. You've always been *so* smart and determined. *You know?* You've always known what you want from life and it always happens for you. You deserve it. You deserve to be *happy*." I said, gesturing to him, tears falling down my cheeks, softly.

I ignored them. I couldn't stop them now. James extended an arm across the table and stroked my cheek gently, letting my tears run down his hand. He said nothing. He just kept his hand there and looked at me with concern. I rolled into it, letting out a quiet breath.

"Thank you." He finally said.

James released his hand.

"Jess, *who did this to you?* I've never seen you like this."

I didn't know how to answer. I wasn't ready to answer.

"I—"

I tried to come up with something. I just looked at him with my mouth open. James seemed so mature in his nature. He was different but still the same. He was still so caring but a James I needed to be reintroduced to.

"It's a long story." I said.

"Well, I've got time," He replied,.

"Well, I was still at Saks until a bout a six months ago. I was fired." I said, as the waiter sat our food down.

James immediately helped himself to a piece of bread and a piece of cheese.

"I'd applied to so many styling and PR jobs to no avail. So, I took a chance on this job that I have now…*or hope I still have*, I'm not sure. Anyway, I'm an assistant for a production company. Well, an assistant to the actor who owns the company. Anyway, he's just really hard to work for." I said. Not a lie.

He looked up at me, cutting into his omelette

"So you're working in film now? That's great. I never would have thought."

James took a large bite, trying to seem as excited for me as I was for him.

"Well, not really, I mean I assist a team of writers and producers." I said, waiving my utensils before cutting into my food.

"I mainly work as the assistant, to an assistant, to an actor." I said, raising my left brow. James looked confused.

"Anyone I'd know?" He asked, with a mouth full of food.

"Um, I'm not sure? Roger Barnes? I really just get his dry cleaning and things like that. His executive assistant was on vacation which is why I was asked on this trip and it's just been a nightmare." I said.

"Oh, I know him. My dad loves his films. How interesting. So he's an asshole in real life, I'm guessing?" He asked, he looked defensive now.

My stomach sunk at the thought of James's dad. One of the kindest and most genuine souls I'd ever met. I began wondering what he thought of me, what his family thought of me, after the breakup. I didn't want to know. I shook my head before responding.

"Um, well, sometimes. It's very long hours, for everyone involved. Tensions can get high but it's fun overall. It *was fun*, I should say. I'm really doing it in hopes of getting some kind of promotion to the PR department. I thought maybe if I could last a year, and really prove myself, that it would happen." I admitted.

He nodded, seeming to pick up on something I wasn't saying.

"I hope that happens for you, Jess,"

"And I hope this is the last time you shed a tear over this job. I hate to see you like this." He added.

The use of my nickname again, gutted me. I didn't realize how long I'd needed to hear it that way, from his mouth. I forced another bite of food, knowing I needed it, feeling my stomach in knots. I needed to pull it together. I didn't want him thinking my life was a mess, no matter how it appeared to him right now.

"Anyway, what's it like living here? I mean, you talked about it constantly and now you're here, actually living it."

I tried to sound excited for him.

"It's as magical as I'd imagined," He smiled, looking down at his food.

"Sure, I miss my family constantly but they come every few months. My mom has retired, which has been good for her." He said.

His tone seemed to change to something more somber.

"*Alice?!* I never thought I'd see the day. She loved her job. *She breathed it.* You're like her in that way, you know? Passionate." I smiled at him intently.

"Thank you." James said.

He held my gaze for a moment.

"Anyway, I've settled in well. I live fairly close to here, actually. This is my favorite spot and one of the few places open before 10am." He said, gesturing around the room.

I asked him what area we were in. The Marais. It was absolutely breath-taking. I caught myself holding my mouth open. I realized *exactly* where we were. The fourth arrondissement, where he'd always dreamt of living. I took a drink of water, as I pieced it together.

"Am I keeping you from work?" I asked, thinking how I must've completely derailed his day.

"No, no, it's fine. I'm not technically working on anything right now. I'm in between showcases." He said.

I nodded, unsure of that meant. I was surprised that he

didn't use my question as an opportunity to get as far away from me as he could.

"I was on my way to meet someone, when I saw you on the Métro. I thought I'd seen a ghost." He said, in a low voice.

He stared at me for a long moment as if he still wasn't sure I was real. "Me too," I whispered.

"I'm sorry to keep you," I added.

"Don't apologize. It's been too long." He said.

I felt an odd sensation in my stomach. *It's been too long.* Did he really mean that? I slowly lifted my hand and placed it on top of his, not knowing what else to do. I just needed to feel his familiar touch. I wanted to tell him how sorry I was after all of these years. How I missed him and that I'd made a terrible mistake after college. But I knew there was very little chance of that being reciprocated now. I didn't know what was coming over me. I was insane for thinking it. I also had no desire to disturb whatever perfect little life he had built here. I also knew I was running on pure emotion and adrenaline and that maybe these feelings were fleeting. James slid his hand out from mine and gave it a gentle pat, before finishing his food. I sunk my head in embarrassment. He probably thought I was crazy. I knew I looked crazy.

I decided to take a few more bites of the food I'd barely touched. I asked where the restroom was and excused myself.

I looked back before rounding the corner to see him staring at me. He quickly looked away and I smiled to myself. I splashed my face with warm water and dried it with a paper towel. I pinched my cheeks to give them some color. I smoothed out my hair before walking back to the table.

The food was clear and James was staring at his hands when I sat back down.

"I assumed you were done," He said, gesturing at the table.

I nodded in response.

"I ordered us a coffee though. Is that alright or do we need to get you back?" He asked, sweetly.

I could tell he wasn't ready to let me go just as much as I wasn't ready to leave. That made me happy.

"No, I'm in no rush to leave."

I was intentional with my words. I looked directly into his eyes when I said it. He cleared his throat and adjusted his watch, looking away.

We spent the next hour catching up and making small talk. He laughed as I assured him that Hanna was up to her usual antics. He told me stories of his first few weeks here and how he was pick-pocked at the Eiffel Tower. I let out a laugh that practically shot coffee from my nostrils.

"Woah, it's not that funny, ok? It's very common here." He joked, pressing his index finger down on the table.

We finished our coffees and I checked the time on my phone. We had been here for three hours and it still wasn't enough time. I could sit here forever talking about anything and everything, as long as he'd listen. We'd always been this way. I'm glad it hadn't changed. I was enamored by how easily we became those ambitious college kids in LA again. We'd both grown so much, in the literal sense too. He was broader and stronger than I remembered. We were suddenly real adults. The way we dressed was more refined, our speech more formal, and our mannerisms new. I wanted to relearn everything about him. I wanted James to learn about me too.

"Im sorry," I whispered.

Like water spilling over a running tub, the words spilled from my mouth.

"For what?"

He seemed confused when I didn't answer. His facial expression changed once he understood. The silence seemed to say what I couldn't.

"I appreciate that." He said, sitting still.

"I'm sorry for everything. You didn't deserve to be treated the way I treated you. I was scared,"

I began rambling. "

I know." He said, interrupting me.

"I mean, I didn't understand it then, but I do now. After all, we were young." He said.

We weren't that young. It was just my only solid excuse. I started crying again, god, I was tired of crying. How many tears were left in me?

"No, it still wasn't right. The way I did it." I insisted.

He shook his head.

"Jess, I get it. You were pushing me away. And honestly if you hadn't, I don't think I ever would gotten here so, thank you." He said, smiling.

I felt taken aback by his perspective.

How could he be so understanding?

"I was so angry and hurt back then. I thought we would spend our lives together. I really felt like we would. Sure, we were younger than most people are when they settle down, but I thought I knew. You felt differently and I could never force you to feel the way I did. I couldn't be that selfish. Besides, you've always known what you wanted and I knew it wasn't marriage. You're driven too, you know? You always put your career first. You're so independent. When you ended things, I just wanted to run away. So I took an internship here, thanks to my aunt, and the rest is history." He said, shrugging.

I couldn't believe what I was hearing. He was over it. He was over me.

If only I'd had a good reason for ending things. If only I'd seen that it all worked out for the better. I didn't. My life had gotten significantly worse since the breakup. I missed him often. I denied it to myself but it was true. I denied it to Hanna too, but I knew she saw though me. A small part of me knew what I had with James was incredibly special. It was a storybook kind of love. It was past life love, finding itself again in this one. It was love at first sight. It was an unbreakable bond.

Unfortunately, it took losing him to see that for myself. We sat there in silence as I hoped he'd say more. I wanted him to still be in love with me, to realize the time we'd lost and offer me back in. I wanted him to say how a day hadn't passed where I wasn't on his mind, but I knew that was wishful thinking. I was selfish and possibly a bit narcissistic for wanting that.

"And you've landed this fantastic job! You're in Paris of all places, you've been to London. You *LOVE* London. You always talked about moving there someday, remember?" James said, searching for my gaze. It was on the table. His tone was reassuring.

I knew if I looked at him, the waterworks would start again. I forced a smile and nodded. I could tell he knew something was wrong. He could always read me like a book. That hadn't changed.

"Right, absolutely." I reassured him.

Giving it my best shot. I wanted to blurt out how miserable I was, and that leaving him was one of the worst things I ever did. I couldn't. I knew it was selfish.

"Can I show you something?" He asked, softly.

My eyes widened.

"Of course," I said, looking up at him.

A large smile spread across his face. "

Okay, come with me." He said, extending a hand to me across the table.

I grabbed onto it tightly as he pulled me up onto my feet.

CHAPTER SIXTEEN

WE LEFT THE RESTAURANT, walking a few miles before reaching a small stone building, wedged between two large apartment buildings. The stone was a dark grey and the door was large and black. It was made of beautifully crafted iron. Two golden number fours hung next to the door.

James squeezed my hand.

"We're here,"

James reached into his pocket and took out a set of keys. He unlocked the door and told me to follow him. I hesitated, in a daze from the touch of his hand.

The door opened to a modern art gallery. The light fixtures were small and bright, illuminating all the paintings on the walls. It was a mix of contemporary and classical pieces, that somehow all seemed to flow together.

"This is my office." He whispered in my ear.

The heat of his breath made my knees weak. I felt goosebumps form on my neck. I stood silent.

"Do you want a tour?" He asked, with his hands in his pockets.

I closed my mouth and nodded 'yes'.

I was knew I sleep-deprived, but I swore he was flirting.

He extended a hand and I grasped it tightly once more. His grip stayed loose this time.

"Obviously this is our— my recent curation which will change in a few months. Back this way, are the offices. James opened a set of French doors to a fairly large room, with four desks placed uniformly throughout. It was beautiful and quintessentially French. We walked down the aisle, to what I assumed was his desk.

I felt my pupils dilate. I couldn't believe what I saw. It wasn't artwork or a view of the city. It was something much more special. A red scarf was messily laid across the back of the desk chair. Without a word, I stepped closer, grabbing it from the chair. I ran it through my fingers slowly, admiring the natural wear of the fabric. It still looked how it did years ago, just more lived in.

James was rambling on about his coworkers and the owners of the gallery. I hadn't heard a word of it. My back was turned to him as he spoke. I felt my eyes well up. I quickly wiped the tears on the back of my hand.

"You still have it," I said, without looking at James, my back still turned.

I continued fingering the material before holding it up to my face. It smelled just like him. The scent overwhelmed my senses with nostalgia. I let my tears silently began to drip onto the scarf.

"How could I get rid of it? It's a masterpiece."

I knew that he was still holding onto some part of me just as I was him. Maybe we never really let go of anyone. Maybe we're not meant to.

When he realized I was still silent, he stepped closer and put a hand on my shoulder. I couldn't bare to look at him, knowing how ridiculous I looked.

"I just can't believe you kept it." I said.

I wiped away my tears quickly and sat it back down, flipping it to hide the wet marks.

"It has has good memories tied to it. That's all that matters. You know I've always been sentimental. And honestly, it's quite warm." He laughed.

I finally turned to him and forced a smile. I knew he could see my faint tears behind my swollen eyes.

"That was such a good weekend." Was all I could say.

James squinted at me, unsure of what I was referencing until it finally hit him. He took a few steps back and leaned against the desk across from me, folding his arms. He was a sight for sore eyes.

"It was one of the best weekends of my life. I got laid in my parent's house." He smiled big, showing off that one dimple on his left cheek.

I rolled my eyes and laughed. I could tell he was intentionally keeping things light. He was avoiding any feelings tied to me. I couldn't blame him.

"Finally, I've gotten you to do something other than cry today," He said, throwing his arms in the air.

I shrugged.

James got up and walked my way, placing his hands on each side of my shoulders.

"Come ere." he said, in his New England accent.

I hugged him tightly and breathed into his neck.

"I miss you," I whispered.

I felt his body tense at the words. Instant regret ran through me.

What was I thinking? What is wrong with me?

"I miss you too."

James ran a hand down the back of my head. Whether he meant it, or not, it was exactly what I needed to hear. He pulled away from me gently, meeting my eyes.

"Should we get you back to your hotel now?" He asked.

"No." I said, almost too quickly.

"I mean, I'd rather not go back just yet. I've had such a long week and this is my free day, after all." I explained.

"Well, I'm not sure what else you'd like to do. I'm sure you've done so much since being here," He said, scratching his head.

If only he knew what I'd actually been doing here. I grimaced at the thought.

"Would you like to see my apartment? It's close by."

I raised my eyebrows in surprise.

"I— I would love to." I stuttered.

He grabbed the red scarf and swung it around his neck dramatically. "Allons-y!" He yelled, leading the way out of the gallery.

We walked for what seemed like a couple of miles. James occasionally pointed out his favorite cafes and shops. Remarking which ones I'd love. It was such a beautiful area. I was almost envious of how far away from LA he was and that this was his life now. He was completely transported into a world that felt so surreal.

Finally, we made our way to a beautiful, white stone building. He opened the door to a narrow foyer leading up to a gorgeous staircase that sat under a crystal chandelier. The chandelier reminded me of the ones in his parent's home.

"The chandelier reminds me of my parent's house. I took it as a sign to move into the building." He said, smiling behind his shoulder at me.

I was in shock that we were on the same wavelength, after all this time. Maybe it was just a coincidence. Then again, we were always the couple finishing each others sentences.

To the right of the staircase, on the wall, was a set of gold plated mail boxes. They could've easily been 200 years old.

"How many people live in this building?" I asked, climbing the next flight.

"Maybe ten people." He said, sounding unsure.

I couldn't help but wonder if he was a neighbor to some beautiful French girl. The kind of girl who was perfect without trying. The kind that was effortlessly low maintenance.

We continued climbing the stairs, my legs feeling weaker by the moment. "The stairs in Paris are no joke.." I huffed, as we reached his unit.

I noticed the number eight was hammered into the wall.

"You get used to it." He said.

I didn't believe that one bit.

He turned the key to the flat and opened the door to his flat. The floors were a dark wood with old scuffs throughout. It was beautiful. The kitchen was small. It sat to the right of the entry way across from the living room.

"Still not much of a tv watcher I see?" I asked, attempting to lighten the mood.

"Well, you know me. Besides, I don't have much time to watch tv these days. Even if I did, I'd probably just beat myself up for not soaking up every inch of Paris, right outside there." He pointed to a small window looking out to another building.

I took off my shoes as he spoke, and carefully placed them by his red velvet coach. He noticed, without saying a word.

"Very fair point. No need for escapism," I said, standing awkwardly in the middle of the room, still in his oversized trench coat.

The flat was an eccentric one. It was loft style with a spiral staircase in the left corner of the living room. The space couldn't have been larger than 800 square feet, which was quit large for an apartment in France. I knew he probably made good money now, but I had no doubt that his parents helped him financially, too. I could only imagine the rent for a space like this, I winced at the thought. I'm sure this apartment was "normal" to him. James had always been humble about his upbringing, but I'd be lying if I said he was aware of his privilege. At least in comparison to mine.

"Do you want to see upstairs?" He asked.

The question lingered in the air for a moment. The energy shifted at the unknown implication of the question.

"Sure."

He nodded.

"After you."

As if I knew where I was going. I climbed the iron stairs, carefully. Finally, when we reached the top, our feet met a plush carpet. The room was exactly what I'd imagine his room to be; quirky, cozy, and clean. There was a large round wooden table and a grand built in bookshelf. He had a large impressionism painting above his bed and smaller one on the opposite wall. I gasped at the sigh of it.

"Is that a Wilson Greer?"

He shot me a surprised look.

"Yeah, it is actually. Wow, Jess, I cant believe you remember that." He huffed.

I stepped closer to it.

"Of course I do. He's your favorite. I just never expected you to own one of your own."

I took my eyes off the painting to see James beaming at me. I brushed my hair behind my ear and continued to look around his room.

The ceiling was lined with large wooden beams. I'd always wanted a flat with exposed beams like that. It reminded me of the homes I'd stayed at in London.

To the left of the bookcase was a vintage record player, to no surprise of mine. On the other side of the room was a large and thick armoire that looked to be 100's of years old. In front of it, sat a small coffee table and two cream colored vintage chairs. They were beautiful and plush. There was no doubt they were chosen by Alice. His bed was full-sized and tucked into the corner of the room next to a small balcony. The double doors to the balcony were far too small to walk through in an upright position, at least for James.

"Wow...this place is beautiful." I said, running a finger over his book collection, most of which I know he'd read four times over.

He said thank you and leaned against the table, watching me intently. James was more pensive and observant than I remembered. "I can't believe you have a balcony...and a haunted armoire." I joked, tapping it with my index finger.

That made him laugh. His laugh was medicine.

"Your mom picked the chairs didn't she?" I asked, in a whisper. His eyes grew wide "uh...yeah, she had them flown in. How did you,"

"Just a guess," I shrugged, interrupting him.

It was more than a guess. I knew Alice and her attention to detail and I knew James loved his mother very much. He knew asking her to decorate his first real apartment, would make her the happiest mom alive. That was the thing about James, he always found ways to make the people around him feel important. I felt my shoulders tensing up and decided to change the subject.

"So where is that extensive record collection of yours?" I asked.

He took a step past me to the book shelf. Having him inches away from me, had me holding my breath.

He opened up one of the lower cabinets to display three rows of vinyl.

"I have just the one for you, a classic." He said.

He bent down and thumbed through them until he found what he was looking for. I turned around to watch him remove the record from the sleeve. I noticed the room had grown darker and turned to the balcony to see the sun was setting. Just as I did, I heard that small scratch of the needle and the music began.

I felt a lump in my throat as Frank Sinatra lowly began humming from the speakers. I couldn't cry again, I don't think I had it in me, even if I wanted to. Instead, I forced a smile and took off his trench coat. I laid it over the back of the chair behind me and sighed.

"This album will never get old. I can't believe you brought it all the way here." I said.

He laughed.

"No, that one is still at my parent's. I found this copy at a vintage shop when I first moved here. It's oddly comforting." He said.

I wanted to ask how and then quickly realized what he meant.

"It reminds me of happy times whenever I'm feeling homesick." He added. There was a long pause. I didn't know what to say.

"It reminds me of you," He said quietly, looking at the floor.

I knew that's what he meant. My cheeks were suddenly warm and I felt my stomach drop. A million things ran through my head in that moment, but I couldn't find a single one to spit out. I wanted to profess everything now, not caring about the repercussions, but I didn't have it in me.

"C--can I see the balcony?" I asked, after the silence grew uncomfortable.

He rubbed the back of his neck and looked at the floor.

"Sure."

James stood up straight walked through the small doors. He almost folded completely in half trying to fit his 6'4 frame through them. I followed behind him and took a deep breath.

We stood in silence as we both leaned over the railing, watching the traffic below.

"Where are we again?" I asked, to break the silence.

"The Marais, which is located in,"

"In the fourth." We said in unison.

James looked at me in suspicion, his blue eyes glistening in what was left of the sunset.

"Right." He said, smiling in surprise.

"Do you remember that day we first met? In the UCLA library?" I asked.

"Yes, of course, why?"

"Well, we'd talked about a lot that day. You told me about your potential thesis. We talked about our majors, and how I loved expressionism and you loved the renaissance." I said.

I remembered how we used to playfully tease each other about which artistic movement was more influential. I looked down at my hands as I spoke.

"Yeah, you were obsessed with Frida Kahlo back then." He scoffed.

"Still am," I laughed.

"Anyway, you told me how it was your dream to move to Paris and to curate your own museum one day. You said you were going to have your own apartment in the fourth, remember?" I asked, trying to jog his memory.

His eyes were dancing as if he were replaying it in his mind.

"And you laughed because you assumed I knew what that was. As if I'd been to Paris, or would have any idea that it was divided into these 11 sections called arrondissements." I said.

James cocked his head back and let out a huge laugh. One that I hadn't realized I'd been desperate to hear.

"Oh, my god that's right!" He said, pointing at me.

"Wow, I can't believe I forgot about that. What an arrogant jerk I was right?" He asked, as he ran a hand through his hair.

It had become slightly oily from the day and a long strand fell into his brow. I realized in that moment, how much more refined he'd become. He'd changed so much, yet not at all. He no longer looked like a history professor, but rather a Ralph Lauren model. His shoulders were more defined and strong. His back seemed muscular too. James noticed that I was looking him over and broke the silence.

"Do you want to dance? For old times sake?"

He asked, extending a hand.

I nodded in agreement and placed my right arm around his neck. The touch of his hand in mine sent a shock through me.

"You…you weren't a jerk" I stuttered.

"You were perfect— are perfect." I said.

The low hum of Frank Sinatra was still playing in the background as I pressed closer into him. He embraced me and let his cheek touch mine, causing my breath to catch. His distant demeanor was thawing now.

"And now you have your dream…" I whispered in his ear, trying not to cry.

He swayed me, remaining silent. I couldn't help but think of how ridiculous I was for not wanting this, years ago. Or even allowing myself to enjoy the idea of this, of us. I thought I knew everything about myself. Yet, these last two years, even the last year, have taught me how little I knew. Everything I thought I wanted was merely an illusion I'd built up. I was infatuated with the idea of so many things, not the reality of them. I was married to the idea that living my life freely, outside the bonds of a relationship, was the only way to be successful.

I realized in this moment, I didn't want to be independent and alone in London. I could be happy living anywhere with someone I loved, building a life with them. In this moment, I realized that love could be the catalyst, not the crux to my happiness. I knew if I could just open my heart to love, every-thing else would fall into place. The only issue was that *it was too late.*

Everything was coming full circle. I felt a warm tear roll down my cheek, I prayed James couldn't tell. I felt his grip on me become tighter.

"Well, I don't quite have my dream," He whispered in my ear.

I felt my body stiffen.

What did he mean by that?

He was letting his guard down. Whatever guise he'd been putting up since this morning was gone.

"I don't have you." He finished.

His words pierced me. Those four words alone were all I needed. They were the remedy to everything terrible I'd been through. Those were the words I never thought I'd hear, from a man who's heart I'd completely shattered. I didn't deserve it. *I didn't deserve an ounce of his love after what I'd done.*

James pulled back from me slightly to look at my face. He gently wiped away the tears that were now streaming down.

"You don't mean that," I whimpered, shaking my head.

"Sadly, I do, Jess."

The use of my name only made me cry more. I'd been surrounded by people who were practically strangers for months now. But here, in his arms, I felt at home.

"I can pretend that I've met someone else, or that I'm happier without you. God knows, I've tried,"

We were standing two feet apart now. He aggressively ran both of his hands through his hair.

"But it always comes back to you, doesn't it? *It was always supposed to be you.* And you know it. That's the wort part. But for some reason, you can't admit it to yourself." He sighed, his tone accusatory.

I took a long pause before responding. This is the anger I was expecting from him earlier. He'd been holding it in. I wanted to believe him so badly, but I was overtaken by the thought of hurting him again.

"James, I'm selfish and hot-tempered, and I react too quickly. I'm unpredictable and I completely ruined what we had," I yelled, as the tears spilled over.

He started shaking his head.

"No. You're passionate. You're ambitious and bold..most of the time." He argued.

He always saw things in a positive light. I loved the way he nurtured the shadow parts of me.

"You were scared..." He reasoned, filling the silence, lowering his voice.

"I knew it then too. I didn't understand like I do now, but I knew, Jess. And that's the only thing that kept me from hating you." He said.

I winced.

"James, I wanted nothing more than to call you after I ended things and tell you how I didn't mean a word of it. I wanted to tell you how I really felt, I did, but I just couldn't. So I pushed you away." I said, covering my mouth and gripping my stomach.

The tightening in my abdomen wasn't going away.

"The way you looked at me that night, I never wanted to see that look again. It still haunts me." I said.

He nodded in silence.

"You know, I stayed in my car all night? I couldn't face my parents after that." He admitted.

I was shocked to hear it.

"I told myself I was going to drive to you and convince you to stay. I wanted to change your mind, but I couldn't do that either. I was frozen. I didn't want to keep you from your career. I didn't want to keep you from your happiness. I didn't tell my parents for a month. Once I finally went home, they knew something was wrong." He said.

I turned around, unable to look at him.

"I should've fought harder, Jess. I don't say any of this to hurt you, truly." He confessed.

"Don't you dare, for a second, blame yourself." I said.

"Look, I don't know what tomorrow looks like or what you want, but maybe after today, you'll understand what I want." He said.

I turned around to look at him again. I took him in, hanging on his every word. He grabbed my hands.

"I want *you*, Jess. I never stopped wanting you, no matter how much I tried. *Do you think it's a coincidence that we're both standing here right now?* Do you think it's a *coincidence* that we got on the exact same train in a city you're completely unfamiliar with? A city where I live, whether you knew it or not. In a city of two million people, we still managed to stumble into the same train. The second I saw you, I couldn't believe it. I even told myself for a second that it wasn't you. I couldn't be so lucky, I thought. The shock subsided when I realized that if this wasn't meant to happen, I would've forgotten you by now. I wouldn't have felt my heart stop the moment I saw you in the Métro." He confessed.

I believed every word he said. He went silent for a moment. I was motionless and in shock, hanging onto his every word.

"I hear you in an old record, Jess. I smell you at the Galleries Lafayette. God, I taste you at the pastry shop. You're everywhere. I couldn't forget you if I tried. I wished this feeling away for *so long*. I thew myself into my work to distract myself. There were days, I hate to admit, that I wish I'd never met you. Only because of how much *I couldn't forget you,* or the pain of losing you. But I'm not going to let you slip away this time." He sighed, running another hand through his hair.

His tone was much softer now, back to its normal decibel. I couldn't believe what I was hearing. Some of it was too much to bear. I wanted to grab onto him and never let go. Everything he was saying was exactly how I'd felt too over these last two years.

"And even if you don't feel the same...I'll be happy knowing at least I got to be here with you today."

His words absolutely sliced me in two.

How could I not feel the same? Surely he knew I did, or I wouldn't be standing here.

There was nothing I wanted to hear more from him, despite how unworthy I felt. I found myself unable to speak.

Instead, I slowly walked over to him and gently placed my lips to his.

He squeezed me tightly to his body, digging his fingers into my back. Soon, the gentle pressure of my kiss turned hard and our mouths opened in unison. We were hungry for one another. Starved. He tasted better than I remembered. His warm and wet tongue brushed the back of my teeth and I felt my body vibrate. We were both insatiable for each other. There was something incomparable to what I felt in that moment. That alone, washed away every single doubt about a future with him.

I was home. I was melting into him, our souls merging into one another. The missing piece was making becoming whole. I couldn't believe that what I'd been fighting for so long. It was more than what I needed, it was what I *wanted.* Our kissing slowed and he pulled away. I didn't want it to stop.

"Can I stay with you tonight?" I asked in a whisper, looking up at him.

He nodded 'yes' without thinking twice, and caught his breath. He leaned his forehead against mine.

"I was hoping you would." He said.

I smiled at his response. I knew that tomorrow I would have to face Roger and the whole of my future, but tonight I wanted to make up for lost time. I wanted to relish every second together.

Suddenly, I felt my phone buzzing in the pocket of my skirt. I took it out, noting the low battery and twenty plus notifications.

"I bet there's a lot of people wondering where you are." James said. Unfortunately, he was right. A text from Daniel read, '*Jess, where the hell are you?!* Please just let me know you're alive.' Amongst the other five he'd sent today. I responded quickly letting him know I was safe and would see him tomorrow.

"Yeah, this line of work is demanding to say the least." I sighed, not wanting to explain anything else.

I wiped my nose on the back of my wrist and asked if I could take a shower. I felt disgusting and cold.

"Of course."

James said that he had a change of clothes for me to wear. I was shocked when I found him pulling women's clothes from the bottom of his armoire. He noticed the look on my face and put up a hand in protest.

"They're my mom's. She did a lot of shopping when she came to see me in the spring, and had to leave some things behind. I think you two are about the same size." He said, handing me a cashmere sweater and a pair of jeans.

I felt relieved to know they were his mom's, selfishly, as if I hadn't spent the last few months having an affair with my boss. My stomach sank at the thought.

"Great, thanks." I laughed.

He nodded respectfully and told me to use whatever I need and that he would be here when I was done. James gave me a gentle kiss on the head.

I shut myself into the small bathroom, putting the clothes on the counter. After a few minutes of fumbling with the mechanics of the shower, the hot water started to sting my skin. I didn't care. I grabbed what looked like shower gel and scrubbed every inch of myself until I was practically raw. I scrubbed my scalp vigorously until the suds were streaming down my face. I wanted to wash away every part of this trip, leading up to this moment. I felt dirty. I felt used. I felt exhausted. I finished up quickly and rang the water from my hair. I wrapped myself in the nearest towel and ransacked James' drawers for something resembling a hairbrush. I found a wide-tooth comb and made due. I slipped into the soft, beige-colored cashmere, deciding to go braless. Realizing I didn't want to wear the same underwear from earlier today, I went commando too.

I scrunched my hair once more ran the towel through it before opening the door. James was putting the record back in it's sleeve and turned at the sound of me.

"Are you hungry?" He asked.

"I could eat." I said, feeling inexplicably bashful, as if we didn't just have our tongues down each others throats on his balcony.

"Great. There's a place just down the street I know you'd love." He said, with a smile.

CHAPTER SEVENTEEN

A<small>RE</small> you sure I'm dressed properly?" I asked, motioning to myself.

James laughed in response.

"Yes. I promise."

He stepped closer to me, looking me in the eyes. I laughed nervously as he grabbed my hand and laced his fingers through mine. My hand was trembling.

I don't know why I was so nervous. I guess I was running on an empty stomach and adrenaline. James was the only person I'd ever let in. I'd never let him in fully, but he was the only person who'd made it this far, friends included.

We'd both grown into what seemed like mature adults, or at least he had. I slipped on my heels on and put his large trench back on. I looked at him intently, feeling like today he had shattered my walls. I wanted to keep it that way. I wanted to stay open for him. He reached into his armoire and grabbed a brown bomber jacket before leading the way out of his apartment.

We walked down the street, hand-in-hand, watching the city traffic in silence. It was a comfortable silence. The kind where there isn't a gut pressure to make aimless conversation.

I caught him smiling to himself every few steps. It gave me butterflies, knowing he wasn't having second thoughts about this. About me being here. After a block or so, he pulled me into the doorway of a dimly lit bistro. He held the mahogany door open for me, as I timidly stepped inside. I was suddenly very aware of my hair still being damp, as the male at the host stand gave me a disapproving look. The stereotype of the French being assholes had proved to be true.

As soon as he saw James, his expression changed. "Ah, Monsieur, James! Salut! Comme ça va?" He asked, gesturing him closer.

James responded warmly as he pulled me into his side, making a statement. The man looked to me and then James in confusion before seating us at a cozy table in the back. The small restaurant was tiled with miniature black and white shapes. The tables and chairs were reminiscent of those in old French films I'd seen. Each table had a small candle and votive lit on it. The space was simple yet romantic. We took our seats and I smiled at James.

"You come here often, I assume." I said.

He answered with a laugh.

"The host was not amused by me....but you on the other hand.." I said, trailing off as I looked over the menu.

I took a deep breath and relaxed into my chair. I finally felt calm for the first time today. It was the first time I'd felt comfortable this whole trip.

"It's my favorite spot. Don't pay attention to André. He's not used to me bringing beautiful women around." He said.

I was relieved to hear that.

He winked at me and looked over the menu. We ordered our food, a fillet for me, and the risotto for him. James picked a bottle of red wine to pair. We began snacking on the table bread. It was the first time I'd had an appetite all day.

"This place is beautiful." I remarked, with a full mouth.

He took a large swig of wine.

"Told you, you'd love it."

I felt like James had done most of the talking today and I felt insecure about it.

"I'm so happy to be here." I said.

He raised his eyebrows as if he was listening more intently. He placed his elbows on the table and leaned in closer, resting his chin on his right hand.

"I promise I'm done crying too." I said.

I laughed nervously, fiddling with my fingers.

"I just can't believe after all this time...we're here. I'm here...with you, I mean. Obviously the circumstances aren't the greatest, but I don't think I've ever felt happier than I do right now. I also never thought my first time in Paris would be so..eventful." I said, taking a drink of wine.

He sat still, listening intently to me, waiting for me to offer up more.

"I never really understood your infatuation with this city, or anyone else's for that matter. No offense, it was charming that you talked about it all the time. I think a part of me always found it cliché though. I always pined after London but there really is a unique magical energy to this city." I rambled on.

He smiled, taking another drink.

"There's nothing like it, Jess." He whispered.

The sound of my name on his lips sent a warm sensation through me. I wanted him to say it 100 more times. But I didn't even think that number would satisfy me.

"To be honest, I'd been so lonely here that the magic had faded a little. The city had lost it's sparkle for me and I'd been so busy with work. You kind of forget how much something means to you once you finally have it." He said, swirling the wine in his glass around.

It was a loaded statement.

"Now, that I can relate to." I said.

"And quite honestly, when you have no one to share it all with, that causes the magic to fade too." He admitted.

He looked at me directly while saying it.

"When we were at breakfast this morning, I wanted you to think everything was perfect. I wanted you to think I'd been so much happier since you last saw me. But when I saw how sad you were, I couldn't bare it for a second longer. I didn't care how much you'd hurt me, I couldn't make you feel any worse." He said.

He was too good. He'd always been too good for me, it only took me this long to realize it. I grabbed his hand and squeezed it. He froze in surprise at my touch.

"I don't want you to be lonely." I whispered.

What I really wanted to say was 'I want to be with you', surely he knew that. He looked at me for a long moment.

"Then stay."

My stomach dropped. I knew this conversation was coming. I could tell by his tone that he was trying to be firm. He was afraid of losing me again. I just didn't think this conversation would happen so soon. Just then, the waiter brought our food and sat it down.

"I would love that. I dread going back to LA, but I don't know how that would work." I admitted.

"When does your flight leave?" He asked.

He was being so direct. It caught me off guard. This morning I was so sure of my choice to leave the agency. Now, I wasn't so sure. *How could I give up something I worked so hard for? How could I give up my dream?* I took a second to answer. I'd almost forgotten that I didn't have a return ticket.

"I actually never bought my return ticket." I admitted reluctantly.

His eyes lit up.

"I was asked to extend the London trip last minute and wasn't quite sure how long I'd end up staying." I said.

I felt embarrassed about the reason why.

"That's great. Stay a few more days then."

I truly wanted nothing more than to stay here for weeks if I could, but my life was up in the air. I'd stay years if it were possible. I wanted nothing more than to stay here with him and escape my reality but I hadn't had a second to gather myself. I'd been so reckless and unlike myself. I knew part of him was worried he'd never see me again and this would be fleeting memory. Or worse, that I'd leave and change my mind, but I'd never been more sure of him until today. Even if that meant we would have to workout something long distance. Maybe I could keep the job in London and take the train to James on the weekend, that was, if Roger hadn't thought about firing me after last night. I needed some time alone to think.

"James, I would love that, truly, but I've got to get home and figure things out." I said.

He nodded and began eating. We finished our food in silence, occasionally looking at each other. We finished the whole bottle of wine and he paid our bill. I stood up, struggling to catch my balance for a moment.

"Still a light weight, huh," He laughed.

"Apparently so."

He wrapped his arm around my waist tightly as we walked out onto the street again. I felt so safe and at ease with him. He always made me feel this way, like I had nothing to worry about when we were together. I felt small, in the best sense of the word. I leaned my head on his shoulder for the rest of our walk. We climbed a few steps before I stumbled slightly and began laughing.

"I'm sorry...gimme a second." I said.

I giggled, hanging onto the banister.

"Nope, up you go." He said, before throwing me over his shoulder.

I let out a loud screech before yelling his name.

"Shhhh!" He said slapping my butt.

"Damn. You've been working out, Locke." I said, squeezing his bicep.

Finally, I was planted on my feet and he was unlocking the door. He kept his left arm attentively on my back while we fumbled inside his place. I took off my shoes instantly and threw them into the living room.

"Oh, no!" I gasped, theatrically placing my hands in front of my mouth.

"What?" He asked, in a panic.

"There's more stairs and if you throw me over your shoulders again I might puke."

He laughed and rolled his eyes.

"Fine. I won't throw you over my shoulder." He confessed.

He scooped me up into his arms in silence.

"I'll carry you the old fashioned way." He said, his face inches way from mine.

He looked so handsome and strong, carrying me like a damsel in distress. I felt like one. I wanted to melt into him again, like I did before. He stood smiling, his eyes glistening as I stayed silent, unable to look away from him. Soon we were ascending the spiral staircase slowly. His strength took me by surprise. I was average wight and height, but it was a lot to carry any normal person up several flights of stairs.

We reached the top story. I expected him to sit me down but he didn't. He used every ounce of strength he had to carry me over to his bed and put me down gently. He walked away for a moment. The lights went off and the moonlight shined through the window, taking their place. He returned quickly, sitting at the foot of the bed. He slowly unlaced his shoes and took them off one-by-one and placed them on the floor.

"James?" I whispered.

He turned to look at me over his broad shoulders

"Yes?"

"Come back to LA with me." I said.

I knew it was a long shot but it was the best solution for both of us.

"Come back while I sort things out. It shouldn't take long, I don't think. I mean, I've never worked a job like this, but I want to sort it out properly," I said.

He cut me off before I could finish.

Suddenly, he was crawling on top of me and his lips crashed aggressively into mine. I relaxed into it. I was in shock, but I couldn't pull away. I slid my hand under his shirt and let my fingers brush the hardness of his abdomen. He pulled away slowly, still on top of me and looked at me in silence.

"Ok."

"Really?" I breathed, before arching myself up to kiss him more.

"Yes, whatever you want," he said in between my lips.

I began tugging at his shirt. I finally got it off of .

"I'll have to work it out with the gallery, but I'm sure it will be ok." He breathed into my neck.

We began to move faster. I was dizzy from the wine and my hands had instinctively began undoing his belt. His warm finger tips were brushing my ribs as he lifted my sweater over my head. I was bare and topless on his bed for the first time in what felt like forever. He was hard as stone.

"I don't think I could be apart from you again, after today." I admitted.

Surprised at the words leaving my mouth. I couldn't control them. I breathed into his neck as he pulled me in closer. He lifted me on top of him and cupped my left breast. I let out a soft moan and undid my jeans. He slid his large hand inside the front and stopped when he realized I wasn't wearing underwear. He looked up at me in surprise. "Lucky me," he breathed.

He cupped my labia before forcing his fingers inside me. I sighed and sat deeper onto his hand, biting my lip in pleasure.

He pushed me onto my back, his fingers still inside me. I wanted to be completely naked and taken over by him. My cheeks were flushing and my body was pulsating. He stood up, tugging the jeans off of me and throwing them across the room. I looked up at him with my legs open. I wanted him more now than I wanted anything in my life. I wanted him to make me feel the way he did years ago. I wanted to forget that I'd ever been with anyone else.

He slowly went to his knees, my eyes glued to him. His hands began grazing my thighs. His head went between my legs. I couldn't help but let out a cry. He'd never felt so good. *Nothing* had ever felt this good. I finished quickly with his head still between my thighs. My whole body trembled around him as I moaned. I said his name as he climbed over me.

"Jess..." he whispered, brushing my hair out of my face.

I locked eyes with him just as he slid himself inside of me.

"I must be dreaming." He said.

It was enough to end me right here. I dug my nails into his back as we moved together in unison. It was as if he was making up for lost time, and he wasn't going to stop until he was completely satisfied. Lucky me. I'd never seen him look so masculine. Before I could catch my breath, we were both climaxing. The second time, even better than the first. He grabbed my hips and rolled over, placing me on top of him.

"I want to see you." He said, in a guttural voice.

I bit my lip and placed my hands on his chest.

"I love you." I whispered.

I felt embarrassed by the single tear rolling down my chin. I turned my head to the left so he couldn't see. I wiped my face quickly before his warm hands found my jaw and moved my head to meet his gaze. "I love you too. I always have." He said, with a furrowed brow.

The room was spinning and my heart was pounding. I buried my head into his neck. Our naked bodies found each other once more and he wrapped his arms around me. I took in a deep breath, unable to get enough of his scent. He was sweet and musky. It was a scent that was laced with more nostalgia than I could handle.

I opened my eyes to look up at him. I didn't want to waste a moment more with him. I never wanted to take him for granted again, not for a second.

Something washed over me. I was suddenly having flash-backs. I thought about when he used to meet me after class every Friday. He would drive us to my favorite spot in the city, to watch the sunset. I could see it so clearly in my mind, a memory I'd repressed for so long.

I thought about the first time his parents came to town, and how proud he was to show me off to them. We laughed all through dinner. I remember how easy it felt to be around them. Like I'd known them my whole life. I thought of a million other moments we shared years ago, as he drifted off to sleep.

He was snoring quietly now.

Finally, I thought about the exact moment we made eye contact today, after years of trying to forget one another. My stomach filled with knots. Our souls instantaneously reunited. It's odd to think of how easily I'd tried to make him a stranger in my mind before now. I was sick at how much I'd tried to forget him. I couldn't believe my eyes hours ago, and now we were here. I was in his apartment, reintroducing myself to his body. I thought by the end of today he'd either tell me that he'd fallen madly for someone else, crushing me into a million pieces, or that he'd never want to see me again. I felt it's what I deserved, honestly, until *now*.

I knew I deserved a love like his. I knew I'd have to forgive myself if we were going to move forward. A small part of me knew I would find him again someday, I was just never certain what that would look like.

So I laid there, happier than I'd ever been, and watched him sleep until my eyes grew heavy.

CHAPTER EIGHTEEN

I AWOKE SUDDENLY to the sound of the reoccurring alarm on my phone. I was beyond surprised that it still had any battery left to it. I rolled over to turn it off, realizing that James must have plugged it in for me. I realized that he wasn't with me in the bed, and I was still naked, covered by a soft throw blanket.

I smelled something heavenly and decided to get dressed. I heard James rustling downstairs as I pulled on the same clothes he leant me yesterday. I ripped my phone from the charger and softly walked down the spiraled stairs. James was standing shirtless, his bulging muscles prominently on display. The eggs he was cooking were sizzling atop the stove.

"Good morning—or bonjour, I should say." I said, in a hushed voice.

He turned around and smiled warmly at me.

"Bonjour," he said back, sliding an omelette onto a plate.

"Are you hungry?" He asked.

I nodded and stepped closer to him.

"Starving," I said.

I brushed my hair behind my ear and leaned against the counter, still watching him cook.

"Great, here—" he said, handing me a hot mug of coffee.

"Have a seat and I'll bring your food over." He said.

He gave me a reassuring smile. I sat looking around the room. It was a charming space he had. It was cozy and clean, not a thing was out of place. Typical James. I was always the messy one.

The small touches that Alice added were apparent to me too, but the other details were so quintessentially James. The IKEA floor lamp in the corner that resembled a lantern, the art history books stacked on the coffee table, and the small Salvador Dali figurine next to it. The books had easily been read five times through, by the look of the spines and the flipped up corners. He refused to use bookmarks which I always found to be blasphemous. I laughed to myself.

James landed a plate in front of me.

"You still like bell peppers right?" He asked.

I shook myself out of my head.

"Yes, of course. I love them." I smiled.

James sat his plate down and took a seat across from me.

"When did you wake up?" I asked, raising an eyebrow.

"Not long ago. I tried not to wake you."

"Thank you, but my alarm had other plans. Thanks for charging my phone, by the way." I said, taking a large bite of my omelette.

It was the best omelette I'd ever tasted.

"Last night was wonderful.." James said, his tone more sober.

"I didn't want to fall asleep." I admitted, taking a sip of coffee.

His eyes drifted up and over my head, as if to avoid me.

"But.." he continued, as a lump formed in my throat.

Here it comes, the let down.

"I can't— I'm not going back to LA with you." He said, finally meeting my eyes.

I was frozen in shock as I stared back at him.

"What... what do you mean, James? Was it something I did?" I pleaded.

He shook his head in disagreement

"Oh, *god no*, Jess. It's not you. I just think it would be best if you went back and got everything sorted on your own. And truthfully, I don't know how I'd explain my sudden departure to the gallery, whether I'm busy or not. I can't just pick up and go, as much as I want to, believe me, I want it more than anything." He said, placing a hand on his bare chest.

I could tell he was trying to be reassuring and logical. I knew he hadn't changed his mind, but the fear still lingered.

"Umm, right, ok. But last night you said—" I stuttered, shaking my head.

"I know. It had been so long since we'd been together, like that. I was caught up in the moment. Now I've had time to think." He said.

I was disappointed but I understood. After all, it had been the craziest 24 hours of my life and I needed to think more practically for once. I'm sure it had been the craziest 24 hours for James too. I owed it to him to take things slow this time and give him space even though I didn't want to.

"Right, I hadn't really even had much time to think about all of this." I admitted, knowing I'd made my decision the moment I saw him today.

"I know, I know, and I want you to have that...to make sure of exactly what you want before you make a life-altering choice." He said, pressing his elbows into the table.

I knew he meant well, but I was starting to get upset. I wanted this. I wanted us but I wasn't sure how I was going to prove it. I forced another bite of food and wiped my mouth.

"I made the choice to alter my life before I saw you yesterday. Choosing to spend the day with you only solidified it for me." I said, moving my food around my plate.

I looked up from my food and up at him. His eyes were wide open and his mouth was slightly ajar.

"This situation with my job is complex and sudden, but I know what's best for me. I've made up my mind. Sure, I haven't sorted out the details but my mind is made up. Are you worried that I'll change my mind?" I added.

I was direct. I couldn't lose him again. James cleared his throat. "I'm honestly not sure. Not that it matters, Jess, I'll be here for you no matter what, but I don't want to be the reason you give up on this career."

There was a short silence between us.

"Besides, there's visas and money involved. Whatever we —*you* decide, it won't be an overnight thing, you know?"

He was right. I hadn't thought of any of this. All I'd allowed myself to think about was him. I had used him to escape every ounce of my reality. I took another bite of my food and he did the same. I took a deep breath, trying my hardest not to be offended. After all, he had every right to tread lightly with me this time, if that's what he was doing. The steaks were much higher this time. However, I didn't have much to lose.

"Have you given any thought to where you'd want to live? Are we going long distance? What's the end game?" He asked.

I felt overwhelmed with all of his questions.

Why did I need to think about all of this now?

I shot him a look.

"I think *you've* clearly thought about it." I said, under my breath.

"I have, Jess. It's hard not to. I've worked hard to be here. I love my life in Paris. I love my job and the locals, and my little bistro on the corner but I also *love you*. You must know that by now. I just don't know if I could give any of this up...but I could potentially, in the future." He said.

He was being honest and he was right. I couldn't expect

him to give anything up for me. I leaned over the table and grabbed his hand.

"Of course not, James. I'd never ask you to. I couldn't, no matter how bad I wanted to be with you." I admitted.

I was taken aback by his offer. I almost couldn't believe it, but then again, he'd always been so selfless. A sudden epiphany washed over me. I'd wanted nothing more than to leave LA for London, or so I thought. Being in Paris with James—not Roger, opened my eyes to it's own beauty and charm.

I was quickly learning that despite how badly I thought I wanted something, life always had a way of showing me something better than I could've imagined.

"You've helped me see so many things in a new light. That includes this city. I could see myself here. I could see *us* here, if that's what you would want." I said, softly.

He slowly lifted his chin and smiled at me.

"Not London?" He asked, lightening the air between us.

"Not anymore. Besides, it's just a train ride away." I said.

We sat smiling at each other for a moment longer, before I leaned forward putting my head in my hands.

"Ugh, I'm a mess! I'm not even wearing my own clothes." I moaned.

"You look great though. I'm sure Alice doesn't mind either." He laughed.

I rolled my eyes and sat back in my chair.

"Ok, I'll take a red eye to LA and call for a meeting with Roger, my boss." I said.

Saying his name in front of him made me feel sick.

"My apartment is month-to-month, so I could put everything in storage and come back to Paris. If that would be ok with you. Just until I have a more permanent living situation." I said, trying to problem solve.

His eyes lit up in that special way.

"I would love nothing more." He assured me.

"As far as a job...James, I'm screwed. I never even thought I'd land the one, much less be searching for a new one. I have savings though, which should help—"

I felt exhausted at the thought of all this.

"It's okay. I'll find you something here. I have connections. Don't worry. A job is the last thing you should worry about." He said interrupting me.

He squeezed my hand to comfort me. Truthfully, I knew he had enough money to support the both of us, but I'd never expect him to.

"We'll take this day-by-day. You're not alone and I'll help in anyway I can." He said.

Before I knew it, tears were rolling down my cheeks. I felt awful for ever doubting a life with someone so reliable and caring. I'd always been so independent. I was on autopilot at this point. I'd never had a single person to lean on. I didn't know how to accept it. I didn't deserve it.

"Ok." I breathed, wiping a tear away.

We finished our breakfast while I looked at flights on my phone. There was one leaving in three hours which was plenty of time to collect my things from the hotel and be off. I suddenly realized that my bag was still in Daniel's room with the room keys inside. *Shit.* As much as I wanted to run away and leave everyone from the company in the dust, I knew I needed to face this mess.

I decided to call Daniel. James had just gotten in the shower, making me a bit more comfortable to make the call. His phone rang twice before he answered.

"Jessica, where *the hell are you?*" He hissed.

"Daniel, calm down. Everything is fine, I'm fine. I'm with, er, a friend. Listen, I need your help."

After Daniel was done berating me, he agreed to meet me at the hotel once he made sure Roger had left. He'd make sure my suitcase was packed and all I would need to do is checkout and turn in my room keys. I was impressed with how quickly we were able to make a plan.

"Thank you. Thank you so much. I *owe* you." I breathed in relief.

"Yeah, yeah, just promise you'll fill me in once were back at the office, ok?" He asked.

I felt a ping of guilt as I realized he had no idea that I'd never be in that office again.

"Absolutely, thank you again." I said.

I hung up and took a deep breath.

"Everything ok?" James asked, stepping out of the bathroom with a towel around his waist.

Slightly distracted by his moist torso, my response was delayed.

"Uh, yes, um.. I've got to get to the hotel by eleven and gather my things. From there, I was thinking I would head straight to the airport."

My stomach sank at the thought of leaving him. I began looking for my dirty clothes from the day before, trying to distract my mind. I found them neatly folded on the plush antique chair by the bed.

"Ok. Would you like me to come with you?" James asked.

I was suddenly nervous. He had no idea the sort of mess I was in, and I had no intention of him finding out. My palms became sweaty as I searched for the right words.

"No, no that's ok. Daniel— the executive assistant is going to help. I mean, he doesn't quite know I'm quitting yet, and I think if you tagged along it might make this whole thing far more suspicious. After-all, I left without a word yesterday. Apparently the team has been worried." I said.

A half lie. Daniel of all people, was worried. Roger could probably care less. James looked confused, but shrugged it off. I felt relieved that he didn't pry.

"But I could bring the car back around and you could

come to the airport with me. I would love to have your company." I admitted.

James surveyed me momentarily. He knew something more was rattling in my brain. He knew me too well. Luckily, he didn't question me. He just nodded in agreement.

I ordered a car that arrived within 20 minutes. I grabbed my phone and ran my hands through my hair.

"Well, Im off I guess." I shrugged.

He grabbed my pile of clothes to hand them to me. I paused, momentarily.

"Actually, I'll leave those here. If that's ok." I said.

I gave him a smile and he nodded reassuringly.

"Of course." He breathed.

It was a small way for me to keep the promise of my return. I knew he saw the meaning behind it in the way he smiled. He walked me down to the car, holding the door fro me like the gentleman he was. "Wait," I begged, stepping back out of the car.

"I- I just realized I don't have your number...unless it's the same." I stuttered.

It was such a weird thing to say aloud.

"Oh, right. Here, it's different." He said.

Of course it was. Everything was different. He took my phone and entered his number.

"To new beginnings," he smiled and handed it back.

I smiled too, appreciating his sunny disposition in contrast to mine. I got back in the car and waved bye.

The driver whipped through unknown narrow streets. I gripped the door handle as my chest became tight. My reality was just beyond the dashboard and quickly approaching. I'd thought so low of Daniel before this trip and I couldn't believe the kindness he'd shown me the other night. I made a complete ass of him and myself. I thought for sure he'd take advantage of my drunken escapades, but he didn't. Instead, he'd shown me more respect that Roger had on this entire trip.

The car arrived at the hotel and my heart began to race. I texted Daniel, letting him know I was here and rushed out of the car. I ran through the foyer with my head down. My pace increased as I headed for the stairs that Daniel insisted I take. Roger would be boarding the train to London, if he hadn't already.

Thankfully, I reached the small door leading to the stairs without any sight of him. I took a deep breath as I had six flights to climb in my heels. I pressed hard into the palm of my foot trying not to make a clatter. My calves ached with each step.

Finally, breathless, I reached the sixth floor. I opened the door, my heart pounding through my ears and saw that the coast was clear. I ran to Daniel's door and tapped gently. The door swung open, causing me to fall forward. Daniel grabbed me tightly by the elbow and looked me over anxiously.

"Daniel, let go of me!" I scoffed.

"I'm just making sure you're in one piece. God only knows where you've been." He said, rolling his eyes.

"Daniel, *relax*, it's a long story but I'm more than fine." I said.

"And without a bra I see." he remarked, raising an eyebrow.

I slapped his arm.

"Perv."

I huffed and turned to look for my purse.

"Well, alright. I expect you to fill me in completely the moment you land in LA, ok? Look, here's your bag. I've got to run. My car is waiting. The keys are inside and your bags are packed tightly in your room." He said, more relaxed.

He didn't have a shred of an idea of what was coming. I felt guilty. He wasn't the slimy womanizer he pretended to be. He was kind and genuine. He was someone I could actually enjoy working alongside now, but it was too late. He was absolutely loyal to this company too. Something I'd never understand. Any doubt I had about leaving it behind was dissolved in this moment. Seeing him cover for me, I realized that he must've done the exact same other employees in the past, maybe even Roger. He was just doing his job but I didn't want any apart of this world.

"Ok. Thank you again." I breathed.

"No problem," He said, putting on his sunglasses and leaving.

I nervously looked around the room, making sure I hadn't left anything behind. I opened my purse and fumbled around for my key card as I opened the door. I turned and briskly walked to my room. Just as I entered the key to unlock it I jumped at a familiar adenoidal voice.

"Jessica."

I felt my stomach drop as I turned around to see Roger staring blankly at me. I couldn't believe this.

Did Daniel set me up? Was Roger here all along? How on earth was this happening?

"I'm just getting my things." I said, flatly and turned back around, refusing to look at him.

My heart was pounding nervously out of my chest. I could barely breathe. I felt so nervous that I could puke, but I tried to keep it together.

"Wait, let me speak to you, please. I've just forgotten my scarf and came back to my room to grab it. I didn't expect to see you here." He pleaded firmly, as he followed me into my hotel room.

My suitcase and travel bag was neatly stacked on the newly made bed. I was amazed to see the care Daniel put into helping me.

He couldn't have set me up. He wouldn't. I grabbed the suitcase by the handle and lifted it to the floor.

"Roger cut the bullshit. *I KNOW ABOUT YOU AND CELESTE!*" I screamed, raising my hand in the air.

His eyes grew wide and he scrunched his large eyebrows.

"*What?* What on earth?!" He asked in a deep voice.

He looked guilty confused.

"Please spare me. It's fine, really. I was stupid to ever think that *this*," I motioned between us.

"Could ever realistically be something. *God*, I think I was honestly just enamored by the idea more than anything." I scoffed at him.

I shoved a scarf into my carry-on and zipped it up before throwing it over my shoulder.

"I will NOT have you speak to me this way. You're... you're-" he stuttered. "I'm what, Roger? *Your assistant?*" I asked, smugly.

"Look, you haven't got a clue what you're saying. Maybe I should be asking YOU why you've just come from Daniel's room, or why you were nowhere to be found the last two nights. I think *you're the one* who owes me an explanation! You left in a drunken mess and Daniel had to bring you back here. Who knows what you two were up to all night." He said, pointing a finger at me.

I might have been willing to talk things through if he hadn't deflected to me and Daniel. His insinuation was beyond offensive. I felt my ears getting hot with rage.

"I know that Daniel tried to dig his claws into me when I first started here but don't think for a second that it was recip-rocated." I spat.

I moved past him with my bags and struggled to open the door. Once I wedged it open I turned to him one last time.

"I don't owe you *anything*." I said, through my teeth.

I wanted to leave it at that, but I couldn't bare having him try and wedge into the elevator with me, continuing this conversation.

"And DO NOT follow me. I'll contact you next week, once Im back in LA." I said.

I made my way down the carpeted hallway feeling anger pulse through me. I viciously pressed the button to the elevator and jumped in, practically shoving into an innocent stranger in the process. I felt relieved that I'd made it out without crying, I'd done enough of that these last few days. It had taken a lot of courage to face him here. I felt cornered. Especially after thinking I'd have at least two days to mull everything over and collect myself. The moment I saw his face, I couldn't hold it in. I couldn't pretend to feel anything other than anger. I'd never been one to burn bridges, especially at a job, but something inexplicable came over me.

As I rode the car back to James' apartment I realized what had prompted me to act so boldly. It was the single fact that all the energy and admiration I had given to Roger was misplaced. I had given him parts of me that only one person could ever deserve. I thought that Roger could fulfill me on some level, or that a man of his age could somehow have higher standards.

It hurt to be proven so incredibly wrong. I laid my head back on the headrest and let out a big sigh. I closed my eyes until the driver alerted me that we had reached my stop. I felt a wave of relief, as well as anxiety, now that I had another mountain to climb. I had to pack up my whole life and prove to the man I love that he should trust me again.

I slowly opened my eyes to see James on the doorstep of his building, sitting patiently. Waiting for me. He'd spent years waiting for me.

I gave him a soft smile and unbuckled myself. He was wearing a thick black sweater with grey trousers. He looked so incredibly handsome that it hurt. He looked like my future. I stepped out of the car and he made his way over to help me with my bags.

"You made it out alive, it seems." He said, in a light tone.

I sighed and cocked my head to the side.

"So it seems. I'm just glad to have my things." I said.

I checked the time on my watch to see that I had about three hours before I had to board my flight. I asked James if I could freshen up quickly before we headed to the airport together. He finished up some work on his computer as I ransacked my suitcase, completely forgetting what all I'd even packed. I pulled out a brown silk skirt that I knew was clean. I pulled on a wool turtleneck and a heavy cardigan to match. I doused myself in perfume before zipping everything up. I was baptizing myself. I grabbed my makeup from my carry-on and put on a neutral lipstick, smudging the same color onto my cheeks to put some life back into my face.

"Here, let me help." James said, as I walked down the stairs.

James was quick to my side. He grabbed my bags and placed them onto the floor. As he bent back up, he stopped to look at me.

"I forgot how well you cleaned up." He said in a sensual voice, low and controlled.

I leaped off the last step, smiling back at him.

"Well, that's a shame isn't it?" I joked.

"Well, I'm happy to have my memory refreshed." He said, pulling me into his side.

After about five minutes outside, a car pulled up. A small black Mercedes with dark tinted windows.

Before I knew it, we were at the departure gate of the Charles de Gaulle airport. I nervously looked over my ticket once more as James guided us in the right direction. I couldn't believe my eyes. The airport was unlike any airport I'd ever seen. The ceilings were low and rounded in some spaces and high in others. The ceiling above the escalators was made up of small square windows that looked out to metal roofing rather than the sky. It was whimsical and quirky and not at all what I had expected. We took the escalator down to an area filled with bars and restaurants, deciding to lounge together until I boarded. I wanted to soak up every last second with James.

We settled in a sleek little restaurant with a view to the tarmac. My stomach rumbled as we sat down. I hadn't finished the delicious breakfast James had made for us earlier today. My mind was too preoccupied. I ordered a salad and some fries for us to share along with a glass of wine. James ordered a beer.

We made small talk for awhile. It was so natural for us to fall back into place with each other. James told me about the work he'd done for the gallery and about his experience when he first moved to Paris. All of it sounded like a fairytale compared to the hell I'd been living back in LA. He told me about the rigorous process of something called *'Guide Conférencières'* that he had endured. He had worked nonstop after we had graduated. First acquiring his masters and then becoming a guide in Paris. It was a life most people would kill for.

"I've always admired how dedicated you are to the things you love. You're steady and determined." I said.

He took a drink of his beer before smiling.

"Well, I try. At the time I just felt like I needed a distraction more than anything. I'd always planned on doing this but everything was fast tracked after we... graduated." He said, clearing his throat.

I moved uncomfortably in my chair.

"I could've been more determined with you." He added, looking out the window.

"Well, I admire you and all you've built for yourself, really, James. I envy it." I admitted, looking out of the window too.

I felt his large warm hand slowly cover mine.

"This is just a bump in the road, Jess. After all, you should be proud of yourself for making it this far and landing such a great gig. Any PR firm would be lucky to have you, even if you haven't specifically worked in PR yet. Look, I wasn't going to mention anything yet, but I know someone who would happily get you in for an interview at their firm...that is, if you're serious about moving here." He said, firmly.

I turned my head back to look at him.

"Of course I am." I breathed, almost offended.

"I mean, that's incredible. Thank you." I said.

I knew he was just trying to help. He didn't want me to feel pressured. And there was always the potential for me to change my mind. I was known to do that. I felt a small flicker of hope for me and my future with James. The fact that he had a connection was the only practical thing I had to count on. I felt myself becoming more and more excited about starting over. About Paris. About me and James. It wasn't what I'd imagined for myself days ago. It was better.

I finished my salad and began shoveling fries into my mouth. We were on our second round of drinks when the tone became more somber. James was fidgeting with a napkin he'd folded into a million squares in silence.

"Look, Jess, there's something I need to tell you," He said rubbing the back of his neck.

I felt my stomach drop. I'd had enough bad news and surprises for one trip, or even a lifetime. I couldn't possibly imagine what it would be.

Is this the part where he tells me there's someone else? Or that maybe he feels like we're rushing into things? Maybe he was the one getting cold feet.

I couldn't imagine what was about to fall from his lips. I sat in silence as my heart rate increased.

"Um, well, my mom..she's been sick, or she was sick this last year." He said, correcting himself.

What.

I sat in disbelief unsure of where this was going.

"I don't really know how to say this," he continued.

"Spit it out." I urged.

"She was diagnosed with cancer." He said flatly.

He was choked up. My eyes grew wide as I couldn't believe what he was saying. Not Alice. *Sweet, sweet, too good for this world, Alice.*

"Luckily they caught it very early and you know, my dad was able to offer some relief with his medical knowledge. She's in remission now." He said, reassuringly.

My hand covered my mouth.

"God, oh, my god." I whispered.

I felt sick.

"I'm so sorry to bring it up now, but I spoke to her this morning, when you left to the hotel. I couldn't help but mention you. I didn't tell her everything, of course, just that you were in town and that alone made her day. You should've heard her perk up at just the sound of your name." He said.

He smiled, trying to soften the serious bomb he'd just dropped on me. He squeezed my hands reassuringly. I could tell he regretted mentioning it to me. My stomach turned at the thought of his mom ever being ill. I began to imagine her under the florescent lights of a hospital, hooked up to IV's. The woman who still sends me birthday and Christmas cards whether, James was aware or not.

Tears welled up in my eyes. The plate of fries in front of me became blurry.

Suddenly, I could taste metal.

I felt something thick and hot run from my nose and just as I went to touch it James froze.

"*Oh, god*, here" he said, handing me a napkin.

A large blob of red blood dropped onto the table in front of me. James took the napkin from me and held it up to my nose, pinching it with his other hand to stop the bleeding. His tall frame was bent down in front of me with his arms extended up. I tilted my head back and took a deep breath through my mouth. The blood ran down my throat.

"No, it's fine....I think it's just the stress of everything." I said.

"I'm so sorry, Jess, really. *Shit.*" He whispered.

He never cursed. I loved when he did. I started giggling uncontrollably. Partially from hysteria and partially from hearing him. I don't think I'd ever heard him curse, apart from the time his modern art professor refused to bump his grade to an A.

"Why on earth are you laughing?" He smiled, his hand still resting against my nose.

"You said 'shit'." I said, roaring with laughter.

He looked at me in bewilderment and joined in.

"You're something else, Jess."

I waived my hand in front of myself, shooing him away.

"I think the bleeding stopped," I said, tilting my head back down.

He removed his hand and sat back in his seat slowly.

"Are you sure you're ok, love?" He asked, looking worried.

I melted in my chair. I never thought I'd hear him call me that again. I bent my head down and removed the napkin to see that the bleed had stopped. I looked up at him and nodded silently.

"Here drink drink some more of this. I don't want you having a panic attack on the flight." He said, scooting my wine glass closer.

I finished off the remainder of the wine in my glass, just as I heard the boarding call for my flight over the intercom. James looked up at the sky and back at me. This was it.

"Well, on that note..." I whispered.

The gravity of the situation setting in finally, he stood slowly before grabbing his beer and downing the rest of it.

He grabbed my suitcase with his left hand and quickly placed his arm around my shoulders. I grabbed my other bags and walked quickly with him towards the gate, leaning into his side the whole way. My heart was racing as we approached my terminal.

I saw a handful of people in line for the flight. I turned to James, stepping out of the way of traffic.

"Here we are," I whispered softly.

I felt myself holding back the words I knew he probably was dying to hear. I felt nauseous, holding them back but I didn't know how to get them out. *Just say it.*

"I'll call you the moment I land, or I guess text depending on time difference." I said, embarrassed.

Say what you really wanna say.

"I have a meeting the following day, so I'll have everything sorted out." I added.

No, not that, Jess.

He nodded, saying nothing.

"I'll be here." He finally spoke.

I felt like he wanted to say more. We both stood there for a moment in thick silence. I couldn't say what I knew I really needed to. I nodded and gave him a smile. I craned my head up to kiss him gently on the mouth before turning and walking to the gate. I felt his eyes on my back as I walked away. I couldn't look back at him to confirm it though. It would hurt too much.

Why the fuck couldn't I just say it? I was about to uproot my entire life for this man.

I made it to the back of the line, two people in front of me and gave in.

"Shit." I whispered.

I turned around to see him right where I left him. He was going to stand there until the gate closed. I knew he would.

"James?" I yelled.

He raised his eyebrows. "

Yeah?" He yelled back.

"Promise me—Promise me you'll be here when I get back?" I yelled again.

Tears began to well up in my eyes. I rubbed my forehead with the inside of my palm.

"I'll be right here, Jess. I promise." He said in the most serious tone I'd ever heard.

And I promise to never take you for granted gain, James Locke.

I smiled at him, holding back tears, as a lump grew in my throat. I turned back around so he couldn't see them fall. I wiped them on the back of my sleeve as the attendant scanned my ticket. This was it. I boarded the plane quickly and prayed that the following days would fly by. I prayed nothing would get in the way of the two promises we made.

CHAPTER NINETEEN

I sat nervously, tapping my fingers on the table. It had only been a few weeks since I had been in this conference room, but it felt like a lifetime since then.

I read the decal, *"Burton Barnes"*, on the glass door for the fifth time. I checked my watch again. Daniel had asked me to be here at 1:00pm sharp and he was late, as always. My palms were sweaty. I kept imagining Roger or Celeste appearing from around a corner.

I knew it wasn't possible but *still*, it terrified me. I personally knew Roger was staying behind in London. *Thank GOD.* I'd written his itinerary. We still hadn't spoken since the trip and I was fine with that. There was nothing left to say. I was happy with a clean break. Although, he might have won some brownie points with me if he'd texted a 'sorry', or begged to me to stay working for the company.

The moment that I landed back in LA, I sat down and crafted my termination email. My ego was telling me that this was a huge mistake, and that I was throwing away nearly a year worth of hard work. I didn't care. All I wanted was to get out of this damn town and never make another decision based on fear. All I wanted was to be with James.

As much as I wanted to berate Roger and celeste in the email, I didn't. I addressed it to the team and thanked them for the time and experience I had gained here, partially genuine of me. The plane ride home seemed to fly by because I was so lost in thought. I picked apart of every outcome of me coming back to Paris to be with James. I would be lying if I said I wasn't terrified at the idea, not because I didn't want it, but because I didn't want to mess anything up this time. I wanted to get every moment right. I'd been in contact with James since the moment I landed, just like I promised. He warned me that he might be back at the gallery and that if I don't get a response that I should just call. Even knowing this, I felt a ping of anxiety whenever he didn't respond to a text.

I smiled to myself, imaging James working long hours in his little Parisian gallery. I still hadn't worked out any moving logistics other than booking a company to help me get my things into storage. I'd drafted a 30-day notice to my landlord too. It was a start.

Suddenly, I saw the flash of a blue suit. It was Daniel. The person who didn't respond to a single one of my texts or calls since I'd been back. He paced quickly around the corner and into the conference room. He had a sullen look on his face. I shifted in my seat. The gust of wind he brought into the room filled to with that strong scent of his. I had no idea what to expect from Daniel. I had no idea how this was supposed to go.

"Jessica," He said cordially, straightening his collar.

"Hey." I whispered.

I looked up at him from my chair as he took a seat in his. He took a deep breath and unbuttoned his suit jacket.

He was began opening the thick manilla envelope in his hand. "You know, don't you?" I asked gravely.

He finally looked me in the eyes. "

Yes, I do." He said matter-of-factly, straightening the stack of papers on the table.

This wasn't like him to be so serious. It was the most professional he'd ever looked. Daniel was the only person I knew who could truly make light of any situation. I didn't realize until now, how much I admired that about him.

"Daniel, please know I wanted to tell you everything but-"

He raised a hand to stop me.

"Jess, it's ok. Really. Let's just press on." He said, sternly.

I nodded in agreement as he laid the papers out in to stacks of three. He grabbed the first stack and explained that they were NDA's and termination papers.

"Uh...okay, well, I'm going to need to read over these." I said, fighting for more time.

I felt the urge to explain myself to him. I wanted him to know how much I appreciated him now too. I wanted him to know I didn't hate him. He had helped me more than he realized and I felt like I was abandoning him. I was disgusted at the formality of all this. Although, I knew it was probably the most logical for Roger's sake and the company. Not that he should worry. I'd never say a word about any of this, I wanted to forget it all together.

I skimmed the pages quickly, knowing it was all perfectly reasonable. So, signing away my intellectual rights was almost therapeutic. Just as I signed the first line, Daniel cleared his throat.

"You know, I really didn't know he'd gone back to the hotel? I would never do that to you." He said, looking at the table.

I looked up at him slowly, glad he was finally braking the ice.

"I know, Daniel. Thank you for clearing that up." I assured him, warmly.

I reached for his hand, but he pulled it away and smoothed out his hair. In truth, I didn't know his part in it. I had my doubts. But he'd proven himself respectful to me after all these months, finally. So, I decided to give him the benefit of the doubt. Besides, he'd shown me more respect than Roger had.

I looked back to my paper and signed the next line. The third page stated that I was "not to disclose any addresses or usual whereabouts of any employees of the company."

A knot grew in my stomach. A flashback of my naked body hunched over the top of Roger hit me. *I felt sick.* I shook my head at the thought and finished reading the small stack. I wanted this burned out of my brain.

"Right, here is a severance from the company and a paper stating you received it." Daniel said.

"Sign here."

He slid the paper closer to me along with a check. I skimmed the paper that stated that my severance of *$14,000.00* was given to me. I choked on my spit at the number.

"F-fourteen thousand?" I stuttered.

Daniel finally cracked a small smile.

"You think I'd let him get away with anything smaller than a double digit?" He said.

He winked at me, softening his demeanor. The contrast of my first week versus the current one was night and day.

"Daniel...I-"

"Just take the money and shut up, princess. I really don't want to go back to the bank today. Besides, you did so much while I was gone. Think of it as a bonus." He said, straightening his jacket and leaning back in his chair.

I laughed in shock.

I finished signing the next stack of papers, agreeing to turning in all keys and other company property. I slid the papers his way. I leaned back, prepared to ask a question I never thought I'd have to.

"I'm not the first girl to leave on these terms am I?"

He looked me over slowly, running his tongue over his front teeth. He nodded slowly, affirming my suspicion.

"You tried to warn me didn't you? You tried to warn me in your own way." I said, in a whisper.

Piecing it all together. I laughed to myself. I couldn't believe it. I didn't want to, anyway. I suddenly realized that maybe that's why he'd come onto me so quickly. Maybe he thought he could beat Roger to it in some way. Maybe he thought he could win me over and then extinguish it before it had gone too far, distracting me from Roger. Regardless of his motives, I knew from here on out, that I was grateful for him. This crazy mess had lead me back to James. It had opened my eyes to parts of myself I didn't know were still there. I couldn't resent anyone for that, not even Roger.

Daniel gathered the papers and gave me a reassuring look. We stood in unison. I walked over to his side of the table near the door.

"Right, well, I'll be seeing you then." He said, before I wrapped my arm around his neck, pulling him in for a hug.

His body tensed up in response. He gave me a gentle squeeze and then stepped back.

"Thank you, Daniel." I said, softly.

I stared into his eyes momentarily, hoping he would feel the truth of my words. He looked away quickly.

"You know, I'm going to have loads of work now, don't you?" He joked, pointing at me.

"Well you better get to it then, shouldn't you?"

I stepped out slowly and adjusted my purse on my shoulder. He watched me walk away, not caring that I saw. I gave him a wave and a smile through the glass and walked to the elevator.

I pulled out my phone and found his message thread.

> "Don't be a stranger. Xoxo"

I texted as I stepped into the elevator.
Daniel immediately responded.

"You know I wouldn't dare, Jess. xx"

I smiled to myself, feeling a sense of freedom wash over me. It was the end of a chapter for me and simultaneously the beginning of a new one.

I checked the time on my watch, *2:03pm.* I was due to meet Hanna for coffee soon at our favorite shop. She had no idea about James, or the fact that I'd decided to move across the world for him, or us. I honestly wasn't sure how she was going to take it. I was her only real friend in the city and she was mine. Surely she'd known this day would have to come eventually. The idea had to have been more real for her when I accepted the job at company and even more-so when I was asked on the trip.

I walked towards the entrance of our favorite café, on the corner of sunset boulevard. I saw her luscious blonde hair through the window and made my way inside. I walked over to her as she slowly lifted her head.

"Jess!!!!" She squealed.

She shot up and wrapped her arms around me. I felt my body melt instantly at her embrace. I felt like it had been an eternity since I'd seen her sweet face.

"God, its good to see you." I breathed into her neck.

"Come. Sit, sit, I ordered us our usual." she said.

"Thank you, H. Looks delicious."

I took a large sip of my dirty chai, realizing it was the last time I'd be having it in this café.

"Sooooo tell me everything. I can't believe you're quitting." Hanna said, waving her hands in front of her.

I kept my gaze on my drink.

"It's...*it's complicated.* How about you recap *YOUR* trip first. Gimme a second to breathe. Mine's just a lot to digest and I've truly missed you. I feel like I haven't seen you in years." I admitted.

She seemed concerned but went ahead and told me about

her time in Italy. To my surprise, she told me that her and Richard were no longer in contact. He'd decided to reconnect with his wife and hoped to still keep things going with Hanna on the side.

"I told him, I may be a hussy but I'm no home-wrecker."

"You are NOT a *hussy*. Besides, do people even use that word anymore?" I asked.

"I'm so sorry though, H. You know, I always had a feeling there was a little more to you two than you let on. I mean it's not like you to go global with these types of guys, much less watch their kids." I admitted.

I expected her response to be defensive but she just shrugged in defeat.

"Well, I got three new bags and some shoes out of it, so it wasn't all for nothing." She joked.

"Besides, I've been promoted to buyer at Saks and I am genuinely excited for it. No more sugar daddies." She said, proudly.

I almost spat my drink out in front of me.

"Hanna, that's great!"

"Congrats! When do you start?" I asked.

"Next week! It was such a surprise. Henderson made me aware of the position and set everything up for me. I just needed a change and it felt right. Besides, the pay is pretty sexy, so I don't need to entertain anyone but myself for awhile." She smiled, checking out her glossy manicure.

"Cheers to that." I said, lifting my glass.

"Now, tell me about your trip. I can tell you're stalling." She pressed. I took a deep breath and cocked my head back.

"Buckle up." I breathed.

I told her everything. Every single detail as if I were recounting it to a detective. I knew she'd have questions and I was trying to save time. She sat across from me in pure shock, her eyes growing bigger with every detail. I told her about James, and how I felt the universe was pushing us back together and how I wasn't going to run this time. Lastly, I told her that my apartment was being packed up and put in storage. I told her I'd decided to leave and start a new life with him, one that I should've started three years ago.

When I finished speaking I shifted my gaze from the spot in front of me to her, just as a single tear fell from her eye. She quickly looked down, wiping away the tear quickly.

"I—I always knew you two would find your way back." she whispered.

I'd only seen Hanna cry once over the course of our friendship and she wasn't even sober. I relaxed and placed a hand over hers, to comfort both of us.

"I think I always did too. I don't know why I fought it for so long." I said, as I felt a warm tear stream down my face too.

It was so cathartic sharing all of this with her. Someone who knew me deeper than anyone else.

"I'm going to miss you so much."

I raised my eyebrows at her. She wasn't the type to be so open with her feelings. She'd always been the stoic, the surface level one. I knew she was human and that deep down she felt everything. Seeing it in real time was a different story.

We were both embarking on new versions of ourselves. A part of me felt sad, grieving the versions of ourselves that were fading almost instantaneously in front of us here in this café.

"I'll visit often…and you will too." I said, reassuring her with a pat on the hand.

"I mean it. And we'll talk everyday, no matter what." I added.

She smiled and casually wiped her eyes on a napkin.

"I just can't believe this is all real and happening so fast." She cried. "Believe me, I know." I said, rolling my eyes and looking out the window.

"You know, all i've done is let fear rule my life. I let the worst-case scenarios cloud my judgement. And even though it seems terrible for things to be happening this way, I know it was all *meant* to happen this way. I wouldn't have realized what I truly wanted out of life. I'd still be stuck at Saks and living in my tiny apartment, well, if I hadn't gotten fired. And it's all thanks to you. You've always believed in me. You've always supported me no matter what." I said, fidgeting with the corner of a napkin.

Her eyes glistened at me.

"I know you'd do the same for me, Jess." She said.

We stared at each other for a moment.

"So what about London?"

I laughed slightly before answering.

"I still want to be there someday, but I think at the root of all of this, I just wanted a fresh start, in a new country. Besides, it's only a two hour train ride away. That alone is enough to satisfy me." I said.

With each word we spoke, my new life drew closer and closer. I felt oddly calm. I felt it clicking into place with ease. I decided to invite Hanna back to the apartment to help me mark boxes for the movers. I wanted as much time with her as possible before I boarded my flight tomorrow, one I'd only purchased before meeting her. She gasped at the sight of my empty studio.

"I know. It's weird for me too. It's the end of an era."

I ordered us a pizza and uncorked a bottle of wine while we waited for it to arrive. I handed her a sharpie and told her which boxes to mark.

"How do you own more pairs of shoes than me?" Hanna yelled.

We finished marking just as the pizza arrived. We dug in and polished off the bottle of wine quicker than we should have.

We spent the rest of the night reminiscing over our earliest college memories. We went from tears of laughter to tears of sadness as the wine sat in. The minutes faded into hours and before we knew it, it was 10pm.

"It's time to call it a night." Hanna said, with a yawn.

I nodded in agreement, folding my arms into my torso and looking around my empty space.

"Thank you for helping me, really." I said.

"You didn't need my help. You wanted my company." she smiled.

I pulled her in for a long hug, squeezing her tight.

"I love you." I said, a lump growing in my throat.

"I love you too." she exhaled.

It's the first time we'd ever said that to one another.

"Now, get some sleep." she said, pulling away.

She grabbed her bag from the counter and slipped back into her heels.

"I'll text you the moment I land." I promised, before she left my apartment for the last time.

I turned around, slowly taking in the emptiness of the space. All that was left was the bed frame, which came with the apartment, and the mattress I'd bought when I first moved in. I had no choice but to leave it, otherwise I'd be sleeping on the floor.

I had three suitcases stuffed and ready to go by the door. Stream-lining my wardrobe and life into them was the most challenging part of this whole ordeal. At the end of the day, I knew this was all replaceable. The only thing that wasn't, was James.

Part of me wanted to sell every last bit and raid the designer thrift stores in Paris. Or blow my entire severance on the Champs-elysées, I couldn't decide.

I walked over to my windows, that overlooked the city. I stood, looking it over in a way I hadn't before. I felt grateful for everything that had happened get me here. Every bit of it had lead me to this exact moment, one I could have never foreshadowed for myself. I walked to my front door to lock it and turned off the lights. Every sound echoed loudly off the empty space.

The street lights and cars now lit up my studio like a snow globe for the last time. I walked to my bed and tucked myself in under a throw blanket. I laid my head down on the mattress and let the city of angels sing me to sleep one last time.

CHAPTER TWENTY

I BOARDED my flight to Paris with more anxiety than I'd ever felt in my life. I was chewing my gum so fast that I bit my cheek. My past was in a storage unit and my future was about 5,000 miles away. My brain was on a hamster wheel. I'd been playing through the various scenarios and conversations I would have.

Would James change his mind before I landed? Would I change my mind and hurt him all over again? No. Absolutely not that. Would his parents disapprove and convince him that he was crazy? No, surely Alice would be thrilled. Would I quickly grow to hate Paris? Not a chance.

All I knew was that I loved James. It was the only thing I'd been sure of in a long time. I put my carry-on in the stowaway overhead and went to the toilet before takeoff. I felt so nervous, like I was going to meet James for the first time. Everything felt new again, as if we didn't know each other. In a lot of ways we didn't. There was something exciting about getting to know each other all over again. I wanted to know him all over again.

When did he wake up in the morning? Did he still take his coffee black (unless we went to a café)?

I decided I couldn't be sad about the time we'd lost

together. It made more sense to be excited for what was to come.

I squeezed myself into the ridiculously small airplane toilet, and looked myself over in the mirror. I tried to imagine what James would see. I fished my lipstick from my purse and reapplied it. I was wearing a pair of straight-leg jeans, Chanel flats, a silk chemise, and the grey blazer that belonged to him. The blazer was oversized on me but it looked good. I hardly doubted James' large shoulders would be fitting into it now anyway. It was an homage to the invisible string that held us together these last few years. James had no idea I still had it.

I arrived at my seat to find an elderly woman seated next to me. I gave her a cordial nod as I shimmied past her.

"Hello." She said, with a warm smile.

I sat down and fastened my seatbelt, focusing my gaze outside of the window. I dug through my purse to find my lipstick once more. I couldn't help but fidget. The woman next to me must've noticed.

"Is this your first time flying?"

I laughed.

"No, no its not. I'm just a little nervous." I responded.

"Ah, well what takes you to Paris?" She asked.

I didn't quite know how to summarize for her, and I didn't want to.

"Uh, I'm traveling for work. It's actually my second time there this week. Hopefully I'll stay for awhile." I smiled.

"Wow, very exciting." She said, and nodded.

"Well, what about you? Have you been to Paris before?" I asked. "Many times...I used to live there, with my husband." She said.

I paused with my lipstick still touching my bottom lip. I wasn't sure exactly what she meant but I could only assume he wasn't alive. I looked her over. She had to be in her early 80's at the least.

"He died about ten years ago." She said, reassuringly.

"I go back every year to visit him—well, his grave. I still have an apartment there, but I have grandkids in LA that I can't stand to be without. I know he understands though."

I sat frozen for a moment, before I told her how sorry I was that he had passed.

"It's okay, dear. We had many happy years together and for that I'll always be grateful. Besides, he's still with me." She said, clutching a large medallion hanging from her neck.

It looked to be a large coin of some sort.

"Although, you never really think about what life is going to be like without someone until they're gone. There's no way to prepare for it." She added.

"That I can understand." I said, softly.

I placed my makeup back into my purse and slid it under my seat. "Oh, do you?" She asked, raising her eyebrows.

I let out a laugh and nodded.

"Yes, well, it's complicated, but I met someone in college. He was perfect—is perfect—but I was young and scared and I let him go."

I looked down at my fingers that were tightly laced together.

"But we found each other again, recently, it was quite kismet actually. Anyway, it turns out we're still crazy for each other. Even after these last couple of years apart." I said, with my hands in the air.

"Is he handsome?" She asked.

Her question took me by surprise. I laughed nervously and brushed the hair behind my ear.

"Wildly handsome...more than before, which I didn't think was possible." I gloated.

I told her about how we reconnected, the very brief and concise version, that is. I told her about the scarf and how the blazer I was wearing was his too. She gasped, marveling at the sweetness of it, and touching my arm. I admitted that I was not only here for work but to be with James.

"I had a feeling there was more to your story." She said, proudly.

I asked her to tell me about her late husband. They met one summer when she came to Paris. She was attending Le Cordon Bleu and he was a local native working at his family business. They stumbled into the same smoky bar one night and got married three months later.

"Back then you didn't wait. At least we didn't...when you know, you know." She said, patting the back of my hand.

My stomach churned at her words. I'd always known, and that's why I fought it.

"So....when do you think you too will get married?" She asked.

My cheeks turned hot.

"I —I'm not sure. We've only just gotten back together. I mean, I'm living out of a suitcase. I haven't even thought about that yet." I said.

She sat quietly, listening intently.

"I think he was going to ask me when we graduated college. He was about to move back home for the summer and I just had a feeling.... That's when I ended things." I admitted.

Shame seeped through my tone.

"It's only natural, you know? Independent women rarely see the value of men because they never had one to value in the first place. I bet your daddy wasn't around." She said, flatly.

I nodded involuntarily. This woman saw right through me. I should've been offended, but I couldn't be. She was right. I'd never even given it enough thought to see it her way, either.

"Oh, I don't mean to offend you, dear. Am I right though? Was your father ever around?" She asked.

I felt like I knew her. I felt like I could trust her and even If I couldn't, who's to say I'd ever see her again?

"Um, no." I said, shocked.

"Me neither. I think I see a bit of myself in you, honey. I

was hesitant at first with Henry. I wanted to be one of the first female chefs. You know, back in my day that was lofty of me. I wanted to come back to LA and open my own restaurant. I wanted to be like Audrey Hepburn in Sabrina, and I somehow thought I couldn't do it if I got married and had kids like my friends. I was wrong. I knew I couldn't imagine a life without Henry and I was determined to make it work no matter what. So, I finished my schooling and eventually, Henry came back to the states with me. We built a life here and I had my little restaurant. It was a small, but proud establishment. I kept it open for twenty years and earned critical acclaim too. *And you know what?* I couldn't have done any of that without Henry." She gave me a matter-of-fact look.

Her perspective was refreshing. Not only had I never had a solid male figure in my life, but I'd also never had a strong female one either. I was always fending for myself. I smiled at her, letting her know I understood.

Just then, the flight attendant came around with drinks. I opted for wine to calm my nerves and she asked for a coke.

"I'm sorry, I didn't even get your name." I said, taking a sip.

"It's Carol, what's yours, dear?"

"I'm Jessica." I said, extending my hand.

She shook it gently. Her hand was warm and soft.

I thought briefly of all the things she must've seen in her life. I thought about how lucky she was to have lived so long and accomplished so much. Our conversation faded into a much lighter one. We talked about our favorite places in California and all the places we'd traveled. She told me all about her children and grandchildren. Eventually, our conversation came to an end and she got up to use the toilet. The wine must've done it's job a little too well as I felt myself nodding off. I leaned my head against the window and let my eyes grow heavy.

I awoke alarmed, as a flight attendant was tapping on my shoulder.

"Ma'am the flight has landed. We're disembarking now." the attendant said, flatly.

I looked around to see that half the plane was empty and that Carol was gone. My eyes were so glossy I had to rub them to see. It was the best sleep I'd had in weeks. I sat up slowly and stretched. I grabbed my bag from overhead and looked over the plane once more, hoping to find Carol. She was nowhere to be found.

I grabbed my phone from my pocket and turned off my airplane mode. Time seemed to be moving slowly. I was about to step off of this plane and into my new reality. I felt 21 again. Nervous and dressed up, waiting to meet up with James, except this time it wasn't at our spot. It was in Paris and I had more to be nervous about. I put my phone in the pocket of my blazer. I stopped in my tracks as I felt something brush my hand.

It was a small piece of paper. I opened it and read,

Jessica, it was lovely to meet you. Follow your heart, it will never lead you astray. - Carol xx

with a phone number on the back. I smiled to myself, holding it to my chest before putting it back into my pocket. I knew right then, that this was a sign from the universe that I was on the right track. I hurried out of the plane, impatient to be in James' arms again.

The moment I stepped into the airport, my eyes searched for him. When I didn't see him, I checked my watch. I looked at the time on the screen above me, 3:45pm. I knew I shouldn't panic. He would be here. He promised. I walked a few more steps forward, looking down the hall. I decided to wait ten minutes before heading to baggage claim. My palms began to feel clammy and I was nauseous. I looked up and around once more, searching for him, seeing no one that even resembled him. I took my phone from my pocket. No messages or missed calls.

Five minutes passed and then ten. I made a small circle in the area I was standing in and watched as people reunited around me. I walked over to baggage claim, feeling defeated. James had never been late for anything a day in his life.

My mind began to imagine the worst as I watched the metal conveyer belt spin. I recognized one of my bags and quickly grabbed it. I looked around the room once more for him. Nothing. Tears began to well up in my eyes, making it hard to see. I tilted my head back letting them run from the corners of my eyes.

Relax. It's going to be ok. Whether he shows up or not.

I grabbed my other two suitcases with a struggle and walked towards the exit. I began walking quickly, the tears falling faster, I couldn't hold them back. I was exhausted and terrified at the thought of him backing out. I was terrified that this was all for nothing. I was terrified that he'd come to his senses. I stopped in the middle of the walk way to wipe my tears away. People brushed me and shoved past me, the airport was much busier now.

I looked up to see a tall figure running through the airport. *Someone else's husband or boyfriend coming to greet them. Great.*

The figure was holding a large bouquet of pink flowers and shoving people out of his way. *Jesus, people really had some nerve in Paris.*

I scoffed and moved to the side of the baggage claim. I cocked my head to the side, taking a closure look at the man who was running. My mouth opened wide. I couldn't believe it.

It was him.

"Jess!" James screamed, as he ran closer.

"Jess, stay right there! Im coming!" He called out.

He was running faster now, that red scarf swaying from side-to-side. My heart sank at the sight of him. As he got closer, I could see his rosy, hushed cheeks. I dropped my bags and ran towards him, slamming into his chest. I felt relief wash over my whole body.

"*It's you*" I whispered into his chest.

"I'm so sorry," he said, trying to catch his breath.

"I promised you I'd be right where you left me, but there was traffic and everyone was walking so slow." he said, as I began sobbing.

He huffed, trying to catch his breath.

"I promised." he whispered, again.

James breathed into the top of my head before kissing it. He was struggling to catch his breath as I stepped back to look at him. I wanted to take him in fully.

He was holding two dozen peonies, my favorite. I was shocked he remembered.

"These are for you." He said, extending his arm to hand them to me.

I took them and held them close to my chest.

"I can't believe you remembered," I breathed.

"Of course, I remembered. It's been a couple years, Jess. Not a lifetime, even though it feels like it. Here," he said, grabbing my suitcases from the ground.

"Let's get out of here. I've got a surprise for you."

We ran through the Charles de Gaulle airport. I struggled to keep up with his long strides, which was hard since he was 6'4.

We reached the arrivals where a black car was waiting for us. I followed James to the trunk to help with my bags, when he came to a stop, looking at me inquisitively.

"Is that my blazer?" He asked.

His brows scrunched up in that adorable way. He squinted and stood motionless.

"I was wondering if you'd notice." I smiled sheepishly,

pulling it closed.

"It looks better on you." he winked, shutting the trunk.

We slid into the car and he slammed the door shut. I cozied up to him. He placed his hand on my thigh. I relaxed into his touch. He gently kissed me on the cheek before I turned to kiss him on the lips.

"I'm so happy you're here, Jess. I wasn't sure you'd come back." he admitted.

"I wasn't sure you'd be waiting for me when I got back." I said.

"Yet, here we both are." he said, softly, kissing me once more.

I felt so at peace with my decision to come here. It felt better than I could've imagined. It felt right.

"It still smells like you, you know?"

"What?" He asked, with a confused look.

I laughed, not realizing how weird that sounded.

"The blazer. I've had it in the back of my closet since graduation." I admitted.

"I'm glad you kept it. But you should still expect an invoice from me soon." He joked.

We both shared a laugh. I laid my head on his shoulder, fixing my gaze to the city whipping by. We laced fingers and sat in comfortable silence. I'd never felt more at home than in this moment with him. His presence had always felt like that to me. It was a homecoming. I was relaxed and calm. I felt like I could breathe easier than ever. The sun was setting as we arrived at his apartment. We took my luggage inside, where James had a bottle of champagne waiting for us, *Bollinger Brut*, my favorite. It was the same champagne that James Bond drank in *'Diamonds Are Forever'*, my favorite Bond book.

I laughed softly, into the back of my hand, as he popped the cork "Diamonds Are Forever" I remarked.

"I was wondering if you'd catch that. I saw it at the market and couldn't resist." He smiled.

I could tell he was satisfied with himself. He raised a glass, "Welcome home," he said, staring into my eyes.

I took a large sip before wrapping my arms around his neck.

"I do feel like I'm home, finally." I whispered into his neck.

He stood frozen for a moment before stepping back.

"What is it?" I asked nervously.

"I have something for you." He smiled.

He had already done so much to make me feel special, I couldn't possibly imagine what it could be.

"James...you've already," I said, before he interrupted.

"Ah, ah, shhh..just open this." He said.

It was a box as big as my head. Plain and white, like one a cake would come in, with a silver bow on top. It was heavy. I opened the box slowly to reveal something shiny and round. I moved the tissue to the side to see that it was a helmet. It was a glossy cherry red. I lifted it up into the air and turned to James.

"And what on earth do I need this for?" I laughed.

"Come on, i'll show you." He extended a hand and lead me down the stairs of the building.

In the minuscule space between the two buildings, was a red Vespa moped.

"Is this yours?"

"Well, yeah, how do you think I get around? Well, apart from the Métro," He shrugged, before pushing my right shoulder playfully.

"Jump on," He said, taking a seat.

I began to get a little nervous. I'd never been on a Vespa or anything similar for that matter. He shoved his head into a helmet and turned the key. I pushed my new helmet over my semi-fresh blowout and straddled him from behind. My palms became clammy.

"Eh, I don't know about this, James." I said, nervously.

He turned to make sure I was secured and backed us into

the street.

"Hold on tight, ok?" He yelled, zipping us down his street and into the setting sun, completely disregarding my worry.

"Okay!" I squealed.

I had no idea where we were headed, but I felt like I was lost in a dream. The crisp autumn air bit our faces as we whipped around every little corner. He weaved us through moving traffic, telling me that he'd had this Vespa for awhile. It wasn't as bad as I thought. I straddled him tightly and kept my grip tight to his chest. It was refreshing to see such an adventurous side to him, one I was excited to get to know. I grasped his waist and buried my head into his shoulder, closing my eyes. I felt his speed slowing down so I opened them again. As we descended down a cobble-stoned street, the tip of the Eiffel Tower came into view. By the time we were at the end of the vacant street, the full scale of the Eiffel Tower was in front of us.

"Wow," I breathed.

We came to a full stop and stepped off the moped, placing our helmets on the handlebars.

"This is my favorite street, Rue Saint-Dominique. It's not as crowded as most streets with this view." He said, marveling at it just as I was.

We stood there for a moment silence, the last bit of golden sun showering over James' perfect face.

"You never get tired of this do you?" I asked.

"I don't think that's possible." He said, opening the seat to the Vespa and pulling out a small picnic basket.

He guided me over to a small park bench on the side walk and opened it.

"I'm sure you're starving." he said.

"I'm always starving."

The basket was filled with pastries and various cheeses, along with a thermos and two plastic wine cups. I grabbed a croissant and took a large bite. The bread melted on my tongue just as the first one I'd had. This one tasted better, though.

I smiled at James, noticing that the sun had completely gone down. The Eiffel Tower was lit now and beaming amongst the crowded buildings that had been here for hundreds of years. James poured us a glass of wine and took a sip.

"I don't think I'll ever get tired of seeing you here next to me." He said.

His eyes were sparkling in the dancing lights. I stopped chewing my bite of brie and brushed my hair behind my ear. I felt at a loss for words. Nothing I could say would truly match how I was feeling, there were no words to describe it. He always knew exactly what to say though. He had always been so eloquent.

"I should hope not. After all, my whole life is in the three suitcases back at your place." I joked.

He gave a half smile. I felt silly for always resting on my humor, especially in situations like these, but it's the best I could do.

Jess, come ON! Say something else. Say how you FEEL.

"I don't like the word 'never', but I could never imagine another day without you, James." I blurted.

I kept my gaze on his, intentionally. He leaned over the picnic basket to kiss me softly on the lips. He was speechless. *That wasn't so hard.* We ate the rest of the food in the basket and drank the wine in the thermos. We lost track of time, dancing in the street and laying on the park bench, gazing at the stars.

Eventually, we rode back to his apartment and spent the rest of the night making up for lost time. We explored every inch of each other, drunk off the champagne bottle, now floating in a pool of water that was once ice. For the first time in months, I let myself get lost in time. I allowed myself to get lost with James, like I never had before.

CHAPTER TWENTY-ONE

Six months later

We pulled into the drive of that breath-taking Victorian house I'd stayed in years ago. It was just as I remembered, not a thing had changed on the outside. I was curious to know if anything had changed on the inside, though. I could smell that Spring was in the air here in New York. I felt so lucky to be experiencing real seasons again back in France. The lack of snow in Paris was surprising, but the cold winter had been lovely.

James had rented a Volvo just as he had last time we visited his parents. I knew he'd done it for me and I was just as thrilled as last time. We'd spent the last six months getting reacquainted with one another and creating a routine together. We spent our mornings talking over coffee and planning our days together. It was bliss. We'd spent countless evenings with his friends, who were now my friends too. The time had flown and we were happy, but I knew James was dying to get home. It was longest amount of time he'd gone without seeing his family. For me, it was the longest time I'd ever been out of the country. We had been fighting the hurdles of the attaining a visa through the European Union.

Luckily, we were able to work out a way to secure one and we wanted to share the news in person, with his family.

James slowly pulled the car into the long driveway of his parent's home. The leaves on the trees were slowly blossoming out front. I released my hand from his and gave him a smile. His eyes were reflecting in the light from the fixtures on the porch. He looked dreamier than ever as he smiled back at me.

"You ready?" He asked, quietly.

I nodded in response, feeling equally excited and nervous. So much had changed since I had been here last, for both of us. He walked over to my side of the car and grabbed me by the hand.

"Everyone is excited to see you." He said, squeezing it reassuringly.

I felt relieved to hear him say it. I knew I shouldn't feel guilty for all that had happened, but a part of me did. We climbed the small cement stairs in unison and James grabbed the massive lion shaped door knocker, pounding it twice. Nerves sank in just before Paul opened the door. He was smiling.

He had grown a dark mustache and was wearing glasses, completely transforming the vision I had of him in my mind.

"Hello, you," He cheered, grabbing James by the back of the neck and bringing him in for a hug.

Paul released him and turned to look at me.

"Jessica, darling.." He whispered.

I felt the corners of my mouth turn up.

He spread his arms, welcoming me in for a hug. I could've cried just then. He was as warm and welcoming as he was, when I first met him.

"It's so good to see you." I whispered.

He patted me on the back before releasing me.

"Come on in. Alice is waiting for you in the living room."

I wanted to take off running and find her, that's how excited I was. Instead, I kept a steady pace with the guys. We took the semi-long walk into the main living room. The fireplace was lit and the overhead light was dimmed.

As we entered the room, I saw the back of what I thought was Alice's head. She was sitting in a large armchair. It was hard to tell at first glance, but it looked like her hair was wrapped in a scarf. As we rounded the corner she jumped up from the chair.

"You're here!" She screeched throwing her thin arms around me and James. Her touch was cold.

I hugged her frail frame and stood in shock when she pulled away. She'd always been thin, but was now at least 20 pounds thinner. Her skin was a pasty shade of pale. No color to it. She was as beautiful as ever, but she didn't look like the Alice I remembered. Her eyebrows were sparse and she didn't seem to have any lashes. A result of her treatment I assumed. The scarf she wore on her head was a green Hermés scarf. It was beautiful and complimented her baby blue eyes, the same as James'.

James had only briefly talked about Alice's cancer with me. Once crushing me at the airport. And then once more after that when I was settled into the apartment. He was always quick to change the subject when it came up. I knew why, but I had questions.

"Oh, how i've missed that sweet face." She said, lovingly to me, as she cupped both sides of my face with her cold hands.

I looked into her eyes, something I'd avoided doing since we stepped into the room, and broke down.

I gave her a half smile and pulled her in for another hug, partially to hide my face. As she pulled away, I felt that large painful lump form in my throat. I averted my eyes to the ground.

"I'm sorry, I have to excuse myself to the restroom."

I nearly sprinted to the nearest bathroom, unable to remember where it even was. It had been so long since I stepped foot in this house. I could feel everyone's eyes on my back as I left the room.

After a couple wrong turns, I found a small bathroom and shut the door behind me. I ripped a tissue from the box and pressed it firmly to both tear ducts. I tried desperately to sob in silence as to not make a scene, not that anyone could hear me if I did. This house was huge. Seeing Alice in such a fragile state was something I hadn't prepared myself for in the slightest. I naively thought she'd look like that same old Alice. My Alice, who loved me before she even knew me. It was in that moment that I realized why I'd grown so fond of her. She'd always loved and accepted me unconditionally. Even after me and James' split. Maybe she always knew we'd find our way back to each other too, just as Hanna did.

I tilted my head back once I realized that it was going to take a while to gain my composure. I let out a low whimper just as I heard a gentle knock on the door.

"It's me." I heard James whisper.

He knew what was going on. He'd always picked up on my emotions easily, not that I was being discreet. I took a deep breath and told him to come in. A look of serious worry was painted on his face

"Oh, look at you, Jess."

I was distraught at the sound of my name. I began sobbing hard and put my face into my hands. He brought me close to his chest and began stroking my hair.

"Its ok, its ok. *She's fine, Jess.* She's perfectly healthy."

He knew me too well.

"I know, I know....just the thought of her...I-" I whimpered.

James stood there, at a loss for words.

"I can't bare the thought of her not being here. I wasn't prepared to see her like this" I admitted, hot tears streaming down my face.

My breathing became unsteady and I was hyperventilating like a child.

"All this time....I mean what if id never seen you again? And then I-I- found out she was just gone?" I asked, desperately.

I looked into his eyes now. He was tearing up too, at the sight of me or the idea of losing his mother, I wasn't sure. He understood the grief that I was overwhelmed with. I wasn't sure if he'd processed any of this himself. He pulled me into his chest once more and I squeezed onto him tightly. I held onto him until my breathing became steady again. James released me and handed me another tissue.

"You can't blame yourself for everything, Jess. She loves you, she loves all of us, and she knows how much you love her too. We're here now....we have such wonderful news to share with her. Let's enjoy it. Let's make some new memories together, ok?"

I nodded, wiping my eyes for what I hoped was the last time. He placed his hands on either side of my shoulders and gave me a squeeze.

"I've had my fair share of tears too. My mom is everything to me...to everyone. There's no one like her, but she's healthy now, and I don't want to waste another second of her life wondering when she might leave us, ok?" He added, in a more serious tone.

I nodded, feeling calmer now. I turned on the tap and cupped cold water into my mouth and took a drink. I placed my cold wet hands onto my cheeks to help soothe the redness. I fixed my hair and brushed it behind my ears. James stepped behind me, placing is hands-on my shoulders once more.

"You look great." He whispered, kissing the top of my head.

I turned around to kiss him before we stepped out. He was warm and smelled like neroli and light musk, his captivating and comforting scent.

We made our way down the maze-like hallway and into the formal dining room, where his parents and his brother were sitting at the table, talking amongst themselves. Feeling embarrassed, I kept my gaze on the floor and folded my hands together in front of me.

"Jessica, darling, come sit next to me." Alice said, warmly.

I obliged quietly and James took a seat next to his brother, who had grown significantly over the years. I took a seat next to Alice and reached for my napkin. I placed it in my lap just as I felt her cold hand touch my knee. She gave me a gentle pat and a squeeze before taking her hand back. It was her silent way of comforting me. It was enough to bring me to tears again, but I swallowed the lump in my throat and took a large gulp of the wine in front of me.

"Okay, everyone help yourself. We're doing it family style tonight." Paul said, breaking the silence.

In the center of the table was a three large silver dishes. One filled with heaps of mashed potatoes and the other two with vegetables. In the center was a large platter of what looked like chicken picatta. Paul began serving Alice as James and his brother served themselves. James took my plate from me and kindly made filled it. The mood became lighter as the evening progressed. Ethan recounted anecdotes from his semester at college. I picked at my food, too emotional to eat it all. I pushed it around hoping no one would notice.

I was fairly silent until Alice asked me about the visa process, to which I happily announced that I was approved.

"Wow! That's incredible! How did you do it?" She asked.

James had gotten me a job at a PR firm, but I hadn't actually started yet. Daniel had kindly emailed over a letter of recommendation for me that was addressed from Roger, to my surprise. I had no doubt that Daniel had forged Roger's, signature, seeing as how Roger would never say that I was "wise beyond my years"

Or at least, I couldn't imagine it coming from him.

Whether it was the letter, or James' connection, I was beyond grateful to have landed the position.

"Well…" James began to say.

Everyone stared at him blankly. I tried to hide the smile growing on my face.

"We had our ways," he added, looking my way.

Paul and Alice clapped loudly.

"I'll get the champagne!" Alice exclaimed, bouncing up from her chair.

I looked at James sheepishly and smiled. He was grinning from ear-to-ear. I'd been trying my hardest to keep my ring hand out of sight all night. James had popped the question late the night that I had arrived back in Paris. After all we'd been through, in the course of a week, I couldn't imagine a better way to prove my love to him. I said yes without hesitation, and stayed awake staring at it's beauty long after he'd dozed off. I watched the sun rise and lifted my hand above me to watch the light reflect off the diamond.

It was a gold ring with an oval diamond that was placed horizontally in the setting, surrounded by two smaller, triangular cut diamonds. It was a 1930's vintage piece that James had bought from a local jeweler. It was the most beautiful thing I'd ever laid eyes on.

I leaned into James and whispered, "Wait until they here about this," briefly raising my left hand.

"What are you two talking about?" Ethan asked, just as Paul placed five crystal champagne flutes into the table.

Alice sauntered around the corner with the champagne.

"Okay, who wants to do the honors?"

"I will." James said, cooly.

It was the sort of tone he took when he was hiding something. He loved to act nonchalant during big moments like these. It was something I never understood, but knew was a dead giveaway that he was excited. He popped the cork and filled everyone's cups before lifting his glass.

"To health," he motioned to his mom.

"And to love," he motioned to his dad and brother and then to me.

"*My bride-to-be, Jessica,*" James said, at last, lifting his glass to mine.

Alice stared at us with her mouth open. She looked at Paul and back to us. Paul yelled with excitement and Ethan joined in. I looked back to James before taking a sip of champagne. He pulled me into his side as Alice ran to us.

"You're...you're really getting married?" she began to cry.

I nodded in confirmation and held up my left hand. She grabbed in firmly and looked at James before planting a kiss on his cheek and then mine.

"My god!! It's beautiful but of course it is! My son has my taste doesn't he?" she smiled, wiping a tear from her cheek.

I felt my eyes welling up again at the sight of her happiness. I sat my champagne flute on the table and pulled her in close to me. I squeezed Alice tightly, as she stood a good foot smaller than me.

"I love you, dearly." she whispered to me.

I closed my eyes tight.

"I love you too, Alice." I whispered back.

"I knew you'd come back one day."

I stood looking at my soon-to-be mother-in-law through my tears. She was the mother I'd always hope for but never had, until now. Not only was I gaining a husband, I was gaining the family I had always wanted.

"I'm just glad to be welcomed back." I admitted, looking at my shoes.

"Alright, time for dessert in the den!" Paul yelled, clapping his hands together.

I walked over to James, who'd joined his dad and brother across the table.

The rest of the night felt like a dream. We were walking on air. The contrast of this night and the one I had first spent here was remarkable. Unpredictable. I didn't even recognize the girl that sat at this table, terrified at the prospect of marriage. Now, I fit into his family like the corner piece of a puzzle. Maybe I always had. This was exactly where I belonged. It was where I was destined to end up and there was nothing scary about that.

We spent the rest of the night getting tipsy on champagne and playing charades with his family. Alice couldn't help but ask me dozens of questions about wedding planning.

Had we set a date? Would it be in France? It should be in France.

I was happy to tell her any and all thoughts I had. I happily asked for her input and showed her the few images I had saved to my phone.

The night grew late. Paul had carried Alice up the stairs and off to bed, not long after Ethan excused himself. I marveled at the way Paul cared for Alice, knowing that James inherited every ounce of goodness his father held.

I rested my head on James' shoulder and fidgeted with my ring.

"It's so beautiful. I can't stop staring at it. I hope I never get tired of it." I said.

I felt him smile against my head.

"Me too."

We decided to head to bed too. James walked past his bedroom and I asked what he was doing.

"We're staying in here tonight." he said, opening the door to the stunning pink room I'd stayed in last time.

I saw no reason to object and followed him in.

"I know how much you love this room and to be fair, I've never gotten to stay in it." he shrugged.

He had unzipped our suitcases and placed them on the ottoman towards the foot of the bed. I removed my earrings and placed them in a small crystal dish on the bedside table.

"Can I admit something?" I asked.

He raised his brows in reply.

"The last time I smoked a cigarette was in this very room." I cupped my hand over my mouth dramatically.

"In front of my mom's vintage curtains? *Jess....*" he said, sarcastically.

"I thought you'd be more upset than this. You hated when you caught me smoking!" I laughed.

"Well, it's very french of you, I have to admit." he said, taking his shoes off and laying on the bed.

I crawled over him, the fabric of my dress stretching over my butt tightly. I caught his eyes dance to it instantly before he squeezed it.

"You know...we could try and reenact that night in your old room." I offered.

A devilish smile painted across his face before he turned off the lamp on his side table. Gently, without a word his left hand grazed my right breast. I craned my neck up to press my lips to his. I slowly forced my tongue inside his mouth, our breathing getting heavier. His hands found my bare legs as he pushed my dress up and over my hips. He rolled on top of me and I heard him unbuckle his belt. He pulled my sweater dress over my head and threw it on the floor. We spent the rest of the night righting any wrongs from that first week that I stayed here.

After two blissful days with James' family, soon to be my family, we made the road-trip to my hometown. Westport, Connecticut was a small coastal town that I hadn't been back to since freshman year of college. My mother had begged me to come home that Christmas. It was the last one I ever spent in Westport. She spent the whole week complaining about work and getting drunk on eggnog. Our relationship was strained and she never made much of an effort to see me.

"Los Angeles is nothing but a wasteland of wannabes and yuppies. I don't see what keeps you there." She'd always say.

I didn't disagree with her, but she was exactly what kept me there. Even though I hated LA, I always pretended to enjoy it, knowing I'd never hear the end of it from her. She'd never wanted me to move away, not even to NYC. But she didn't make staying here any easier. I couldn't bare the thought of staying remotely close to the state of Connecticut. Nothing tied me to this place, not even friends. I only had one close friend from high school. Her name was Elizabeth and we lost touch after high school when she got married.

We were two hours into our roadtrip when James reassured me it was going to be great. He was genuinely excited to meet my mother, which put me more at ease. She still lived in the same house we grew up in. He would probably die in that house too. She wasn't a fan of change. It was a small two-story house with three bedrooms and two and a half baths. A decent size for just the two of us. I had no doubt that it would seem like a Nanny's quarters compared to James' parents house. My mom must've been doing well as I heard from her less nowadays. I never told her when me and James broke up and I didn't plan for her to ever find out. To my advantage, this would probably make our engagement more palatable to her.

"Do you think she still has your room decorated the way it was when you left for college?" James asked, cheerfully.

"I would imagine so, not that there's much left other than furniture. I think I packed everything with me when I left for LA." I sighed.

"What a shame." he joked.

"I'm curious about high school Jess."

I rolled my eyes as we drove past the "Welcome to Westport" sign. My hands began to sweat as we sped closer to my mom's house. It was odd driving through my hometown and noticing the small ways it had changed. So much had stayed the same though.

"It's charming." James said.

"It kind of reminds me of Saratoga."

I agreed, chewing the inside of my cheek. I checked my phone, hoping for a message from my mom saying she needed to cancel. Wishful thinking. I studied James for a moment. He was excitedly tapping his fingers on the steering wheel and humming along to the radio. My anxiety melted away once I realized he was happy just to know everything about me. James had shown me into his world many times over, and I hadn't even given him a glance of mine. I was choosing to spend the rest of my life with a man who I hadn't completely letting in.

I relaxed into the headrest and focused on the road.

Deep breaths. Deep breaths.

We drove down main street, putting us less than two minutes out from the house.

"That's the frozen yogurt shop I'd always beg my mom to take me after school." I said, pointing to my right.

"Wow, I can't believe Henderson's is still in business. Some things never change." I laughed to myself.

James flashed me a warm smile before I told him to take a left. We pulled into my small neighborhood. Most of the houses were identical.

"Here we are," I breathed as we pulled into the driveway behind a car I didn't recognize.

The house still looked the same; bright white paint with a small staircase leading up to the porch. There was an American flag hanging out front and a large potted plant near the stairs. I smiled, realizing the small garden gnome I'd painted in fifth grade was still where my mom left it. We unbuckled our seatbelts and I walked ahead of James up the porch.

"Woah, slow down there." James said.

I was eager to get this over with. I wanted to rip it off like a bandaid. I checked my watch for the time. 4:15. I knew full well that my mom was probably uncorking her evening wine.

Please god, don't let her say anything embarrassing.

I rang the doorbell with James right by my side. I squeezed his hand tightly before my mom opened the door. *Here we go.*

"Hello, stranger!" She cheered.

I stood examining her briefly before giving her a hug.

Something was different about her. She cut her hair...or did she dye it?

"Hi. You look different." I blurted out.

"Well, I'd hope so, I haven't seen you in a good few years." She replied, shutting the door behind us.

"Aren't you going to introduce me to this fine young man?" She asked, looking James up and down. I touched my forehead.

"Oh, sorry, mom. This is James."

He extended a hand to her and shook it firmly.

"It's lovely to meet you, Marisa." He said, in a genuine tone.

I stepped further into the small foyer, noticing it was painted a different shade of green than before. It was was lighter and more inviting.

"Can I get you two something to drink?" She asked.

"What kind of wine are you having this evening, mom?" I joked as we followed her into the kitchen.

"Oh, I'm not having wine. I can offer you a Coke or some water. I don't drink anymore." She said.

I turned to her in shock.

"Since when?" I asked.

"Oh, about a year now. I gave it up cold turkey. It was my New Year's resolution. I was getting so fat and well, anyway, you don't want hear about all that." She said, playing it off.

"Oo I'll have a Coke Zero, please." James said.

I shot him a look.

"*What?* You know my mom doesn't keep soda in the house." He replied.

He didn't catch the fact that I was shocked at my mother and not his drink choice.

"That's great, mom. I'll have a coke too." I said, motionless.

She grabbed two cans from the fridge and handed them to us.

"Well, do you want me to show you around? I've done a few renovations since you've been here." She said.

I raised my eyebrows and looked around.

"Yeah. I can tell. The place looks great. Are these new countertops?" I asked, grazing my fingers over the cold granite.

I'd only ever seen laminate growing up.

"Yes, it was the first thing I was dying to change." She gloated.

"Come on, I'll show you two upstairs." She urged.

We followed her up the narrow, carpeted stairs in a single file. She turned to the right.

"This used to be Jess's old room. I decided it would make a great gym since I hate going to the recreation center in town." She said, waving her arms in exhaustion.

I was shocked to see the walls were bare and painted in an eggshell white. Not at all like the baby pink I was used to growing up. There was a large mirror on the East wall and a treadmill. A small rack of weights sat to the left of it. There was a plasma screen tv mounted in the corner of the room where I used to have an antique lamp.

"Wow, mom. Everything looks great." I said, trying to be supportive.

I couldn't help but feel a little sad at all the change.

"Thanks, hon. I've sold ten houses in the last two months so I thought it was time to spruce the place up, as a treat." She smiled and motioned for us to exit.

She had retired from teaching and got her real estate license. Clearly it was a good career move. We headed back downstairs and into the living room, where she invited us to sit. Her furniture was new too. I took a seat on the brown mid-century modern couch next to James, and she sat in an armchair across from us.

"I got your postcard." She said flatly.

She was always flat with me.

"I couldn't believe you were in Paris, not that it feels any closer than California." She added.

I shrugged and told her it had happened unexpectedly.

"James had gotten a job there and I followed suit. I like it a lot better than LA, that's for sure." I said.

I'd told James that keeping things concise and vague was what best suited me and my mom's dynamic, which was undoubtedly why he was remaining silent.

"You know, you're just like your late grandmother. I wish you could've met her. She loved to travel anywhere she could. I can't say I inherited that trait. I'm terrified of flying and boats make me sea sick. If I can't drive there, I'm fine not going." She said, light-heartedly.

I bit my cheek trying not to impose my opinion.

"So, what exactly do you do, James?" She asked him.

He cleared his throat.

"I am an art curator for a local gallery. I'm also a part-time tour guide. I give guided tours of the Louvre and other museums in Paris." He said.

Mom's eyes lit up.

"Wow, that's incredible. Maybe you can help me choose some artwork to put up around here." She said, motioning around at the walls.

"Actually, my mom, Alice, is an interior decorator. She would be much more suited to help you with that. I'm sure she would be happy to help you with any decorating needs." James said.

"Is that right? How neat. I'll have to get her number before you leave."

"Yeah, I think it would be good for you two meet, especially since we're getting married." I blurted out.

The words fell right from my mouth. I couldn't hold it in any longer. James and my mom both shot me a surprised look. I was ready to get this visit over with and I hated small talk. James laughed nervously.

"That is if I have your blessing." He added.

My mom took a long moment to look both of us over, her mouth wide open.

"Well, of course you do! I mean, I'm shocked. I must say. I never thought my little girl was the marrying type but congrats! Let me see the ring!" She exclaimed.

I was surprised at her chipper reaction. Giving up drinking seemed to do her more good than I could've imagined. I placed my left hand in front of her and she rotated my finger.

"How gorgeous...it's vintage isn't it?" She asked, looking at James.

I was surprised that she remembered my love for antiques.

"Yes, I wanted something as special as she is, Miss Chadwick." James said.

"Call me Marisa, please." Mom told him sternly.

He nodded and smiled at me. She looked at us both for a long moment.

"Well, I know I don't know you very well, but I can tell that you'll take good care of my daughter. She's always had a steady head on her shoulders too, so I know she's making the right choice. Congratulations to both of you." She said, as her eyes began to well up.

"Oh, mom." I said, getting up to hug her.

"Thank you for saying that."

"Yes, thank you for your blessing, Marisa." James said.

She smiled at us as she dried her eyes. For the next hour we sat with her and caught up. She told us all about getting her real estate license and we told her about our life in Paris.

She had a million questions for us including, "Do people really drink wine and smoke all day?"

She asked, almost as if that would suit her.

I was embarrassed to say the least, but James found it entertaining. He laughed.

"Yes."

For once in my life, I found myself enjoying the company of my mother. She had changed so much in the last few years and so had I. James seemed to keep great conversation with her, which surprised me. I thought they'd have absolutely nothing in common. I was silly to think his warm charm could be wasted on anyone.

Eventually, we said our goodbyes and I promised to call more and send more post cards. We pulled out of the driveway and watched her wave goodbye all the way to the end of the street.

We had a few hours to kill before boarding our flight back to Paris. I wanted to show James where I grew up, just as he did with me three years ago. We stopped into the yogurt shop I'd shown him on the way in. I made him get my favorite flavor combination peanut butter, tarte, and cappuccino with white chocolate chips.

"You know, it's surprisingly good." He admitted, shoveling the whole thing within minutes.

When we finished I took him to my favorite book store where I bought Pride & Prejudice and re-read it ten times that one summer. "And yet it still took you this long to commit to me. So what does that make you? Pride?" He joked.

I swatted his shoulder and finished my yogurt. Once we were done, we drove to my high school. We sat in the parking lot and I told him stories of when my mom would routinely forget to pick me up. I'd be crying on the bench, feeling beside myself.

"Wasn't she a teacher?" James asked.

I laughed.

"Yes, but a middle school teacher at a school ten minutes from here."

"That's still pretty bad." He winced.

"I know."

We talked about our first crushes and our favorite teachers. I told him about all the times I'd gotten in-school detention for being late to class because I hated school.

Lastly, we drove to my favorite spot in town. A small park with a white gazebo in the center of it.

"I used to spend all of my summer's here, just reading and listening to CD's." I told him.

"I would sit here listening to old jazz CD's my mom picked up at garage sales and imagine what my future husband would be like." I said.

"I thought you didn't dream of that sort of thing." He said, playfully. "I did, I've just never told anyone."

"So what was this guy like? Tall, dark, and handsome?"

I shook my head no.

"More like tall, blonde, and blue-eyed with good manners." I said.

He pulled me in close and stared at me, examining my face.

"Good fashion sense too." I added, jokingly while staring back at him.

"Thank you for bringing me here today, Jess." James whispered.

His tone was serious now.

"You're lucky to have been raised by your mother. She truly cares for you and she did it all on her own. It's incredible." He said.

I'd never given it much thought. She really had done the best with what she had, whether I wanted to believe it or not.

"It's crazy to think that every point, up until now, lead us to each other, isn't it? We both were born on the same coast and decided to go to school on the opposite one. What are the odds?" I asked, looking up at him.

"Whatever they were, they were the same ones that put us on that train six months ago." He said.

I felt a lump growing in my throat. I pulled him in and wrapped my arms around his neck tightly.

"Lets go home." He breathed.

He lead the way back to the car, holding my hand tightly.

"Let's go home." I echoed, as I buckled my seatbelt.

ACKNOWLEDGMENTS

THANK YOU TO CHLOE WADE FOR INTUITIVELY UNDERSTANDING MY VISION FOR THE COVER. THANK YOU FOR ALSO BEING PATIENT WITH MY PROCESS. HUGE THANK YOU TO MY FRIENDS FOR BELIEVING IN ME AND BEING EXCITED TO READ THIS. THANK YOU TO WHOEVER PURCHASED MY BOOK AND IS READING THIS NOW. I HOPE YOU LOVED IT, OR AT LEAST LIKED IT. IF NOT, THAT'S OKAY. THE FACT THAT YOU'RE HOLDING MY ART MEANS THE WORLD TO ME.

CPSIA information can be obtained
at www.ICGtesting.com
Printed in the USA
LVHW052329210723
752880LV00016BA/607

9 798218 245191